ELLIE HAYES AND THE HIMBOS

VANESSA KING

FOREVER

New York   Boston

Forever
Hachette Book Group
1290 Avenue of the Americas, New York, NY 10104
read-forever.com
@readforeverpub

First Edition: November 2025

Forever is an imprint of Grand Central Publishing. The Forever name and logo are registered trademarks of Hachette Book Group, Inc.

The publisher is not responsible for websites (or their content) that are not owned by the publisher.

The Hachette Speakers Bureau provides a wide range of authors for speaking events. To find out more, go to hachettespeakersbureau.com or email HachetteSpeakers@hbgusa.com.

Forever books may be purchased in bulk for business, educational, or promotional use. For information, please contact your local bookseller or the Hachette Book Group Special Markets Department at special.markets@hbgusa.com.

Print book interior design by Jeff Stiefel.

Library of Congress Cataloging-in-Publication Data
Names: King, Vanessa (Vanessa L.) author
Title: Ellie Hayes and the himbos / Vanessa King.
Description: First edition. | New York : Forever, 2025. |
Identifiers: LCCN 2025026255 | ISBN 9781538774588 trade paperback |
ISBN 9781538774595 ebook
Subjects: LCGFT: Fiction | Romance fiction | Novels
Classification: LCC PS3611.I58666 E45 2025 | DDC 813/.6—dc23/
eng/20250610
LC record available at https://lccn.loc.gov/2025026255

ISBNs: 9781538774588 (trade paperback); 9781538774595 (ebook)

Printed in the United States of America

LSC-C

Printing 1, 2025

ELLIE HAYES
AND THE HIMBOS

To Jeanne.
When I started this project,
it was for you.
It turned into something else along the
way, but it's still yours.
I hope you don't mind sharing.

ELLIE HAYES
AND THE HIMBOS

himbo *noun*

him·bo ʻhim-(,)bō

: a large (broad, tall, muscular) attractive man, lacking in intelligence or common sense but inherently kind and respectful. Other traits can include (but are not limited to) unbridled enthusiasm, limited situational awareness, and unwavering devotion.

1

I ROLL MY SHOULDERS BACK and take in a deep breath, then knock on the front door of the brick bungalow, planting what I hope is a friendly, open smile onto my face. But just as I bring my hand back to my side, the smile slips. Something isn't right.

It's the smell.

Another whiff and the scent clicks into place. It's unmistakable, conjuring deep voices emanating from locker rooms, matte black cans of body spray, and multistep handshakes tailored to the narrow parameters of traditionally acceptable masculine intimacy.

It's 100 percent grade-A *dude*.

And it's not supposed to be here.

I turn, pivoting on the heel of my pump to squint at the "room for rent" sign at the end of the driveway, where the rideshare just deposited me. It's there, in all of its hot-pink, bubble-lettered glory, the glitter highlighting the words *private bath* catching the fading twilight this Friday evening with the same flair that snagged my attention Monday afternoon.

The sign's unapologetic femininity had me prepared for fellow ladies, the proximity to UT Austin and a single room on offer all but guaranteeing students. It would be perfect. The sunny coeds would keep me hip to social media trends, while I introduced them to overlooked rom-coms from the aughts. They would turn to me for guidance, and while my ten-plus years of life experience had left me a bit jaded, in time, I would be softened by their fresh enthusiasm. We'd end up as linked emotionally as our ovulation cycles would be synced.

Derivative? Sure. But I'd woken up blind in my right eye that morning and clocked the Pepto-pink sign while en route to the first of two specialists who would tell me that they had no explanation for my condition. My boyfriend of five years had responded to my situation with a resigned "Now what?" that made clear how misplaced my optimism had been when we signed a two-year lease on our apartment last fall. And if being a medical mystery in a domestic situation of dubious stability wasn't reason enough to dabble in a little escapism, Wednesday's neurologist diagnosed me with optic neuritis: swelling on the optic nerve that's preventing my brain from interpreting what my eye is trying to see. The kicker? Fifty percent of the time, the condition is the first sign of multiple sclerosis.

I was tossed into an MRI machine the same afternoon, and in the panicky day and a half I waited for my results, that glittery posterboard became a touchstone. My immune system might have turned on my nervous system, and I may no longer be able to ignore that the doomsday clock on my relationship is seconds to midnight, but there could be sisterhood in my future, and evenings spent in shared admiration for Nancy Meyers's kitchens.

It was freak out or fantasize, and I chose the latter.

So it's with a touch of desperation that I scan the porch, hoping to disprove what my nose is telling me. A pair of dark blue sneakers sits to the side of the battered welcome mat, which, I realize, is conspicuously devoid of an *L*: WE COME.

Ick. Never mind. I get back to the shoes, which dwarf my silver Fluevogs. I try rationalizing. My college roommate had huge feet! Or...maybe they belong to a boyfriend?

Heavy footsteps sound from inside the house, and I gather more evidence. There's a triangular rack of dumbbells in the corner, the numbers on the weights ranging from 25 to 50, and to the right of the front door, I note a flash of white. I angle my head to use my good eye and find that the mailbox has been labeled with a torn piece of paper reading THE DAWGHOUSE in incriminatingly masculine scrawl.

I cling to the hope of a house of endearingly raunchy, yoked ladies, one among them, perhaps, with a closet full of clodhoppers. I'm still struggling to spin the DAWGHOUSE signage when the door opens. The scent I'd identified hits me in a cloud of concentrated *bro*, and a young man towers over me from the doorway. He's cute, with wide dark eyes and a blond fade that speaks of regular maintenance. Early twenties, I'd guess, based on the softness of his cheeks. He's a baby. A dude*ling*.

He cocks his head. "Hi?"

My desperation morphs into defeat; my imaginary bestie squad has been deposed by the bro-iest of bros. He might be a puppy, but he's the physical embodiment of the body spray I'd recognized. He's even dressed for the gym, wearing a T-shirt with the sleeves cut off and armholes extending almost to his waist.

But I'm determined to recover some shred of that sidelined fantasy; *The Proposal* has something for everyone. I straighten and plaster on my winningest smile. "Hi! I'm Ellie."

The dudeling continues to stare, the information, evidently, not meaningful to him.

"I'm here about the room?" I venture, feeling the corners of my mouth slip.

His wide eyes widen further. "*You're* who texted about seeing the room?"

I screw the smile back into place. "Yes. Oh! Did I not include my name?" He shakes his head, and I offer an apologetic grimace. "Sorry about that…" I trail off, hoping to inspire an introduction in return.

"Grant," he says, voice distant. He takes a step back, pulling the door open further. "Come on in?"

Despite the ongoing mental and emotional whiplash, some sense of self-preservation manages to bubble up. I am about to follow an unfamiliar man—a puppy of an unfamiliar man, but an unfamiliar man nonetheless—into an unfamiliar space without relaying my whereabouts to anyone who might come to my aid or collect my remains.

A week ago, this would have been madness. But a week ago, I wasn't half-blind, freshly dumped, soon to be unhoused, and waiting to find out if I have a debilitating nerve condition. Because even though my MRI showed no sign of nerve damage, it's possible that I'm in an early, undetectable stage of MS. Another flare-up in the next six months would be confirmation. My boyfriend, Cole, couldn't hack it long enough to get through tonight's semi-celebratory dinner, so here I am, having put all of my eggs in this fabulously misrepresented basket.

So I step into the bungalow.

Grant joins me, leaving the door open, which is appreciated. Inside, two more youths sit in lawn chairs, one reclining with his legs dangling over an armrest, eyes glued to his phone, while the other, whose seat is so low he's basically on the floor, sits with a video game controller in his hands, attention firmly on the first-person shooter lighting up a massive flatscreen TV.

I scan the rest of the room, but there's not much to take in. Nothing on the walls, no coffee table, and the only source of light is an audibly unbalanced ceiling fan. There's a recliner toward the back of the room, just past the lounging guy, and between it and his folding chair, an end table I'm sure is meant to be a nightstand. There's a beer bottle on the surface, and the lounging guy reaches back for it without lifting his eyes from his phone, takes a swig, and then puts it back down. No coaster. I suppress a twitch.

The one playing the video game turns his head nominally, offering an overly loud "Hola!" without looking away from the game. His curly dark hair is so voluminous, it buries his headset. The sound's high enough that I can make out the rat-a-tat of gunfire.

The guy with the phone looks up. He stares at me. I stare back, because good God, this kid is *stunning*. He's all chiseled cheekbones and dark-eyed smolder, with sideswept hair coiffed to careless perfection. I'm actually appreciative of my single-eye status; it's like staring at the sun.

Granted, some of my awe wears off when his jaw slackens—dumb confusion isn't a good look for anyone—and I wave. His brow furrows, and it's another few seconds of silent observation before he takes in a breath, holds it, then lets it out on a thoughtful "Huh." He extends a socked foot to nudge the guy playing the video game, who turns to face him. The pretty one bugs his eyes insistently, pointing toward me, and gamer boy finally looks my way.

"I already said—*ohmigoodness!*" He heaves himself forward to stand, and the tiny chair rises with him, the armrests gripping his backside. He staggers forward in a crouch, reaching back to free himself from the lawn chair with a high, self-conscious giggle.

"That chair is *very* small," he says, and rises. We're the same height in my heels, and he's built like a compact linebacker, his barrel chest rising and falling in quick, panicked breaths. "I am Diego!" he announces in a shout that has me flinching. He frowns, then gasps. "Oh!" He tears the headset from his head, sending askew the blush-pink scrunchie partly restraining his curls. A few coils spring loose, and he smooths them back, heedless of his controller and headset.

"I am Diego," he repeats. His volume is normal this time, but his chest is still heaving like he's come in from a run. "So sorry for my rudeness. I didn't know you would be…" The hand still bearing the headset extends toward me, making a vague, circle shape. But whether he's indicating my gender, the ten-plus years I have on him, or the plunging neckline of the halter dress I selected when the evening's direction had promised champagne and not sudden singledom, I don't know.

He glares at Grant. "This is not a *roommate!*" he insists. "This is a pretty lady! *You…*" He returns to me. "*You* are a pretty lady."

It comes out more as an accusation than a compliment, which

is good; given the overwhelming suck of the past five days, a compliment from this puppy probably would have made me cry.

I smile. I think I like Diego. "I'm Ellie."

"Ellie," he repeats, like my name is the key to resetting his expectations. Apparently, it is, because his face lights up with a smile so large, his cheeks threaten to overwhelm his eyes. "Okay! Nice to meet you, *Ellie!*"

The pretty one continues to observe from his spot in the lawn chair. "And you want to live *here?*" he asks.

While I can't rightly say that *want* has anything to do with my current situation, I'm also not inclined to lay out that my boyfriend proposed "a break" while I wait to find out if my body has decided to turn on my nervous system, and that, frankly, I'd rather set myself on fire than spend another evening under the same roof as him. So I nod.

He considers this. Then shrugs. "Aight." He gets back to his phone.

"That's Alistair," Diego explains. "He just got back from a shoot. *He's a model,*" he adds, conspiratorially. I nod. Of course he is.

"So it's the three of you? No girlfriends or..." I stop myself shy of saying *actual adults?*

"Nope," says Grant. "Just us. Though my brother was here for a while. He had the back room while his place was getting remodeled." He chuckles. "Ian was *so* ready to get out of here."

Looking around at a living room that appears to have been furnished with the contents of the lost and found of a public pool, I don't doubt it. Good for him.

"Is the back room the one that's available?" I ask.

Grant's brow wrinkles, then relaxes. "Oh, yeah! Do you want to see it?"

"It's what I'm here for," I remind him.

Grant brays out a laugh. "Right! Cool. Let's—"

A vibration picks up in my purse. My chest squeezes uncomfortably, but my lips twitch into a smirk. Took him long enough. I'd already ignored the *You okay?* I received while waiting for my ride, and Cole's *Ellie???* had arrived as I'd messaged Grant about looking at the room.

Three pairs of eyes dart to the clutch humming at my side, then back to me. The only other sounds in the room are the tinny gunfire drifting from Diego's headset and the incessant rock of the ceiling fan.

The phone stops, and the tension in my chest releases some.

"The room—" I start, and the buzzing picks up again, rattling against my hip. The guys cock their heads in tandem, a chorus line of curiosity. I sigh.

"Excuse me." I fish my phone from my purse. Filling the screen is the familiar, handsome face of my abruptly, emphatically *ex*-boyfriend, Cole's too-pretty lips captured in a smile. It's a far cry from how I'd left him at the restaurant, eyes rounded in shock, my "Go fuck yourself" hanging in the air over our cozy two-top. His mouth had still been open when I excused myself from the table, which in retrospect I regret doing. He'd just dumped me in a public setting, thank you very much. He didn't deserve politesse. I'll have to consider that a moral victory.

I glare at the image, a sliver of hurt intruding on my anger. We were supposed to be celebrating. Even if today's MRI results were more of a semicolon than the period I was hoping for, I was happy. I got dressed up; I'm wearing boob tape, dammit! We'd been on a downward trajectory for months; what was another night of willful ignorance? But before we could even order, Cole announced that he was "just not strong enough for this, too."

The memory of that *too* cuts deeply enough that I wince. I swipe the screen to find the option to block his number.

"Ellie!" Cole's voice explodes from the receiver.

I swear under my breath. *Damn stiletto tips.* I'm constantly flubbing on my phone because of my nails, but I just can't give them up.

"Where are you?" he continues.

I frown. He doesn't sound mad or worried, more…exasperated. Which is annoying. I'd like to think that one's long-term partner's sudden disappearance from a dinner together would register as more than an inconvenience. At least when that long-term partner is *me*.

"You can't just leave like that in the middle—"

I end the call, and a few taps later, succeed in putting the thing on do not disturb. I'll figure out how to block him later.

I look up to find that I am once again being observed like I am part of a zoo exhibit. I brace for the inevitable onslaught of questions.

Who was that?

Did he dump you? Why?

How do you feel about the dissolution of yet another relationship as a direct result of your defective body?

The imagined interrogation is enough to have me blinking back tears. Anger shudders through me. *No.* I've managed to get through this week without crying once. And while the greater implication of the breakup might be worth a few tears, Cole, who, despite two years of cohabitation, still doesn't know where we keep the goddamn salad spinner, is *not*.

Steeled, I raise my chin and wait.

All three men dissolve into laughter.

Grant points to the phone, one side of his mouth hitched up in a smirk. "He sounded like a *tool*."

"Right?" Diego chuckles, back to his eye-encroaching grin. Alistair snorts.

Grant nudges my shoulder gently. "Seems like you could use a beer."

I look from bro to bro to bro. That's…it? No commentary. "A beer?" I manage, still floored by their lack of reaction. What they overheard was downright delicious! If I'd listened in on that, I'd be dying for details.

"Ah! A beer!" Diego returns to his seat, deposits his headset and controller, and turns to me with a sweaty, unopened bottle.

I start to shake my head, then stop, letting my good eye land on the label. Shiner Bock. When was the last time I had a Shiner? Between Cole's aversion to macrobrews and the never-ending supply of options that comes with dating a wine rep, I can't think of the last time I'd had *any* beer. It sounds perfect. "That would be great, actually. Thank you."

"My pleasure!" Diego twists off the cap and extends the bottle to me. I swear, he bows slightly as he hands it off.

I raise the beer appreciatively, and Grant does the same, while Alistair reaches back for the drink defacing the end table behind him and Diego scrambles to his chair for his bottle.

"Cheers?" I offer.

"Cheers!"

We clink bottles, though Alistair doesn't deign to get up to toast. I drink. I don't know that I consciously decide to chug the whole thing, but I commit, the mental middle finger to Cole and his snobbery and weakness and every other character flaw I've spent years overlooking absolutely worth the watering eyes.

I finish with a gasp, then blot my eyes. I silently thank the bighorn on the label. Good *God*, that hit the spot.

They're staring again. Even Alistair gawks, dazzling features slack in shock.

"Dude," they chorus, the single syllable coming out with no shortage of admiration. I'm oddly proud.

"It's been a day," I say flatly.

"No shit," says Grant, and he lets out a little laugh. "So, you want to see the room?"

2

THE SPACE IS SIMPLE. Just a bedroom, as advertised, with honey-colored hardwood floors and exposed beams. No odor beyond the stale air of an unused space, and nothing so obviously unacceptable that my good eye can pick up on it. There's a mattress pressed against one wall, wrapped in plastic, though I'm not sure if that's good or creepy, and past it, a darkened doorway, what I presume is the bathroom. And the windows! I don't know if it's the influence of the beer, which I am absolutely feeling, or the sheer scope of the divided panes of glass dominating the south wall, but I could swoon. My plants would be so happy here.

Behind me, Grant clears his throat. "So, um...This is it? Bathroom." He points to the door I noticed, then to the one we entered through. "And the rest of the house. Obviously."

My apprehension sparks back to life. I'd made a point not to peek into any of the rooms we passed as Grant led me down the hallway, lest I spy something that would send me running from the place before I'd gotten a chance to scope out the one on offer. But a shared kitchen. If I go through with this, I'll be sharing a kitchen, laundry room, and common areas with three unknown variables in lawn chairs.

My memory drifts to the substandard living conditions of male friends and guys I dated in my undergraduate days. Suspiciously stiff towels. Microwaves so crudded up, they had to be pried open. One guy I worked with had a pump bottle of dish soap in his shower in lieu of body wash.

Even Cole, who was, by most metrics, a functional adult when we met, fell soundly into the category of hapless male. Dishes made it to the sink but could never quite travel the last three feet into the dishwasher. Shoes abandoned in the living room, little land mines to tumble over in the dark when going to the kitchen for water. He couldn't cook and barely cleaned, and I tolerated it all because in my mind, that was how I made up for my own deficiencies.

But it wasn't enough. *I'm not strong enough for this, too—*

My face must betray some of the ugliness running through my head, because Grant's brow puckers in worry. "There's a lock?" He crosses to the door leading to the hallway, closes it, and turns the dead bolt. He makes a minor production of trying to pull it open, then unlocks it, letting the door swing into the room.

"Great!" The false cheer in my voice is grating.

"Cool. And you're good with the rent?" He recites the price that had been on the sign, a mid-triple-digit sum I haven't paid since my own undergraduate days. "And no deposit or first and last or anything. But there are utilities," he adds, solemnly. As if a share of this place's utilities would make a dent in the savings I'd get from reducing my rent by a good 65 percent.

"Absolutely," I say, happy to contribute something fully

genuine. And very happy to think about Cole's rent skyrocketing. *You strong enough for* that, *y'dick?*

"If all this is too weird, you can just, like, bounce?" Grant points to a third door on the far wall. "That'll let you out on the same side as the driveway." I blink at the unexpected out, and he blanches. "Not that I want you to! But you seem…grown-up?" he says, which is very diplomatic. "And I'm sure we seem *way* not. So I get it if you aren't into this. No hard feelings."

Points for self-awareness, Grant. "I'll keep that in mind."

"Cool." After another moment of silence, he starts to edge toward the door to the rest of the house. "I'll give you a minute?"

"Yes!" The word comes out tight. Reality is threatening to close in, and I refuse to subject this innocent bystander to whatever that might look like. "Thanks."

"Rad. See you in a few!" He laughs, adding, "Hopefully!" before stepping into the hallway and closing the door behind him.

I take in one long, slow breath, holding it until the urge to scream passes, and exhale. This is fine! It's stupid and impulsive, and I'm actively dreading the moment I'm going to have to look at the kitchen, but…it's fine. I need it to be fine.

I stroll over to the mattress and scan the tag taped to a corner. *Final Sale. Ian Hammond, pickup,* and a date going back almost a year. I squint at the price. *Damn.* He got a good deal, but this thing was pricey. I send the room's former tenant a silent kudos.

While I'm peering down, my left eye picks up a flash of light, and I angle my head toward my phone, still in my hand. I brace myself. Incoming call. *Heather.*

My stomach drops. If my notoriously call-averse friend has resorted to dialing, then I've already missed at least three texts of increasing intensity. Plus, she's with Mark, her roommate. The man's a drama teacher. He literally can't help himself from escalating a situation.

I fake a smile as I answer. "Hey, H—"

"Ellie, what the hell?" Heather's voice comes out sharp against my ear. "Why is Cole blowing up our phones, and why aren't you responding? I've sent you, like, four texts."

Called it.

"Why does Cole even have my number?" Mark grumbles, which bodes well. If he's open to petty grievances, then we're well out of range of hysteria.

"He's asking if we know where you are? Weren't you two going to dinner?"

"We were…" I say, and let the incomplete statement hang. I've been avoiding this conversation all week. I'd reached out to Heather that first morning, in case her biology background might hold the secret to my mysterious blindness. Instead, Mark joined the conversation and I found myself talking down two semi-hysterical secondary educators. And while calming them did a nice job of easing my own nerves, it didn't seem like the time to introduce the possibility of a soon-to-be-dissolving relationship.

Now isn't any *better*, but there's no avoiding it. I take a crinkly seat on the mattress. "But before we could even order, he proposed that we 'take a break' from our relationship," I say, loading Cole's words with the disdain they deserve.

Twin gasps brush against my ear.

"Oh, my God, Ellie! Are you okay?" Heather asks. "Where are you?"

"I'm fine," I say, sidestepping the second question. "I just needed a minute."

"What did *you* say?" Mark's voice is edged with wicked intrigue.

"I told him that he could go fuck himself." There's a bloom of pride in my chest at the recall. That was not very "Ellie" behavior. Kind of like everything that's followed.

Mark's laugh is a bright cackle. Heather snorts.

"It's been a long week," I say, and groan at the understatement. "It's been a long few *years*, but this week in particular has been more than enough." A bitter laugh pulls free from me. "Which is funny. That's how Cole felt, too! 'We've already been through so much,'" I quote. "'I don't think I'm strong enough for this, *too*.'" I grit my teeth. The final word twists just as painfully as it did at the restaurant.

The silence on the other end of the call speaks volumes. We don't have to be face-to-face for me to know the look they're giving one another, the wordless anxiety as they try to determine whether I've opened the floor to the subject of my notoriously uncooperative body.

Unbidden, my free hand comes to rest low on my abdomen. When Cole and I started dating, a degree of pain had already been a standard part of my cycle. He'd been so patient and understanding during the stretches of days I'd be "out of commission," murmuring gentle words as he held me on the floor of whatever bathroom he'd found me doubled over in, soothing me in waiting rooms and doctors' offices. When I'd finally been diagnosed with endometriosis and given a treatment plan, it had been a relief for both of us.

But there's no curing the condition. Barring surgery, which my insurance isn't *quite* convinced I qualify for, the most anyone can do is mitigate its symptoms. With the potential for pain lurking in the background of every intimate encounter, it became harder to connect physically. Add to that the fertility issues that are common with cases as severe as mine, the distance that accompanies the possibility that you won't be able to provide what your partner wants in the long term, and the unspoken awareness that you're only staying together out of convenience and respect for a lease agreement, and you have yourself a dealbreaker stew.

"I'm not sad," I insist, but there's a sliver of dishonesty in the words. "Or, maybe, for some past version of us." Or just the past version of myself. The me that hoped that Cole would be different from the guys I'd dated since my symptoms started. We'd make it because he cared enough about me to stay, despite my traitorous body. I'd be enough to make him care. I could do enough and ignore enough and accommodate enough. But it really was only a matter of time.

"Oh, Ellie." Mark turns my name into a sympathetic coo. "Fuck that guy."

"But where are you now?" Heather repeats, inconveniently attuned to my earlier evasion.

"I'm looking at a room that's available to rent. Near Hyde Park," I add, hoping the allusion to the stately Austin neighborhood north of the university will inspire confidence.

"How did you find the space so quickly?" Mark asks.

"I saw the sign for it on Monday."

Another loaded pause. *Shit.* I fall back onto the mattress, the plastic cold against the bare skin of my shoulders and back. Heather's never outright expressed her dislike of Cole, but she never had to;

her face always did it for her. So I am unsurprised when she asks, "And *why* were you noticing rental signs Monday?" with particular venom.

"When I came into the kitchen that morning, I was still trying to figure out what was going on. So I had my hand over my left eye." I demonstrate, even though they can't see me, and my field of vision is reduced to the sliver I've retained in my periphery. I drop my hand, bringing the ceiling back into view. "And when Cole saw me, his reaction was 'Now what?'"

The rumbling of disapproval over the receiver is deeply satisfying.

"Ellie!" Mark says. "Why didn't you tell us then?"

"I was half-blind and no one knew why," I remind him. "It wasn't a priority."

"Ellie." Heather's voice is a warning.

"Why didn't you just go to our place tonight?" Mark cuts in. "We're not even there!"

A fair question. They're at a teaching conference in Houston and won't be back until tomorrow. And I had considered their address when I opened the rideshare app outside of the restaurant, but I'd dismissed the thought just as quickly.

I don't know if it's the buffer of the phone call or exhaustion— or, again, the beer—but I fess up. "Because you get an alert any time your front door's unlocked, you'd see that it was my door code unlocking it, and then one of you would call and I'd have to have this conversation. And I really, *really* didn't want to have to talk about this—any of this—tonight.

"It's not you," I assure them, because it isn't. It's everything else. "I've been being handled with kid gloves for years now, and

I'm tired of it. Constantly getting asked how I am and being told that I'm *so brave*, when what goddamn choice do I have?"

My voice rises as I talk, and I pause, forcing myself to reel it in. "Either my vision will come back, or it won't. Either I'll end up with MS, or I'll be okay, and we can add this episode to the list of shitty, weird things my body is so fond of throwing at me." I sigh. "And…yeah. Screw Cole. I'm not spending another night in that apartment. That was his plan, by the way. That I move into the room I use as my office, and we'd reassess in six months."

Mark sucks in a breath. "Like, your exact diagnosis window, those six months?"

"The very same. In this scenario, I presume, I'd be waiting for my vision to go out again—if it comes back in the first place—or for a tingling sensation in my limbs, or sudden lightheadedness, or some other symptom in the packet of maladies the doctor handed me today, and Cole would be chilling in the next room. He—" My next breath hisses in through gritted teeth. "He actually thought I'd accept that. That I'd be desperate enough—"

"No." Heather's voice is hard. "You're done with him."

"And he was done with *me*," I remind her, hoping to undercut any point she might make about my having settled or me being too good for Cole. Because it wasn't enough.

"Ellie—" she starts anyway.

"Any improvement on the eye front?" Mark interjects, like he's trying to defuse a squabble between cast members but will tell us to "use it" in our performance.

I take the out. "It fogged up in the shower this morning. My neurologist said that'll happen with extreme heat or physical exertion."

"At least it keeps things interesting?"

"You know how I love surprises," I grumble, which gets a laugh out of both of them. If there's anything I'm known for, it's my absolute resistance to surprises. Ditto disorganization, stretches of unstructured time, and substandard levels of cleanliness in any context. As far as people go, I might not be the best time, but I'm always guaranteed to be on time!

"Thank you for checking on me," I say. "You should go back to your mandatory fun."

Mark groans. "Ellie, the deejay just played a version of 'Hey Ya!' with lyrics about *cell division*. It's unbearable! And you're not even here to provide commentary!"

I smile. We interned at the same high school while we got our teaching degrees and were offered contracts there after we graduated. It hadn't been smooth sailing for any of us, but Mark stuck with it after being offered the coveted drama teacher position, and Heather found her footing with the science department. I'd bowed out after my single-year contract expired, focusing instead on the part of the experience I'd enjoyed: writing lesson plans and designing units of study. My business is still gaining traction, but I've landed some big projects; my online bundle for instructing *The Odyssey* was recently picked up by an entire school district in Denver. A welcome boon...even if it's going to be consumed by my deductible.

"Just don't commit to a place tonight, okay?" Heather implores. "Go to our place, put on some comfies, and veg out until we get back tomorrow. We'll plan from there."

"Which is to say that we'll come home to a spotless apartment and review the plan you've already come up with," Mark amends.

"You'll humor our suggestions, then execute your original plan because you'll come up with the best solution, anyway."

"True," I laugh, but throw them a bone. "The comfies are a great call, though."

"See? We're helpers." Heather sighs. "Hang tight, girly. I'm so sorry we can't be there."

"It's fine."

"No, it isn't," they chorus.

"You're right. It really, really isn't."

Something in my voice must betray how close I am to tears, because Heather's voice is uncharacteristically gentle when she says, "We'll see you tomorrow. I love you!" Mark sends his love as well and offers me the last of the exfoliating mask concealed in the butter penthouse of the fridge. I end the call as Heather gripes at his betrayal; he'd been hiding it from her.

While the screen is still illuminated, my eye lands on the bright pink icon of the rideshare app. I glance at the door Grant left through, then turn my head to look at the one that leads outside. It would be rude, but I could leave. I can pop over to my friends', ditch the boob tape, don some pjs, and start making lists in a desperate attempt to maintain order in my crumbling life. Not too different from a regular Friday for me.

I grimace. God, that's grim.

A text from Cole appears at the top of my screen. *I'm at home. Please come talk.* I glare at the message. *Home.* If there's anything I am sure about, it's that the two-bedroom apartment we've been overpaying for over the past two years is no longer my home.

A tentative knock sounds from the door to the rest of the house. "Hey...Ellie?" It's Grant. I unpeel myself from the mattress and rise with a crinkle of plastic. When I open the door, I find him and Diego shoulder to shoulder in the hallway, Alistair behind them. Diego waves.

"We, um..." Grant clears his throat. "We worried that you might be sad—"

"Do you want cheese?" Diego interjects, shouting over his roommate.

"Do I..." I blink. *"What?"*

The shorter pup thrusts his arm forward, hand up in offering. Resting on his palm is a single package of string cheese.

I stare at the offering. They have brought me cheese.

"We looked online for what helps girls when they're sad," Alistair explains, his expression guarded as he waits for my reaction. "Cheese was the only suggested thing we had."

My chest gives a little squeeze, and I press my lips together, blinking furiously against a week's worth of tears. They brought me cheese!

Three pairs of eyes go round in horror.

"Oh, no!" Grant's voice is pure panic as he shakes his head. "If you don't like cheese, we can find something else? We just don't have much in the kitchen. Maybe a banana? Or we're about to go out—" He grabs at Diego's still outstretched forearm.

"No! The cheese is great. Thank you." I relieve Diego of the string cheese, and his hand drops to his side, his frame going slack with relief. "I've had a rough week. And this"—I hold up the package—"is the sweetest thing anyone's done for me since I woke up Monday." I dab at my good eye, where a tear is threatening to fall. "These are gratitude tears."

The guys let out a collective "Ah!" of understanding.

I peel open the package, revealing an inch of shiny, off-white mozzarella, and take a bite. The three watch me in silent satisfaction at a job well done, Alistair craning to see from behind the other two.

I swallow. "Thank you, really. And you're right. I'm kind of down." I frown, accepting the gauntlet of questions I'm about to endure. "My boyfriend broke up with me tonight."

"Oh, shit!" Grant's brows are high. "That *sucks*."

Diego shakes his head, all empathy. "I'm sorry, Ellie."

I nod, waiting for a follow-up. Seconds pass. That's it. Once again, no prying. No prodding for gory details. Just an acknowledgment: This sucks, and they are bummed for me.

"Well, he *tried* to break up with me," I continue, curious how long this suspension of inquiry will hold. "He started it, and I finished."

"Sounds more like a tie," says Alistair.

"That—" I consider the reframing. It's almost cheering. "Thank you, I'll take that."

"You're welcome."

I smile and help myself to another bite of cheese. I'm ravenous, I realize. Before my appointment I'd been too nervous to eat, and after, it hadn't been a priority. I think back to the menu I'd been perusing before Cole brought up his bullshit "break." I was going to order the burrata. I could kill for a burrata right now.

Grant's shoulder rocks forward from a shove from Alistair, and he clears his throat. "If you want to take some time to decide about the room, that's no problem. But if you think that more cheese would be good, we were gonna go get pizza? If you wanna hang out?"

"And we're having kind of a party later," Alistair adds. "No big deal, just some friends."

My instinct is to decline, but before I can find the words, a tendril of something I can't quite identify winds through my rib cage. There's a charge to it, a call to action.

I pop the rest of the cheese into my mouth and chew, using the oversized bite to buy myself time to think. I *am* hungry. And it's not as though I have anything else to do. And if I discount the sheer farce of me hanging with a trio of college bros…

Why the hell not?

I swallow and then grin, the expression feeling foreign on my face. Foreign, but welcome. Made even more so when all three of the guys beam back.

"Can I get another beer before we go?"

3

28…29…30!

I spit the mouthwash into the sink and turn on the tap, watching the water rinse away the purple liquid. Oh, blessed, minty relief. I nod my thanks to the bottle of Listerine, as well as the dusty Spider-Man Dixie cup dispenser beside it. Mouthwash had been an *excellent* choice.

One of very few excellent choices I've made in the past few hours, because I am *drunk*.

I rest my hands on the bathroom counter and examine my reflection in the mirror. At least I still look presentable. Or…I think I do? It's hard to tell. The mirror is stippled with water spots and toothpaste, and—I lean back to take in the smudges running the width of the glass, gripping the counter as I teeter on my heels—based on the smudges, someone's used their finger to sketch a gigantic dick and balls on the glass after a steamy shower. A collegiate cave drawing.

Squinting through the artwork, I fluff my hair, arranging the front of the dark pixie cut into a state of classy dishevelment.

Then, I check the wings of my eyeliner; the left, and as much as I can make out of the right. Not smudged. More an indication of quality product than a measure of my current state, but I'll take it.

Next item of business: Do I need to throw up?

My lips screw to the corner in thought. *Nah.*

Though it wouldn't be the worst idea. I'd shotgunned beer two because Grant didn't think I could do it a second time. The pizza offset some of its effects, and I probably would have been okay if I hadn't taken up the bartender on his offer of a round of shots. Twice. And then had another beer. Or two? I smile. One had even been a Bud Light. *Take that, Cole.*

Thinking about him makes my chest hurt, and I scowl. *Ugh.* Cole. Proposing a "break" because of my stupid, screwy body.

My heart stutters, and the vision in my good eye blurs with tears. The booze has softened my defenses. I imagine the outlines of the more aggressive worries pressing against the walls I put up, their sharp edges tearing through and bringing reality crashing in with them—

"No!" I roll out my shoulders, standing tall—with a steadying hand on the counter—and blink back the tears, forcing myself to breathe. This is not the time for that. Right now is fun-times memories with Ellie. Like...the last few hours with Grant and his roommates! They are delightful. Sweet puppies, all. Even if Alistair speaks exclusively in declaratives and they've adorned their bathroom mirror with a penis.

Anyway! There was pizza! And the bar we hit *after* pizza was having a trivia night, and I crushed it! I waggle my eyebrows. I swept the classic *SNL* category, even if I'm not sure the nineties should be considered "classic"—I was born in the nineties and I am not "classic," thank you very much. And then we were kicked out because I was "disrupting the game" by "shouting out answers" while "not actually on a team," therefore "ruining the experience for paying participants." But I got everything right, and the guys were amazed, and that's what matters. But mostly what matters is that I *dominated*.

And now, I am at the house, enjoying a party filled with dudes. *Dudelings!* And it is time for me to go back to the dining room and soundly crush said dudelings in flip cup. *Again!*

My smile is huge. Oh, my jerk of a body is going to make me pay for tonight, but that is a problem for Tomorrow Ellie. Ellie of Now is Queen of the Collegiate Cave-Pups, and it *rules*.

But this mirror…this is unacceptable.

The corner of my bad eye picks up a familiar shade of blue, and I cock my head to confirm that it is, in fact, a bottle of Windex. *Serendipity!* My preferred all-purpose cleaner! I pick it up, then snag the stiff hand towel from where it hangs beside the light switch.

I look back at the mirror. A good queen leads by example, and my subjects must learn to recognize a civilized level of cleanliness.

It is decided: I shall tidy.

The tribute to masculine pride is erased in a series of sprays and wipes, though the more stubborn toothpaste flecks require that I pry at them with my thumbnail—my nail tech is always getting on me for using my claws like a multitool—before I work my way down to polishing the faucet, which sounds like a euphemism, but it is not.

As I wipe, the lightbulbs above the mirror catch my attention. There's a gray cast to them, as though coated in a layer of dust.

This will not do. I hike up my dress and clamber onto the counter, then pause. Bare feet would be inadvisable on the bathroom floor, but high heels on the counter sounds like danger times. I wiggle my toes until my shoes slip off my feet, thudding onto the floor. I wiggle them even more. Oh, those are not going back on tonight. Or ever, maybe.

Back to work! A queen never shirks her duties.

I'm considering my approach to the bulbs—spray and risk creating a mystery paste, or dry-wipe and risk inhalation—when there's a knock at the door. I reply with an "It's unlocked," that, if I'm being honest, sounds pretty fucking regal.

The door opens, and behind me, a deep voice asks, "The hell are you doing up there?"

"I'm tidying," I say primly, and turn to the—good Lord—*truly* massive man now filling the doorway. "Whoa. You are a *lot* of dude."

His responding shrug is apologetic, which is adorable. "I get that a lot. What do you mean you're tidying?" His "What do you mean" sludges out in one long "Whaddumean?," which suggests he's as sauced as I am. *How festive!*

"I mean that the bathroom is gross, so I'm cleaning it. Look at this." I use the nails of my thumb and forefinger to pick at the grime on the nearest bulb, and release it to fall in one solid sheet.

The man follows the drifting ick, frowning as the gray mass settles on the counter. "Ew."

"Quite."

He hikes his thumb toward the door. "Mind if I shut that? I need to pee."

"You're in the right place," I say, supportively, and resume decrudding the bulbs. For the sake of decorum, I position myself so I can't see the man's reflection, though even with his distance from the mirror, one broad shoulder is visible around my own reflection. I focus on my task and try to ignore the unmistakable sound of someone who stands to pee.

Another panel of gray detritus comes loose. Isn't dust mostly dead skin cells? I grimace. *So gross.*

The toilet flushes, and a fly is zipped. I hear, "If we're cleaning, I'll do the toilet. That's not fit for a lady's eyes."

To say nothing of a queen, I think.

Or not, as the big guy says, "Queen?" I pretend that I haven't accidentally spoken my thoughts aloud and thank him for his offer. The toilet is, indeed, foul.

A cabinet opens and closes, and he scrubs the toilet as I wipe down the remaining bulbs. He extends a polite "Excuse me" to wash his hands, and I step aside, focusing on eliminating the smudge my shoulder made on the mirror when I stood.

Satisfied, I decide it is time to get down off the counter. But as I turn, my heel hits a wet patch. I gasp, going into free fall. I'm coming down hard—

Until I'm not. Strong hands grip my waist, and I let out a grunt unbecoming of a lady of my status. My hands close on beefy shoulders, and I find myself staring down into a pair of remarkable gray eyes.

The hands at my waist give me a little squeeze, guiding me to a kneeling position on the counter, making us eye level. "You okay?"

"Yeah, I'm—" What *am* I? Other than super drunk, sharing a space with a large, unfamiliar man, and probably overdue for a threat assessment.

"Assess away."

I frown. I'm thinking out loud. That's no good. But I accept his invitation, leaning back as far as I can without releasing my hold on his shoulders, because they feel really nice. He's dressed in a light, fitted sweater in a pale blue, with a white crew neck tee underneath. The sleeves of the tee are obvious under the sweater, creating rings around his bulging upper arms.

"It's hard to find things that fit me," he says quietly.

"It looks very nice," I say. "But tight? I hope it's not uncomfortable."

He shrugs, as though resigned to his ringed fate. "Sleeves are never big enough around."

"That must be difficult." I look him up and down. And side to side. He's truly a landmass of a human; I can't fathom how much height he'd have on me if I were on the ground. His shoulders are so wide, it wouldn't be a stretch to imagine him having to turn to the side to get through doorways.

"It's happened," he mumbles, so self-conscious that I let out an "Aww!" of sympathy. One of my hands shifts from his shoulder to pat his cheek. He closes his eyes, pressing the side of his face into my palm with a faint, satisfied smile. His face is smooth, like he's only just shaved, and is so, so warm.

Even without those exceptional eyes, this fellow is a treat to look at. He has a firm jawline and defined cheekbones, not so high as to be pretty, but striking. Thick brows, too, and dark lashes. All terribly manly. Very appealing.

I have completed my assessment and identified him as a sexy man.

His eyes flutter open. "*You're* pretty," he says, as though extending an olive branch. "I like your hair. I like short hair on women. I like the shape of your head," he adds, which is an embarrassment of likes, but the unsolicited flattery makes my chest feel mushy. Which I hope I hope I *hope* isn't a sign of impending vomit.

"You seem very…" He frowns. "Fancy."

I cast aside any fears of vomiting. "Fancy?"

"Cause of how you talk? Or the dress."

I beam. "Thank you! I'd been saving it."

"And your nails," he adds. I lift my hand from his face, and he cranes his neck to inspect my nails. "They're very long. How do you use your phone?"

This is a good question. "Carefully?"

He nods, seeming to take this in, then cocks his head. "Do you always clean bathrooms at house parties?"

"Only when there's a dick on the mirror," I say, but I'm totally absorbed in this man's face. His eyes really are amazing. He half smiles, letting me know that I probably just said that "amazing" bit aloud, but I can't be bothered to be embarrassed because that smidge of a smile makes his eyes *sparkle*!

I lean forward on my knees to look closer, pressing my hands against his very firm and—*ooh!*—very warm chest—for balance. His eyes are dark gray. Slate. The color of a Weimaraner's coat. A lesser woman might compare them to storm clouds, but I show tremendous restraint as I study them. Gray, with flecks of gold. Amazing! How does someone even get gray eyes?

"Genetics?"

I blink. That came from the eyes' mouth. The eyes' *owner's* mouth. Which—I allow my attention the multi-inch trek required to consider his lips—is very nice.

And very close. *We* are very close.

I wonder what his lips feel like. Intrepid explorer queen that I am, I lift a hand from his chest and use my index finger to trace along the line of his jaw, grazing his lower lip. "Soft."

The lips part slightly, tongue darting to taste where I'd just touched. Ooh, *tongue!*

I gasp. I've just had *the best* idea! "I'm going to kiss you, if that's okay," I tell the lips, already preparing for launch. But as I initiate, the hands at my waist hold me in place, stopping me from making contact.

"Are you drunk?"

I shake my head. Silly question, lips. "I'm not *drunk*. I'm *Ellie.*" And I'm the queen. And I'm coy. And kinda sexy. But sad. And maybe a little scared—

Lips frown, the lower one jutting out in the most delectable way. "You're Ellie and a *queen* and you're coy and sexy, but sad and scared?"

To my horror, my eyes sting with sudden tears. I freeze, my mission to lips forgotten. Because of all of those things, I am mostly the last one.

I am *scared.*

I force my next breath in slowly, painfully aware of the way it shudders through my chest, like hiccupping sobs in reverse. The stunning eyes I'm staring into soften, the tenderness among the storm clouds threatening to undo every careful bit of scaffolding I've erected to keep myself upright this week. The fears press against my defenses.

I push back harder. "*And* I'd like to kiss you, Tall Man. Please? Are *you* drunk?" I ask, because it seems like a good question. I'm smiling again. We are so good at questions!

Lips smile back, angling closer. "I'm not drunk, I'm—"

Tumbling forward, I finally make it to his lips. They part upon contact, the tip of his tongue eager and teasing. The hands at my waist slide up my bare back, pulling me closer. The whole front of me is warm and melty and soft, the chest and abdomen of Man Mountain a solid slab of heat. It's like a hot stone massage at every point of contact, a soothing firmness.

For a second, I'm sure my eye is going to fog up, but I don't let myself think about that because I am still the queen.

And coy and sexy, but no longer

even a little bit

scared.

4

I.

Feel.

Like.

DEATH.

My stomach is a burning, roiling riot of alcohol fumes and acid.

And my head is pain. Concentrated misery throbbing in time with my heartbeat. It stabs against my eyeballs, which are so gritty with makeup residue, I can feel last night's mascara through my closed eyelids. For the moment, I keep them shut; best to reduce the number of parts receptive to pain.

Today will be a total write-off. Hell, it'll be a miracle if I'm even at 75 percent *tomorrow*.

And yet, a smile stretches across my face. I had a *great* time.

Tentative optimism has me reaching across the mattress to check for a possible gray-eyed bedmate, but as my left hand skims over what feels like terrycloth, it seems I'm alone. I brave a peek, slitting my eyes: just me. Me, covered with, if the crinkling is any indication, a sleeping bag, lying on a red-and-white-striped beach towel. There's a large fold-over tag still sewn in the far corner of the towel. A new towel, then. How nice.

My solo status rouses a flicker of disappointment, but it's probably for the best. If I look even as remotely as hellish as I feel, I'd hate to alarm my mystery hunk.

Though I could go for a co-misery snuggle.

Or the release of death.

Or...Taco Bell.

Eyes still partially open, I spot my phone beside my pillow. It vibrates with an incoming text, but I leave it. I'm not ready to let reality intrude on this surreal bubble of pain and giddiness. My head is splitting and I got kicked out of a bar last night! I cleaned a bathroom and made out with a stranger! Who was that guy? And who the hell was I?

I close my eyes, replaying the session's highlights. We kissed, which *I* initiated! Five years since my last first kiss, and *I* made the first move! And the kissing was excellent, with hands going all sorts of happy places. Definitely a butt guy, my mystery man. He found my tush and held on!

And then—

I frown.

And then...it is now. My memory is a soggy blur from the butt-grab to the unkindness of daylight. Save for that enthusiastic hold on my backside, I've got nothing. I know that there was no sexual activity; even with the current barrage of sensations in my body, I'm clued in to my nether regions enough to know they stayed on the bench last night. Though, in other erogenous zone news, I've exceeded my boob tape's recommended usage period by who knows how many hours. That's going to be rough later.

Okay! So. I blacked out—not great—but I was safely tucked away with makeshift bedding. I'll call that a draw. I'm not super sure where I am—also not ideal—and I'm—I hold a hand over my left eye, cautiously opening my right—nothing but a blur in the outside corner. Still half-blind, then. Crud.

So that's two in the con column for my current state, and that's ignoring the dumped, homeless, and potential MS of it all.

But I'm still smiling. I *went* for it.

And now I'm violently hungover in an unknown location.

Still smiling, though!

Granted, that smile slips into a grimace as I push myself into a seated position for a better view of my surroundings. The sleeping bag falls to my lap with a crinkle of nylon. Other than the bed, which is simply a mattress on the floor, there's nothing in the room. Incredible light…

Clarity! The Dawghouse! With the collegiate puppies! Where… I might live now?

My other senses are slowly emerging from the booze-soaked haze, and I register the dull thump of bass. *And*—I inhale through my nose—someone in the vicinity is cooking bacon.

The bacon is my motivation as I knee-walk my way to the end of the mattress. There, I find my shoes—ugh, no thank you, heels—and a pile of laundry. On it is a sticky note reading, FOR ELLY ALL CLEAN! The note must have been written after the sticky was put on the clothing; there's a hole poked into the paper at the bottom of the exclamation point.

I look over the stack of sweatshirts and shorts and smile. First, they give me cheese, and now, they've conjured comfies from who knows where.

I put the clothes aside for later and swing my legs off the mattress. Standing is precarious, but once upright, I make it to the door without incident, then open it and step out. The bass is louder, and the bacon smell blessedly thicker.

"Hello?" No response.

I continue down the hall, noting an abundance of fuzzy gray mounds running the length of the baseboards. The off-white walls are bare and pockmarked with years of thumbtack punctures and residual tape. There has to be a constant flow of students through this place.

I pass an open door and peer in to find a bedroom. It is masculine collegiate in its purest form. The unmade bed has no headboard, clothing litters the floor, and in lieu of curtains or blinds, dark sheets have been pinned—no, *duct-taped*—over the windows.

Leaning in the doorway in my achy, dehydrated state, I feel ancient. This is a world for which I have zero context. I don't know if the posters on the walls are for bands or video games or some strain of comic book movies. The desk is a wasteland of textbooks and slim black cans of what I'd guess is an energy drink. I shake my head and move on.

The next door leads to the bathroom I enjoyed with my mystery man, and I take advantage of the facilities. I study my reflection as I wash my hands. Other than the telltale puffiness of binge-drinking after thirty, I look less haggard than I feel. I clean up the raccoon eyes with my fingertips and give my hair a fluff. Man Mountain had liked my hair.

Grinning, I shake my head and reach for the mouthwash. I

gargle and swish—thanks again, my minty friend—and replay what I can remember. That *happened*!

I spit and rinse. *And* I'm feeling almost human. Things are looking up!

For exactly three seconds.

Then I lurch for the toilet and violently expel the contents of my stomach.

One hideous, sweaty minute later, I'm back at the sink for a second helping of mouthwash. This time, the refresh isn't hijacked by my body's attempt to rid itself of the many poisons consumed last night, and I step back into the hallway, leaving none the wiser.

I pass a window—and backtrack.

It's a view of the backyard. A black frame sits on a concrete slab by the back fence. Grant is hanging on to one of the bars bracing across the top of the frame, doing...something. His legs swing forward, then pump back, and a moment later, he's levered his torso above the bar. I don't even have time to wonder how he'll get down before he reverses the route, swinging himself below the bar. Another launch has him vaulting up again.

A few feet away, Diego is committed to some other bonkers feat of strength. He has a barbell held across his chest and shoulders, with thick weight plates on either end. He squats, then straightens to a standing position, shoving the bar up and over his head with a grunt loud enough to hear over the music they're blasting. In one movement, he brings the bar back to his shoulders, squats, straightens, and sends the bar up, repeating the cycle...again...and again...

I've lost track of how many times the two repeat their respective endeavors when Diego announces something I can't make out.

Grant replies with a cry, propelling himself above the bar one more time. "Fifteen!" He lowers himself to the ground. The two knuckle-bump as they change spots, immediately getting to work on the other activity.

"They didn't even take a break," I marvel.

"Yeah. That set is for time," announces a voice.

I wheel to find Alistair on my right, wet-haired and glistening, wearing only a towel. Protective instinct has me returning to the window, for fear that looking upon a god in its purest form will extinguish the vision from my remaining eye. *Jesus.* I don't even understand what I just saw. An eight-pack?

When he joins me at the window, he's on my bad side, limiting my view to a sliver of shape and motion. "Diego's on bar muscle-ups, and what Grant's doing is just a thruster. It's a quick grind. Twenty-one, fifteen, nine. Of each."

Wow. "I can't imagine doing a single one of either. Let alone forty-five."

"Nah. The bar muscle-ups can take years to master, but there's always alternate movements. And thrusters are basic. It's the weight and volume that wear you down."

I understand none of this, but it's nice of him to try to explain. "You're not out there?"

"I gotta hold stuff in my shoot on Monday. Can't shred myself on the bar."

Before I can process the implication of the "shred" comment, Alistair says, "C'mon," and moves farther down the hall to a door. He shoulders it open, and his towel slips from his waist to flash me his entire posterior.

He recovers in time to spare himself further exposure, bunching the towel together as he continues to press open the door. He brays out a laugh. "Almost showed off the goods."

I just raise my brows and step onto the porch. There are no words.

Alistair keeps a hand on his towel as we cross the patio, still strewn with last night's fallen soldiers. I don't know that I made it out here, but if I had, I'm disappointed in myself for failing to rouse anyone to consolidate the recycling.

By the time we get to the yard, the guys have traded places again. They move through the final round with the same speed as the previous sets, and I lose all thoughts for beer cans and the unbroken skin tone of Alistair's backside as I watch them work. It's incredible.

Diego spots us. "Ah!" he grunts, the bar overhead. He brings the bar back down, squats, and extends. "Morning—" Squat, extend. "Ellie—" Squat, extend. "Did you sleep—" Squat, extend, "Well? Nine!" He brings the bar to rest at his chest, then drops it to the ground with a thud. "That's time!"

"Howdy, Ellie!" Grant drops from the bar and fetches his phone from a little stand on the frame, silencing the music, then bumps knuckles with Diego, and the two join Alistair and me.

Alistair extends a fist to each of the guys. "Looking strong. Overextending at the top of some thrusters, though, Grant."

"I felt it, too," Grant replies, shaking his head at himself as he rolls out his shoulders. I remain agog. How is he not incapacitated right now?

"As long as you know. Imma get dressed." Alistair bumps me with his shoulder. "Ellie just saw my ass," he says, chuckling, and departs.

Diego shakes his head. "We're *always* seeing his ass."

I nod. "This is what you do? To maintain—" I motion toward them, hoping it conveys their general vitality without having to directly address the fact that each appears to have been hewn from marble. Because neither of them is wearing a shirt, and it's hard not to stare. Grant is a tribute to long, lean, athleticism, while Diego is a stockier version, softer, but powerfully built. They gleam in the spring sunshine, breathing heavily, but steadily. The way they've bounced back from last night's activities brings to mind the adage that youth is wasted on the young, but considering what they just did with their youth, I'm going to settle on being jealous.

"My brother owns a gym," Grant explains. "Actually, we were gonna talk to you about that—oh!" He interrupts himself. "Were you okay in back? We kind of threw together the stuff for you to sleep on."

"Yeah, thank you! I appreciate it. I'm just sorry you had to take care of me."

Grant waves me off. "Nah. It's all good." He chuckles. "You were *awesome.*"

I don't believe I've ever been dubbed "awesome" before. I can't help smiling. "Thanks?"

"Seriously!" he insists. "You, like, *crushed* that trivia game. You could have been your own team and totally won."

"And you're so good at flip cup! Do you think that your nails are an advantage? They're so elegant. *You're* so elegant," he says, voice dropping off into shyness.

My smile expands to a grin, which, oddly, relieves some

pressure on my aching skull. "Thank you. That's very sweet," I say, otherwise unsure how to respond. I'm not accustomed to this degree of unfiltered flattery. A gal could get used to this.

"It looked like you had a great time, too!" says Grant. "I'm so glad, especially after how your night started."

"I still cannot believe you were dumped at a restaurant," says Diego.

The reference abrades my freshly stroked ego. Except for that inventory of misfortunes when I woke up, I haven't spared a thought to the general unpleasantness of my reality. Some of that could be simply prioritizing my hangover and the exploration of my surroundings, but the guys have been a welcome distraction.

"At least it ended up a tie," I say.

"Hell yeah!" Grant raises a hand for a high five, and, why not? We slap palms.

He grins and pivots toward the frame they were on earlier, like he's just remembered the three-subjects-ago thread of conversation, "Yeah, we coach at Ian's gym, and also work out here." He points to an open-sided shed. Inside are black weight plates, as well as an assortment of dumbbells and some kind of round, handled weights in yellow, orange, green, red, and purple.

"You wanna get in a few pull-ups? You'd have total freedom of movement in what you're wearing. Oh! We left stuff for you to change into. C'mon!" He starts walking toward the house, leaving me several conversational turns behind.

I follow him and Diego, still trying to formulate a response to the offer to do pull-ups, as if it were a given that I'm capable of performing them, when I remember the laundry that had been at the end of the bed. "Where did you get clo—"

But the guys gasp in unison, breaking into a sudden run for the open back door. I can make out a shrill beeping, and Diego's dismayed cry of "The bacon!" before he dashes inside.

Bacon?—Ah! I congratulate myself as it clicks. They'd been cooking bacon. And the beeping is a smoke detector. Which means that the bacon is burning.

Then I'm running for the door, too. "The bacon!"

5

THE BACON IS NOT ONLY burning; it is actively *ablaze*. Flames are leaping from the pan when I arrive to find the three men in the kitchen, panic in their voices as they bicker over what to do. Alistair's on a chair, poking at the buttons on the wailing smoke detector, while Grant swings a broom, fanning the air. Diego moves toward the stove with a pitcher of water.

"No!" I cry, and they freeze, Diego stopping so suddenly, some of the water spills. "It's a grease fire. Water will make it worse." I lunge for the stove and turn off the burner, dodging the inferno still raging in the frying pan. "Salt?" I ask. "Or baking soda?"

Three pairs of eyes blink at me through the smoke. Grant gives the air a broad swipe with his broom.

Shit. "Fire extinguisher?"

Grant points toward the cabinet below the sink. "Down there, maybe?"

I lurch for it, yanking open the little door. The space is a clutter of cleaning liquids and sponges, but a red canister peeks from behind the pipes. I grab it, knocking over a sticky bottle of dish soap. Crossing back to the stove, I scan the directions on the side of the extinguisher. I've never had to use one before, but I pull the pin, aim the hose, and squeeze the handle. White foam explodes across the stovetop, and the fire is out.

No one moves. My heart is racing, and the smoke detector is still going off, the sustained wail rattling my skull. I may vomit again.

Eyes watering from the lingering smoke, I gesture toward Alistair, still on the chair. He's replaced his towel with a pair of black boxer briefs with an inseam bordering on negligible. I'm going to be able to draw this guy from memory before noon.

I point to the hateful disk still screaming above him. "Don't bother with the buttons. See if you can get the battery out."

He gets to work, and I look to the others. "Open every window you can. The doors, too. Let's get some air in here."

Diego gives me a thumbs-up, and Grant nods emphatically, like he's grateful for the direction. They leave the kitchen while I put the fire extinguisher back under the sink, righting the soap I knocked over, and close the cabinet. The smoke detector cuts off mid-beep, but my ears are ringing. I brace myself against the sink, hands gripping the porcelain rim as I take in long, slow, vomit-abating breaths.

When I'm confident enough that I'll be retaining whatever's left in my stomach, I face the kitchen again. The smoke has cleared some, and there are scorch marks across the stovetop. "How long had that been cooking?" I ask.

"Dunno." Alistair's still on the chair, holding the smoke detector in one hand and the nine-volt battery he removed from it in the other. Frowning, he raises the battery to eye level, then, after a moment's consideration, sticks the business end to his tongue.

He lets out a little "Yip!" at the resulting shock, then chuckles, his smile dazzling. He extends the battery my way. *"Feisty."*

I decide that a response isn't necessary and cast my watery eye over the room. The counter is a clutter of dirty dishes, last night's empties, and dark plastic tubs covered in aggressive fonts declaring tens of grams of protein per serving. The only solid foods I see are a speckled bunch of bananas well past their prime, whatever bacon might be left in the package, which is precariously close to the stovetop, and some protein bars. I pick one up. *Tastes just like birthday cake!* Wouldn't bet on it.

Grant reenters the kitchen, still brandishing the broom, Diego behind him. "Ellie, I'm so sorry about that! We were trying to get a head start on the breakfast tacos you said you'd make, and we decided to get our workout in, but I guess that was too long. Or we had the pan too hot?"

I toss the bar back onto the counter. I said I'd make breakfast tacos? That…tracks.

"You wrote out a list of stuff we'd need to pick up, but I was going to get what we didn't already have after we worked out. You made a couple of lists, actually." He reaches into the pocket of his shorts, fishing around until he finds a folded slip of paper, and hands it to me.

It's a Michael's receipt that I still need to expense, but written on the back in a vibrant teal brush-tip marker is a list in my distinctive handwriting. The heading reads *Taco Fixins*, followed by the groceries Grant mentioned, but it's the list farther down the receipt that catches my eye. *To-dos in the face of suddenly single status.* Lord. Even three sheets to the wind, I just can't help my neurotic self.

Division of property, it begins. *Find a place to put said property—go through with the Dawghouse? Recoup my half of deposit/first and last*

from apt with Cole. Hate him. Many expenses ahead. Deductible, etc.
Part-time job? This color is too whimsical for this task.

"I love your handwriting." Diego taps the paper. "Your *A* looks like a star!"

"Thank you." I frown at the teal-tinted rambling. "Did I go over this with you guys," I ask, wondering how thoroughly I'd detailed my plight, "or was I just scribbling like a weirdo?"

"Mostly like a weirdo," says Alistair, who seems content to remain standing on a chair in the middle of the kitchen.

"We, um, have an idea, for the part-time job, if that's cool?" says Grant, managing to break the offer up into multiple questions. "Because Ian's looking for someone to work the front desk at his gym. Like, help members check in, handle the social posts, do some cleaning—"

"Was it you who cleaned that bathroom?" Diego interrupts, the question bursting from him with the same intensity with which a detective would reveal the name of the murderer in a whodunnit. I nod, and he, once again, beams. "I could tell that someone had made it fresh. It was nice to greet my face this morning without having to move around a giant penis."

Grant points to Diego as though his contribution proved a point. "So, you're obviously qualified for the gym job. And, um…" He swallows, eyes darting from Diego up to Alistair. "We might have a solution for another item on there."

"You have some thoughts on the blue I used?" I ask, glancing back at my list.

"Way too whimsical for a list with 'deductible' on it," says Alistair. Before I can worry about how much he might have read into that, he adds, "We want you to move in."

I huff a laugh, but Alistair doesn't respond to his own punchline. "You—" I look from him to the other guys. "Seriously?"

The guys glance back and forth at one another. Grant resumes the role of spokesman. "Yes?"

"You do remember that I'm way, *way* older than y'all, right?"

Grant shrugs it off. "So's my brother. That was never a big deal."

"And you're way more fun than Ian," Diego adds. "No offense, Grant."

"Nah. Ian's boring as hell."

I tap my chest. "*I* am boring as hell. Last night was an outlier."

"Which makes it even cooler that you owned us in flip cup!" Grant persists. "You're funny and fancy and smart, and—" He uses the broom to indicate the scorched stovetop. That's absolutely coming out of their deposit. "You know how to avoid a grease fire!"

"True," I say, not quite believing that I'm actually entertaining this. But other than the massive gap in ages, interests, and standards of cleanliness, why not? Aside from what might, I realize, be a minor case of alcohol poisoning, I had a damn blast last night. So, provided there are no further flirtations with death by booze, why can't I simply postpone reality for a little longer?

When I left my neurologist's yesterday, the paperwork he handed off included a copy of the email exchange he had with my gynecologist, Dr. Selah. A courtesy, as endometriosis patients appear to be at a higher risk of developing other autoimmune diseases, predominantly MS. The numbers aren't significantly higher, but, as per the good doctor, "They're not negligible."

Dr. Selah's reaction had been priceless: *Can't this woman get a break?*

That same insistent energy that had me accepting the guys'

offer for pizza sparks to life. Maybe I can! *This* can be my break.
I can manage my own business from anywhere, and it's flexi-
ble enough that any schedule I end up with at this gym can be
worked around. If I can do this while coddled in an onslaught of
blind admiration, it sounds like a win-win.

Provided one looks past the nightmarish state of things around
the house. Which, even with only one functioning eye, I cannot.

"That is so generous—" I start. Grant and Diego's faces fall.
Alistair is looking at his phone, produced from who knows where,
but his brows twitch down in some degree of disappointment. It's
like I've declared that Christmas is canceled.

"That's a *no*," Diego grumbles.

"Not at all! I'm just"—*trying to come up with a polite way to convey
that I find your standard of living unacceptable and that if every trip to
the restroom carries the threat of Chia Pet toes, I'm not going to make it a
week*—"wondering if you'd be cool with me helping you elevate
things around here a bit."

They nod, eyes going distant in thought or incomprehension.

"Like, clean the bathrooms. *Properly*," I clarify. "Shop for more
than protein bars."

"We don't even buy those," Grant says, leaning into the broom
like it's a wizard's staff. "We get them from Ian."

"Because we're usually broke," says Alistair.

"Budgeting!" I say. "I can help you with that, too. Get you set
up with an app."

"You would do all of that?" Alistair asks, sounding genuinely
interested.

"It's what I *live* for." I tap my sternum again. "Boring as hell,
remember?"

Grant brays out his distinctive laugh. "Oh. You're gonna be *perfect* for the gym."

"And here! Food in the fridge, no more penises on the mirror," Diego says. "Oh! Could you help us with cooking, too? Like, show us how?"

"Absolutely," I say, and his whole face lights up. "To be clear, I won't be your maid. I'll help set up a baseline for the house and get you more comfortable in the kitchen, but if we're doing this, it's something you'll have to maintain." I've done enough man-coddling. This isn't simply me imposing my standard of living on three collegiate males. I'll be sparing future partners the indignity of pube-dusted bathroom floors and the burden of undoing years of learned helplessness. This could change lives.

A tendril of excitement begins to weave through me. Cole's "Now what?" from Monday takes on new meaning. Now what? *This!*

"Like a mentor. For adult stuff," Alistair muses.

Grant shrugs. "I'm in. It's what? May? And we're gonna be here at least through May of next year. So, even if you wanted to just try it for a little while—"

"A six-month lease!" I say, plucking the timeline from the no-man's-land of my con list. I reach out a hand to shake on it. "Do we have a deal?"

All three grasp my outstretched hand, chorusing, "Deal!" The resulting handshake is vigorous enough to jostle my upper body, and I'm reminded of the adhesive support system rigged up beneath my dress.

"Great!" I say. "First order of business: Do we have any cooking oil?"

6

FROM THE BACK SEAT OF Grant's ancient Jetta, Diego takes in an exaggerated inhale, releasing it on a sigh. "Is it you who smells so good, Ellie? It's like a cookie in here. The kind with the cocoa and chocolate. What is that, Alistair?"

"A macaroon."

"Ah, yes. Like a macaroon."

"That would be the spray oil," I say. The only options earlier were a store-brand coconut oil spray and a still sealed bottle of rosemary-infused truffle oil with a HomeGoods sticker on it. Lord only knows how three dudes with an empty fridge ended up with truffle oil.

Unwilling to be marinated, I opted for the spray. It actually worked really well to release the adhesive; I'll have to make a note of it when I post a review of the tape.

"That's genius," says Alistair. "Full-coverage moisture in a fraction of the time. I should try that."

I nod, but I'm not sure that the switch would make a dent in Alistair's skincare routine; that guy's product lineup puts Mark's to shame. He even had a few basic makeup products for me to pick through after I washed off the remnants of last night's face. I may still *feel* like death warmed over, but the five-minute beautifying routine has made me *look* less like a corpse.

Changing into the clothing the guys had rounded up was also restorative. While I have zero doubt that the pile was all keepsakes from my hosts' sexual conquests past, the desiccated Tide pod adhered to one of the hoodies supported their claim that it had all been washed, and I dove in. After vetoing anything in UT's distinct burnt orange, I settled on a pair of black running shorts, a top with a built-in shelf bra, and a blue hoodie. They even had flip-flops in my size.

Comfortably dressed, features drawn in to a degree of discernibility, and my tummy lined with a base of oven-cooked bacon (a revelation to the trio, though I don't know that it's any less a fire hazard when they forget that they're cooking in the first place), I'm feeling a solid 63 percent human, and up to a field trip to my workplace-to-be.

While I try to count the protein bar wrappers and discarded energy drinks littering the floor of the passenger side, Grant and Diego pepper me with factoids about the gym. It's in a decommissioned firehouse, and named Firehouse Fitness, which Diego thinks is very clever. Grant's brother opened it after an injury ended his weight-lifting career a few years back.

"Saturday morning is the big endurance class," says Grant. "We usually come, but we stayed home so you wouldn't wake up to an empty house. That would've been weird."

I smile. "Thank you for that." It's remarkable how these guys can be so clueless and yet totally thoughtful. Full hearts, empty heads, the lot of them. I love it. I still can't believe I've agreed to *live with them*, but I love it!

"We're here!" Diego leans between the front seat to point to the building ahead, which is, for all appearances, a classic firehouse. It has two large truck bays, the garage doors open to the increasingly balmy Austin morning. The driveway has been covered in green turf, and a series of tractor tires lean against the fence that separates the gym from an alley. A red awning stretches over the turf, casting what must be blessed shade over the sweaty bodies littering the ground.

And holy *hell*, are there bodies.

At least a dozen people are sprawled on the turf while a handful of athletes wrap up their workout. One guy is using a jump rope impossibly fast, the line slipping underfoot twice between jumps. A woman, middle-aged and in a T-shirt reading BUT DID YOU DIE? is jumping onto a low wooden box, then hopping off the opposite side, before turning around and going back again. Over, and over, and over, just like the guys with their workout earlier.

"Excuse me" I hear, and I step aside as a fellow who cannot be less than seventy shuffles past me. In each hand is a green handled ball, like the ones in the guys' shed, held down at his sides. Every muscle in his—I blink—his *incongruously jacked* arms is corded and taut, and as he crosses some invisible finish line, he releases the green things to the turf with a guttural cry. He throws up his hands, fingers still curled around phantom handles, and gasps out a laugh as others shout their support. A few of the downed athletes clap, but the older guy isn't done yet. He picks up a jump rope from beside his weights and begins jumping.

His approach is the single hop I'm familiar with, but he gets in some doubles, too. As he works, the initial guy concludes to some applause, then joins the fallen, but no one who's finished leaves their spot or starts putting away their stuff. They just watch and offer encouragement. Except for the gal at the box; it's all hop, hop, hop over there. The guys had a box in their setup, too. Looks questionable. Questionable, but…fun?

"How old is that guy jumping rope?" I ask.

"Tom? He's, like, seventy-five? He lives next door. Came in the first week to yell at Ian about the music being too loud, and we gave him a trial membership. He's been here ever since."

I nod, watching him continue to jump. How many is he going to do?

"Then, Tom recruited a bunch of his neighbors," Grant is saying, "and they're all here, too. That crew rolls in for the five a.m. class during the week."

"They do coffee at Tom's after," chimes Diego. "It's really cute. He makes espresso."

"Tom has diabetes," Alistair says, his voice low. "Type two. His doctor had been trying to get him to pick up some form of activity for years."

"Better late than never," I offer.

Alistair makes a dismissive noise. "Better to *not* get diabetes in the first place."

Grant shrugs. "You gotta take charge of your body while you can."

While you can reverberates in my brain with all the subtlety of a gong. It rouses my awareness of the six-month diagnosis window from where I'd banished it after shaking on the lease. How long might I have to take charge of my body?

My whole body flashes hot, my heart rate spiking in vicarious thrill as I watch the athletes work. It's the feeling I'd get before a race at swim meets in high school, the thrum of anticipation, the itch to move. I *want* to do this.

While I can.

In a lot of ways, my body is an unknown. I can read the signs of oncoming pain and do my best to mitigate when it arrives, but I've never explored the limits of what my body can *do*. Can I do a pull-up? If I tried, would I be able to do the double-jumps?

There's a rope hanging from a beam extending above a window on the second floor of the building. It's thick, like the ones people climb in gym class in movies and on TV. I've never had to do that, and I don't know how long I'll have to find out if I can.

MS isn't a death sentence. To quote my neurologist, patients "die with it, not from it," and the majority of people living with MS remain fully ambulatory even decades after being diagnosed. But there's no question that the condition would have a significant impact on my life.

My pulse thrills again, adrenaline surging through my limbs until they tingle with the need to move. I want to know what I can do. More than that: I want to have command of my body and push it to do more than whatever it's capable of now. I want to do thrusters and muscle-ups and carry those ball things with Tom. Maybe have an espresso.

The *now what?* has been actualized. This is *it*. I'm going to do *this* while I can.

I'm filled with a sense of purpose as I stride through the nearest bay door.

And freeze.

He's here.

7

MAN MOUNTAIN. My toilet-scrubbing makeout partner, he of the gray eyes and the compelling butt-grab, is *here*.

I caught him in profile before I froze up, but now he's facing me, greeting Diego with a high five in the center of the room. He's wearing a navy baseball cap with yellow stitching, and lifts it to run his fingers through his dark hair as Diego starts speaking.

The memories wash over me. Me, raking my nails over his scalp. He'd liked that. I'd liked the feel of his hair. Very soft. And I'd liked the growling sound my nails had pulled from him, and the way he'd cupped my butt immediately after...

I shake my head to clear it of the libidinous fog. My brain is slow on the uptake, but two and two are easing together. Man Mountain was the only house party attendee of an age at which one might reasonably own and operate a business, and if there's anyone in my recent experience who I'd guess had spent time as a professional weight lifter, it's Mr. T-Shirts Don't Fit My Arms. Now, here he is, at the gym Grant's brother owns. Either this place's clientele is *casual drop-in for a hangout* close with its staff, or...

"So, Grant." My voice squeaks. "Just wondering, is Ian *quite* tall?"

Grant brays out his laugh, moving to where I've planted myself. "Oh, yeah. He's gigantic—*oh*!" The bright revelation in his tone has me bracing for the inevitable. "You probably saw him last night! He hadn't been able to come out with us, but he dropped by the house. He was in a rough spot, like you. He doesn't usually drink, like…at all. He's probably feeling shitty today, too," he adds, elbowing me.

My smile is a grimace. "Yeah. We met while I was cleaning the bathroom. He, uh…" My booze-soaked brain offers a flashback: Ian's hand sliding from my waist to cup my breast, me yelping—actually yelping, like a kicked Yorkie—at the resulting pull on my boob tape.

Really could have lived without that one, brain.

"He handled the toilet," I finish. The memories continue to unspool. His eyes had gone huge with worry, his big hand flying away from my chest as he apologized. I'd been quick to reassure him that I was fine, and tried to explain the situation before opting to simply show him. He was intrigued by the product, giving my boob an exploratory poke through the tape, but disappointed by how inaccessible it made my assets.

Not that it kept him from enjoying what he *could* partake in.

Heat blazes across my chest at the recall of teasing fingers outlining what the removal process confirmed was a very thorough and unflattering arrangement of tape and cleavage.

I fight to keep hold of the memory. He'd done a fine job with what he had to work with, running his knuckles along the outsides of my breasts, grazing the length of my cleavage with his fingertips. Taking his time, watching my face for a reaction, grinning when I gasped...

"Hey, Little Hammond!" a female voice hollers, yanking me back to the present.

Grant laughs, turning to face the turf. "Just a sec," he tells me. "I gotta go get yelled at for missing the workout." He trots off, abandoning me to my plight.

I will myself to focus. I don't know how to play this. Regular me would...well, regular me would never have been in this position to begin with. Break from Reality Ellie is in charge now. And between the unholy cocktail of revived horniness, the thrill of adrenaline that hit me out front, and the morning's ever-present threat of vomiting, she has her work cut out for her.

Ian's still talking to Diego. I watch as my name forms on Diego's lips. Ian lists forward slightly, as though to better hear him, and repeats "Ellie?" just loudly enough for me to hear him over the din of the gym. Diego points in my direction, then waves at me. Ian's gaze follows.

He blinks, otherwise immobilized, and we stare at one another over the felled athletes on the gym floor. I'm pleased to find that he is as good-looking as my bleary memory had me believe. And relieved for his sake that this T-shirt fits him better; no rings around his biceps, which, now that I'm seeing them without the cover of a sweater, are something to behold.

Lordy. His whole *person* is something to behold. The man's pecs are as big as my head. Literally; I confirmed last night by pressing the side of my face to one and having him compare the two in the mirror.

I suppress a cringe. So smooth, Ellie.

I kissed this specimen of a man. Freshly single after five years, and I'm the one who made a move. Shame there are so many gaps in my memory, though. If that boob flashback is any indication, he is skilled. And I'm supposed to work for him?

Ian recovers first. He saunters toward me, a half smile hitching the corner of his mouth as he weaves between the bodies on the ground. He's trying so, *so* hard not to laugh, his face is twitching with the effort. "Good morning." He looms so large, I might as well be sitting down.

"Hi," I say.

"I didn't think I'd see you again so soon. Or…ever, actually." I catch a hint of cinnamon on his breath. Had there been cinnamon last night? I have a weakness for cinnamon.

He looks me over, more of a wellness scan than an appraisal. "How are you?"

"A little worse for wear, but I at least woke up in a bed."

"Good for you." He nods toward the corner of the gym. "I came to on the floor of the pro shop."

"Oof," I say, navigating a torrent of disappointment that he hadn't even started in bed with me, relief at the same fact, and curiosity about how he got here. Given the state he'd been in, if he drove, I'm writing him off as both potential employer and subject of recovered lust.

He finally loses the fight against his smile. "Diego," he turns and calls over his shoulder, "you mind wrapping up this class for me? I'll pay you for the full hour—"

"Absolutamente!" Diego replies, and jogs past us to position himself in an open garage doorway. He claps his hands to get the attention of everyone inside and on the turf. "Good morning,

friends! I will lead your cooldown while Ian talks to Ellie! We met her last night! She's going to live with us and work here!"

The floor squeaks with the sound of sweaty heads turning to take me in. It's unsettling, like someone's given the command to an army of undead.

"Everyone say *Welcome, Ellie!*" Diego instructs.

The room echoes with a chorus of "Welcome, Ellie!" that's both hospitable and reenforces the legion of the damned thing. I wave.

"Ellie is very good at flip cup and has beautiful handwriting," Diego continues. "She also taught us that you never use water to put out a grease fire! That makes it worse!"

"Oh, girlie," says an older woman propped up on her elbows a few yards away. She's wearing the most violently pink lipstick I've ever seen away from a drag show. "You're either very brave or very desperate."

"Both," I concede, which gets some laughs from the fallen.

Diego redirects the crowd's attention, saying something about scorpion pose, and Ian motions for me to follow him. We head toward an arrangement of couches and chairs between the pro shop and the front desk, which is conspicuously devoid of an attendant.

"Have you been hydrating?" he asks. I shrug, and he moves to a mini-fridge on the counter. Pushing past the cans I recognize from Diego's room and Grant's car, he produces a pair of large, squarish bottles of purple liquid. He hands one to me with a "Try this."

"Electrolit?" I ask, reading the label aloud. It's all in Spanish.

He unscrews the cap of the one he holds. "More effective than

Gatorade, but when buying it by the armload, it's less shameful than the stuff meant for toddlers with diarrhea."

"Thank you." I unscrew the cap and lift my bottle toward his. "Cheers." The containers connect with a thud, and we drink. It's not bad. The grape flavor is strong, with a hint of salt.

Ian watches me as he drinks. When he lowers the bottle, he's half smiling again, setting off a fluttering sensation in my chest. We each take a seat, me on the couch, him on one of the boxy armchairs opposite it. "What do you remember about last night?" He's not needling me, just curious.

I appreciate that he's not making a big deal about this. "Not a lot. We had—" My face *ignites*. "Fun?"

"I'm glad you think so, too." He cocks his head. "I can't remember much, either. We, uh…" He holds his hands up, palms together, fingers entwined, then pulls his hands apart.

"Disengaged?"

"Sure. And then you fled the scene."

"No!"

"Yes."

"Did I at least thank you?"

He laughs. "No idea. I ended up outside, and then woke up around seven on the floor with no memory how I got there. The Lyft receipt helped. I tipped two hundred percent," he muses. "Then I coached. After I showered. Where I also threw up."

"Gotcha." So, that's that. Glad he took a rideshare. "Sorry about bailing. I—" I'm not sure what to say or what I detailed last night. "I'm in a weird spot right now. As far as"—I raise my hands, forming an arc above my head to encompass me—"all of my life."

"So, that includes the breakup, subsequent homelessness, moving in with the guys, and wanting the front desk position here for supplemental income?"

I blink. "How did—"

"Diego can get a lot of information out at once. He doesn't breathe much. It's caused problems with his lifts." He tugs on the rim of his cap. "You get the lowdown on the job?"

"Checking people in, routine cleaning, social posts…" I say, recalling the list of duties the guys mentioned, and he nods along. His eyes really are the most incredible color. And did I miss the cleft in his chin? Because it is *pronounced*. It would be very much in keeping with Drunk Ellie to have run a finger along that space, maybe make a sawing noise.

Nope; that's a memory. I did do that. *Jesus.*

I meet Ian's eyes again and realize that I've let the silence go on long enough to develop a charge. It seems smart to ask, "Where are we, exactly, as far as last night?"

"Like you said. We had fun."

"And that's…all?"

"Why?" That smile hitches at the corner of his mouth. I want to lick it. Hell, I may have last night. Stupid, brined brain.

"Because we'll be working together."

His brows draw together, but the smile is still teasing his lips. It's adorable. "I haven't hired you yet."

"You're going to hire me. I'm a competent adult with an intense commitment to cleanliness, as you well know. Just because we—"

"Just because we what?" Ian grins. "Your majesty."

"You've been wanting to say that since I came in, haven't you?"

"It's been *killing* me."

I glare at him on principle. His grin only spreads wider, if that's possible. It shows his canines, which are more pronounced than on most people, giving his grin a feral appeal. I'll just assume that I mentioned that last night.

"Are you looking for an out from the job you're trying to convince me to give you, or would you rather itemize what each of us did in that bathroom?"

I manage to lift my chin, but God help me, I could really go for some itemization.

"We were drunk. We have established that it was fun." He tips his head, considering, and that lick-tempting half smile hooks the corner of his mouth again. "I *think* I remember it being fun, anyway. Pretty hazy, overall. But you need a job, and I need someone who can use the computer without getting distracted by their own reflection in the monitor." He nods, and I follow his eyes to spot Alistair in his preferred state of shirtlessness, inspecting himself in the full-length mirror in the pro shop. His immaculate form is almost enough to distract me from the general disarray of the shirt display beside him, which is an eyesore.

Alistair flexes, every muscle on his right side achieving anatomy book–level definition, then nods approvingly. "Looking *cut*," he determines...to himself.

I wrinkle my nose, turning back to Ian. "No promises there. I fluff my hair a lot."

"I've noticed."

"What?" One hand flies to my scalp, fingers tousling my roots.

"You've done that three times since we've been talking. Not a problem. You've already strung more sentences together than I've ever heard from Alistair, and you've yet to pull up a cat video on your phone *while* I'm talking to you, so you're an improvement on Diego, too."

"Good to know the bar is so easy to meet."

"The bar is *underground*."

"So we agree that having witnessed one another in a compromised state will not impact our professional relationship. And the fact that I'm going to be sleeping in your bed? Old bed. Old bedroom!" I say, stumbling over every noun with increasing volume, like I might drown out the one that came before. I wait to crumble into dust, but Ian just laughs.

He shrugs. "It is pretty weird that you're moving in with them."

"Very brave and very desperate," I remind him, though he hadn't sounded judgmental, just…accurate.

"For what it's worth, I never used that mattress. It wasn't deep enough for my bed frame," he adds, and gestures upward. Confused, I look at the ceiling, finding only exposed ductwork and I-beams. "There's an apartment on the second floor," he explains. "I lived with the guys while it was being renovated."

Ah. That explains why he ended up here in the wee hours. "And yet, you passed out on the ground floor?"

"I couldn't even make it onto a couch, so, no. Stairs were not in the cards."

I smile. Most people wouldn't own up to something like that. It's disarming. And *hot*. Accountability is deeply appealing.

But I'm not here to be seduced by compelling character traits. This is me, in defiance of everything "me," agreeing to be employed by a man whose tongue has been in my mouth. "Then I will be professional and acknowledge your role as owner-operator with all the respect it deserves."

"Outstanding. Welcome aboard." He scoots to the edge of his seat, hand extended, and we shake. His palm is warm and dry, with calluses that have just enough scrape that I now know what caused the roughed-up snags along the fabric backing of the boob tape.

Ian releases my hand, expression going thoughtful. He sniffs the air. "Do you smell coconut?"

8

"SO. THAT'S ME. HOW WAS the conference?" I ask and take a drink from my coffee. In the time it's taken me to recap my past forty-ish hours, the beverage has cooled to a non-scorching temperature, and I enjoy a few sips while waiting out Heather's and Mark's stunned silence.

Heather's staring at me in open disbelief, while Mark's wide, dark eyes travel from me to the backyard, where Grant and Diego are working out on the concrete slab by the rig. Today's workout is another partner effort, alternating jumping over the plyo box with performing a burpee, leaving only a split second between each other's turn over the box. The spectacle is riveting, a ballet of coordination and timing with potential disaster written all over it.

Grant lets out a loud grunt when he hits the bottom of his next burpee, and Mark gasps, turning back to face the table we're seated around on the patio. He and Heather have been blowing up my phone since last night, when they arrived home to find their couch empty of the friend they'd last heard was half-blind and unhoused, with zero sign of me ever having entered their apartment in the first place. I texted to assure them that I was fine and promised to explain everything over coffee this morning. Was it impolite of me to send a photo of myself seated for dinner at the Ping-Pong table with my new roommates before turning off my phone? Perhaps. Especially since I was the only one wearing a shirt, though Diego was in an apron. A practical consideration; he'd helped cook.

A barrage of texts expressing various degrees of thirst and dismay had been waiting when I turned the phone back on to send them my new address. And if their desperation made them all the more willing to pick up some of my stuff from Cole's, so be it. It was on their way!

Heather finally blinks. "The only part of this that tracks is that you cleaned a bathroom. The rest..." She gestures toward the guys, then back at the house, then to me, and my apparent newfound enthusiasm for hoodies; I haven't changed into the clothes they brought over yet. "No. None of this makes sense."

"Oh, I don't know," Mark says, his attention drifting back to the spectacle of vitality. "If anyone is going to be seduced by a man cleaning a toilet, it's going be Ellie."

Heather frowns at me. "You got kicked out of a *bar*. You. You, who are..." She searches the air for a sufficient word, then points to me. *"You."*

I raise my chin primly. "*I* was being a *nuisance*."

"What does that mean? Who even are you right now?" she demands.

"And you're living with these glorious creatures," Mark adds, voice trailing in admiration as he observes the sweaty duo. Grant and Diego have switched from box jumps to the less flashy but still remarkable kettlebell snatches. I'm not sure how much the green ones weigh—fifty-plus pounds?—but with the guys' finely honed form, they practically float up and overhead.

"Plus one more," I remind him. "Alistair's inside. He's a model."

"Oh, so, not like those *fuglies*," Heather deadpans.

"And they're going help me learn how to do all that," I add, pointing to the rig.

Heather looks at me as though I've started speaking in tongues. I take no offense; nothing in our shared history would lead her to believe that I'd ever engage in the kind of activity that would produce the amount of grunting we're hearing now.

"Working at the gym gets me a complimentary membership, which I'm expected to use." Ian had explained that he requires everyone on staff to have a functional knowledge of what goes on at the gym. We're going to have a goal-setting session for "focus and intention." So hot.

I waggle my brows. "I did a pull-up yesterday. Kind of. Or a chin-up? Whichever one has you hold the bar like this." I raise my hands, palms facing me, trying to remember what Grant called it. He'd been the one coaching me on the rig after dinner.

"With those claws?" Mark reaches for the hand nearest him, pulling it toward him to inspect the stiletto tips. He gets me.

"All intact! And I'm *sore* from it." I cross my arms over my chest, feeling the achy muscles on the outside of my rib cage, below my shoulders—traps, maybe? "For the first time I can remember, I'm sore because of choices I made, not because of my fucked-up body, and it's..." Empowering? Addictive? Filling a void I hadn't known was there? "It's a nice change. That's how I'm approaching the next six months. A change. A break from Regular Me and more whoever I was Friday night. Let loose. Try new things." I gesture to the workout area again. "Engage in feats of strength!"

Mark nods, then grimaces. "Do they know about your eye?"

The reference conjures an echo of the disappointment I felt when I woke up this morning to no improvement in my right eye. "*No. And they're not going to.*" I say firmly. "I don't need their sympathy or for them to start calling me 'brave' for rolling with my body's most recent choice in punches." I catch Heather's frown and press on before she can speak up. "I feel good about this! I need something to focus on while I wait out this diagnosis window so I don't end up obsessing. So I'm going to get strong. And I'm going to live among adoring himbos and teach them how to maintain a functional household. It's perfect. I get to feel useful *and* appreciated."

This makes them both laugh. My incompatibility with altruism is what made my solitary year in education so painful. Call me petty, but this gal needs positive feedback—not something with which high schoolers are particularly generous. And when a day's "success" was so often limited to a freshman writing out the word *for* instead of the digit, any sense of my usefulness went out the window.

"I made an omelet earlier, and when Diego saw it, he begged me to teach him how to make one, and I did! And he did an excellent job." Mostly. It was more overdone than *I* like, but it was a solid go for a first time, and he beamed with pride at the outcome. It was more fulfilling than anything I did in the classroom.

"And your himbo king at the gym?" Mark leads.

I tamp back a scowl on Ian's behalf. He's no himbo. Sure, he's beefy, and has displayed the requisite amount of kindness one finds in such a creature, but I've seen no sign of the endearing dimness that would change his classification from *hunk* to *himbo*.

Not like my roommates, who, between the battery licking and bacon burning, have proven consummate examples of the breed.

"He doesn't need to know, either. We're keeping things strictly professional. Friday was a one-off. He's still eye candy," I concede. "But I'm not looking for a relationship, and casual sex isn't exactly in my repertoire, not when I have to consult a calendar first. The plan is to sock away my hourly wages so I can have everything lined up for when it's time for real life again. If six months pass without incident, then great! I'll have an apartment deposit and first and last and will take everyone out for a nice dinner to celebrate. But if there's going to be a mountain of medical bills in my future, I want to get a head start."

"You're planning six months out. What happens if you have another nerve attack before then?" Heather asks, finally getting to what I suspect I sidelined earlier. In any other scenario, it's exactly what I'd be asking.

"I can't control whether or not that happens," I say, painfully aware of how tightly the words come out of me. "That's why I'm trying to get a handle on everything I do have control over while I can. Everything I'm talking about has an asterisk denoting *while I can*. I'm going to save money *while I can*. I'm going to get strong *while I can*. I'm going to be useful and functional and independent—"

The final *while I can* gets stuck in a knot of emotion. Mark gives my hand a squeeze. I squeeze back in thanks.

"I'm going to take this time for *me*," I say. Articulating it gives me some of the same kick I felt at the gym yesterday. The lump in my throat dissolves, and I sit up straighter.

Heather shrugs. "You playing house mom to these guys is pretty inspired. It's just a departure for you."

"In quality of life, maybe," Mark says. "Like you said, I think this setup is perfect. Presuming you get them to a certain standard soon. Because I don't see you sticking it out if they don't start living like humans in the next few days."

"We're already making great strides." I extend my arms to indicate the tidied deck. "An hour ago, this was littered with empty cans and Solo cups. But now, totally civilized."

"Snow White and the Three Himbos?" he asks with a grin.

"I have made it abundantly clear that I am not their housekeeper. I will help to set a baseline and lay out a course of action that will keep it maintained, and then it's up to them."

"And if they slack?"

"I am not above nagging."

"What plans do you have for the gym?" Heather asks.

I shrug. "I'm going to work the front desk, run their social—"

"And gradually integrate yourself into every element of the facility's operation until it runs like clockwork," she finishes.

"How do you know it doesn't already run like clockwork?"

"Because you would have had a competence boner about it."

I nod. Fair.

"Ugh!" Alistair's wail comes from inside the house. A moment later, the screen door bangs open, and he joins us on the porch, clad in what I can only describe as a Speedo.

Mark chokes on his coffee, and I thwack him on the back as Alistair erupts with "You see this shit?" He motions to his torso. "It's got *shimmer*!"

The three of us are forced to take a closer look. Indeed, Alistair's immaculate form is shimmering in the late morning sunshine.

"This is some goddamn *Twilight* crap," he grumbles, wiping

a hand across his abdomen. He studies his palm for a moment, then looks over his fingertips at us, brows twitching slightly when he sees that his audience consists of more than just me. "Oh. Hi."

"Alistair, these are my friends Heather and Mark."

Alistair greets them with the quick chin-lift traditionally meant to convey *s'up?*, then resumes his study of his glittery torso. "I'm gonna use the hose."

Mark's coughing fit kicks off anew, a high, thin *"A hose?"* getting rasped in on his next breath. Heather takes on this round of back thumps.

"Why do you want a hose?" I ask.

"I'm not rinsing this off inside. You said we'd be deep-cleaning the bathrooms today. I don't want to give us more work than we'll already have." Alistair examines his arms. "I don't even know what it is. It came in the other day with a bunch of skincare stuff from my cousin in Korea. I thought it was bronzer."

"Are you going to want a towel after?"

"Nah. I'll air dry. Thanks, though."

"That was a suggestion, not an offer," I clarify, reenforcing the non-housekeeper nature of our arrangement.

"Cool," he says, attention back on his abdomen. We look on, as helpless against the pull of his perfection as the tide is to the moon, as he traces a finger around each segment of his abdominals, creating a pale outline of his six-to-eight-pack in the shimmer. He completes the path, then, using the same finger, pokes his belly button with a high little "Boop!"

The *boop* at least breaks the spell, and I shake my head. *Ellie Hayes, this is your life.*

Chuckling at himself, Alistair strolls to the edge of the porch, disappearing around the side of the house.

Heather slumps in her seat. "That's just your new normal?" I nod, electing, for the sake of Mark's esophagus, not to mention yesterday's flash of tush. "Sure. So. How are negotiations going with Cole? When we went by, he wanted to know where you were staying."

The reference to my ex wipes away the lingering sortilege from Alistair's display. "He had the temerity to text that he was worried about me yesterday morning."

"Like he hasn't lost all claim to that, the *shit*," says Mark, voice still thin from coughing.

I smile at my friend's loyalty, and the fact that the response I'd sent Cole had said the same thing. "Thanks again for picking up those bags."

Heather smirks. "I should have known you'd have coordinating luggage."

To Cole's credit—not that I'm willing to extend him much—he had been willing to pack up a good portion of my clothing at my request and had braved the wrath of Heather and Mark when they went by for it. Granted, I'd made the packing portion pretty easy for him; my preference for compartmentalization extends beyond the arguably less-than-healthy approach to my inner life. Drawer organizers were removed from the dresser and placed into suitcases, the underbed storage containers for my rarely used winter clothes simply put in the back of Heather's car, ditto my toiletry and makeup organizers. It's fitting, really, how easy I make it to extract myself from a partner's life. My body made the relationship severing simple, and my organizational skills made clean lines around the bulk of my possessions.

All that's left are the bigger items and car retrieval. I'd be tempted to make a clean break and send him a bill, but there's no way I'm parting with my plants, and I like my stuff: the couch I bought with my first big check from a school district in Wisconsin, the bed frame I already had when we moved in together (the masculine urge to sleep at no higher elevation than that of a mattress remains incomprehensible to me), and the dresser I refurbished last summer. The guys have offered to help me move when the time comes, and I am not above exploiting their excitement for non-foldable seating if it means that I get to see Cole's reaction to my perpetually shirtless roommates.

But before I can overwhelm Cole with their virility, he and I are going to have to divide our combined stuff. Disentangling from a partnership of five years is going to take some time, no matter how well defined my margins were. Determine who gets the food processor (me) and who gets the Vitamix (him). Decide whether to open individual accounts for streaming services or if we can continue splitting them but maintain separate profiles (I'm going to propose the latter, but I reserve the right to secretly fuck with his algorithm; enjoy the content recommendations based on your sudden love for K-dramas, asshole).

Then there's the emotional fallout, which I suspect will plow into me the moment I sit still long enough for it to catch up. But for now, it's as though there are too many potentially debilitating elements trying to get me at once, and they're all bunched up in the doorway to my awareness. The MS prospect, the dissolution of yet another relationship due to my traitorous body, and its offshoot, the suspicion that my ever-growing list of physical maladies and personality flaws have rendered me unlovable and doomed to die alone, are scrunched together, waiting for a care-less, examining tug from me, and then it'll be a dogpile.

The backlog of emotions presses against its confines, and I imagine myself turning away. I have better things to do. Like getting strong. And ignoring the occasional sexy flashback of the time I spent in the bathroom with my now boss. I have a job to start tomorrow, a household to establish, and so many lifts and movements and skills to work on in the coming weeks, I won't have the time to pick at that scab, anyway.

A shriek pierces the air. Alistair has turned the hose on the others, who'd collapsed onto the grass following their crushing session by the rig. He alternates aiming the water at Grant, then Diego, who protests loudly in Spanish, before returning to Grant.

"Dude!" Grant yells. "Not cool."

Diego charges with a roar, sacking his assailant. With a whoop, Grant joins the tussle, the hose writhing beside them. In seconds, the patch they're rolling in is a wreck of muddy males.

"Someone should probably stop them?" says Mark, craning to observe from his seat.

"My influence ends at the edge of the porch," I say. "As long as they clean off before they go in, they're welcome to mud wrestle."

Diego emerges from the fray and army crawls toward the hose. He aims it over his shoulder, spraying the other two, who either laugh or shout at the water.

"Well," Heather says with finality. "The next few months are certainly going to be interesting."

"For all of us," Mark mutters, his stare gone thousand-yard. "*Jesus.*"

9

"GOOD MORNING," SAYS IAN, as the guys and I stroll into the gym a little before eight on Monday. He peers at the plate I carry. "What's all this?"

"Ellie made us treats while we cleaned," Diego tells him.

Yesterday had been busy. Heather and Mark went home once the wrestling match wrapped up, and after the guys had sufficiently de-mudded themselves, we gathered for a chat about expectations for the coming months. They were open to my plan to elevate the household's baseline for cleanliness, with the understanding that they'd be responsible for upkeep. I got a breakdown of their coaching schedules, Grant's and Diego's summer classes, and Alistair's upcoming modeling gigs, and assigned nights for cooking lessons and meal prep, as well as days for laundry and grocery shopping. We'll tackle finances next week.

Then, the cleaning began. Any enthusiasm they may have had was smothered by mountains of dirty clothes and the realization that *all* the grout in the shower is supposed to be white, not, as Diego had thought, an orange that faded *up* to white. Grant got

Windex in his eye. Something hard struck Alistair in the face while scrubbing the toilet of his and Grant's bathroom, and he refused to continue without protective eyewear. I had only one recourse: bribery.

In my classroom management course, I'd been dismayed to learn that there was a possibility that my students wouldn't see the intrinsic value in, say, discussing the ubiquity of human cruelty in *A Separate Peace*. In such situations, my cohorts and I were advised to provide external motivators to keep students productive and engaged. Rice Krispies Treats were my go-to, and based on everything I'd learned about them in the previous day-plus, I figured that these three would also be receptive to edible incentives. In a moment nothing short of serendipitous, my search of the kitchen provided all three necessary ingredients, though the marshmallow portion came in the form of stale Peeps—remnants of discounted pre-assembled Easter baskets Grant purchased last month.

Morale was restored. Alistair found goggles and tackled the bathroom, scrubbing and sanitizing so thoroughly, I had to ask him to crack a window to release the bleach fumes. The living room, if the hand-me-down recliner and lawn chairs let it be called that, was tidied and mopped, and every inch of baseboard in the four-bed, three-bath bungalow was wiped clean.

I multitasked, cleaning the stalactites from the microwave and wiping down cabinet fronts and work surfaces while devoting one burner to continuously melting Peeps. The guys refueled so often that I ended up wrapping individual squares just to slow them down.

"I don't know that distributing sugar bombs at a gym is good practice, but we do have plenty." I hand a blue-tinted square to Ian.

He thanks me, and I am gratified as he immediately unwraps the treat and takes a bite. He lets out a groan of pleasure, and the gratification turns to something warmer and more southerly on my person.

"Jesus," he says around a second mouthful. "Why is this so good?"

"I brown the butter," I say.

"Whatever that means. *Wow.* I haven't had a homemade Rice Krispies Treat since…"

"Mom, probably," offers Grant.

Ian's chewing slows, then stops.

Grant had said the same thing yesterday, but it had been mentioned offhand, like it was something their mom had made for them when they were kids and simply didn't do for them as adults. But as I watch, a shadow crosses Ian's expression. There's more to it than that.

He swallows, then rewraps the square, leaving it on the desk, and nods to the computer. "We can start with a breakdown of the desk stuff and then do a tour."

My eyes flick to the treat he's—abandoned? rejected? put aside to be savored later, perhaps while recalling the precious moments he spent worshipping my décolletage—and I move to join him on the opposite side of the desk. "Sure."

The system Firehouse uses for checking in members is similar to what I used for attendance the year I taught, so most of the time at the computer is devoted to Ian creating a new admin login for me while I mentally inventory a host of Friday night memories evoked by his proximity. There *had* been cinnamon.

It takes only a few minutes to go over the specific responsibilities of the front desk position: minor cleaning, laundering the towels on hand for wiping up sweat and disinfecting equipment, stocking the little shop of Firehouse Fitness–branded gear, and familiarizing myself with the list of members who most often run afoul of the "no dogs on the gym floor" policy. I also get a tour of the locker rooms, which are utilitarian but clean, and the storage area, home to the cleaning supplies and the gym's washer and dryer, and I spy a peek of a stairwell behind a door.

"That leads to my apartment," Ian explains.

"Ah! Friday night's insurmountable ascent."

"I swear to God, I'm not back to one hundred percent yet," he grumbles, and steers us back down the hallway to the gym floor, where members have started to gather near a large flatscreen monitor and a whiteboard. "*Never* again."

Ian raises a hand in greeting to a member and asks me, "What's your experience with cross-training?"

"Is that what you do here?"

"What *we* do here? Yes. So, I'm assuming zero experience?" At my nod, he asks, "How about Olympic lifting?"

"I don't even know what that is." I offer it up like a boast.

"Have you done weight training of any kind?"

I shake my head. "I swam growing up, rec leagues and then in high school, but none of the teams I was on ever had us lifting. I've used free weights in workout classes, but I wouldn't know what to do on my own."

"You probably put on muscle pretty easily."

"How can you tell?"

Ian's smile is wry. "The musculature of your back."

"What do you—never mind," I say, recalling the open-back styling of Friday's dress, the side zip of which remained imprinted on my skin as late as yesterday afternoon.

Ian's smile lingers, and I wonder if he's dwelling on the memory or trying to jog his further. Or if he'd even want to. He'd been happy enough to see me Saturday, but that could have been out of concern for my survival, given the condition I'd been in when he'd seen me last.

"You're a compact lady version of me," he continues, and I file that away to obsess over later. "With the right approach, you'd be a beast in no time."

"I don't know that beastly is what I'm going for, but I'd like to see what I can do."

"Now's your chance. If you'd like to start your shift with the WOD, I can check in the stragglers." He points to the members by the whiteboard. "The eight thirty class starts in five."

"WOD?"

"Workout of the day. Today's will be a good first one for you. It doesn't include any advanced movements, and we'll go over modifications, anyway."

"The WOD it is," I say, and Ian accompanies me over. The screen displays the same attendance software as the front desk but is set up to show little photos beside the names of the class's participants. The workout itself is written out on the whiteboard. It looks…unpleasant.

I'm frowning at the prospect of five four-hundred-meter runs when movement in the periphery of my bad side has me turning. It's the woman with the pink lipstick from Saturday; Babs, according to the name accompanying her picture. She smiles, her lips as brilliant a shade today as they were this weekend and in her photo. There's pink woven into her hair, too, breaking up the gray bob. Babs is a *signature color* gal.

"Hi, there!" she says. "Ellie, right? How are things going with the boys?"

"I've already resorted to bribery, but my feet are no longer sticking to the bathroom floor, so we're making progress!"

She rolls her eyes good-naturedly, hands going to her hips. "Those boys are such sweethearts," she says. "But I do worry about them sometimes. All *four* of them."

"Four?" I ask, and she winces, pressing in her lips, as though she's said too much.

"We include Ian with them," she admits, casting a furtive glance toward the gym owner, who chats with another member a few yards away. "Though, I would hope that his bathroom floors aren't sticky. There's a *touch* of the same..." She frowns, shifting side to side as if to jostle loose the right descriptor. "*Immaturity* about him."

"Oh?" It seems Babs is a gossip. Outstanding.

She waggles her finely etched brows. "What did you think of the room for rent sign? Wasn't that *snazzy*?"

I laugh. "I take it you were responsible?" I ask, needlessly. If Grant is the embodiment of the body spray that hinted at what lay within the house, then Babs is glitter and hot pink in human form.

"They didn't tell you? It's my rental property. One of them, anyway. I'm your landlady," she says, loftily. "The amount of money Ian's flushed away by not insisting those boys find a fourth for that house is criminal. I've been getting on him for months, but he wouldn't hear a word of it! I put up that sign last weekend." She huffs a long-suffering sigh, then grins. "Was it the glitter? Did the sparkle reel you in?"

"It was certainly a factor," I say, bursting with curiosity. "So, Ian's been covering the rent on that room since he moved out?"

Diego jogs up then, clapping his hands for everyone's attention as he welcomes us to class, and Babs and I are prevented from further discussion.

She winks. "You get settled in. Then we'll talk."

"I hate Kelly," I say from where I lay sprawled on the floor.

As Diego explained, today's workout, Kelly, is one of many benchmarks revisited throughout the year. Athletes keep track of their performance on each and try to improve their respective scores. Kelly, the hateful bitch, is done for time.

The fourteen-pound ball I'd used for wall balls—squatting in front of the rig, then standing "explosively!" as per Diego, and launching the ball up to a target, then catching the ball and repeating the motion another twenty-nine goddamn times *per round*—rolled to a stop by my head after I finished/collapsed. I nudge it aside, letting it disappear into my blind spot, currently cloudy from the pressure my elevated body heat puts on the optic nerve. I just threw and caught that thing 150 times. I never want to see it again.

Babs laughs; she's right next to me, but her breathing is already more regular than mine. "You think this is bad, wait until you meet my namesake. Barbara *sucks*."

Ian peers down at me from where he's perched on the box I used for the third and, arguably, worst portion of the exercise: box jumps. Even at twenty inches, they were as harrowing as I'd suspected. Diego advised that I focus on form over speed, which chafed my more competitive impulses, but after my compromised depth perception led to some close calls with the edge of the box, I was happy to take it slow.

"You did well for day one," Ian says, casually tossing a lacrosse ball up in the air and catching it. "How are you feeling?"

"Oh, *great*," I pant. "You know it's brutal when a quarter-mile run is the least offensive element of an activity."

"Even with the breaks between each round?"

"Those were *not* breaks." The three-minute windows between each set went from being a relief to a period of anticipatory stress, me huffing and puffing as I watched the clock tick down to the next run with an increasing sense of dread.

"And why are wall balls so terrible?" I rail. "It's just half sitting and throwing."

"It's a compound, high-intensity movement," Ian says. "A large number of muscles in your body are putting in maximum effort. You're squatting, and that's all the powerful muscles in your lower body, and the muscles in your upper body contract to execute the push-pull phase as you throw the ball."

"To a *target*," I add, ignoring the faint tug of attraction at his knowledgeable breakdown of the movement. I think of Heather's comment yesterday: competence boner, indeed.

Ian turns to glance at the targets dotting the top bars of the rig, black discs about a foot or so in diameter. "They probably spiked your heart rate, too. And after the box jumps…" He frowns, then lets out a little laugh. "I hadn't thought about the individual components. If you aren't used to this kind of workout, your legs are probably jelly. Kelly *sucks*."

"Kelly *sucks*," I say, the sentiment echoed by several others on the floor around me.

Ian watches me, brows raised expectantly, that half smile tugging at his mouth as he gives the ball another toss and catch, toss and catch.

I scowl, conceding. "And I loved it."

I really did.

Since Saturday, I've done a stellar job of not dwelling on any of my life's unpleasantries. The guys have kept me busy; when there's a chance your roommates might mace themselves with household cleaners, you have to stay on point. It's the downtime when the intrusive thoughts creep in, calling to me from the crowded doorway. Lying in my borrowed sleeping bag last night and finding no thrill in being on a mattress Ian *hadn't* used, it was all too easy to indulge in some self-pity. If not for the sudden burst of digital machine gun fire that had me shrieking from the room to remind Diego, my now wall-neighbor, to use his headset when playing *Call of Duty*, I might have fallen down a hole of despair.

But for the past hour, I have been in survival mode. My focus was on dialing in the rhythm of my squats and ball tosses and not letting my impaired vision earn me fourteen pounds of pleather sphere to the face. Every one of the 150 box jumps required my full concentration, lest I mistime it and shred my shin. The run was the only portion when I could have slipped up, but by the second round, I was so focused on psyching myself up for what would follow that I couldn't spare a thought for anything but keeping myself moving.

Nothing but blessed silence from my worries.

Ian laughs, extending his free hand to offer a fist bump. I feebly bump back; I earned it. "You were grinning the whole time."

"Was I?" I ask, as surprised by the news as I am interested in the fact that he had been watching me closely enough to notice.

"Or gritting your teeth really aggressively. *All right! Finish strong!*" he booms and claps, his attention on someone past me. I turn to the rig, where the final two athletes, Russ, a tall, heavyset guy with a thick dark beard and blindingly white tube socks, and Maggie, who'd been doing the box jumps on Saturday, grind out their final set. Maggie had scaled up, positioning her box to the twenty-four-inch side and using a twenty-pound ball; no wonder it's taking her longer.

Other athletes clap, too, and I contribute a whistle. The two finish at the same time, Maggie walking it off, striding past Ian for a fist bump and continuing down the length of the gym floor, while Russ takes a seat on his box, whooping loudly and announcing, between gasped breaths, "Let's do it again!"

I turn back to Ian. "Is everyone always so supportive? Folks were cheering and giving high fives as we passed one another during the runs." I figured that Saturday's enthusiasm had been a critical mass thing. I hadn't expected it in today's much smaller group.

Ian nods. "There's something to be said about shared suffering. It creates a bond."

"A trauma bond," says Babs.

"I'll take box jumps over battlefields, I guess," I say.

"You say that now, but wait until you eat shit on one of these things." Ian taps the lacrosse ball against the side of the box he's on. "Everyone here has dinged their shin on a jump at some time or another. Fucking *kills*," he says, then cocks his head, as if considering. "But also makes you feel alive?"

"Cheating death will do that," Babs mutters.

"What has you here so late anyway?" Ian asks, leaning on his side on the box, closer to the older woman. "I don't usually see you during daylight hours, other than Saturdays."

"I volunteered to come later on the chance I'd get to gab with the new girl," she says, smiling at me. "I'm supposed to report back to the five a.m. crew."

I laugh, surprised to be a novelty. "Was that a warning, or should I be flattered?"

Babs shrugs, her skin making a sticky, sweaty sound with the movement. "Eh. Our lives are a little slow."

Ian bounces the lacrosse ball. "And all of you gossip like old hens."

"Hardly," she counters. "The gym is a constant source of intrigue."

"It isn't," Ian tells me, and levers himself up in a smooth movement. He hands me the ball. "You're going to need this." He nods to my pink-loving new pal. *"Barbara."*

"Coach," she says in parting, and Ian strides off.

I eye the ball he handed me. "I'm going to need this?"

"You'll use it as we stretch. Find a sore muscle in your back or shoulder, then lie with the ball on that point. Hurts so good," she says.

I'm not so sure, but I'm willing to go with it.

"Interesting that he handed that off to you," she muses. "There's not always enough to go around. That he didn't give one to me, his respected elder..." Babs gives the ball a meaningful look. "I call that *intrigue.*"

My shift begins after I shower. I tidy the locker rooms. I clean all the windows in the facility. I use the stick vacuum to get into every neglected nook and cranny of the place, unearthing balls of dust that could've eaten the ones the guys eradicated yesterday. I do laundry. The clothing and towels among the lost and found items are no longer stiff.

I rearrange the dumbbells to correspond with the number of pounds written on the storage racks, and am intercepted by Grant, who takes advantage of my proximity to the weights to show me how to use them. Rows and curls I knew about, but I'm introduced to tricep kickbacks, which are hateful, and am humbled by how hard a time I have with snatches, which he and Diego made look so effortless in the yard yesterday.

But by three, I've cleaned to my satisfaction, the guys are off to classes or, in Alistair's case, a photo shoot, Ian is coaching, and I have nothing to do. The free time looms; I can practically hear my maladies closing in.

Ian stands in an open bay door, cheering on a group of runners in the two thirty class coming back in from a four hundred. As the last member staggers past the threshold, Ian comes over. The fleeting look of yearning he sends his abandoned Rice Krispies Treat does not escape my notice. Mostly because I made a point of moving it to my good side so that any such look would not escape my notice. "You've been keeping busy," he says.

"I have been. I don't have a lot to do while the classes are going on," I say with a glance at the group currently enduring Kelly. "And I've taken care of everything in my job description."

"You're quick. If you have other work to do?" He shrugs. "Or just enjoy the downtime."

I grimace. "I don't do downtime. And I'd work, but I'm waiting to hear back from a district about supporting materials for my *Of Mice and Men* unit."

Ian cocks his head in a motion so like his brother, it makes me smile. "What *do* you do?"

"That is a conversation or another day. Right *now...*" I straighten and strum my nails over the legal pad I found while organizing the office supply drawer. "I've made a list!"

"A list?" Ian's attention has shifted, keeping an eye on the progress of his class. I nod anyway.

My need to be useful borders on pathological. I have to be engaged in an activity that contributes to something. Cleaning is a solid outlet, but, as proven by the guys yesterday, anyone— provided they have the proper motivation and clearly established standards—can do that. And with the humbling experience with Kelly still fresh and Alistair's insistence that my snatches are, in his words, "slow as shit," I needed to assert my competence.

"Little things I noticed around the gym." I read aloud from the pad. "Places for touch-up paint, and there's a spot in the flooring that's sticking up a bit," I say, and peer over the edge of the legal pad to spot the circle of chalk I drew around the area as a warning to members. "A hamper or something to replace the cardboard box you're using for lost-and-found stuff. A bold, new vision for the pro shop." I'm excited about that; I can already feel the future orderliness radiating from the space.

It's a touch more Regular Life Ellie and Her Desperate Need for Organization to Maintain an Illusion of Control than is in keeping with the spirit of the next few months, but Break from Reality Ellie wasn't going to be completely free from that, anyway. Not when Standard Me can clearly be put to good use.

I expect Ian to express appreciation for my initiative, but

instead, his brow puckers. Confused, I glance at the gym floor, assuming that something there is what has him scowling.

"The pro shop is fine," he says.

"It's—what?"

"The pro shop does what I need it to. And this is a gym," he continues, and faces me, his brows still low. "Stuff's going to get dinged up, so the paint and all that doesn't matter. And the lost and found doesn't need to be anything but a box, anyway."

"It doesn't *need* to," I agree, politely. "But it would look nice—"

"Don't worry about it."

"I'm not! I just thought, you know, fresh perspective—"

"Leave it."

Ian's voice has an edge that surprises me. It surprises us both, if the silence that follows is any indication. I watch, stunned at the sudden severity of his expression as he works to smooth it into something closer to his usual, friendly one.

"I appreciate the list," he says, but his tone makes clear into which sunless crevice I might shove said list. "Save that energy for your roommates." He starts moving toward the gym floor. "I don't need to be a project, too."

I stare after him, the sting of reproach heating my cheeks.

So much for intrigue.

10

"Y'ALL READY?" I ASK, as my roommates survey the ingredients for tonight's dinner. We're starting simple: a monstrous batch of pork meatballs they will either inhale all at once or enjoy for the next few days as leftovers. I'm still trying to determine how to portion with this crew; the past two nights have looked like a plague of locusts passed over the Ping-Pong table.

Grant chirps out a cheerful "Nope!"

"But that's the point, right?" says Diego, pulling his curls up into a small poof on top of his head. "So we will be in the future."

"Exactly! And I appreciate everyone chipping in. There's going to be a lot of ball rolling," I warn. Then I wait out the giggles from the guys for having referred to balls and explain, "We will have over four pounds of this stuff, so I need all your hands."

"All hands on balls!" Alistair singsongs, like he's calling a boat crew above deck. He's styled from today's shoot, his hair sculpted in a high, shiny pompadour. He's still in makeup, too, contoured to the ridge of the uncanny valley, though I suppose it photographs well.

Again, I wait out the laughter, and we get to work. Diego and Grant chop basil, mint, and parsley, while lemon zesting and ginger grating has been delegated to Alistair. I season the ground pork and incorporate what they chop, keeping a watchful eye on everyone's digit-to-blade proximity. After a few reminders to keep their fingers tucked in, I'm fairly confident that encouraging conversation won't result in accidental bloodshed, and I consider how to approach the subject of the massive chip on Ian's shoulder.

The last hour of my shift was endured in chilly silence, and I was relieved to meet Seth, the friendly, ginger-bearded evening coach, who took over at the desk at four. I've replayed the conversation with Ian on a loop and can't figure out where I went wrong. There's a fine line between "helper" and "tedious know-it-all, against whom entire groups are united in their shared contempt," and I'm no stranger to being on the wrong side. But this was touch-up paint!

I open with something light. "Is Ian particular about what he eats? He didn't finish that Rice Krispies Treat today, and I don't want to bring in snacks not everyone can enjoy."

Grant pauses his chopping, staring off into the middle distance. Then he gets back to work. "Not really."

"Did he not finish the treat, Ellie?" Diego asks, wide eyes on me...as he chops.

"Watch what you're doing. And it's no biggie. Just aiming to be accommodating."

"Ah!" He beams, then looks down at his knife work. "So thoughtful."

I shrug, registering a sting of guilt at his praise for my fabricated consideration, and get back to Grant. "You'd mentioned that your mom had made them?"

"Oh, yeah. Or she *did*, but she died, like, seven years ago."

My chest squeezes so tightly, I let out a squeak. I freeze, hand outstretched to take the zest Alistair has shaved, and stare at Grant, who continues to passively butcher the mint. "Grant! Oh, no. Oh, I'm so sorry!"

He shrugs, looking up to extend a shadow of a smile. It breaks my heart. "That's nice of you. It was *rough*. I was in middle school, and Ian was..." He frowns in recall. "Shit, he was already out of college and competing and stuff. She'd been sick before, like, when I was really little? But I don't remember any of that."

I just nod. I am a prying asshole. And I have no idea what to do. My go-to is to offer a hug, but my hands are covered in ground pork. My backup is to provide food, and we're already doing that. Way to go, Ellie.

"The anniversary was Friday, actually," he continues, his smile looking a little more heartfelt. "It's why we had friends over. We always do something to make the day less sad."

"It's why Ian was hammered, too," Alistair adds, which is also heartbreaking.

I feel less guilty about steering the conversation as I sidestep my faux pas with a change in topic. "How did the three of you end up living together? Was it the gym, or—"

Grant laughs. "Oh, man, me and Alistair go *way* back. We've been friends since first grade."

"Our *moms* were tight," Alistair contributes, his emphasis on *moms* turning the word into a direct reference to my misstep. Beautiful, beautiful butthead.

"And freshman year, we were roommates!" Diego says. "We moved in here last fall."

Ah! Another in. "And Ian was here then?"

"Yeah! While he fixed up the apartment at the gym. That setup is so sweet. You should check it out. Oh, dude!" Grant pivots to Diego, pointing at him with his knife. "He got a great deal on a sound bar for up there."

Good Lord. Maintaining a direct conversational flow with these guys is like trying to reroute a river bare-handed.

"Didn't he already have something like that?" Alistair asks, not looking up from his ginger. "Those speakers he had when we were in high school, when your dad was overseas?"

"Just your dad?" I ask, confused.

"Dad's an engineer," Grant explains. "And he got a job with an oil company in Saudi, when I was, like…fourteen? So, I moved in with Ian. 'Cause out there, all the international employees and their families live on some compound. When kids reach high school age, the company pays for them to go to boarding school in Europe. And that would have been cool and all, but…" He shrugs, losing some levity. "It was good to be here."

I nod. Based on the timeline Grant's provided, that move would have been within a year or so of his mother's passing. It would have been a huge change for anyone, but so soon after losing his mom? And to then get shipped off to a boarding school on yet another continent? Ian taking him in was more than "good"; it was a mercy.

The thought makes my heart feel mushy.

"How was it living with your brother in high school?" I ask, imagining Ian at a parent-teacher conference. If I'd been faced with him at a meet-and-greet the year I'd taught, I don't know what I'd have done with myself.

Oh. My. God. The year I taught I had one class of seniors. They're the same age as these guys now. I'm living with youths who could have been my students. The *horror.*

I scrub the realization from my mind. "I'd imagine it was pretty rowdy, given there was a midtwenties dude providing the only oversight?"

"Uh, *no,*" Grant says flatly. "He was such a dick! Everyone figured I'd have this sweet party life because of him, but he was the worst! He never bought us beer. And since he was always prepping for comps, I ended up eating whatever weird, super healthy shit he had around. Even though that was mostly stuff from sponsors." He nods at Diego. "The ones hounding you look *way* better."

"What's this now?" I ask Diego, giving in to the swirling stream of consciousness.

Diego reverts to his toe-grinding-in-the-dirt humility. "A meal box company has offered me a sponsorship. They'd send me food. I'd cook it, post about it." He places his knife on the table and pulls his phone from his pocket, then begins to thumb the screen. "But they want me to film the cooking part and post the videos online." He shrugs. "I'd just make them look bad."

Diego shows me the phone, and I lean in to read the screen. It's the social account of Built Box, a meal box brand aimed at athletes. I swipe through their offerings with a meat-free knuckle. It looks like a good balance of stuff, tailored to whether a customer is in a heavy training cycle—whatever that means, though, based on what I'm seeing, it requires a staggering amount of food—or cutting—which is trimming down? Recipes are included, pretty basic, but still requiring a general knowledge of how to cook.

I tap on the subscription link. "Good Lord! This is *steep*. What were they offering you?"

"Oh, like, a few months of boxes? More, if it was successful. I do have many followers."

I flick to Diego's profile. I have to do a double take. "You have over a hundred thousand followers, Diego."

He beams. "Cool, right?"

"How?" I don't mean to sound as baffled as I am, but he doesn't seem to mind.

"It began with my fitness journey! Also, I dance a lot between sets when I lift," he adds, with a smooth hip-shimmy. "I've been told that I am very charming."

"Diego, that is an excellent word for you. Also, you're sitting on a gold mine."

Diego looks over one shoulder, as though for the aforementioned gold mine. "A what?"

"This is a huge opportunity, if for no other reason than to get something very expensive for free." I hold up a finger to pause the conversation, then point at the bowl I'd been adding their chopped herbs to. "The rest of your stuff will be for garnish. It looks like I have everything we need integrated, so it's time to roll." I scoop out a golf ball–sized portion of meat and herbs and roll it between my palms until it takes on a spherical shape. "Don't roll too long or the fat will warm and make everything stick to your hands. Got it?"

Each of my roommates takes an appropriate amount of meat and gets to rolling. I inspect their work, giving feedback where necessary, and the conversation resumes.

"I don't know how much of it is because they want me," Diego says, and I'm amazed that he's maintained the thread after the minutes-long pause. "Or if it's because I coach for Ian. When they found out that I work for him, they hoped he'd do videos *with* me, like, because he was a pro? And that's kind of a big deal to have someone like him endorse them."

"He's that well-known just from weight lifting?"

"In the weight-lifting community, he's *huge*. He still gets commissioned to train some top competitors, and he consults like crazy. But back in the day? He'd have probably qualified for the Olympics if he hadn't gotten hurt."

"Really?" I ask, legitimately curious. So far, I've refrained from digging into Ian's background beyond what's on the Firehouse Fitness website, which is pretty vague. Ian Hammond, owner/operator, some letters I assume indicate coaching certifications, and that's it.

"You see the black tubs on the shelves in the laundry room at Firehouse?" Alistair asks, and I nod. "That's all his trophies and medals and stuff."

"That's a lot of bins."

"He was *really* good," Diego says.

"*Is* really good," Alistair amends. "He can't go as heavy now, but his form is dialed *in*."

"And that's why they wanted Ian to be involved?"

Diego nods. "But he didn't want to. They'd still have me without him, but I know they were disappointed. They liked his credibility."

"And his connections," says Alistair.

"Why wouldn't he do it?" It seems a little crummy.

"He's weird about stuff like that. Sorry, Grant," Diego adds, hastily.

"Nah, it's good. He is a weirdo. Like, he's been real private since he got injured, and after everything with Denny?" Grant sighs, letting his cheeks puff out exaggeratedly. "Scandal!"

"Denny?" I ask, though my brain prioritizes *scandal*.

"Ian's mentor!" Grant takes up another wad of meat to roll. "He coached Ian all through college and into his professional career. They were *tight*. And after Ian got injured, Denny hired him to coach at his gym. But when Denny sold it…" He scrunches his nose. "I guess that was my senior year? He announced he was gonna sell, and everyone thought Ian would go for it, 'cause he had his big settlement from getting hurt."

"It was at a competition," Diego adds. "There's video online. So hard to watch. His knee, it went—" He holds up his meat-speckled hands, palms facing one another, then jerks them violently toward the left. He shudders. "The knee is not meant to go that direction."

"Fucking *brutal*," Alistair agrees.

I have my own Greek chorus of beefcakes over here. "So, did Denny not sell to Ian?"

"Nah. Ian went and started Firehouse himself. A bunch of clients followed him over, which created more drama, 'cause the guy Denny *did* sell to accused Ian of poaching, which is BS. They were his personal training clients. That was separate from gym membership."

"And that guy couldn't program for *shit*," says Alistair, uncharacteristically impassioned. "In less than a year, half of his members ended up at Firehouse."

All three guys nod, chests puffed out, like a meaty, physical barrier against Ian-related slander. It's more endearing than menacing, but I'm not going to storm the castle tonight. They've already revealed plenty.

"To recap," I say, and elect to skip the passing of the Hammond matriarch. "You moved in with your brother in middle school, instead of going overseas with your dad. Ian was competing then, got hurt, then worked for his mentor, who, later, wouldn't sell him his business. Ian started Firehouse with the clients he retained, and other members from that old gym followed later. Scandal ensued, and…" I look from contributor to contributor in case I missed something.

"And we were all roommates when we were freshmen," Diego adds.

"Yes! Also…" I look at the dozen perfectly formed meatballs he's amassed on his cutting board. "Great work. Now, more recently, you, sir, who has a social following the size of *Montana*, have been approached by a sponsor, who would also like Ian on board—"

"Not regularly. Just, like, a guest. Ian wasn't interested, and I can't cook, anyway—ah! *Yet!*" Diego uses both hands to indicate the spread of ingredients on the table, extending far enough that Alistair leans back to avoid his pork-covered reach. "I can't cook *yet*, but *you* are teaching us! Oh, Ellie, would you help me? Like, in the videos for Built Box?"

The introduction of yet another subject takes a moment for me to process, but I nod. "I would be okay with that, I guess?" I say, thinking aloud. "But you'd have to check with them. They probably wouldn't want some rando in the kitchen with you."

"I'm sure they would be fine with it! You're on a fitness journey, too," he says. "And you're very pretty. And you know how to cook! Oh, Ellie, this could be so fun! And maybe, after I get better in the kitchen, you won't have to babysit me. And we would get free food! And free is good!"

I nod, because free is good, and I've had an abundance of information hurled at me in the past few minutes. And hanging over it all is a new question: Why wasn't Ian's mentor willing to sell to Ian, his presumed successor?

Fortunately, I have the feeling that there's another source of information that would be more than happy to dish…if I can get myself up in time for a five a.m. class.

11

IT TURNS OUT, I CANNOT get myself up in time for a five a.m. class. Not because of the objectively inhumane hour, but because when my alarm goes off at four thirty, I find that my body is exclusively a host for muscle soreness. Glutes, hamstrings, quads, biceps, and all the other groups I don't know the name of scream in protest at the simplest movement.

It's awesome.

"There's just so many places that ache!" I marvel, and wince at the complaints from my hammies as I take my seat at the front desk. There's less discomfort since I've been hobbling around for a few hours, but I'm still keenly aware of every overworked muscle. I *earned* this!

"As your body gets used to the exercise, it will be more of a two-day turnaround on the soreness," Ian tells me, his smile bemused. I grin back, doing a little happy dance in my seat. There had been no trace of yesterday's hostility when I came in, and he's been genuinely sympathetic of my muscle pain, which made his suggestion that I knock out today's WOD at eight thirty seem more like confidence in my resilience and less like a revenge scheme. And while most of the chalk marking the rise in the flooring has been wiped away, the spot is also more level today; perhaps there is room for subtle improvements after all.

He laughs at my celebratory wriggling, treating me to a view of the canines I'm now confident I mentioned on Friday night. Heat rises in my cheeks, and I look away, busying myself with the sign-ins.

I googled him.

I'd been curious after the guys' infodump and threw myself down an Ian Hammond rabbit hole. Even for someone with zero frame of reference, it was clear to me that the man was and, given how often and recently he's been written about, continues to be a big deal in the industry. At his peak as a professional athlete, he had too many sponsorships to count. I've been spotting the remnants of them all over the gym, like a name-brand scavenger hunt: the plyo boxes, his shoes, even the big fridge in the corner of the pro shop are all from companies that sought him out to represent their brands. These days, multiple professional sports teams contract with him for their lifting and conditioning programming, and he's regularly tapped to contribute workouts for training publications.

There was a ton of video of his glory days. A lot of amateur footage taken on phones at gyms, as well as official clips from competitions. Seeing him perform the lifts with such ease and control was breathtaking. Again, I know nothing about any of this, but he was hefting huge amounts of weight and making it look like a breeze. Even when he was straining, veins bulging and face red with exertion, it was compelling. Real-time documentation of an athlete committing to his performance.

And then: the photos.

The videos I could view somewhat objectively. The focus was on the motion and power on display. The spectacle took precedence over the shape of the individual performing them. Looking through the photos was...*different.*

Most were harmless. Ian on a tiered podium, holding up a trophy. Ian in a shoe campaign. Ian captured at the top of a pull-up. That shot must have been taken after Grant moved in with him, because the teenaged junior Hammond is in the photo as well, his grin latticed with braces as he dangles one bar over on the rig they share.

Ian profiled in a men's magazine, demonstrating proper snatch form. Ian examining the contents of a ready-made meal kit. College Ian, still an amateur; Ian as a professional. Ian as a guest coach at gyms across the US. Ian as a guest coach in gyms abroad. Impressive. Competent. Appealing, but not inherently lust-inducing.

But the top hit had been a *nude.*

Evidently, there is a tradition of athletes being photographed free of the clothing that would otherwise prevent a viewer from fully appreciating the extent of their fitness. I had not been aware of this practice until last night and feel that I might be entitled to financial compensation.

Ian was posed in what the caption informed me was a split jerk; a high lunge stance with a loaded barbell held overhead, forward leg, mercifully, intentionally, blocking the camera from capturing his assets. It wasn't sexual. It was something to be admired; a testament to what the human body is capable of. A physical state honed over years of dedication and commitment, every line of muscle earned. It was art.

And he was *fuzzy*. I've never had much of an opinion on chest hair, so long as it isn't completely absent or alarmingly excessive, but to see the expanse of his impressive torso capped with a dark dusting of hair was a revelation. I *liked* it.

He also appeared to be roaring. Mouth open wide, teeth bared, those feral canines of his brought into striking relief. That's what tipped the image into sexyland. Now I have questions. Is roaring a standard part of his lifting routine? Are there other outlets for roaring? Could *I* make him roar? I elicited some groans on Friday, and a low, rumbling sound similar to recordings of a jungle cat's purr. But a roar? That would be gratifying.

"Did the computer freeze up?" Ian asks, rousing me from my fuzz-appreciating reverie. How long have I been sitting in front of the monitor?

"Nope! Just noticed a new sore spot." *And thinking about your man-fuzz. Is it soft?*

I'm adding myself to the upcoming class when a familiar voice says, "Good morning." I smile to see Babs in the open garage bay, a vision in her signature hue.

"*Barbara,*" Ian grumbles.

She ignores him, instead leaning a not-so-casual elbow onto the counter above me. "Ellie, will you be joining the eight thirty class again?"

"I just signed up."

"Excellent. We'll partner for the back squats." She winks. "Plenty of time to chat."

The WOD is divided into two parts, focusing on back squats first, and finishing with a cardio session. We warm up as a group, then gather at the rig as Ian goes over the fundamentals of the lift. For something that amounts to not quite sitting and then standing back up, there's a lot to think about. Don't pitch forward. Don't let your knees shift toward one another. Don't stare at the profile of your employer's splendid backside, which you can now visualize bare, the hollows and lines defined in tasteful shades of black, white, and gray, as the muscles engage and release throughout his demonstration. Do not make eye contact with your new friend Babs at any point during these proceedings, and certainly don't respond to the eyebrow raise she shoots you.

Later, Babs stands with me as the third member of our group, Helen, does her squats. The three of us are close enough in height that we won't have to change the position of the j-hooks in the rig, where the barbell sits between sets.

"Helen was part of the initial swarm of women who showed up when word got out that there was an eligible bachelor running the show," Babs explains.

Helen laughs, pausing as the top of her squat. "Let's not forget that I was eighteen months postpartum and still trying to recover my pelvic floor." She resumes her squatting. "Jump rope's still a problem. Gravity always wins in the end."

"Try giving it another thirty years," Babs gripes.

"I was recruited by an old sorority sister," Helen continues. "But Marcia only made it a month. She's more barre than barbell, and Ian wasn't receptive to her wiles." She reracks the bar, and I step in to remove a twenty-five-pound plate from the nearest end of the bar, while Helen removes one from the other side.

We might be matched for height, but Helen is way stronger than either of us.

"That ended up being the case for most of— *Do you mind?*" Babs complains as Ian approaches. He's been monitoring the class, giving feedback and correcting form. *Hot.*

He looks to me. "You comfortable with this weight?"

"I got up to 95 on the first set, and that felt fine," I say. "115 seems reasonable."

"Let's see your setup."

I find the correct placement for my hands on the bar, then duck beneath it, positioning it on the more muscled part of my shoulders, as Ian had on his considerably more developed "meat shelf," mindful not to let the bar press against the top of my spine. I straighten and step back from the rig, standing with my feet shoulder width apart.

"Good. Take in a breath, brace, and get down to parallel," he instructs, and I follow along, performing each step as directed. "Up—don't let your knees come toward each other."

When I'm back in a standing position, he nods. "Go ahead and finish the set." I do, my awareness of the weight on the bar increasing with each repetition, but never to the point of discomfort... beyond the soreness I started with. It's actually kind of helpful; I am keenly aware of every tortured muscle participating in the lift.

"Good. One thought," he says, as I rerack. "You're coming forward onto your toes. Keep your weight in all four corners of your feet. Think about digging in with your whole foot. Don't put too much pressure on a single area."

"Sure," I say, as "competence boner" bounces in my brain in time with my elevated heart rate.

"Are you finished?" Babs asks him, approaching the bar for herself.

"No. Ellie, add another twenty pounds next round. You made that look easy."

"Fine, fine." Babs shoos him away. "Off with you. We're *bonding*."

"Of course you are," he says, resigned, and moves on to the group a few spaces down.

Babs watches him go. "Helen, have you ever made anything 'look easy'?"

"I don't believe I've ever heard the words."

Babs raises her brows at me, conveying a silent *intrigue*.

I roll my eyes. "Keep that up, you're going to give your forehead a cramp."

Her grin is unrepentant. "As I was *saying*, most of that manhunter flock dropped off. And those who stuck around found others onto whom they could project their affections."

"There were four weddings with gym couples within a year of Firehouse opening," says Helen. "And a *whole* lotta babies." She punctuates this with a nod toward the break room, left of our spot at the far end of the rig. Filling the window that looks onto the floor is a group of kiddos under preschool age, observing the class with rapt interest. Grant stands behind them, Helen's daughter, Penny, on his shoulders. Firehouse offers childcare during some morning classes on Tuesday and Thursday, with Grant as sitter. They've been clambering over him like chicks on a farm dog. It's precious.

Penny waves to her mom. Grant waves to me.

"Why did you stick around?" I ask Helen. We step back so Babs can have her turn with the bar.

She seems to consider her answer. "Have you had your goal-setting session yet?" I shake my head. "That was what sold me. Not that the workouts weren't great. But"—she gives me a droll look—"I'm a lot of woman." She gestures to herself, moving her arms to emphasize her generous frame. "I came in expecting to be taken to task for being fat. It's why Marcia dragged me in. She thought it would be 'good for me.'"

"Neat friend," I say.

"Right?" Helen laughs, retrieving another two ten-pound plates to add to the bar. Babs finishes her set, and she and I put the twenty-fives we'd removed back on.

Helen continues as she adds her tens. "Every other gym or trainer I'd met with before coming here gave me a goal weight. 'Here's your metric for success. Hit that, you've succeeded. You don't? You're a failure.'"

Her expression shadows. She crosses her arms, leaning against the bar. "I was done with that. I was told to lose weight if I wanted to get pregnant. Or it was my physician's opinion that my weight was contributing to my fertility issues. And there might have been some truth to that, but *Christ*." She sighs. "When you're fat, that's the first thing you hear for anything medical. 'Try losing X pounds; see how it goes.'"

I nod, having read testimonials after my endometriosis diagnosis. Patients being denied care for years, their doctors insisting that their weight was the underlying issue to the chronic pain. "And it was different here?"

Her face immediately brightens. "When I sat down with Ian, he asked me what I wanted to be able to *do*." She ducks under the bar to set up her lift. "I wasn't told to *be less*. I was shown that I could *do more*. That was it. I knew I'd found my place."

She's quiet as she performs her squats, grinding through the heavier set with the same control she had with the lighter weight. That's fifty pounds more than I'll be working with, but she's breezing through it. I wonder how long it will take for me to work up to that, or if my body will turn on me before I have the chance...

I shake off the thought.

Helen racks the bar, and we busy ourselves switching around the plates. "I'm not going to act like I wasn't open to losing weight," she resumes. "And I have. I have less body fat, but more muscle, so the number on the scale isn't too different from what it was on day one." She lifts her chin. "And that's not how I measure my success here, anyway."

"That's what PRs are for," says Babs, proudly.

"When I get to ring *that*." Helen points to the bell hanging on the wall beside the workout whiteboard. Beside it in—shudder—Comic Sans is a sign reading NEW PERSONAL RECORD? RING THAT BELL! "*That's* success."

There's a thumping sound to our left, and we turn to see Penny pounding the window, cheering for her mom. She presses a hand to her lips, then swings her arm low, blowing a kiss that sends her hand straight into Grant's face. He laughs it off.

Helen blows a kiss back. "And it matters to me that my girl gets to see it. I never had that growing up," she adds. "Never got to see bigger women do anything athletic. Maybe in field events or weight lifting in the Olympics, but even now, you really have to seek that out." She sticks her tongue out at her daughter, who does the same. "Penny will have whatever body she has, but it's important to me that she's seen what bodies like mine can do."

Before I can say anything, she laughs. "I'm sorry. That wasn't too soapbox-y, was it?"

I shake my head as I step under the bar. "I asked. And it's nice to know that you don't have to look like something from the Parthenon to be a powerhouse." I unrack the bar and get into my squatting stance. "My coworkers are threatening to skew my perspective."

Helen laughs, and I brace, starting my set. I'm absolutely feeling those additional twenty pounds, but it's still manageable.

I'm on my last lift when Babs asks, "So, you've seen Ian's nude?"

I seize up, halfway out of my squat. *How does she know?*

"Babs!" Helen chides, but the older woman is laughing. They're behind me, so I can't see them, but Babs must realize that she's thrown me off, as her laughter tapers some.

"Oh, shit. Sweetie," she says, still giggling. "You okay?"

"Ellie, are you stuck?" Helen asks. "Do you need to bail?" Ian had shown how to bail on a lift if we were unable to complete it. It's simple, a matter of releasing the bar and shrugging it off your shoulders, but I'm just out of sorts enough that even those two motions are beyond me.

My legs are shaking. "I don't—"

"Hayes!" Ian bellows from across the room. "Push through! You've got this. Up!"

The command activates some unknown source of strength and I propel myself into a standing position. I rack the bar, stepping into the rig, relieved of the chrome and plates, but feeling the weight of the entire class's attention instead.

Then Ian's at my side, and my awareness homes in on him. "Are you okay?" he asks, voice tense with worry.

While I'd happily keep my focus on the gray swell of concern in his eyes, I glare at Babs, who tries not to smile back, both of us knowing full well that explaining the situation is not an option. "I'm fine. Just lost tension," I say, recalling something he'd warned of while demo-ing.

"Okay," he says, taking in each of us in turn: me, glaring at Babs; Helen still wide-eyed; Babs, unbothered. "Well...don't."

"Noted. Thank you," I say. Ian sends a final, skeptical glance to our trio, then departs. I scowl at Babs, who finally looks abashed. "Are you going to say something about *intrigue*?"

"Girly, that goes far beyond intrigue. That was *dangerous*," she admits. "I'm so sorry." Her serious face holds for another few seconds, then she cracks a smile. She leans in, waggling her brows. "So that's a yes on the nude?"

12

I SHOVE MY PHONE INTO my shorts' pocket and grip the counter in the ladies' locker room, forcing myself to take in slow, even breaths. I shouldn't have opened that email. The subject line was warning enough, but I ignored my mom's all-caps *SO INSPIRING!!* and clicked. Photos of celebrities with canes. The link to an MS podcast hosted by an actress who can no longer even use a cane. Something about a study involving mono, which I had in middle school, so...Why? I didn't read on to find out.

The heavy weight of guilt pulls me deeper into the doom spiral. My parents still don't know about the breakup. They had to deal with enough last week, and after our weepy call with my results on Friday, it seemed cruel to ring them up and hijack their tentative relief with a new source of worry.

That's what I've been telling myself, anyway. But the noble motive hasn't stuck, which is probably why I subjected myself to my mom's MS "research" as penance for not fessing up. I just really, *really* don't want to get into all things Cole again. Sunday's partial unpacking with Heather and Mark exceeded my threshold for emotional excavation, and I'm unwilling to dig any further. The bedrock is cracked enough as it is.

I'm breathing normally when I exit the locker room and walk toward the gym floor. Ian's filling his battered Yeti at the drinking fountain.

"You heading out?" he asks. Tuesday and Thursday I'm scheduled until the eleven thirty class wraps up, and I have Wednesdays off. I still plan to come in for tomorrow's WOD and, hopefully, tire myself out enough for an uninterrupted night's sleep. Tonight will probably be a write-off, because, courtesy of my mother, I now know about urge incontinence, a malady experienced by some MS patients. A lifetime of feeling like you have to pee and getting zero reprieve when you relieve yourself. It sounds like hell; I already have a bladder like a thimble.

Ian frowns. "Something wrong?"

"Nope!" I force a smile and take in another long breath. Because nothing *is* wrong. I just have to shift perspective. I'm fine. I ended up back squatting my body weight earlier; that was cool. And I made a new friend! Helen was really fun to talk to, and what she said about Firehouse showing her how to do more, instead of demanding she be less, resonated with me.

It gives me an idea. "Would you have time to do the goal-setting stuff now?"

"Oh, uh." He checks his watch, casting a glance past me, toward the door to his apartment. "Sure, now's fine. Let's go out front." He gestures me ahead.

I'm just clear of the hallway when his warm hand closes over my bicep. "Sorry," he says, voice low. "Wait a sec." His hand leaves my arm to point at Diego by the rig. There are no classes for the next hour and a half, so he and Alistair are the only ones working out.

Diego has set up two phones to record his back squats from different angles. He hadn't been kidding about dancing between sets; the man was getting down over there while I was cleaning. Now, he's brought one phone to the floor, and as we watch, he gets on his hands and knees in front of it, making what looks like a finger-to-lips *shh!* gesture.

I frown up at Ian, who smiles, mouthing, *"Wait for it."*

Diego gets up, then tiptoes over to Alistair, who's facing away from him, using an ab roller. Alistair starts in a kneeling plank, holding on to the handles on either side of the single six-inch wheel, then rolls forward, extending his arms out as far as he can while keeping them straight. It must be grueling; his body is shaking with the effort.

Diego stops with his hands to either side of Alistair's feet. Oblivious, Alistair rolls himself back to his starting position, then extends, pausing to hold a plank. With a whoop, Diego grabs a foot in each hand, jogging forward with Alistair in front of him like a human wheelbarrow.

Alistair bellows an elongated "Dude!" in protest, but Diego ignores him, continuing to wheel him around, back and forth, in view of his camera setup, giggling maniacally. I have never seen anything more absurd, but I'm laughing harder than I have since I can remember; I have to wipe away tears. Beside me, Ian's laugh is a deep rumble.

Diego slows to a stop, but before he can let go, Alistair tells him to keep hold because, quote, "The burn is *sick*." Diego trots off, steering our roommate around the rig.

Eyes still watering, I gawk up at Ian, who starts toward the lobby. "How did you know?"

"There's a look they all get when they're about to fuck with one another. You'll learn"—he's interrupted by a yawn he doesn't even try to conceal, then finishes—"to recognize it."

"Aww, this is Ian's nap time," Diego coos, circling us with Alistair. He has a great turn radius. "Every day during the break, he's upstairs for twenty minutes of sleepies."

The offer to postpone our meeting out of respect for nap time is on the tip of my tongue, but I force it down. That's a Regular Life Ellie impulse, the knee-jerk response to be accommodating at my own expense. Break from Regular Life Ellie is committed to her fitness journey and knows that setting goals is important. She'd also like to avoid going home to an empty house with only her thoughts for company; if that means intruding on nap time, so be it.

"It's fine," he assures me, and points me toward the large table by the pro shop. As I sit, he rummages through the clipboards I organized yesterday. One has the gym liability waiver new members sign, another is for drop-in guests, and the one Ian grabs now is simply titled "Goals."

Ian takes a seat. "First, any medical conditions that we need to be aware of…" His voice trails to give me the opportunity to jump in.

I shake my head. It's not a *lie*. I'm manifesting: My limited vision is temporary. And I see no need to disclose my endometriosis. I doubt I'll be working out during flare-ups. In my experience, referring to menstruation in any capacity is a free pass out of male-guided activities.

"Fitness history." He taps his pen against the clipboard. "What kind of workouts or sports have you done in the past?"

"I grew up swimming. And there was a fitness center in my last apartment building, so I'd use the stair climber or whatever. Go for runs. Why—" I frown, which is what Ian started doing as I listed. "What? Why is that the face you're making?"

"It's not you, it's the all cardio, no weight training you're describing. Pretty common."

I try to determine whether I should be offended. "Weights are intimidating if you don't know what you're doing. And even with the guidance here, there's the chance I'd get bulky—"

A voice cries out behind me, and I turn to find Diego on his knees a few feet away, taking a break from his turn wheelbarrowing. He sits back on his haunches. "Women always say that! They try us, they like it, but they're afraid of putting on too much muscle, and bail. Why?"

I shrug. "Lots of women don't want to be bigger, *period*. They work out to be *smaller*."

"Is that what you want?" he presses, with a hint of concern.

"That's not my current priority." Not that I'd mind a change in the ratio of my softer to firmer body mass, but my frustrations with my body have been so firmly focused on its betrayals that perceived aesthetic flaws take a back seat. "Give gals a break. It's going to take a lot more than a handful of body positivity campaigns to undo decades of social programming insisting that muscles are for men and that smaller is better for women."

Ian half smiles. "It takes more than lifting to pack on muscle, anyway."

"Like what?"

He leans back in his chair, balancing it on the back legs. It takes everything in me to refrain from telling him to keep all four legs on the floor—a lingering peeve from teaching. Knitting his fingers together, he lifts his hands up and over to cup the back of his head, causing the muscles of his upper arms to shift in the most fascinating way. I care less about the chair legs.

"Past training and exercise. How often someone's training. And the diet component is huge. Your muscles don't grow much unless you feed them. But a lot's genetic. Some people are genetically inclined to put on muscle easily, some aren't. You—"

"Have the back of a would-be beast," I cut in, not missing—or minding—his smile. "How about long, lean muscles?" It was practically a refrain at a yoga studio I used to go to.

Bending to retrieve Diego's ankles, Alistair drones, "Muscles have a point of origin—"

"Where they start," Diego grunts.

"—and a point of insertion."

"Where they attach."

"At both of these points, tendons connect muscles to bones. They're fixed points. They don't get longer."

"How about stretching?" I ask. "Like yoga or pilates?"

"That's an increased range of motion," Diego says, voice straining as he holds plank.

"What about the higher reps, lower weight thing?" I've heard that...somewhere.

Alistair shakes his head. "For real change, you gotta challenge the muscles. Overload them. Increase the weight, add more reps, slow the tempo, take shorter rests..."

"I never learned any of that," I admit. "You guys know

your stuff." They legitimately thought the grout in the shower was ombre, but a crash course in kinesiology they can relay, no problem.

"The more muscle mass, the higher the calorie burn during exercise and recovery. That means that when combined with nutrient-dense foods, a caloric deficit, and quality sleep, the kind of training we do here can help reduce body fat, if you're looking for *lean*. As far as any *bulk*..." Alistair starts rolling Diego away. "You'll just have to live with it."

I blink. It's the most I've heard him say since meeting him.

"That's the understanding we have. For now," Ian amends. "Fitness theory is ever-evolving. Same with food science, which is why there's some new trend every few years. But to put on muscle, you gotta eat."

"I'm not afraid of putting on muscle," I assure him. "Just so we're clear."

"Glad to hear it." Ian sits forward in his chair, bringing the legs back to the floor as he looks over the form. "What would you like to accomplish here?"

"I want to get stronger," I say firmly. "And I want to be able to do more of the movements as prescribed. Short term, get a handle on the general skills, then add more weight. Long term, master more complicated movements?" I nod toward the rig. "Toes-to-bar was pretty humbling." They were a component in today's cardio portion. It turns out, getting my toes to the pull-up bar while I'm *dangling* from it requires strength I do not currently possess.

"You're not too far off. It will come down to fine-tuning." Ian makes a note on the form. "I recorded your final weight from the back squats, and you can test out other lifts in the next couple of days. As you get comfortable with them, you'll see some big jumps in weight, so we'll track that and set longer-term goals." He clicks his pen a few times. "Anything else?"

I let my attention wander across the facility. I probably should have waited on this; two days in, I don't know enough to know what to shoot for. My eye lands on the trio of ropes attached to the I-beams between the pro shop and the gym floor. The ropes have been pulled aside and secured to a hook in the wall, like macho curtain swag. "I've never climbed a rope before."

"It's more about skill than strength to start." He looks me over, and a wry smile snags on the corner of his mouth. "Come on."

"What...now?"

"Unless you have other plans?" Ian leans to peer under the table. I self-consciously tense my legs, lifting them off the seat lest they appear unflatteringly splooty. "You left dominant or right?"

"Left?"

"You'll probably wrap right, then," he says, more to himself than me, and pushes away from the table. "Congratulations. You're going to learn how to climb a rope."

"Try leaning back when you pull," Ian says. "Your feet will come up more, and the higher your feet are when you get purchase, the more rope you'll get to bypass when you stand."

"Makes sense," I grunt. I have achieved little more than Ian's standing height, so we're basically at eye level. The lesson went better than I'd have anticipated, if I'd ever anticipated receiving a lesson on rope climbing. There's a wrap-and-crimp maneuver that was a little hard to get my head around, partly because it was so foreign, and partly because it required that I direct my focus perilously close to Ian's groin. But once I got that, it was smooth sailing.

Before we started, Ian set me up with a bright blue neoprene sleeve to protect my right shin—which gets "wrapped"—from rope burn. I was assured it was a precautionary measure, though I'm on my own for making sure I don't burn my hands during the descent. This was a *touch* dismaying, but I found myself chirping, "Noted!" Go with the Flow Yet Dedicated to Her Fitness Journey Ellie strikes again!

"Mind if I touch you?" he asks.

Every place on my body that has known his hands goes hot with recalled contact. Back, butt, boobs, outer thighs, and the back of my skull all flare so violently, I almost lose my grip on the rope. Some part of my brain not hijacked by my libido produces a "Sure."

Ian places a hand low between my shoulder blades, joining the ghost of Friday night's contact, and the other just above the waist of my shorts; also a repeat visit. Welcome back, guys!

"Keep looking up the rope. I'm going to guide you a little, and on three, pull with your arms and lift your knees." He's close enough that I catch that same hint of cinnamon I noticed last weekend. Is it his toothpaste? Gum? "When you no longer feel me, just stand."

"Gotcha." My hands have started sweating.

"All right. One, two, three!"

He presses against my lower back, controlling the range of the resulting backward tilt with the hand at my shoulders, and I hike up my knees and pull myself as high as I can. Then Ian's no longer holding me, and I stand. I have to loosen my grip as I rise, sliding my hands up the rope, but when I'm at my full height, I've managed to get myself higher off the ground.

Like, *considerably* higher. I stare down at Ian, who smiles. "Whoa." I turn wide eyes on Alistair and Diego, who've finished wheelbarrowing and are clapping for me.

"Well done," says Ian. "Think you can do that again on your own?"

A recently familiar thrill hums in my chest, the *now what?* gearing up for an outlet. "Think you can catch me if I fall?"

"You're not going to *fall*," he chides. "But also, yes."

"Then, yes!" I repeat the motions, not getting my feet as high as I did with Ian's assistance but covering more distance on the rope than I was when we started. "I did it!" And this one was all on my own. My smile is huge, the humming in my chest extending to my arms and legs. My roommates whoop; both raise phones, recording.

"Great!" cheers Ian. "You have another one in you?"

We find out together: yes, again!

I survey the gym from my higher vantage point. I'm only ten or twelve feet off the ground, but it's exhilarating. Back squats have *nothing* on this. I feel like I could fight crime! I look down at Ian, standing on the cushioned mat he situated below the rope "just in case."

"Now, I have to get down," I say, realizing it as I articulate the thought.

"Do you remember those steps?"

"Get the rope on the outside of my knees," I recite, shifting the rope, "loosen up on my feet—" I loosen too much, relaxing my hands at the same time, and then I'm streaking down the length of rope. I don't even have time to scream before I hit the mat with a grunt.

No, not the mat: I've been caught by Ian. "You okay?" he asks in a rush, a gust of cinnamon rustling the hair by my ear. His remarkable eyes are wide with concern. I have a death grip on his shoulders, like I'm trying to climb him. Man Mountain. How fitting.

"How are your hands?"

It takes another second for the question to register, and I release my hold. My nails have left tiny crescents in the fabric of his shirt. Still too stunned to speak, I raise my palms for inspection.

"A little red," he determines. "Not too bad."

This close, I pick up on a rattling sound as he speaks, like he has something in his mouth. "Are you eating?" I blurt.

He frowns, attention darting from my face to my still upraised hands and back. After a moment, he works his jaw, and I watch, rapt, as his lips part. Between his teeth is a bright red candy. *Cinnamon.*

"Ah!" I say, appreciating the resolution to the mystery of his spicy scent. His tongue darts out to draw the candy back in, which is fascinating.

My focus stays on Ian's lips as I regain the rest of my senses. Primarily touch, as I register the hard heat of his chest against my entire right side. I'm being held bride-over-the-threshold style, which is a first and a thing I like very much. Like Ian's chest hair! And muscle soreness. I'm learning all kinds of things about myself these days. And—"I just climbed a rope!"

Ian laughs. "Yeah, you did."

"That's so cool!" I am awash with adrenaline and pride. It's dizzying. Though that could be the pheromones.

"Oh, shit." Ian lifts the arm behind my knees to raise my lower legs. A dark pink line about two inches long angles over the sliver of shin between the sleeve and the top of my shoe. A smattering of crimson beads blossom within the pink.

"Abraded," he grumbles. He lowers me to the floor, keeping a hand at my side as I find my feet. "I'm so sorry. I should have gone over that descent one more time. We'll get that cleaned up."

I'm in my car a few minutes later, admiring the Band-Aid on my shin, when a text populates in the roommate group chat. Diego has wasted no time editing and distributing the footage of my rise and fall, and I watch the replay. I grin, getting another hit of that heady, buzzy high. I really did that. Me and my busted body did that.

I watch the clip two more times. And then I call my mom.

13

HEATHER RESTS HER CHIN ON my shoulder, giving me a hug from behind. "You okay?"

"It looks like the furniture's been raptured," I say, and she laughs, coming to my side to survey what little remains in the bedroom I shared with Cole. The dresser, bed, and nightstands had been mine, so all that's left is the mattress and piles of Cole's things.

"He made zero effort to consolidate," I say, pointing to the phone charger and books on the floor beside his side of the mattress, which I've elected not to take. Bringing a surface on which I've experienced intimate contact with Cole into the next chapter of my life felt...*icky*.

"His drawers in the dresser were still full, and he left a bunch of crap on top." I sigh. "But I was the one to move out with zero warning, so do I have any room to bitch?"

"Are you kidding? His 'break' bullshit absolves you of anything. And he left one of your fancy bowls dirty in the sink," she reminds me. "He's lucky you haven't set this shit on fire."

"It crossed my mind." The sight of one of my handmade

gold-rimmed soup bowls in an inch of standing water and swollen pasta flotsam, its white interior ringed with marinara sauce, had me distinctly incendiary.

"He isn't worth the arson charge," I say, and turn around, Heather following me from the room. I'd convinced her and Mark to try the endurance workout at Firehouse this morning, and once I got Cole's tersely worded text that he'd left on his Saturday group bike ride, we came to pack. The guys arrived about an hour later to load up. Ian even lent them his truck, which was a godsend; Mark overestimated the capacity of his SUV. To my understanding, the Explorer has been relegated to transporting my houseplants, which Mark has been coordinating down in the parking garage for the past half hour. I have...too many plants.

I do a final sweep of the guest bedroom. That mattress is bare, the bedding now bundled in the back of my car, and the only signs of the office furniture Grant and Diego took downstairs are the divots they left in the carpet. The living room is similarly barren, now devoid of my couch, coffee table, and miniature jungle. My favorite chair, a wide-set wingback in channeled navy velvet, waits by the open front door, but I figure Heather and I can manage it. Which is good, because the designated muscle with us is distracted.

By the open front door, Alistair palms Mushu, one of my potted dragon tails. He's draped its long, leafy vines over his shoulders like a boa. Paired with his standard shorts-only status, he has a distinctly jungle-hunk look that I'm sure anyone with masculine preferences would find appealing, had they not witnessed said hunk lick a nine-volt battery.

Like Heather, who is actively ogling. *Lord.* She'd about had a stroke at the abundance of muscled torsos at Firehouse earlier. Ian had been among the few to remain fully clad, but even so, he'd inspired colorful commentary from Heather. I'm going to let her discover the nude for herself.

"This is the last of it," I say, nodding to the armchair, on the chance that it will remind Alistair why he's here. "I don't know how y'all managed to get everything loaded in one go."

"Huh? Oh, no way," he says. "Ian and Grant have made, like, two runs to the house."

"Ian—" My eyes bug. "*Ian's* here?" *Here.* Where I lived with Cole. The same icky feeling crawls over me as when I thought about taking my mattress.

"Maybe? He could be on his way to the house, or at the house, or—"

"You guys said you 'had' his truck," I interrupt. "I thought he'd let us borrow it."

"Nah. He came with."

Ian. How has he been helping this whole time and no one told me? Then again…I glance at Alistair, who's caressing his cheek with the tip of Mushu's bottommost leaf. I can absolutely believe it.

Before I can decide whether to obsess over Ian's unexpected involvement, a door slams out in the communal hallway, followed by the sound of quick, heavy footsteps. Heather shoots me a confused look, and a moment later, Mark bursts through the doorway.

"*Cole!*" he wheezes. "Lobby. Calling the elevator. I took the stairs. *Two at a time!*" Each statement comes out between quick gasps.

Dammit! I check my watch, ignoring the painful squeeze to my chest. "We should have had another hour before he got back."

Mark slumps into my chair, tossing his hands up in helpless apology.

"You took the stairs?" Heather asks him.

"Five floors!" Mark gasps.

"Hell yeah," Alistair says, supportively, and reaches out with Mushu's bottom leaf like a high five. Mark accepts, reaching out limply with his index finger to brush the offered leaf.

Before I can fully appreciate just how routine this degree of absurdity has become, the distinct *clink* of Cole's bike cleats sounds in the hallway. My stomach drops. I fluff my hair, and Heather comes to stand closer to me, giving my hand a quick supportive squeeze. We wait.

A few seconds later, Cole stands in the foyer with his bike, arm through the outrageously expensive, feather-light frame on his shoulder. He looks from me, to Heather, to Alistair, to Mark, then to Alistair again. Or, at least, that's who he's facing; he still has his stupid wraparound shades on, so I can't tell.

He tears off his shades with his free hand, and despite the *this fucking guy* of it all, I stifle a laugh. His face is the shade of red that precedes sunburn, the contrasting white around his eyes so stark, it's like a raccoon's mask in reverse. He forgot sunblock. Of course he did! Because I wasn't here to remind him.

"You're early," I say, not bothering with niceties.

"The wind picked up, so we called it short. Did you hire movers—" Cole's attention fixes behind me, and his eyes go wide. Sunglasses in hand, he points to the empty space where the couch had been. "You took the *couch*?"

"The couch that I bought? Yes. And that's Alistair. Grant and Diego are here, too—"

"They're her roommates," Heather finishes for me, with no shortage of wicked glee.

"Her—" Cole wheels toward Alistair, the clips on his bike shoes grinding audibly into the hardwood, one week having been enough time to abandon my *no footwear beyond the threshold, bike be damned*, policy. He gives Alistair an affronted once-over. "You're, what? *Twenty?*"

"Dude, whatever," Alistair gripes. "I turned twenty-one, like, a *month* ago." He turns to me. "Imma load this up," he says, indicating the plant, which in no way constitutes a load, and extends a curt "Ex*cuse* you" to Cole, who stiffly maneuvers his bike so my bevined roommate can toe on his sneakers and step out.

Cole stares after him, then fixes his pale eyes on me. "Are you living with *undergrads?*" He looks to Heather and Mark. "Did you know this last week?"

"Do you think we'd have told you if we had?" Heather asks. Mark just glares. Probably because he's still catching his breath. He had his butt kicked at endurance earlier.

I don't know what to expect from this interaction, and while I appreciate their loyalty, I do know that I'd rather not have an audience. "Would you give us a moment, please?" Heather nods and helps the still semi-incapacitated Mark from his seat and into the hallway.

Cole purses his lips, and with hauteur subverted by his head-to-toe highlighter-yellow riding ensemble, shifts the bike from his shoulder to hang it on the wall stand beside him. He refused to store his *precious* in the communal bike cage downstairs, so I scoured the internet for an in-unit solution and installed the little rack—custom, because of the hyper-aerodynamic design of his frame—while he was at work one day not long after we moved in. I even used a stud finder.

And he couldn't spare the seconds it would have required to wash a goddamn bowl.

He crosses his arms. "Why won't you answer my calls? You won't even text back."

No *How are you?* No *I've been worried*, or anything relating to the MS prospect. Five years together, and all I get is a pissy *How dare you?* Disappointment settles over me like a physical thing. Not at his response, but because I honestly hadn't expected anything more from him.

I conjure some dirty-bowl anger to combat it. "Because there's nothing to say. You're not strong enough for *this*," I say, pointing at my right eye, "on top of *this*"—I clutch my abdomen. "What's left to cover?"

He tosses up his hands. "That doesn't mean that I don't care—"

"But it does mean that you don't care *enough*. Which is fine," I insist, wanting him to get this through his still helmeted head. "We'd been done for a while, Cole. We both knew it. We could have split amicably and raised a glass of whatever outrageous wine you ordered—"

"The *cab*," he says, with just enough superiority to set my teeth on edge.

"Which is a *red*. Which you know kills my stomach but ordered anyway. On a night we were supposed to be celebrating me, if you'll recall."

"It was going to pair beautifully with my pasta—"

"You are *not* helping yourself," I say, my voice dark.

Cole shuts his mouth, blinking in surprise. That wasn't very *his* Ellie of me.

"Instead," I continue, "you made it clear that you could only be with me conditionally." I look into his still-wide eyes, hoping to convey how painful it is to even say it out loud, but he's looking at me like I've sprouted a second head. "Do you not get how much worse that is than just splitting up? I already deserved better than what we had. So I sure as *shit* deserved better than to sit around here waiting for you to decide whether I'm worth the effort of being with me."

"I never said any of that!" he complains, the surprise replaced by a defensive edge.

I shake my head, the disappointment crushing. He doesn't get it, and there's no point in trying to make him. You can't make someone care.

Cole looks at me and sighs. "Now what?" he asks, with the same resignation he had when I came in with my eye covered. Hearing it now is just as gutting as it had been that morning.

"That's how you reacted when I came to tell you about my eye. Do you know that?" I ask, genuinely curious, though I can anticipate his answer. "When I came to tell you that something *terrifying* was happening to me, your first thought was that it would be yet another inconvenience to you."

He's shaking his head, tiny little side-to-side jerks of denial. "I don't remember—"

"I've obsessed over those two words that just tumbled out of you. I've turned it into a *mantra*," I add, with a bitter laugh, "and you don't even remember saying it."

I hate that I've done that. That I can give him the slightest bit of credit for the changes I've made, even if they were motivated by spite. And I can be mad about the disrespect for my belongings, and my time, since I got to empty his drawers. Those texts I hadn't responded to had asked if I'd "really thought this through," and where I kept the colander. Nothing about my eye or my general well-being. No apology. He's never even asked why I left in the first place.

Shame smothers what's left of my anger. "I made myself so *small* for you," I say. "My wants, my pain, just to avoid inconveniencing you. And I can't even be mad at you for missing it, because I never expected you to notice."

I don't know when the scales tipped, when my desperation to remain relevant and useful in our relationship outweighed the actual affection that should have been its foundation. It's mortifying. Or it should be. Now, only a week removed from that version of myself, it's like I'm pitying someone else. I can extend her some grace, the poor thing. She doesn't even know that she can climb a rope.

"*Hey.*"

I start at the sudden voice and look up to see a familiar figure in the doorway. Or, a chimera of familiar figures, the bottom half in its uniform of shorts and sneakers, and the top half I know from the results of clandestine image searches scorched into my memory.

Because it's Ian's familiar figure. And it is *shirtless*.

Ian fills the doorway, bracing his hands on either side of the frame. Every line and plane of him is defined, perhaps not as sharply as in the years-old photo, but the man remains a vision;

an anatomical chart as rendered by an artist's hand. The expanse of him uncovered makes him loom larger, the position of his arms showcasing the swell of his biceps and pectorals, the angle of his body compelling the eye downward to the segments of his abdominal muscles, and the chiseled *v* that vanishes into his waistband.

And he's fuzzier than he'd been in the photo.

I force my attention upward, but his face is just as staggering. His attention is fully fixed on me, storm-cloud eyes assessing, shaded with concern. He *cares*.

He cares. The realization cuts through me, severing the me I'd been with Cole from who I'm determined to be now, shearing off the weighty disappointment. My smile comes unbidden. No more "Now what?" Just...*now*.

For now.

Ian watches me for a beat longer, then his face softens, mollified. He tips his head almost imperceptibly to indicate Cole, marking him as his intended audience. I assume that my gawking established how unprepared I was to see him, so I streamline my returning nod to convey that while wildly unnecessary, the demonstration of his vitality is nonetheless appreciated. This nod is received with an eyebrow twitch and the tease of a smile. I'm not sure what I'm supposed to get from it, but we've been maintaining eye contact for a good handful of seconds, so it's pretty hot.

Ian steps in, pausing to ease off his shoes, and reaches out to Cole for a shake. "Ian Hammond." Cole's hand, in the fingerless, neon-yellow cycling glove, looks like a toy as he takes Ian's massive paw. I hope one of Ian's calluses snags the nylon.

It is surreal, seeing them beside one another. Not simply the disparity in builds—Cole is fit, but in a refined way, the opposite of Ian's functionally brutish form. It's the vast difference in my life that I'm staring at. Cole, for whom I'd so narrowly defined my limits, and Ian, who's been helping me uncover how much more I'm capable of. It wouldn't take a literature curriculum writer to see the symbolism.

"Hayes?" Ian asks, and I come back to myself. "We got your bed over to the house, but no mattress. Is there one you need from here? Because"—his almost-smile turns into a lascivious smirk, eyes smoldering—"you're welcome to stay on mine."

Oh, God, he is good. *Too* good. Because I'm visualizing the mattress I've been sleeping on all by my lonesome, but my mind has him on it with me, and we. Are. *Naked!*

I cock my head, pretending to consider his proposition as I savor how very, very still Cole has gone in the wake of it. "You know, I think I'll stick with yours," I say, keeping my phrasing vague. "Thank you for sharing it with me." To the fully rooted Cole, I explain, "Ian's my boss."

"Your..." He goggles at me. "Where are you working?" It sounds like he expects my answer to be "a zoo."

"Firehouse Fitness. Ian's the owner. I'm on reception."

"Stop in," Ian says. "We have sports conditioning classes Monday and Wednesday evenings. Very popular with cyclists." Returning to me, he points to the armchair, asking, "Want some help with this?"

"Thank you, that—"

Footsteps thunder in the hallway, and I am as unsurprised to see Diego and Grant burst through the doorway as I am by the fact that they, too, have opted to remove their respective shirts. Did the three of them discuss this, or was there some brotastic vibe exchange that had them all commit to terrorizing Cole via muscle mass?

"And here's Grant and Diego," I say. "My other roommates."

"You are Cole?" Diego growls. He literally puffs up his chest as he closes in on him.

Cole scoots back half a step, clip-bottomed shoes sliding on the wood. "Yes?"

Diego mutters something containing *pendejo*. Grant just glares. He has his arms crossed, hands tucked high beneath his upper arms, further showcasing his considerable biceps. Ian's doing the same, expression passive, but no less intimidating.

I feel myself standing taller, too.

"I'm done here," I say, directing the words to the trio at the door, but hoping that its deeper meaning finds its way to Cole. "We can—" I look where I'd left my shoes inside the entryway, but they're gone. I frown. "Did someone take my shoes down?"

Grant's stern face goes apologetic. "Um…maybe?"

Cole huffs a derisive laugh, and I bristle. So much for getting out of here on top.

"We can handle that," chimes Ian. "Grant, Diego? Think you can manage the chair with Ellie in it?"

The potential spectacle is just compelling enough that I don't insist on walking.

"It would be an honor," Diego bites out, glare still fixed firmly on Cole.

Grant maneuvers the chair into the hallway, then stands to one side of it. "Milady?" he asks with a grin, gesturing to the seat as Diego comes to stand on the opposite side of the chair.

Without even looking at Cole, I step into the hallway, Ian behind me. We silently agree to leave the door open, so that Cole can watch me take a seat in my makeshift throne, the velvet upholstery which had seemed so indulgent when I bought it suddenly fitting.

"Gentlemen," I say, "Let's go home."

14

"THIS IS WHAT, thirty floors up?" Grant asks, craning to take a last look at the rooftop pool as the elevator doors close. Still high from our moment of triumph with Cole, my coterie and I had swept into the waiting elevator without confirming that it was going down, and were promptly shot up twenty-five floors. I'm still waiting for my ears to pop.

"Thirty and falling." I point to the digital readout above the doors. *29...28...* Grant cocks his head, taking in the countdown, and gestures to Diego, who moves to join him.

I stay put in my chair in the corner. I refuse to put my bare feet on the floor. A rooftop pool attracts two kinds of apartment residents: those who will visit the pool exclusively to show off the view, and those who will employ it as a hunting ground for sexual partners. I know that these elevators have seen some things.

Ian leans against the wall beside me. He's on my bad side, and while my vision has cleared up some, he remains a beige blur, the features of his still-naked torso unclear. Not that I'm trying to sneak peeks. I don't think I'll need to; that scene in the apartment has *core memory* written all over it. But I wouldn't mind confirming the accuracy of my updated mental reference.

The car slows, coming to a stop a few seconds later. When the doors part, I expect someone to be waiting to board, but no one's there. Grant steps out, Diego following.

"What are you doing?" I ask.

"A *challenge*," says Grant, and looks at Ian. "Bet we'll beat you to the basement."

The older Hammond scoffs. "Using what? The stairs? No way."

Grant holds out a hand to keep the doors open. "Easy bet, then. Say, twenty-five bucks?"

"What? No. That would be stupid."

"So make it fifty," Diego offers innocently. *Too* innocently. He glances back at Grant, and I pick up on something familiar in his expression. Something...conniving?

Whatever it is, Ian is too focused on his brother to notice. He crosses his arms over his chest. "*Fine.* Fifty bucks says we'll get to the basement before you."

"We're on!" Grant releases the doors, looking way too confident for a guy who's about to run down twenty-six flights of stairs *and* lose half of his month's entertainment budget. Not that he knows I've set one yet; we're going over that Monday.

The doors begin to close, but just before they do, Grant shoots out a hand, pressing them back again. He points at Ian. "That's fifty for *each* of us."

"Sure. I'll be taking fifty dollars from both of you in however long it takes for you two to get down there *after* we do," he adds, with a nod my way.

"You sure about that?" Grant leans in farther, hovering a

finger menacingly over the panel of floor buttons. He punches the 21. And the 17. And the 4. And the 8…

Ian straightens, back separating from the metal wall with a peeling sound. "Grant—"

With a shit-eating grin aimed at his brother, Grant splays his palm and draws it down the columns of numbers, illuminating all but three before retreating.

"Grant!" I shout, half laughing at the unexpected cunning.

"You shithead!" Ian bellows as the doors begin to close.

Grant lovingly extends his brother the finger. "Enjoy the ride!" he singsongs, then darts around the corner with a *whoop!* Diego giggles madly. The doors shut.

I do a quick tally of the floors we'll be visiting. He managed to miss the 5, my old floor, making it less likely that we'll be enduring a second encounter with Cole, but we have twenty-three goddamn floors before we get to the basement.

I turn to Ian with a grimace. "There is a second elevator, if you'd like to try your luck?"

Ian shakes his head. "This is what I get for underestimating them."

"Suit yourself," I say, not minding the prospect of our forced proximity. I turn to face him, sitting up on my knees so I don't have to crane my neck as much. "Well, thank you for helping me move. Sorry that it's about to cost you a hundred dollars."

He smirks. "It's fine. It's been…interesting."

"Oh?"

The elevator comes to a stop, chiming a bright *ding!* before the doors open. I hadn't noticed the ding earlier. That's going to get old.

No takers, just a large 24 painted on the wall and an oversized print reading "Alright, Alright, Alright." The car waits for ten seconds before the doors close. Twenty-two to go.

"Interesting, seeing where I used to live?" I continue, eagerly. "Or interesting because you can't find a better way to describe the experience of demoralizing my ex?"

Ian ducks his chin and reaches for the brim of his cap, but for once, he isn't wearing it. Instead, he ruffles his hair, reminding me of how soft it had felt between my fingers the night we met. "I know that I can have an impact."

"An *impact*?" I repeat, not bothering to hide my laugh. "Such a tame word for turning a man to dust at the sight of your dominant masculine form." His brows raise, and I roll my eyes. "*Please.* Like yours is ever *not* the dominant masculine form. When Heather saw you this morning, she shouted, 'Whose *horse* is that?'"

He huffs a laugh. "That was a first." He runs a hand through his hair again, then rests his forearm against the back of the chair. "*Impact* is what our dad says. We got our height from him. When I hit a growth spurt in high school, he sat me down to talk about how intimidating size like ours can be. To women, in particular, it can be threatening. So be aware. Don't loom, don't corner, leave an exit clear..."

"Grant must have gotten that Dad chat, too," I say. "He left the front door open when I went into the house the first time. It was really thoughtful."

"Good." He nods, more to himself than me. "Dad also said that if dealing with the kind of guy who'd be..." He seems to search for phrasing.

"Angling to have yourself described as *dominantly masculine* again, Mr. Hammond?"

"If a guy's so fragile that the sight of me can take him down a peg, then he deserves to be."

I prop my chin in my hand. "Fair enough. But how'd you know that Cole fit the bill?"

The elevator settles at the next floor; I've already lost track of how far we've gone. The doors open, but Ian's eyes don't leave mine. He watches me with the same stormy concern he wore when he entered the apartment earlier. My fingers curl, digging into the plush fabric of the chair. It's disarming, being on the receiving end of a look like that. I don't know whether to rally my defenses or surrender.

"Whatever happened with him left you desperate enough to move into the Dawghouse," he says, firmly. "Anyone who could do that is clearly lacking."

My skin tingles. He *cares*.

He's quiet for a moment, eyes going distant. His gaze is still unfocused when he says, "That night in the bathroom, I don't know if you remember, but you said that you were…"

His eyes meet mine again, and heat spreads from my cheeks to my chest…and lower. "*Several* things, but sad was one of them. And for a second, before we—" He raises his hands and lets his fingers link briefly before separating. "You looked it. More than sad. Like…diminished. And I saw that again in your apartment."

The words generate more than tingles. My body is *sparking*.

The urge to tell him everything is so fierce, I have to physically brace against it. I run the scenario: the mystery pain, the breakups, the hope I felt early on with Cole, and the relief of my endometriosis diagnosis before the relationship's gradual breakdown. The degree to which I'd allowed myself to be diminished—ten points to Ian; *diminished* was a quality word choice—my eye, and the fear and uncertainty that quietly dominate every spare moment and thought.

The urge passes before the elevator reaches its next stop. Confiding in him might relieve me of some of the burden, but to watch the concern in his eyes twist into pity is an indignity I'm unwilling to risk.

"We'd been over for a while," I say, the go-to line worn to edgeless. "It was just shitty timing on his part."

"That's vague," he complains, and my thrill at the fact that he cares enough to point this out is outweighed only by how appalled I am that it takes so little to thrill me.

I don't know if it's me or my ever-present instinct to please, but I add, "Seeing him reminded me of who I was when we were together. Who I'd become with him by the end. And I don't want to be that person anymore."

"Hmm." He eases himself into a half-seated position on the arm of the chair, bringing him close enough that I feel the heat radiating from his body. "Still vague. But very dramatic."

I let out an involuntary laugh, and he smiles.

"It's embarrassing," I say, which is also true. "You saw Captain Day-Glo. I stuck it out with *him*. He stopped caring—" I halt, my chest tightening. It's exactly what happened. Cole stopped caring. I've lost all humor as I add, "And I kept trying, anyway."

I force myself to meet Ian's storm-cloud gaze. "I like being useful. I genuinely enjoy doing things for the people I care about. I like making their lives easier. *Better.* And when the cracks started to show, I filled them by leaning into that. I took on more and more around the apartment, prioritized the things he liked or wanted to do. And he was appreciative at first," I add, more for my benefit than Cole's. "But it didn't take long before all that became routine, too."

It wasn't enough.

"I can understand someone not seeing the value in maintaining a pristine toilet," I say, the example inane, but real. "But he stopped caring that I did. That things like that matter to me. And then *that* became routine. I started to expect less and less from him, and he delivered. He didn't value what I did. And by extension, he didn't value me."

"And you stayed," he says. No judgment, just an observation.

"I convinced myself I didn't need it. The consideration. It was either that or believe I didn't deserve it," I say, and wince. I could break my own heart thinking about that too long.

Before I descend fully into melancholy, I force a smile. "Still vague?"

"Oh, *very* vague," he determines. "But I think I get what you're saying. Or…*not* saying."

"I wasn't a doormat," I say, insistent.

He gives me a droll look. "You're *literally* seated in a throne right now. You couldn't be a doormat if you tried." His brows go low. "It takes more than one person's effort to make a relationship work."

"No amount of ironing in the world can make up the difference—" A memory strikes me. "I ironed the shirt he wore to dinner that night!" I blurt. I'd forgotten about that. "I was pressing the skirt of my dress, and he asked me if I'd do his shirt. He was planning to dump me within the *hour* and still asked me to iron his goddamn shirt." I scowl, incensed anew. *"Fucker."*

Ian chuckles. "And that's not who you want to be now?"

"Hell no!" I say, though I do find ironing quite soothing. "Now, I'm someone who can *climb a rope.*"

He makes a thoughtful sound. "More like someone who *knows* that she can climb a rope. You already had the strength; you only needed the mechanics."

"Then, someone…who can back squat her body weight?"

"What, Tuesday's workout? That was a set of *five*," he scoffs, but his tone is light. "Your one-rep will be heavier than that. Another fifteen percent, at least."

"Oh. *Nice.* So, I guess," I muse, "I'm just a gal who's learning what she's capable of."

He grunts. I don't even pretend that I'm not into it. "Still vague. And saccharine."

"Oh, shut up," I complain, but I'm grinning. He smiles back.

There's still a question hovering between us, the why of it all. Why the cracks developed, why I'd been so devoted to patching them, why it had been Cole who finally acknowledged that we were done. Why that had made me sad.

And I have a why of my own. Why, if Ian remembers I'd said that I was "a lot of things" in the bathroom that night, he has yet to comment on the fact that I'd been scared, too.

When I walked into the apartment with Heather and Mark, the lingering reek of my desperation had hit me like a slap in the face. Not the dying gasps of my relationship with Cole or the time I'd wasted denying the end of our run, but the despair of those final days in that space as I waited to find out what the hell was happening to me. If I was going blind, if I was succumbing to a degenerative nerve condition, and the knowledge that I'd be going through it with one less person's support.

And while I'm becoming a back-squatting, rope-climbing himbo wrangler, discreetly jonesing for her boss, if I end up with MS, there's a chance I'll lose all of that, too. And how much more desperate will I be then, knowing how much more I could have been?

I suppress a shudder as I pull up my amended mantra. *Now.* Focus on *now.*

DING!

I turn to see what floor we're on. Nine to go.

"You don't have to be useful."

"What?" I twist back toward Ian. He's settled his head in his hand, elbow propped on the chair, bringing us level. He is so close.

His eyes fall to my lips, then meet my gaze again. "I get that it's your thing, being useful. But you don't have to be useful to other people to have value. You can just…be. *You.*"

The words wrap around my sad, scared, stupid heart.

"You say that like you know who that is," I say.

"You say *that* like you don't." There's worry in his reply. *Care.*

I smile and risk a look at his lips. "I'm finding out, remember?"

He is so close.

The elevator's movement sets us rocking, and while I've long since adjusted to the subtle swaying, this time, I let it shift me a few critical inches. I forgive myself for believing that Ian does the same and take it as my green light. I'm not sad or scared as I close the space between us and kiss him.

Barely. A brush of lips, dry and soft. It's over in an instant.

I don't know that I've actually broken contact when I whisper, "Thank you."

He sucks in a breath, our faces so close that the movement of air tickles my lips. The sensation compels me to lean in for firmer contact, my lips parting. His fingertips ghost over my jawline, encouraging my head to angle, the tip of his tongue—

DING!

We flinch apart as the doors grind open, the distance between us still negligible. But instead of the stillness that's followed our arrival at the last umpteen floors, the car jostles with the boarding of our first passenger. Ian's attention shifts.

He leans back farther. *"Alistair?"*

I wheel to face the doors. Alistair observes us as though he's strolled into Firehouse to us chatting at the desk, not huddled together in an enclosed space, drowning in one another's pheromones and our faces within tongue's distance of one another.

"Oh, hey." He raises Mushu, whose vines he's now angled like a sash across his bare torso. "Ellie, can I hang on to this guy? Like, keep him in my room while you're living with us?"

I settle into a seated position, as though the taste of cinnamon isn't swirling in my mouth. "Sure?" My head clears enough to process what he's asking. "I'll let you know when to water him." I can barely hear myself over the rush of blood in my ears. "That's Mushu, by the way. He's a dragon tail."

Alistair's brows raise, and he cocks his head, as though reevaluating his worldview in light of this new information. *"Sick."* Then he frowns. "Dude, your old place sucks. The elevator is slow as shit."

15

"HOLA, FRIENDS! I AM DIEGO and with me is my roommate, Ellie! She's very grown-up and helpful and teaching us how
to live like we are not animals. And we're teaching her how to be
strong! Ellie, flex with me!"

Diego raises his arms in a classic muscle-man pose. I join him
in front of the tablet, the screen showing us in the middle of the
kitchen, Built Box's logo bordering us on one side and the livestream's chat in the other. As I flex, I catch some of the viewers'
commentary. Grapple303 thinks I need to work on my lats. *Rude.*

"As we work together, she will get bigger and stronger! And I
will get better at cooking…and maybe a little bigger, too?" Diego
wraps his arms around himself in a hug, shimmying his hips.
"More muscle means more Diego to love!"

I smile. He is charm incarnate.

The kits arrived late yesterday afternoon, which we would
have known to anticipate had Diego checked his email since Tuesday. Built Box had been more than happy for me to join, despite
my "negligible online presence"—their words—and wanted to

get the ball rolling. They included the filming releases we signed, scanned, and sent back, and a more detailed contract for Diego, which he spent some time with while I was unpacking. The base offer was bumped up to complimentary meal kits for the whole household, but in bigger news, he'll be seeing a percentage of sales for redeemed coupon codes exclusive to his viewers.

As Diego continues his introductory bit, I do a final inventory of the ingredients. Today's kit is a take on traditional Middle Eastern kofta, combining beef with onion, herbs, and a spice mix, rolled into balls that can be grilled or, because I am unwilling to introduce fire, baked. The process is similar to the meatballs we made last week, the herb chopping and onion grating well within Diego's wheelhouse, leaving him free to engage with his audience.

The guy is a natural. He maintains a steady stream of chatter as we take on each element of the recipe, answering questions in the chat and injecting moments of humor, and I only occasionally have to redirect his attention to the food prep. When he warns viewers not to overhandle the meat when they roll their balls, the aside inspires a burst of raunchy commentary from the chat. Big "balls" humor crowd.

Prepped and rolled, the balls go in the oven, and as we prepare the accompanying side salad and dressing, he continues to engage. There are many dance breaks.

Then, the moment of truth. When the balls have cooled, we each take a bite. They're decent but underseasoned; the salt in the spice mix was not enough to carry the flavor. I chew and wait for Diego, who's front and center, to respond with his standard sunshine.

But his brows come down as he swallows. "I need more flavor. It's good, but tastes good *for* you, you know? And sometimes that's what you want." He smiles, dreamily. "I feel that way when I have a delicious soup, and it makes me feel cozy, but without being too heavy. But this is the kind of healthy tasting that feels like something is missing. Oh!" He turns and points to me. "Ellie, the bottle you used the other day, to give that chicken soup more...what was it? *Umami!*"

"Fish sauce?" I say, worried about what his sponsors might say about him adding ingredients to something they claim to be all-inclusive.

"It could be helpful. Come, friends!" He plucks the tablet from the stand. "Let's go on a field trip to the refrigerator." He crosses to the fridge, pulling it open, but careful not to expose the camera to the inside. He wags his finger at the lens. "No, no, no! No other sponsors or name brands! This is all about Built Box." He winks. "And some experimentation." He plucks the fish sauce from the shelf in the door. "This will boost the flavor, and...ah! I think you'd also want something with spice to step it up. Everyone has a little spice on hand, yes?" He dangles a bottle of sriracha in front of the tablet. "Let's give it a go!"

He shakes a few drops of fish sauce onto the balls we've sampled, following with a dab of hot sauce. He raises his to the tablet. "Round two!"

I toss back the rest of mine, and—oh, wow! "Diego, this is perfect!"

He nods, smiling as he chews. "So much better! And, friends, you saw that it only took a tiny bit of each? A little bit goes a long way with flavor!"

"Is that dinner?" asks Alistair, appearing in the frame. He's clad solely in a tiny pair of shorts and his house slippers. I half expect him to be wearing Mushu again; he's been taking the plant for regular "tours" around the common areas.

I wheel on him. "Dude, you can't be coming in here in your *man panties!* This is *live!*"

"Oh, really?" Alistair moves between us, peering at the tablet, but we're hardly visible amid the sudden barrage of messages from viewers and floating red hearts. "Huh. *Cool.*" He waves, then points to the waistband of his microscopic undies. "These aren't *man panties*, or whatever. They're Italian. I'm in a campaign for them coming up. Should—" He turns to me. "Should I, like, name drop them or something?"

"Let's keep this focused on one merchant," I say, though in the chat BUTTStough95 demands, *drop the deets bro!*

"Rad." He peers at the balls on the cooling rack. "These any good?"

"Yes! Let me enhance one for you," says Diego, wielding his sauce bottles. He administers them to a ball, and steps back so our roommate's the only one on screen. As Alistair considers the offering, Diego produces a small remote from his pocket and uses it to make the camera zoom in on his friend, altering the angle so that when he takes a bite, it's just Alistair's immaculate features, his eyes closing as he savors his sample. The chat is alight with fire emojis and inappropriate suggestions for what else he might put in his mouth. Some people should not be allowed online.

The camera zooms out as Alistair swallows and opens his eyes. *"Yo,"* he says, and holds up a hand for a high five. Diego slaps his palm before they grip one another's hands, pulling one another close enough to bump chests; the ultimate in dudely approval.

"This is awesome," he determines, and they separate. "So, is this one of the loading kits or one for a cut cycle?"

"Excellent question!" Diego cheers. "Built Box has versions of this kit for both. This was the loading one, so it came with ground beef, which has a higher fat content. But if you want a leaner option, you can choose ground chicken or turkey!"

"Sweet." Alistair leans toward the tablet again. "Hah! People want me to take off my underwear."

"Sorry, friends. This is not that kind of livestream." Diego says, sounding politely empathetic. "But if you'd like us to take something off, how about 30 percent off your first month's subscription with Built Box using the code STAYSTRONGMYFRIENDS at checkout?"

I give him a thumbs-up; that was a solid transition from sexual solicitation to self-promotion. I glance at the checklist of Built Box's requests for the stream, but the guys covered the last items. "Diego, I think we're done here. Thank you again for joining us!" I say, and step out of frame, grabbing my phone to cue Diego's chosen outro music. I hit Play, and Diego picks up a quick series of very hip-focused dance steps.

"Until next time, stay strong, my friends!" He flexes again, Alistair and I joining him, then we are out.

For a moment, we stand in silence, the only sound the music still playing on my phone.

Then Diego lets out a whoop and sweeps me into a rib-crushing hug. "We did it!"

We hear back from Built Box in less than a minute. Diego puts them on speaker so I can contribute, but the conversation is largely an onslaught of praise and bro-speak. I envision a board room filled with beefy dudes giving one another high fives and exchanging back slaps.

Eventually, a female voice chimes in. "Ellie? Hello there! This is Veronica. I've been coordinating with Diego. As these continue, will you be participating?"

"Only as long as I'm needed," I say, not sure if the angle in her question was hoping for more or less involvement on my part.

"For now, that would be ideal. You work great together. We'll see what the numbers are ultimately, if there's any viral traction, and what feedback we get. But for now, you have an excellent dynamic. Very…mentor-mentee. And your friend…" She clears her throat. "Alistair, was it? He could be a good addition. Coming in, testing things out. In, ah, whatever he happens to be wearing…"

Or not *wearing*, I think, casting a glance at the guest in question. He's loaded up one of my nice bowls with salad and a serving of balls and leans against the kitchen counter, seemingly unaware of his objectification. "In this house, it's pretty much a guarantee."

"As long as it feels organic!" There's some murmuring in the back of the call, and Veronica replies in a terse, hushed tone before clearing her throat. "We were also wondering if Diego's employer, Mr. Hammond, might be interested in participating."

Diego's face falls. He casts me a wary glance. "He doesn't do—"

"We'll work on him," I say. Diego bugs his eyes at me, but I press my index finger to my lips. "He's been lying low, but I think he'd be willing to make an exception for our man Diego."

"That's right! Our man Diego!" cheers one of the men, and the receiver once again erupts in a cacophony of dudely enthusiasm.

Eventually, the cheers wind down, and Veronica wraps up the call. She doesn't say anything about the fish sauce.

Diego stares at his phone as the screen darkens, then goes black. He'd perked up slightly during the last round of cheers, but he hasn't smiled since Veronica mentioned Ian.

I elbow him. "Congratulations. You did a tremendous job."

"You really think so?" His voice is tentative.

"You have excellent instincts. You were right on about needing to boost the flavor, and fish sauce was inspired."

He stands straighter. "Yeah?"

"I don't think I would have come up with it." I shrug. "Honestly, based on what I'm seeing, and the other boxes we received, I don't know how much you're going to need me."

"But you're way faster at chopping things than I am."

"That will come with experience."

Diego's phone chimes with a video call, and he's back to his full wattage. "It's my family!"

"Take it! Alistair and I will clean up," I say, rousing a muffled "Huh?" from Alistair.

Diego nods and takes in a long breath. "Thank you, Ellie. This means a lot to me. I don't know if I would have ever taken them up on the offer if you weren't helping me to start."

"I'm happy to. Now, go! Be celebrated!"

He grins, letting out an excited *eep!* before taking off for his room. When he answers the call, the cheering is so loud and varied, it sounds like a soccer game is on the other side of line. His door closes, but I can still make out the muffled sound of his voice.

I smile again, but it drops as I recall Diego's reaction when Ian was mentioned. Grant said that his brother's been private since his injury, but after looking him up the other night, he's obviously taking on other opportunities. So, why not make an appearance if it could give Diego a boost?

"Ian wasn't interested." That's what Diego said when he first told me about Built Box. I'm not mad, just disappointed. I'd thought—hoped?—that Ian would show more care.

Pairing Ian with the word *care* launches me straight back to yesterday—not that I've strayed too far from the memory since.

Alistair never mentioned the intimate scene he'd interrupted; whether that was a courtesy, cluelessness, or adherence to the Dawghouse's no-pry policy, I don't know. But the remainder of the ride was endured in painful silence, broken by the last few *ding*s of the elevator and Alistair's muttered plans to Mushu about the plant's upcoming placement in his room. When the doors opened for the final time, we were bombarded, Grant and Diego crowing about their victory and the money they were owed, and Heather and Mark peppering me with questions that all amounted to *Did Cole die when he saw Ian? Please say yes!*

After my chair and I had been delivered to my car, Ian had taken Grant and Alistair to the Dawghouse with the last truckload. This left me barefoot in the parking garage with my friends, who were more interested in relaying the "moment of cinema" that was Ian's reaction to hearing that Cole had arrived (the wordless shirt removal had been vivid, but the way he'd "flown" up the stairs had been a particular standout to Mark, after his own scramble) than helping me load my damn chair, and Diego, whose presence prevented me from revealing what had happened in the elevator. In the time it took to find my shoes, rearrange the contents of the Prius to accommodate my chair, and get home, Ian was gone. But not before he'd assembled my bed—complete, of course, with "his" mattress.

Such care. Such sexy, sexy care.

A shiver creeps up my spine, and I roll out my shoulders to suppress it. No doubt, it's a turn-on because I've been denied basic consideration for so long. I almost cried when the guys offered me cheese the night I showed up, and a week later, I'm hot and bothered because a man did me the kindness of spending five minutes with a drill. After devoting most of his afternoon to helping me move. And parading his shirtless perfection in front of my ex. And waiting for my okay to proceed with said parading, which required a scorching, prolonged exchange of glances…

The storm clouds, heavy with concern. That extra beat he waited to make sure I was okay before the cheeky half smile. The toned *v* that vanished into the waistband of his shorts, which I'd registered before the glances but is just a *really* compelling memory, so I'm adding it to the exchange. Along with his pectorals. And the swell of his biceps. And the *fuzz*.

And the kiss.

I've been trying to convince myself that it was just a friendly physical expression of appreciation, but not even a seasoned self-deluder like myself is going to pull that off. We were going back for more when Alistair showed up, and we both know it; I felt his tongue.

Heat blossoms across my chest, a competing flare of warmth teasing below my waistband, piggybacked by no small amount of anxiety at the knowledge that I'm going to be seeing him again tomorrow. What is that going to look like? Another laugh-it-off exchange is too much to hope for, and while there's a good chance we'll just pretend it never happened, part of me doesn't want to. And by that I mean my mouth parts. And my pants parts.

I grit my teeth, shifting my hips. I need to find some real flaws in that man, *stat*; camera shyness and an aversion to touch-up paint are not going to do it. Which is alarming in its own right! In any other man, the latter would be an immediate turn-off. He's literally overtaken my sense of order. Inconceivable.

I'm still frowning when I look up and see Alistair topping off his bowl with another helping of meatballs. When he sees me watching, he looks back at the heaping pile, then to me, and rolls his eyes. "Whatever. These bowls are rad, and I feel fancy as hell when I eat out of them." When I don't say anything (What is there to say? The fancy factor is why I started collecting them in the first place), he lets out a whine, shoulders sagging. "*Dude.* I'll wash it when I'm done!"

"Alistair," I assure him, crossing the room for a bowl for myself, "I didn't doubt you for a second."

16

"ELLIE?"

I let out a yip, tumbling back from my crouched position beside the laundry basket. I'm flat on my butt, heart racing from the start as I look up at Helen and, at eye level, her daughter, Penny.

Penny steps closer, reaching out a kiddie travel cup of Goldfish crackers.

"Thank you," I say, and she shakes a few onto my palm.

"What are you doing?" Helen asks.

I munch the Goldfish and consider my response. "I officially moved out of my old place this weekend. I ended up with an extra laundry basket and thought we could use it for the lost and found stuff," I say, not mentioning that I'd been expressly forbidden from upgrading from the decrepit box. I'd been transferring items from the semisolid cardboard and into the basket when Helen found me. Ian hasn't been downstairs since I started my shift, and I'm hoping to get everything moved over and the box disposed of before he shows.

The laundry basket plot came to me as I lay in bed last night, stewing over today's inevitable awkwardness. If Ian responds poorly to my defiance, then I can be indignant at his rejection of my good deed and use it to combat any weirdness. The same goes for if he fails to notice it or is generally indifferent. And if he actively ignores the new addition, then I can ignore the butterflies I've been grappling with, thinking about the graze of his tongue and that gentle touch he placed at the side of my jaw.

There is a chance that this is self-sabotage on my part. And while I've never employed mild insubordination to combat an inconvenient sexual attraction, I've had enough "helper" moments backfire to know that this could generate a response that would take the shine off Ian, gentle touches and all. Like when I was teaching and recommended that the vice principal try a lavender rinse to neutralize the brassy tone of his beard. We'd been friendly up to that point, but my next performance review had been scathing. He was not invited to my happy hour sendoff.

Self-sabotage cuts both ways, however, and my imagination was more than happy to provide. The last and least likely outcome is that Ian is so taken with the improvement that he gives me carte blanche to attend to everything on my list of suggestions, culminating in the moment I reveal to him the stunningly appointed pro shop, at which point he sweeps me into his arms and we bang it out on one of the weight-lifting benches.

Entertaining this outcome became its own source of sleeplessness. Fortunately, having been reunited with the contents of the top drawer of my bedside table, I was able to *release* myself from the scenario and fall into contented sleep.

Helen nods. "Good call. I hate fishing through that thing. I always think I'm going to encounter something..." She wrinkles her nose, shaking her head. *"Yielding."*

I laugh and get back to moving items over. It pains me, but I'm no longer folding them, for expedience. "And what are you up to today? You coming to eight thirty?"

"Nope. It's Monday, so no childcare. We're on a walk. Penny wanted to come by to see her *beloved*."

I toss the last orphaned water bottle into the laundry basket, then rise, grimacing at the crackle of my knees. "Her what?"

"Penny!" Grant trots over with a smile. "How you doing, Monster?" He kneels in front of her, one arm curled in a flex, bicep straining against the sleeve of his T-shirt. "You wanna kettlebell?"

In answer, she hands her Goldfish container to her mother, then curls her arms and legs around Grant's forearm. He pulls her toward his shoulder, like he would a weight, then drives her up and overhead, his arm fully extended.

Penny giggles madly. "Again!"

"We're not doing this right, hold up," he says. With the help of his free hand, he pushes up to standing, child still suspended. "There we go! How's the view?" he asks. He lowers her to shoulder height. "Better here? Or—" He dips his knees, then drives his Penny-weighted arm to full extension. "Up high?"

"Up high!" she calls, smile brilliant.

Helen bumps me with her shoulder. "Her *beloved*. Grant's ruined her on sitters."

Still dip-driving the preschooler, Grant lifts his chin at me. "Do you have a sec? We want to try something. If it works, maybe we can add it to warm-ups. If you could take a video—please?" he adds. "Ian's lying low for once, and I don't want to bug him to come down."

"Sure," I say, turning to glance at the box I still need to dump. "Will it be quick?"

"Oh, totally! Yo, Penny, we gotta even out. How many times up was that?" he asks, and offers Penny his unoccupied arm.

She frowns in thought as she switches sides, a little wrinkle appearing between her barely there brows. "Seven reps?"

"Seven it is!" He heads to the floor, walking and launching at the same time, Penny again a ball of giggles, Helen and me trailing behind.

There are still a few minutes before Diego's class starts, and members mill around, most congratulating Diego on the livestream, but some have broken off to linger close to the middle of the gym, where Alistair stands with his phone. He's in a circle formed by one of the big bands we use for assisted stretches. A second band has been looped through the first, linking the two to create a figure eight.

Grant steps into the empty band, then squats to let Penny dismount. "Here's what we're going for," he says, and shows me his phone. On the screen, two beefy men have arranged themselves in bands like the guys have laid out. They bring the far sides of their respective bands to about waist level and assume a high, four-legged position, facing opposite one another. An unseen person counts down from three, at which point each man scrambles forward, creating a tug-of-war with the bands. Much grunting ensues.

"They go at it forever," Grant explains, scrubbing the video forward. The men are sent into overdrive, but even sped up, they don't make much progress; the bands stretch only so far. The showdown ends when one man loses his footing and slingshots backward several feet, his partner staggering forward with the sudden slack.

I grimace.

"It doesn't always work out that way," Grant says, and flicks to another video. This time, it's one man-beast with a much smaller guy. It's no contest; the beast ends up towing the scrapper out of frame. "That one was probably staged, though."

"And this would be for warm-ups?" Helen asks, looking over my shoulder.

"If it's effective. Could be great for hammies 'n' glutes, but maybe quads, too?"

"We also wanna see who'd win," Alistair adds. He's wearing a shirt for once. Kind of. It's been cut into a crop, his abs still exposed.

"Ah." I open the camera app on Grant's phone. Alistair puts his away before both men situate their bands then assume the bear-crawl position from the videos.

"Everybody, circle up," Diego calls, gesturing the class our way. "We'll enjoy the show, then start our warm-up!" They form a spread-out oval around the guys, settling in to watch.

I start recording. "We're rolling. Ready when you are."

"Cool! Penny?" Grant asks. "Wanna start us? Just do ready, set, go!"

Penny stands straighter at the assignment. "Ready, set...go!"

Grant and Alistair charge in opposite directions, clambering on all fours. The bands go taut in seconds, and the struggle begins. As in the video, there is much grunting, but the guys are well-matched; neither gives the other an inch. From here on out, it's all endurance.

"Come on, guys, let's go!" bellows Russ, clapping his hands and eliciting a few more cheers from the crowd. But seconds pass and the guys remain at a stalemate. The time on the video creeps up; a minute in, and nothing has happened—

Then Alistair gains a few inches.

A moment later, he eases forward more. But when I look at Grant, he doesn't appear to have lost any ground. A flash of color below his shirt catches my eye, the black of a waistband, and bright blue below...

Helen gasps. "Oh, no! Are his—"

Before she can finish the statement, the band has pulled Grant's loose workout shorts down his legs, pinning them to his shoes with its tension. Thank God for compression shorts; otherwise we'd be getting to know Grant even better than I've come to know Alistair.

Grant's scrambling to maintain his position, blue-clad backside wriggling, band and shorts at his feet. The band goes tight again. Grant continues to struggle, but the movement just shifts the band farther down his shoes, until they grip only the toes of his sneakers. He holds himself in a tense plank, his body shaking from the effort, but the band slips anyway.

Without the resistance of the band, he staggers forward, splatting onto the gym floor. The band snaps back—

CRACK!

A shriek pierces the air, and Alistair drops.

"I think my *nuts* are in my *throat*," Alistair wheezes. His voice comes out high and thin, his eyes watering as he lies curled on his side, hands cupped between his legs. "For *real*. That band shot my nuts through my body and into my *throat*."

"That can't happen..." Diego turns worried eyes on me. "Can it?"

Alistair's shriek had been followed by a collective cry of sympathetic pain from the onlookers, and the eight thirty class closed in on the felled model. Several of them share Diego's troubled look.

"What if my balls are weird now?" he wails, voice still strained. "I got an underwear shoot coming up!"

"Y'all, this footage is *gnarly*." Grant laughs, watching the recording as he walks back from the break room. Eyes not leaving the screen, he hands me the ice pack I'd asked him for.

I offer the pack to Alistair. "It should conform to the, ah... *affected area.*"

"Thank you," he whimpers, drawing it back to his crotch. He sucks in a gasp, then sighs.

"Is there protocol for moving the victim of potential testicular trauma?" Helen asks.

"Too bad Maggie's out," says Russ, referring to another regular. "She's a doctor."

I nod, not sure what to do, either. "Diego, can your class work around him for now?"

"Way ahead of you!" Diego holds up a stack of the little orange cones we use to mark distances in running drills. "These will keep him safe. People here respect the cone," he says, and busies himself outlining his fallen comrade. It looks like a crime scene.

He nods at his handiwork, then claps for the attention of his class. "All right! We will leave Alistair to recover. Let's take the warm-up to the turf outside! Follow me!" he hollers, and jogs out the open bay door, the class following him obediently.

Russ joins the departing ranks. "Good luck with your balls!"

Grant is still replaying the video. He holds it up so I can see, advancing to the final seconds, backtracking to when Alistair pulled ahead—

By literally *pulling* ahead. I reach for the screen and expand the image of Alistair's outstretched arms. The ends of his fingers appear to vanish just before his biceps bunch in a curl.

"The flooring!" I hop over Alistair's crumpled form, finding the spot where a trace of the chalk I used to highlight it my first day still lingers. The corner is raised a little more now than it was then. I kneel down, wriggle my fingers into the space, and am able to wedge under it to gain purchase. "It was up just enough."

"Dude!" Grant brays. "You cheated and got *wrecked* for it!"

"You lost your shorts," Helen reminds him.

"Yeah, but, like, *honestly.*"

Alistair just groans. He's rolled onto his back, ice pack still over his crotch. Poor guy.

"What's going on?" Ian's voice buzzes in my bones. "Is that Alistair?"

Ian strides toward us, brows low under the rim of his baseball cap. By the time he gets to us, no one has said a word, though I suspect that I'm alone in being gagged by the memory of having fantasized about him until battery-assisted completion last night.

Ian looks at us expectantly. Still silence.

Then Penny approaches him, cracker cup extended in offering.

His face relaxes, and he takes a knee, palm raised as she shakes out a few Goldfish. My heart gives a little flutter at the sight.

"Thank you," he says. Rising, he adds, "Is anyone going to tell me why Alistair is on the floor?"

"We wanted to try a new warm-up activity," Grant chirps. "It was pretty effective. My quads are burning! But, um, Alistair got racked in the nuts."

"There's video, if you'd like to see," Helen offers.

"Banded tug-of-war," I say, finding my voice. "The band slipped off and snapped into Alistair. But! That was after he pulled himself forward with this!" I point down at the raised spot. "It's up again."

Ian comes closer, enough that I feel his body heat. My breath catches. That element had come into play in my nocturnal imaginings.

"Do you think it's the humidity?" I ask, hoping to overwhelm the screaming inside my head that last night's masturbatory session was not only wildly inappropriate but has also made this interaction about a thousand times more difficult for me, because my imagination went *off* with this man. "Making the tiles expand and contract? Or the foundation settling? Or maybe the installer just screwed up…"

"I'll deal with it. I've fixed it before, I can fix it again."

"Like you did last time?"

The question comes out of me innocently enough, but I can taste the judgment. And based on the sudden furrow in Ian's brow, he can hear it.

"It's probably just a mistake made when it was installed," I add, aiming for diplomatic.

He tugs on the brim of his hat, eyes on the flooring. "Oddly enough, *I* installed it."

Goddammit, anyway.

"Oh, yeah!" says Grant. "I remember that. It took you *forever*! You had to measure a bunch of times."

"I did," Ian agrees, and looks at me. "And yet."

"It could still be the foundation," I mutter. "Or…something."

"Sure," says Ian. "Or something."

The words are heavy with self-reproach, and a twinge of guilt goes off in my chest.

"All right," he says, and nods to Grant. "Let's at least get him off the floor."

Alistair groans, but when Grant and Ian each offer a hand, he lets them pull him up to standing without further complaint. Once upright, he leans into Grant like a crutch, and the two hobble toward the lounge. Penny joins them, Goldfish at the ready.

Another sigh, and Ian leaves, too.

I glance over at Helen, who cringes sympathetically. "I didn't know he did the flooring," she says quietly, but whether in apology for not warning me or genuine surprise, I can't tell.

We're almost to the lobby when Ian stops. "Hayes," he says, darkly. "Did you do something to the lost and found?"

Oh, hell. *That.*

"I had an extra laundry basket after Saturday," I say, and while I'd known that I'd been on point when I named the "last and least likely outcome," I can't help being disappointed that we're on course for *Ian responds poorly / I can be indignant.*

I hold my chin high. "That box is actively decomposing."

"It's *fine*. A little weathered—" he starts, picking up the box. One corner of it remains adhered to the floor, the rest of the cardboard collapsing as limply as if it were one of the towels I pulled out of it earlier.

He frowns, glaring at the box, and tugs more firmly. The corner releases with a wet, peeling sound, leaving a pale ring of torn cardboard...and revealing a cockroach roughly the size of a cell phone. Ian and I jump, retreating reflexively as the bug scrambles in circles.

Penny darts forward, and before anyone else can react, upturns her snack cup and uses it to cover the roach. When she steps back, the cup shudders with the activity of its occupant. *Ugh.*

It is not without a sense of vindication that I raise my brows at Ian. "Still calling that *fine*?"

He sighs, looking oddly defeated as he eyes the flaccid cardboard still in his hand. "I'll put this in the compost bin," he grumbles, and heads out the door, his usual stride more of a trudge, the former box flapping at his side.

My stomach falls. This wasn't part of any of the scenarios I ran last night.

The cup scrapes against the floor, moving along with the massive bug.

Helen cringes. "We're never using that cup again."

17

I PLUCK OUT MY EARBUDS, put them back in their case, and watch the battery light go from green to amber. The department head in Tampa had to squeeze in our call before teaching a zero-hour, but through my grogginess and her commute, we finalized the units she'll be purchasing for the fall. She even requested a custom plan for *The Outsiders* to celebrate the book surviving a challenge from the district. Stay gold, Hillsborough County.

To top it all off, as of the beep of my alarm an hour ago, my vision is completely back to normal. I cover my left eye, using the now fully operational right eye to check the time on my laptop monitor. Six fifteen a.m. on a Thursday and everything's coming up Ellie!

Beneath my feet, the floorboards shudder the way they do when folks are coming and going from the front door. I drop my hand, eyeing the door to the rest of the house. I'd picked up the same vibration several times while I'd been on my call. Now that my ears are clear, I'm catching voices, too, and they're not all masculine.

I rise from my desk chair in pursuit of answers and coffee. But when I open my door, the one that connects to the hallway is also closed. The voices beyond it are louder; it sounds like a dinner party out there.

I open the second door and am greeted by—"*Babs? The hell?*" I ask, not bothering with niceties, because, seriously: *The hell?*

Babs stands a few feet away, peering into Diego's bedroom. She's dressed for the gym, her wilted hair telling me that this is a post-workout visit, not pre. "Good morning, Ellie!" She gestures into Diego's room. "Nice to see that he finally has some proper curtains. The sheet arrangement was such an eyesore." She smiles. "I was about to knock. Will you be joining us soon?"

"*Us?* Who is *us?*"

"Follow me," she singsongs, and I trail her down the hall, mildly annoyed at being given mysterious commands in my own home...even if, technically, the house is hers.

I look into the kitchen as we pass and freeze. Diego's furiously grating zucchini into a bowl, one of the Built Box kits open on the prep table beside it. He's wearing my apron.

Before I can ask him what he's up to, Babs grabs my hand, pulling me farther down the hall. "Diego's such a sweetheart, putting together snacks for us on short notice."

We emerge from the hallway, and I again stop short. Eight gym members are gathered in the living room. Half share Babs's sweaty glow, but others are dressed for work, seated on the couch and the lawn chairs, which have been rescued from their exile to the back porch.

Grant comes in from the dining room with a folding chair under each arm. "Morning, Ellie! Did you get our texts?"

"My phone was on do not disturb. What—" I'm interrupted by a knock at the door.

Helen enters. "Hi, hi!" She accepts a folding chair with a smile and stops to take in the living room, scanning the space until her eyes land on me. "Ellie, my God. You've transformed this place!" She elbows Grant as he moves past. "Now I can actually drop Penny off over here with a clear conscience."

"Thank you?" I say, my confusion reaching a new level. "What has you here?"

"I'm the delegate for eight thirty and nine forty-five," she says, arranging her chair at the far end of the couch. "I'll speak for the parents."

Babs hands me a cup of coffee, which I accept by reflex. I take a sip, belatedly wondering if it might be laced with something, given the bizarre scenario currently unfolding.

"Sit down!" she insists, pointing at the lounger, which has been pulled from its usual spot in the corner. As I do, she plops into the open space on the couch. "You know me and Helen, of course, and Tom," she adds, as Firehouse's favorite type two diabetic sits on a folding chair, raising one of my gold-rimmed mugs in greeting. "Russ's here, too, and you're familiar with a few of the afternooners..."

This prompts waves and calls of "Morning!" from members I recognize more from profile photos than personal experience, including Jacob, the gym's number-one violator of the "no dogs on the floor" policy. Bleu Cheese, his dappled Frenchie, croaks out a low bark from his spot in Jacob's lap. Alistair, on a folding chair beside them, gives the dog a scratch.

Babs points across the room. "Maggie's a floater—"

"My schedule at the hospital shifts every few weeks," Maggie says. "So I can do mornings and afternoons. I'm representing the evening gym attendees."

"Sure," I say, the abundance of information explaining exactly nothing. "And why does any of this mean that you're all here, at"—I check my watch—"six twenty-two in the morning?"

"It's a delegation!" says Babs. "A meeting of the minds."

"An airing of grievances," Tom grumbles.

Babs shushes him. "We're not *aggrieved*." She leans back, looking toward the hallway. "Diego, hon, you coming? We're about to get started."

"Sí!" he calls, and I hear the slap of his slippers as he trots to the living room. He's still wearing the apron. "Chocolate zucchini muffins should only take another ten minutes," he tells me, and takes a seat on the last folding chair. "Tinkering with an extra Built Box."

Babs returns to me. "The thing is, Ellie, we've been watching you."

She lets the statement hang for a moment, but before I can determine whether that was a threat, she continues. "Someone who can't pass a crooked picture frame without straightening it isn't going to take kindly to the sad little stash of T-shirts and protein powders that calls itself a pro shop. *You* have ideas for Firehouse."

"I have a whole list of ideas," I say. "And when I shared it with Ian, he shot down every item. *Firmly.* No touch-up paint, keep the lost and found in a crumbling cardboard box, hard pass on overhauling the pro shop. He made it abundantly clear that he wasn't interested."

"But you still went in with a replacement for the lost and found," Helen reminds me.

"That was...different," I say, not missing when Babs arches a brow at the brief pause. "I had an extra basket. When did you decide to ambush me, anyway?" I ask, hoping to sideline any further inquiry.

"We've been entertaining the idea since you arrived," Babs replies.

"And after Helen mentioned yesterday that you replaced the box," Tom says, "the timing felt right."

"That the sort of thing that counts as news in the group chat?" I ask, aiming my annoyance at Helen. She shrugs.

"I knew that y'all would be up early," Babs continues. "So I messaged Grant after five a.m. wrapped."

"You woke me up," Grant complains from his spot in the low-slung lawn chair.

"And I apologized for that." Babs turns her attention to me, expression imploring, but serious. "This is our community, Ellie. Firehouse matters to us."

"Probably saved my life," Tom adds, and I recall what the guys said about his health when the gym first opened. It's enough to soften me on their scheming. I cast another glance at Helen, thinking about what she'd had to say about what Firehouse meant to her. She offers a little smile, like she's read my mind.

From the far end of the couch, Russ of the white tube socks hefts a sigh. "It's hard to see something you care about hovering on the brink of greatness, when one nudge could level it up."

The statement hooks me as if it were a physical thing. He perfectly articulated how I've been feeling. It's like Babs's earlier comment: The gym is a beautiful painting in a crooked frame in desperate need of straightening. And dusting. And some Windex.

"What are you thinking?" I ask, adding, "Purely out of curiosity," as the energy in the room perks up. Best to temper expectations.

"Finances," Tom blurts. "Ian got a settlement after his injury—you know about the injury, right? His knee at the competition?"

He grimaces, and raises his hands, making the now-familiar gesture to mime the accident. "The settlement is how he got the building, paid for the buildout, remodeled upstairs. Now, he didn't spend *everything*—"

I shoot him a look, and he scowls.

"The amount of that settlement is public knowledge," he says. "And it's easy to find a sale listing. As for the remodel, he had to file design permits with the city—"

"Tom, you need a hobby," I say.

"Foam art is not enough," he says, glumly. "But Ian! He invested *nothing*. And I don't doubt that there are recurring payments for things he isn't aware of. Lord, people never keep track of what they're being auto-billed for."

Tom's sigh is so paternal, it's endearing. "I was an accountant. I've offered my services, but no! Won't let me touch it. Have you seen the billing system?" He shakes his head. "Total mess. Ian's doing it all on his own, and it's not good."

"How and why have you seen what Ian uses for billing?" I ask.

"Professional curiosity!" he says, as though it would have been a betrayal of his vocation not to have pursued the information. "And I got Grant to give me the login to the computer up front a while back." He shrugs, conveying at least some guilt at the invasion. "I told him I needed to check my email."

Grant straightens. "Wait, what?"

I pinch the bridge of my nose. I'm changing that password the moment I go in today.

"Ian jumped into gym ownership totally blind," Tom continues. "He'd been coaching since his injury. Worked for his mentor, the fellow who trained him, for years. This guy, Denny, was close to retiring, and Ian figured he'd pass the business on to him—"

"Passed Ian over," Babs interjects with scandalized relish. "Sold it to another trainer."

I nod along, the information lining up with what the guys told me. "Do we know why?"

The room erupts in a collective "No!" but a number of eyes turn to Grant, who shrinks back into his cramped seat.

"We've been trying to figure it out since day one," says Maggie. "I was a member there. It was a great facility. Not too different from Firehouse, but they did more community activities. In-house competitions and meets, and there was a bake-off at one point..." She shrugs. "Little things. But they added up."

"All that wasn't enough to keep you there after Ian left?" I ask.

"There are little things, and there's why I was going to the gym in the first place," she says. A petty part of me wonders how much of her reasoning aligned with the motives of that initial flock of single ladies at Firehouse.

"If we could circle back to our wish list, I'm supposed to put in for more childcare times," submits Helen. "More hours during the week, and weekend coverage."

"That's on the list," Babs assures her, and returns to me. "There *is* a list. I'll share the Google Doc with you."

"It's color-coded," Helen adds. "You're going to love it."

"And yet, you still had this gathering?" I ask, exasperated, but unsurprised. And more than a little intrigued at word of this meticulously organized document.

"We felt it would be more impactful to propose this in person."

"Then why me and not Ian? It's my understanding that

interventions are more effective when the intended recipient is present. And if it's so many of you coming together—"

Several guests shift to look at Babs, who avoids my eyes.

Heat rises to my cheeks, a thread of panic lacing through my sternum. What does she know? *"Barbara."*

"We just thought—"

"You just thought."

"It was thought that if you came to him with the backing of the gym members as a whole, he'd listen." Her lips quirk, threatening a smile. "And if he's more receptive because it's being delivered by someone in line with his sexual preferences—"

I glare at her, ignoring the weight of the stares of the rest of the room. "I'm not *seducing* Ian into letting Tom handle his finances."

Tom's shoulders sag in disappointment, and I don't know what it says about me that I'm charmed that the man is so committed to number crunching that he's open to pimping out a relative stranger to keep doing it.

Babs remains undeterred. "The way you've taken on housebreaking the boys—"

Alistair lets out an affronted grunt. "It's not like we piss outside…"

"Well—" Diego cocks his head thoughtfully, but he elects not to finish his statement.

She continues over them. "It stands to reason that you might be able to extend your influence to one more *overgrown* boy."

"In a purely professional capacity," Helen hastens to add.

"He doesn't want to be my project the way the guys are. His words," I add quickly, wondering if they might take offense to being labeled a project. God, from Ian, the man they practically worship, it would probably be worse...

But all three shrug and nod. "I feel like we've been a pretty successful project so far!" Diego cheers.

I smile back, but it slips just as quickly. Sexual implications aside, Babs's reasoning is deeply presumptuous and leaning harder into the tradition of emotional labor of women than I'm comfortable with. Though she did get ahead of that a little by noting my undeniable air of competence; if I were a complete bonehead in addition to being female, I doubt that efforts would have been made to recruit me.

I look at Grant, wedged in his tiny chair. He meets my gaze, his eyes going wide enough that I elect not to interrogate him. But I cut a glare to let him know that I will be pursuing this later. Ian's hangups do seem to stem from something. And if that something can actually be addressed, then maybe there's hope to straighten this dusty picture frame after all.

Still, I'm not totally optimistic when I say, "I will bring all this up gently. It's possible that a consensus might be enough to motivate him to listen." As the room perks up again, I hasten to add, "But like I said, I've tried."

"So we can send you that list? We'll give you editing rights," Babs adds, as though that would seal the deal. "No one had even thought about the lost and found box before now. It was an *excellent* call."

I wave her off, silently registering the praise.

Somewhere in the room, a phone goes off, chiming an alarm. "Perfect timing!" says Diego, popping out of his seat. "Who wants a sweetie?"

18

I REST A HIP AGAINST the counter in the break room later that morning, watching the steady trickle of the coffee into the carafe. I close my left eye, focusing with my right: The vision's hazy, courtesy of my standard workout fog, but there's no question that my sight is otherwise back to normal.

Smiling, I turn to face the room.

"Do you think that we can request more of those muffins from Built Box?" Grant asks. "They were amazing!" He lies on his side on the floor beside Penny, who assembles something with Legos. All of the other childcare kiddos have been retrieved.

I nod. "I don't know how Diego managed it. I was sure they were going to taste like dirt."

"Talking about Diego's muffins?" Helen asks, leaning in from the doorway. Penny turns at the sound of her voice, proudly holding up her work in progress. Helen gives her a thumbs-up—"Looking good, kiddo"—then points to Grant. "You sure you're okay back here for another fifteen? I'll shower quick."

"Take your time!" he says. "My personal training client won't be in 'til ten."

"Thank you!" She slumps against the doorframe, eyeing me warily. "Have we been forgiven for this morning yet?"

"We're good," I assure her.

She smiles, miming wiping her brow, and freezes, hand still raised, as Alistair passes her on his way into the room. Her eyes follow his shirtless form seemingly unconsciously, tracking him as he crosses the space. He opens the door of the fridge, leaning over to look inside, and as he's cut off from her line of sight, the compulsion to watch him is severed, and she drops her hand.

"Still could have gone without the 'Ellie seduces Ian into letting Tom file his taxes' angle," I say, just on principle. Helen laughs.

Alistair closes the fridge, shaking a premade protein drink. "Really?" He uncaps the shake. "I didn't think that'd be a big deal, since you two keep making out."

The silence that follows is so complete, I flinch at the click of Penny's Legos.

Alistair takes a drink, then screws the cap back on. His brow furrows as he takes in the three people staring at him. "What? You and Ian?" He crosses toward the door, shaking the bottle. "Like, that first night you showed up? And this weekend? *The elevator?*" he presses, as though trying to jog my memory.

I stare back, incredulous, but his attention has shifted to the only person in the room unfazed by the bomb he just dropped.

"Yo, Penny! How 'bout some knuckles?" He extends his fist toward Penny, who does the same, bumping hers to his. "This kid rules," he says to no one in particular, and excuses himself as he walks past Helen and out of the room, oblivious to the wreckage left in his wake.

Grant stares at me, slack-jawed, and then busts out a huge smile. I'm unwilling to go there, so I look to Helen.

She shrugs, decidedly not shocked by Alistair's revelation. "Babs and I were here that first Saturday morning. We noticed your reaction to Ian. We figured there was a story there."

"There's no story—" I start, but Helen taps her neck, pressing just below her jawbone.

"The man had a"—she glances quickly at her daughter, then mouths—*"hickey."*

"I—" My denial gets caught in my throat as a memory unfurls. A quick flash of nuzzling into that tender spot, an experimental lick, then a suck, and the groan it pulled from him that had me going full sexy leech.

My silence speaks for me.

"Congrats, by the way." Helen's smiling now. "You've succeeded where *many* have failed."

"With my brother!" Grant brays out a laugh. *"Gross."*

"And this is common knowledge?" I ask.

"No!" Helen's assurance comes quickly. "Mostly five a.m. Due to Babs's rallying efforts. So, Maggie. And Tom. And…"

"So there's a not-insignificant number of gym members who are comfortable with the idea of me employing my feminine wiles to get Ian to upgrade the pro shop?"

"Whatever gets the job done," Helen offers. "All right, I gotta shower. Penny, love, see you in a few!" Her daughter gives a thumbs-up in acknowledgment, and Helen departs.

When I look at Grant, I expect to find him still reveling in the new, apparently gross news of my dalliances with his brother. Instead, he's frowning, eyes distant before meeting mine.

"Did we ever tell you what happened to his knee?" he asks. "How he was injured?"

"Your summary was enough to keep me from watching the video."

He grimaces. "Have you noticed how, whenever folks grab extra plates, we stack them in the center of the rig until we need them?" he asks. It takes me a moment to visualize, but I nod. "It's because of that. Ian was warming up his back squat at a competition and, dumped his bar, but the guy behind him had his plates in Ian's space. So when Ian bailed, the plates on one end of his bar hit the stack, bounced off them, and collided with the back of his right knee."

He holds his hands up, just as Diego had during the original telling, and, also like Diego, and Tom this morning, jerks his hands to one side.

I am never watching that footage.

"Took him *out*. Ended his career. And, I dunno. Maybe he's super controlling because of it. Since something someone else did screwed up his life, he wants to call all the shots here."

"That's pretty insightful," I say, impressed. "If you put that theory in an essay, with that support, I'd give you full points."

He smiles, and it's quiet for a moment as we watch Penny's fastidious work with the Legos.

"I know he's a hardhead, but have you brought up anything to him?" I ask. "Any ideas?"

Grant shakes his head. "He's my big brother, y'know? He's

already done so much for me, so, like, it feels weird to tell him I think he's not getting something right."

"I get it. It can be hard to confront a superior about anything. But when that person is also family, and the business is theirs, it's probably too close to home."

"He worked so hard to put this together. And after the way things shook out with Denny, his mentor?" Grant pauses, watching me until I nod that I recognize the name. "I know he wants to prove himself. He…" Grant grimaces. "I'm sorry. That's Ian's thing. It feels like a"—he mouths *dick*—"move for me to go off about it. It's not mine to share, y'know?"

"If it's not your story to tell, it's not your story to tell," I say, though my curiosity is piqued. "But…" I try to decide how I want to ask the next question. "Is your only concern that he's sensitive, or…" It feels wrong to even allude to aggression, but I haven't even been on the scene for two weeks. Who knows what might be in the background. "Does he get…*mean?*"

It takes Grant a moment to cut through my vagaries, but when he does, he laughs; I am awash with relief. "You know better than that! Ian's not some rage monster. He can be grumpy, but it's *Ian*. He cried at *Inside Out*." His eyes widen. "Oh, dude, do *not* tell him I told you that!"

I mime locking my lips and throwing away the key, but *God*, is that inconveniently hot.

"Cool. So, yeah. We don't want to hurt his feelings. He's a softie."

"Who cried at *Inside Out*," says Penny. Grant lets out an affronted gasp. "He watched it with us," she says, deadpan. "We were at your house."

"Dude," he warns. She just smiles. This kid does rule.

"Was it Bing Bong?" I ask her.

"He's not really gone, you know," she says, deeply serious. "*We* remember him."

"Penny, I love that. Thank you," I say, and smile. And keep smiling. At her cleverness, at the thought of Ian, crying at the demise of an imaginary friend in a kids' movie. At Grant's earnestness and the excessive but charming dedication of the members of this gym, how wickedly sore I'm going to be later from today's workout, and I don't know…The generally bonkers direction my life has taken, I guess.

For now, I remind myself. This is my life, but not really. Not forever. Because that would demand more hope than I can afford.

"Did you ever work with little kids?" Grant asks, rousing me from the ugly thought.

I shake my head in an emphatic *no*. "I chose secondary ed for a reason. In my experience, that demographic tends to be sticky."

Penny meets my eyes and presses two Legos together with an admonishing *click.*

"Present company excepted, of course."

She nods and gets back to work.

Grant laughs. "I like 'em. I miss them when they leave, like, when they're old enough for school. Kids are so lucky, getting to go learn. Every day they find out something totally new. Can you imagine, being this little nothing blob of a baby person, and then learning, *bam!* Sharks! There are giant fish that can eat you and also they die if they stop moving. Did you know that?" he asks me, eyes alight.

"They have to keep water moving over their gills to breathe," says Penny.

Grant beams. "Yeah, they do!"

"They probably won't eat you," she drones. "More people die every year from falling coconuts than from shark attacks."

"We looked that up. But I'm the one who told you about the gills," he reminds her.

Penny waves him off. "I need a red two by three," she says, fishing through the bricks.

Grant grins, joining in the hunt. "That's gotta be a fun thing about teaching, right?" He passes Penny her desired brick. "Like, sharing all the stuff you know? Or discovering things along with them? Seeing what they come up with?"

"The sharing was the best part," I admit. "When my heart wasn't being broken by how little they actually cared about what I was trying to introduce them to. Between that and the unrelenting bureaucratic bull—*nonsense*," I say, catching myself from swearing in front of a preschooler. "I ended up so discouraged after one year, I left."

Grant frowns, and an echo of judgment crawls over my skin. "Whoa. It must have super sucked for you, then, if you decided to split. Cause you don't do anything without *really* deciding to, you know?"

I appreciate his generous interpretation. "There were moments. When they'd get really into an assignment or, like you said, come up with something on their own. Near the end of the year, we covered *Romeo and Juliet*. I had a student who hadn't once spoken up go on a tear about how Romeo comparing his love to the moon wasn't a good measure, because the moon changes size!" I smile at the memory. "She was fired up about it after, too."

"And with little kids, that's what every day must be like!" He cocks his head. "What do they even do in school?"

"Other than learn that sharks exist?"

"Right? They're getting introduced to everything around them, and themselves, too. But also, not? I mean, beyond basics, and all the puberty stuff in middle school or whatever, do kids even learn about how their bodies work?" He frowns, pausing, and I try to catch up to his stream of consciousness. "Basic nutrition, maybe? Oh, man, don't get me started on the food pyramid. Diego was showing me what he's learned about it. It wasn't even based on science! There were *grain lobbies* involved! I didn't know there were people working for, like, *Big Grain*, but they're why there are crackers at the bottom of the pyramid. Those are garbage!"

He cocks his head. "Where was I going with that?"

"Kids learning about their bodies," Penny supplies.

"Thanks. Yeah, bodies and stuff. So, I don't think I learned anything beyond 'muscles move you' and 'bones give you structure.' Nerves—"

—are at risk of being betrayed by another system and corroded to debilitation—

"—relay information?" He shrugs. "Everything else I picked up from Ian. I'd watch him, and would try movements, but also learn how it all came together. It was cool, having that opportunity. Do you know if there's anything like that in schools?"

"I have no idea," I answer, increasingly curious about where he's going with this. "But I could ask around. Heather played volleyball in college, and she's the coach for the team at the school we worked at. She could probably ask."

As I speak, I notice that Grant's spine has straightened, his eyes bright. I continue, "Or…set you up to talk to the PE folks at the high school? Or one of the elementary schools?"

"You think? That would be sick. Maybe I could help out?"

"There would probably be a background check or paperwork to do, but…" I eye him. "Grant, do you want to teach phys ed?"

He rears back. "Oh, I don't know that I could do that. I'm already so far into kinesiology, and switching would mean a lot more school…" He angles his head, warily. "Right?"

"There would be some for the teaching credential itself, but as far as content, I bet there would be a lot of overlap with your kinesiology courses."

"Really?" His voice is bright with enthusiasm.

"No harm in asking."

He nods, but his smile fades. "I dunno. It would still be more work, probably, and I don't want to let Ian down, y'know?"

"No." I frown. "Why would that let Ian down?"

"'Cause I'm taking after him? He insisted that I get a degree because Mom would have wanted it. And kinesiology made sense, since I'm training folks. *Dude!* This is teaching, too!"

"Totally," I agree. "And you're really good at it. For a twenty-one-year-old to manage a group of people who are two to three times his age, that's no small thing. If you can do the same with a bunch of kids, you'd be golden."

"What, like, here?" he asks. Before I can answer, his jaw drops. "I could do kids classes here! Maybe not ones as young as Penny, but elementary age? Or kids the age I started! Middle or high school? Like, off-season stuff! Sports conditioning!"

"That's inspired," I say, and mean it. "It could be a great opportunity for the gym."

Grant is alight. His smile is huge, and his eyes have gone distant, head bobbing slightly like he's trying to work out logistics.

"Float it to Ian," I say. "He'd be more likely to consider the idea if he sees how excited you are about it."

Grant nods but doesn't look convinced. He sighs, but a moment later, a wry smile crosses his face. I suspect it's the expression I'm supposed to look out for, the I'm-about-to-fuck-with-you face.

"Are you sure you can't ask him? You know, 'cause of your *special connection*."

I groan, and he barks a laugh.

"I'm done!" Penny hands Grant her brick creation. "I think it's a fish. But also a car."

19

A LOW SOUND COMES FROM the gym, and I look up from the phone, waiting for a follow-up. Nope. Nothing. I get back to the screen, trying to find my place in the short story, and my eyes land on the time—*Oh, snap!* It's been twenty minutes since I clocked out.

I shove my phone into my bag and stand, my butt smarting from sitting on the slatted locker room bench for so long. I'd only meant to scan the list of "approved" short stories the district in Georgia had sent me, but I started looking up the plot summaries of the ones I didn't know, which quickly turned into finding them online. Bradbury's "The Veldt" is wonderfully macabre, but I don't know where I can use it. I push open the door and step into the hallway. Maybe for an inference activity?

I'm at the drinking fountain when I hear Ian's voice.

"What do you mean, you've spent your dining-out budget for the week?" he's asking. "It's only Tuesday."

"Dude, I just got so hungry, and I wasn't thinking about it!" It's Grant.

"How tight a leash are you on—" Ian's quiet for a moment, then says, "That's a pretty reasonable amount, Grant."

"Come on, man. Please?"

I emerge from the hallway, ready to play bad cop before Ian has to, but I don't see him, just Grant. I have to look past my roommate to spot Ian, who is, oddly, kneeling in the center of the room. He sees me, and hastens to rise, and I notice him wince, favoring his right leg.

I start for him without thinking. I'm about ask if he's okay when I see his right knee. It's scummed up, covered in the black that always transfers from the floor surface, and beneath that, clearly abraded, shiny and pink. Did he trip? How—

Ah! I look at the floor. Sure enough, the uneven square is sticking up more than usual. When I return to Ian, he is committed to avoiding my eyes. "So, it finally happened."

"I'm sure you're loving this," he says, with an audible edge.

I frown, stung that he'd think that. "No, actually. I prefer victories without bloodshed." I turn to Grant, who is also focusing anywhere but me. "What's up?"

"Nothing!" he says, too loud to be natural. I wait; short of red hands, unnecessary volume is the ultimate indicator of guilt.

He cracks in seconds. "I was thinking about going for tacos."

I cross my arms, feigning confusion. "Weren't you lamenting earlier that you'd blown your entire dining-out budget on that spread at the food truck park last night?"

Grant continues to study the floor. *"Yes."*

"Then, that's on you. You can't just hit up your brother."

"Yes, he can," says Ian.

I blink up at him. *Really?* "Well, *yes*, literally, but that's not exactly in the spirit of our arrangement." I nod at Grant. "We have a fridge full of leftovers and premade meals at home. If you're already going out, just go home."

"But…" Grant's brow pleats, lower lip protruding like a petulant toddler. "I want tacos."

"Then make them at home," I singsong with a pout of my own. I look to Ian for backup.

His expression has taken on the hardness I glimpsed when he showed up to mess with Cole. Without the shading of concern, it is chilling. This can't be about tacos. Is he hanging on to the flooring thing?

Ian reaches into his back pocket, producing his wallet. "Hey, Grant, would you mind going to Torchy's?" he says, pointedly naming the Austin-native taco chain. "I feel like a Brushfire. And, you know what?" he adds, smile so saccharine, I'm sure his teeth hurt. "How about you get something for yourself? As a thank-you, for running this errand."

"Um…sure? It's what I was about to do anyway—"

"Thank you!" Ian gives me a superior look as he hands his brother a twenty. I glare back.

"That's probably not gonna cover it," says Grant, interrupting our stand-off. "I was thinking I'd do queso, and that's already, like, seven bucks, then at least four tacos—"

"You can eat the Brushfire yourself. Just take the money," says Ian, and returns to me.

"But *dude!*" Grant insists. "That's yours!"

"Grant!" Ian digs in the wallet again and hands off a ten. "Go get your lunch!"

"Sweet!" Grant snags the second bill and heads for the door. "Thanks, Ian!"

We watch him go. When the door clatters shut, Ian lifts his chin.

Unbelievable. "You're looking pretty smug for a guy who's out thirty bucks." I shake my head. "Did that feel like a victory in some way?"

"*You* didn't win."

"And neither did Grant," I say, ignoring the fresh sting at the pleasure he's taking in undermining me. Where is this coming from? "How is that helping him? That's not what he needs, Ian. It's not what any of them need—"

"And you would know, after playing house with them for a few weeks."

"Um, *yeah.* Given that the alternative appears to be simply enabling them—"

"What are you talking about?"

"Are you kidding? What am I *not* talking about? You are actively facilitating their slacking. Here's money for lunch, Grant! Diego, you scheduled a haircut at the exact same time as a class you've been running for the better part of a *year?* I've got you covered?" I scowl. "Don't worry about finding a roommate, guys! I'll fork over several hundred a month to cover the rent."

"How— *Babs,*" he growls, in a way that would be appealing if not for the circumstances.

"Where does it end? At some point, they're going to have to succeed or fail on their own. If for no other reason than to give yourself a break. Even here—"

"For Christ's sake, Hayes!" He brings both hands to his face, fingertips nudging back the rim of his cap so that when he draws his hands down, the hat perches atop his head. "What is so wrong with my business that you're so compelled to fix it?"

"All I was going to say is that the guys can contribute more around here. Relieve you of a five a.m. or two, but if you really want me to dig in," I continue, more than ready for this conversation, "you *know* that I have a list."

"The gym is *fine*."

"Don't you want better than fine?" I ask, my voice rising. "You've done something incredible with Firehouse. The heart and soul of this thing is you. You're why people stay. You're a knowledgeable, effective coach. You care about your members and staff. You change lives! Hell, you may have saved Tom's. But the state of this place doesn't reflect that."

"This is not why I brought you on. I needed someone who could check people in and not use fifteen exclamation points in a social post. Not Lady Bird *goddamn* Johnson."

"I don't know what that means!" I spit. "But I don't think it's exactly the purview of a First Lady to point out that this floor should have been fixed properly before *someone*" —I gesture to his still-red knee with both hands—"ate shit on it!"

He opens his mouth, then shuts it again. His cheeks are pink.

"And while you may not have brought me on to elevate this place, a good portion of your membership thinks I should. They have a whole litany of suggestions, but they're too afraid to bring it up with you."

He blinks. "What?"

"Your pathological aversion to accepting help has them desperate for someone who might listen to them. They just want to contribute! The guys, too! They want to be part of it."

"I have a way of doing things here. The guys…" He seems to consider his words for a moment, jaw flexing, his lips pressing together. "I don't want to bog them down with any other gym stuff. They're dudes in their early twenties. They're fine."

"Why can't they be better than fine, too?" I am at my limit. Not just with Ian's hardheadedness, but the entire social structure that expects so little from fully capable postadolescent males. "You have such high standards for their performance, for the performance of the athletes here, for yourself, most of all. Why don't you expect them to be capable of keeping a toilet fit for company?"

"You don't need to dissect everything they do! Not everything is for you to fix."

"I'm teaching them how to do laundry, Ian, not fundamentally changing who they are."

"Who they are?" he echoes, incredulous. "*You* don't know who they are. You're acting like you have all the answers, when you don't know the first thing about them."

"I know plenty."

"Really?" He squares up, placing his feet like he's about to initiate a lift. "What do you know about Alistair, then? Are you aware that he's already graduated?"

"He—what?"

"A *year* ago. And he was the valedictorian of his high school graduating class. Went in with a load of credits. So you probably don't know what he majored in, either?"

I hate that I can't deny him the pleasure of being right. But also…*Alistair?*

He shakes his head. "No? Of course not. Because that would

require *asking*. Going beyond what you think you know about them, based on, what, exactly? A shitty bathroom and an empty fridge?"

Again, I have nothing.

"You're telling me that I don't have faith in the guys, when *everything* you're doing is based on assumptions you've made about them! Honestly, Hayes, what is your deal? Did that ass with the bike really turn you into this? Is this any different from the 'you' you were with him? Still 'filling in the cracks'?"

The words cut in so many ways. "This is nothing like that," I snap. "I am not that person!"

"Yeah, well, you're not their goddamn *mother*."

The air pulls from my lungs in a rush.

Intellectually, I can see this for the revelation it is. His mom died. I'm living with his brother, filling in a lot of blanks that a mom might. This is the extension of his grief and loss and so many complicated feelings that time will never heal.

But he's laid me out with the one-two punch of my oversights and assumptions and the reference to the role that my scarred, ravaged insides will, statistically, barring significant medical intervention, never allow me to experience.

I don't know how to react to that.

So I don't.

I just cross the room and walk out the door.

20

I SCRUB AT THE DIRT beneath my nails, working to dislodge a bit of grit from the cuticle of my right index finger. Rage-weeding hadn't been on my list today, but I needed somewhere to direct my energy. When I stormed into the house earlier, I'd hoped that the guys would have left something for me to do, but all of the common areas were tidy. Even the kitchen, where I found that one of my gold-rimmed bowls had been used. Not only had whichever roommate who'd enjoyed it *not* left it in the sink with pasta detritus, but he'd hand-washed it and placed it in the rack to dry. Like an adult.

I lift my chin. I am making a difference, *Ian*. Not "fixing" them.

I wouldn't use that specific verb, anyway. Sure, moving in with them was influenced by my desire to mold them into men who know better than to mistreat bespoke dinnerware. But it's not like that's a *bad* thing. It's about expecting more from a person because you know they're capable of more. So what if it's largely based on observations about the three of them and not especially tailored to their specific wants and interests? It's all baseline stuff!

Everything we're doing at the Dawghouse is something they had the capacity to do on their own; they just needed someone to light a fire under them.

Which is exactly what I *didn't* do while I was with Cole. With Cole, I was the enabler. The *Ian*.

Ian, who can bite me. And *not* in a sexy way.

But...I sag against the sink. He can also bite me in a sexy way. Presuming that he ever gets his head out of his butt and acknowledges that I'm right.

Which I *am*.

And so is he.

Once again in a huff, I dry my hands and return to the bedroom. A hulking shape fills the doorway to outside. I let out a yelp at the same moment I realize it's Ian. Because of course it is.

"Shit, sorry!" he says. He makes to step into the room but stops short of entering.

I hold a hand to my chest, heart still thundering from the fright...and *him*. "It's fine. Just wasn't expecting you." I check the time. "Shouldn't you be coaching?"

One meaty shoulder rises and falls. "Diego's covering. I need to apologize. I was a dick."

While not quite the white flag that would qualify him to bite me in a sexy way—not that I entertained that image for a portion of the time I spent weeding (Lies! I did!)—it is sufficient to grant him entry. I gesture him forward, and he comes in.

Toeing off his sneakers—ugh, the consideration!—he does a slow scan of his former dwelling. "It looks good," he says, pleasantly. "The plants make a difference." When his eyes meet mine, his smile drops. His brows draw together. "Grant's told you about living with me when he was younger, right?"

"Yeah," I say, not bothering to feign ignorance. I gesture toward my throne, tucked between Kronk the fiddle-leaf fig and the bookshelf in my reading nook. "Have a seat." I pull up my desk chair for myself.

He sits, tugging off his hat and running his fingers through his hair. "I was twenty-seven. And living with me meant that *he* started living the bachelor life at fourteen."

I wait him out, easing the rolling chair closer. Even though I know the basics, I like hearing this straight from him. I don't like that I find it *sexy*, but that's hardly his fault.

"Between my training schedule and, generally, being a late-twenties *idiot*, I didn't get in a lot of lessons on laundry. As long as his grades were okay and he came home when I asked, we were good. But now…"

His frown deepens to a thoughtful scowl. On any other man his size, the expression would be intimidating, but on him, it's like seeing a Great Dane puzzle over a chew toy. "You're highlighting every way I failed him."

I recoil so violently, my seat rolls back. "Failed? You think you *failed* him?"

His shoulders tense, like I'd made the accusation, not repeated it. "Everything you're having to teach him—grocery shopping, laundry, how to live like he wasn't raised in a barn. It's all stuff I didn't fill him in on back then."

"Plenty of actual parents do worse," I say, thinking of what I saw when I was teaching. "Snowplowing every bit of resistance their kid comes up against, or helicoptering them until they've been so micromanaged that they can't even get dressed on their own. Granted, he does spend a lot of time without a shirt on." I shrug. "At this point, Alistair's skewed my perspective on how much exposure is normal in their demographic."

This gets me a laugh, and some of the tension leaves the space between us. "Grant's a good kid, Ian. A good *man*. That's more important than whether he presorts his laundry."

Ian half smiles, but it doesn't reach his eyes.

We're close enough that I nudge him with my socked foot, and he looks at the point of contact before making his leisurely way up to my face. For a moment, I forget whatever insightful thing I was going to say. The man just took a very thorough scan of my leg, thank you very much. "If you're bent on taking responsibility for the gaps in his knowledge, you also get to take credit for the good parts. He's kind and thoughtful, disciplined about the things he cares about. Those things aren't taught. They're modeled. So if you're the primary influence, he learned all that from you."

Ian is back to puzzling over the imagined chew toy. I have to stop thinking about this man in canine terms. That's some deeply weird Dr. Moreau nonsense.

But he's looking considerably less domesticated when he meets my eyes. There's something assessing in his gray gaze, and the trace of heat I'm seeing suggests it's about more than my flattering observations. I am again entertaining thoughts of biting...

"You!" I blurt. "The impact talk, about size and leaving a door open. Your dad was abroad, so that was you." He nods, and the confirmation does nothing for my sexy bite thoughts.

He clears his throat. "You're a good influence, Ellie. He's learning a lot from you."

Something in my chest goes soft at the compliment. "It helps that the payoff is quick. He learns to grocery shop, he eats better. He cleans the bathroom more often, he doesn't have to wonder whose hair is clogging the drain. He keeps his room decent, he'll probably get *laid* more."

Ian smirks.

"I—" I have to clear my throat against unwelcome emotion. I could skip over this, but it needs to be said to fully clear the air. "I'm not trying to replace anyone."

His eyes tighten. "I shouldn't have said that."

He's watching me too carefully, so I press on before he can ask why that had been my breaking point earlier. "And it *is* a little self-serving. You've seen me in action. There was no way I was going to survive in this house with dicks on the mirrors and mysteries in the microwave. And—" I grit my teeth. He's been vulnerable; I can, too. "You weren't off base. I did assume a lot when I came in here. And I was already in the habit of picking up slack."

"With Cole." He says it like an accusation. Or maybe I just decide to hear it as one.

"Just your standard expression of deep-seated issues around being needed and useful to demonstrate to others that I'm worth keeping around. Maybe a means to compensate for past failures to prove to myself that I'm not a loser. Normal stuff." I pretend to shrug it off.

Ian's eyes widen. "Jesus, Hayes."

"I can be painfully self-aware. It's a great defense. Acknowledge your faults before anyone else has a chance to use them against you. If…you want to try it?"

His expression shutters, but not as completely as it has in the past. "I have a hard time accepting help. It feels like…" His brow furrows. "The gym is what I'm good at. Or it's what I'm *supposed* to be good at, now that I can't compete. I'm assuming you know—"

"How you were injured and coached for your mentor who didn't choose you to take over his gym when he retired so you started Firehouse on your own with the settlement money and your sterling reputation?" I say, stringing the words together on a single breath.

One corner of his mouth quirks, threatening a smile. "Diego's wearing off on you."

"Maybe. I'm still stuck on why your mentor wouldn't sell to you."

The almost-smile flattens to a pained line. "Denny said that I didn't have it in me to run a place. According to him, I lacked 'business acumen.'"

He pauses, brows high, like he's waiting for me to tell him his mentor had been right.

"*Dude,*" I say, and genuinely wince. "I am needling at *all* your insecurities, aren't I?"

He barks out a surprised laugh, one that rouses something in my memory. I'd gotten some of those out of him the night we met. Good for me.

But a moment later, the humor's gone. "The man was a second father to me. He knew me better than anyone, and he didn't trust me with what he'd built. He didn't think I could do it."

A response dances on my tongue, but I wait him out. I can connect the dots, but the teacher training says that the lesson will have more meaning if he draws the lines himself.

"That fucked with me. *Hard*. And I know it's something I should be able to get over, but every time a member or one of the guys or *you* point out something that needs improving or a new way of doing things, it's confirmation that Denny was right. I don't have it in me."

Again, I wait.

"But, Hayes? The nuts and bolts of operating the gym? I *hate* it." He falls back into the chair. "I just want to coach and help people the way I'm good at, you know?"

I pounce on the connection. "I do! It's why I don't teach. I *sucked*. But I found a way to continue doing what drew me to the field in the first place. My business lets me develop creative ways to work with books and gets me paid for it. It's all I wanted. Without the endless meetings, bureaucratic bullshit, and the general indignity of intercepting a note that reads 'Miss Hayes has *a* apple head.'"

Ian laughs. "A what?"

"Apple head. My hair was rounder then. And I used the note in a refresher on when to use *a* and *an*, so I got some use out of it. But you can find a way to do that, too. You don't have to do everything. Did Denny do his own taxes?"

"No."

"And did he treat gentle suggestions like they were monuments to his fallibility?"

He glowers but shakes his head.

"Then why should *you*? You've got the most important part: the actual content of the gym. Find a way to delegate the bullshit."

"I assume that you already have a list of ways I can do that?"

"Not just me. Your members are a wealth of untapped

resources. Let Tom do the accounting! You'd be doing him a favor. Retirement has the guy bored out of his gourd."

Ian grunts, but I press on. "You did just say that you hate that part."

"I'll talk to him."

"That's all I ask. Except not really." I hold my hands up in supplication. "I am begging you, *please* let me redo the merch."

Another grunt.

"Please? If I do it and you hate it, I'll put it back—"

"Really?"

"No. That was a lie. *But*," I add, generously, "I would give you veto rights to any arrangement I come up with."

His arched brow asks the second *really?* for him.

"Just let me do it so I'll lay off?"

"Now, that's a compelling angle."

"I could be offended by that, but I'm getting what I want, so I'll let it slide. We can talk about website copy and community outreach later. Food drive, roadside litter cleanup, free workouts in a park once a month…"

"Hayes," he warns.

"I said later! Most of those aren't even my ideas. Five a.m. has a Google Doc. Which you don't get to be butthurt over," I warn, just as he threatens to frown again. "You've built something that has generated a whole community, and communities tend to get vocal. It's all out of love, you know. You've given them so much." I smirk. "The least you can do is make them itemize your deductions."

He takes in a long breath. "As long as you filter the suggestions first, fine. I'm open. But…" He eyes me. "We're good?"

He cares.

"Better than good. We've come to a mutually beneficial arrangement." I reach out my hand, and he takes it in his for a shake. I allow myself the indulgence of thinking how easily he could pull on our joined hands and let the wheels of my chair roll me right onto his lap.

I give an exploratory tug, inching forward enough that I know the scenario is physically possible. When I let go, it is an act of pure self-preservation.

"Okay," he says, and puts his hat back on. He stands to leave, and I follow him to the door, leaning against the doorframe as he steps back into his shoes.

"Speaking of mutually beneficial arrangements," I say, "why won't you help Diego with the Built Box stuff?"

He straightens, brows low. "Are they trying to renegotiate?"

"What?"

"I went over their contract with him. It was pretty boilerplate, not too different from agreements I've signed in the past. They were definitely undervaluing him, though. That's why I pushed him to require the coupon code and a cut of sales."

"I had no idea. I—" I shake my head at myself. "He told me that you hadn't been interested, back when they asked about you. So I assumed—"

His lips quirk at the word. "That I was just being a dick?"

"I don't know. I'm sorry. I should have asked."

He nods, expression thoughtful, and his posture changes. He brings his hands to the top of his head, the movement causing his T-shirt to pull against his pectorals, flaring out his lats, his biceps bunching. Does he have any idea what even the slightest shift does to his body?

"I don't want Diego to think he's gotten something because of me. He earned that sponsorship. Built Box didn't even connect us until after they reached out to him."

"He made it seem like you were a major part of the draw."

"They got more enthusiastic after he told them that he worked for me. That knocked some of the wind out of his sails, and…" He shakes his head. "It's just business for them, but he was questioning himself after that, why they wanted him, if it had all been a scheme to get to me. I hated seeing it." He tugs on the rim of his cap. "It made me not want to reward them with my presence."

I hug my arms around myself, lest I launch myself at him. It's too much. His reasoning, his care, his stupid lats. I have to laugh; it's either that or lick his face. "That was quite the journey. You started out noble"—*hot*—"then got spiteful"—also *hot*—"with just a touch of ego at the end." Back-on-the-sexy-bite-train *hot*. "Would you mind if I plotted that into a unit? It would be a great fit for character arcs."

"Jesus, Hayes," he grumbles, but he's half smiling. "Is your brain ever off?"

"Not if I can help it. That's when the invasive thoughts close in."

His expression goes serious. "Is that more of your admitting-weakness thing?"

"I'm sure you're loving it," I tease, recalling his sour comment at the gym earlier.

"No," he says firmly. "Not for you."

Heat floods my face and chest. I'm desperate to ask him why, while also recognizing how thoroughly any number of responses from him would undo me. The silence that follows is heavy.

He pushes his hands into his pockets and goes down the steps. "Goodnight, Lady Bird."

"That does not get to be your parting shot!" I follow him out. He's already on the gravel path I weeded. "What even was that?"

He throws his head back in a laugh, and if that's as close as I get to drawing a roar out of him, then so be it. I feel it in my bones. "You don't celebrate the legacy of Lady Bird Johnson? Some Texan you are."

"I'm a transplant. And, *duh*. I know she was First Lady."

"Look her up. I think you'll agree that the comparison fits."

"Hmph. Does that mean I'm no longer queen?"

His eyes glitter in recognition as he continues down the path, walking backward. "Hayes, please. This is *America*. Pretty sure we fought a war so we didn't have to acknowledge royalty."

21

THURSDAY EVENING, HEATHER and Mark post up in the dining room to chat with Grant. While they won't be of much use as far as info about elementary-level stuff, our teaching program required that we intern at a middle school as well as the high school where we ultimately worked. The two of them had been deeply involved in the junior high's extracurriculars, whereas I saw much of my free time that semester divided between trying to convince myself that I hadn't made a multi-thousand-dollar mistake in pursuing my master's degree and in waiting rooms, hoping to find out what was causing my abdominal pain. At least I got an answer; for the hours they put in, all Mark and Heather had to show for it was an abiding hatred for *Annie* and a sneaking suspicion that very few seventh graders were wearing deodorant.

They've been talking for the better part of an hour, and when I looked in earlier, Grant was taking notes. He still hasn't talked to Ian about his change in plans, but it says a lot about his commitment that he's taking the process so seriously.

I'd taken to the couch with a book, but I keep losing my place on the page. I used my day off yesterday as a rest day, though my body needed the break less than my exposure to Ian. I did brush up on my American history. Lady Bird Johnson's pet project was the Highway Beautification Act, which, minor controversies aside, sounded right up my alley. She also worked to tidy DC, planting millions of flowers on National Park Service land around the capital. She was a big believer that beauty would make the US a better place to live. Better, one might submit, than "fine."

She also had one hell of a hair helmet. Which is what made her instantly recognizable when I spotted her image on my desk this morning, gracing the glass of a novelty prayer candle. There's one on my nightstand, a white elephant gift from the school, with Dolly Parton fashioned in the style of a Catholic saint. They're all over Austin, done by a local company, with a slew of celebrities and historical figures.

Taped below the icon was a note in Ian's distinct, blocky writing, reading, "Our lady of better than fine."

Hot.

I close my book. Alistair stands at the end of the hallway, eyes distant in thought, or…not-thought, possibly.

Or *not* not-thought. He'd been valedictorian of his high school graduating class, after all. And I'm overdue for my apology tour. No time like the present.

"Alistair," I start, "I know basically nothing about you. I've been remiss. And I'm sorry."

His head quirks to one side, but he doesn't seem particularly affected by the statement. "It's cool. I keep to myself a lot. I have a rich inner life."

It had been *not* not-thought! I gesture to the lounger. "Sit! Tell."

"Like, what's in my head right now? 'Cause right now, I'm just pissed because I have an underwear shoot on Tuesday, and it's gonna fuck up my weekend."

"Oh, man," Grant groans, coming in from the dining room with his notebook. "That sucks. For *all* of us," he adds, pointedly.

Heather frowns, she and Mark joining me on the couch. "What? Why?" she asks, unaccustomed to the unspoken rule of the Dawghouse: One doesn't request elaboration from fellow residents. But after my spat with Ian, I'm thinking that I might have misinterpreted their acceptance of my silence. Just because I wasn't forthcoming doesn't mean that no one else wants to be asked about themselves. With these three having such a long history together, they might just take for granted that they know everything about one another. I'm the interloper. I should have been asking all along.

"I gotta cut my water weight." Alistair eases into the recliner, draping himself across the armrests. "It makes the muscles look more defined. So shitty, though. Dieting is bad enough, but when I'm dehydrating like that, I swear, the last day? I can *smell* water nearby."

"He's a dick the whole time, too," Grant says.

"You would be too if walking past a sprinkler had you drooling. Actually..." He frowns. "I don't think I can even produce saliva at that point."

"Is that level of dehydration even safe?" Mark asks.

"Fuck no. But it's not long-term. And it only comes up every now and then. I'm used to it because of the other stuff I used to do."

Heather's brows quirk upward. "Other stuff?"

"He used to do bodybuilding competitions." Grant laughs. "Until he was *banned*."

"Banned?" I ask.

"Because of my penis."

Heather's "Excuse me?" is a squeak.

Alistair groans, letting his head drop onto the armrest. "When I competed, I'd do my individual program to 'Like a Rock.' Because my body is hard. Like a rock. Like, every time the song would go, 'Like a rock,' I'd flex. To go along with the song."

"That's…" What is someone supposed to say in this situation? "Very literal."

"Exactly. And I'd do a standing backflip at the end. As a finale. But my abs were so tight, doing that meant that sometimes my dick would pop out of my shorts."

This time, Mark squeaks.

"My mom always let me know," Alistair continues. "She'd be in the wings—she'd help me out backstage. So good at coverage for my tanning stuff. And she'd"—he makes a downward motion with his hand, as though tucking in a shirt—"'Tuck it in, sweetie!' But I guess some people thought I was doing it on purpose."

"To be fair, folks probably aren't expecting full-on dick at an event like that," Mark offers, reasonably.

"I guess," Alistair concedes. "It was still sucky that I got banned, but I was already over it. And that's kind of where I am with modeling, too. The money's good, and I'll be putting away a lot more now, with your draconian-ass budgeting," he says to me, accusingly.

I shrug; I'm more impressed with his use of *draconian*, even if I don't think it applies. My guidelines are hardly written in *blood*. "So, what are you saving for? A place of your own?"

"Med school."

"Med—" I goggle at him. "*Med* school?"

He nods, lazily confident as ever, but *med school*? For *him*? I'm really trying not to make assumptions, but…Doctor Tongue Zap?

Grant laughs. "Yo, Alistair was a *nerd* back in the day."

"I'm, like, real fuckin' smart. A lot of people don't know that, because I'm also hot, but yeah. You know how people know you're smart, Ellie? Even though you're hot? It's like, she's a smokeshow, *and* I bet she could recommend a good book? But with me, people see that I'm hot, and the most they can hope for is a rec for a good body spray."

"And what self-tanner to avoid if they'd rather not look like a sparkle vampire?" Heather offers.

He brays out a laugh. "Right? That shit took forever to come off." He shakes his head, examining his palms as if for lingering shimmer. "But, for sure. I've been accepted into a few programs—"

"Aren't you only twenty-one?" Mark asks.

"Yeah. I came into UT with, like, half my undergraduate degree in the bag. But I didn't want to be buried under a mountain of student debt. And there's scholarships and stuff, but I'm cool taking my time right now. I'll only be this"—he gestures toward himself with both hands; as always, we have no choice but to take him in—"for so long, you know?"

Heather rolls her eyes. "I think it's pretty safe to say that barring disfigurement, you'll just transition to a silver fox and end up representing different things."

"Prolly. But I might start looking into those scholarships again, see what I need to do if I want to enroll in the next year or whatever."

His eyes flit toward me, and for the first time, I see something other than vacant self-possession; the man is capable of doubt. "Do you, um, think that's something you could help me with? Because there'll be essays, and personal statements 'n' shit, and I kind of write how I talk. I used to be better," he says, pushing himself higher in the chair, though he's still half reclining. "Like, talk better, but I think I'm out of practice. I've had my brain off for a *while.*"

"Absolutely," I say, happy for the chance to make up the time I've been underestimating him...even if it had been based on every interaction I've had with him up until—and kind of including—now. "And if you want to prime your brain a bit, I have it on good authority that I'm the right person to ask for a book recommendation."

He frowns, then the lightbulb clicks on. Good Lord, he really has turned off his brain, hasn't he? "Nice callback."

"Alistair..." I shake my head, but I can't help but smile. "You are a mystery. Wrapped in an enigma. And, generally, very little else."

"And sometimes a plant!" He chuckles to himself for a moment, then cocks his head, brow furrowed. "It's probably gonna take a while to get my brain back in gear, yeah?"

"I'll start a reading list."

22

IAN STANDS IN THE DOORWAY of the storage room Friday, eyeing me. "That's it, by the way. That's *your* 'I'm-going-to-fuck-with-you face.' You have one now."

"I don't know what you're talking about," I say, but I can't get the words out without laughing.

He grunts, smirking, and joins me at the table I use for folding laundry. "Should I assume it's related to why Helen couldn't look at me on her way out just now, and why Babs was *very much* looking at me?"

"May I remind you that you gave me total access to everything in the bins for pro shop decor," I say. I spent the past hour going through the bins of Ian's accolades for inspiration. He's given me the go-ahead to take on that entire section of the lobby, and the Coffee Coup has agreed on a Saturday early next month to tackle everything he's approved on the wish list, with a grand reveal that evening. I'd asked Helen and Babs back here to see if they'd be interested in taking on one particular element of my vision. I've ceded total control to them, which I think shows tremendous personal growth on my part.

Ian grins, and there's a feral edge to it that makes my toes curl. "You found the nudes."

"Babs did. She found the file while we were talking. You should have warned me."

His smile dares me to ask why he hadn't. "And ruin the surprise? Where's the fun in that?"

I told up an outtake from the series. The photo I have dubbed *The Roar* remains the indisputable winner of the day, and while there was no shortage of quality runners-up, the most delightful discovery had been among the candid shots. "Mr. Hammond, might one call this a *cock sock*?"

He laughs. "If only they'd printed it in color. It was highlighter pink."

"Oh, Babs would have loved that," I say. He'd been captured in conversation with another man, who's holding some kind of reflective screen. The resulting light has washed out the definition in Ian's abdomen, but the contrasting darkness of his chest hair is stark, as is the apparatus over his penis.

The length being suggested by the sock varied from shot to shot, leaving the ladies and me no choice but to speculate how accurately it portrayed the resting state of Ian's unit. There's no question that the man is, as Babs put it, "proportional," though there were some shots where the sock was stretched to an inhuman—but entertaining—size.

"I suspect she loved it anyway," he says, and moves on to the other photos from the shoot. He pushes through the stack, laughing when he gets to a shot of himself in a squat, the sock obscene. "I put an empty Dr Pepper can in it at one point. Which ended up being pretty humbling once I took it out. It was a little roomy in there after that." I laugh, and he reaches for another stack of photos. "Did you get anything done back here, or did the cock sock derail you?"

"I've been very productive, thank you. Those are the ones I'd like to use out front," I say, indicating the pile he's flipping through, then tap the papers beside it. "And I've compiled some newspaper clippings and articles, but let me know if there's anything I missed that you'd like up. Or"—I point to the nudes—"anything you'd rather we not include."

"Thank you for that. What's—" He plucks a stray photo from the table. It's of a family of four standing on a beach, smiling as the sun sets behind them. The outfits speak of a mother with specific aspirations. "Was this in with the others?"

I nod, watching for his reaction. "It was stuck to the side of one of the bins."

Ian lets out a little laugh. "The Hammonds do Hawaii," he explains, but it's obvious. Grant can't be more than twelve in the photo, but he already has the bright smile I know so well, his hair sun-bleached, nose and cheeks the faint pink of almost-sunburnt. Ian also looks like himself; not as broad as he is now, but filling out that flowered shirt in a way no Trader Joe's employee ever has.

However, when Helen found the photo, it was the seniormost Hammond who had us fanning ourselves. Talk about *impact*. Their dad is like a window to future Ian, the laugh lines around his eyes a hint of Man Mountain to come. He's not as brawny as his son, but they're matched for height. I've never been drawn to facial hair, but the familiar smile peeking out from beneath the mustache makes a compelling case for broadening my horizons.

"Did this end up on a Christmas card?" I ask.

"It was our last one," he says, the words carrying a note of surprise. "How'd you know?"

I can't help smiling. "Did your mom pick your shirts?"

"Yeah?"

"They're complimentary enough that nothing clashes, but aren't so coordinated that you look like servers at a tiki bar. Classic vacation-mom move."

"She did that every family trip." His voice is distant with recall. "The last night, we'd go out to dinner somewhere kind of fancy. She'd tell us, 'Wear something nice,' and when we griped, she'd throw shirts at us and we'd put on whatever it was."

I grin. *Stealthy.* Exactly how I'd go about it. It makes me feel a distant camaraderie with this woman I've never met. I return to the photo, and my smile fades. A woman I never *will* meet. I search for signs of her sickness. She's as tan as the rest of the family, with shoulder-length brown hair streaked with sunshine. She's on the slimmer side, but I wouldn't suspect that she was harboring a fatal illness. "You said it was your last Christmas card?"

"She was gone the following spring."

"I'm sorry. I've never lost anyone close. I can't imagine what that must have been like. Or how it still hurts."

"Those first few months are a blur. We kept moving, literally. Always in action, finding things to do. That's Dad's default, 'go, go, go,' and structuring everything to the point that he can't even stop to think. Or—" His eye twitches slightly; a subtle wince that screams for me to wrap myself around him. "*Hurt.* The day after we lost her, he was packing up her closet."

His voice thins with pain, and it's like that moment making

meatballs with Grant all over again. I want to offer some kind of creature comfort, but I don't know what would be appropriate. So I just listen.

"I hated him for it. But even then, I saw it for what it was. He needed a project. He handled all the funeral arrangements, wrote the obituary, called the people she'd wanted to eulogize her, showed us what book passages she wanted read—"

"Book passages?"

"Some quotes she liked. Poems. My reading compared loss to a break that doesn't heal properly, and learning to dance with the limp." He frowns, but the expression is more thoughtful than discontent. "I hadn't thought about that in years. It's...accurate."

I look pointedly toward his right knee. There's a faint red mark left from Tuesday's abrasion, blurring the white, barely there scar from his old injury. "You'd know in more ways than most."

"I...do." He half smiles. "I hadn't made that connection. My knee thing wasn't until way later, but..." He shakes his head, gaze going inward. I wait, selfishly cheered that I've contributed.

"Goddamn Christmas cards," he says. "She was really good about those. Always did the 'year in review' letter, too. *Grant lost four teeth in two months, and Ian had a pregnancy scare with his college girlfriend. Not grandparents yet, but there's always next year!*"

Ian shakes his head as I choke on my laughter. "She held *nothing* back. It was mortifying. At the time," he adds. "Now they're kind of nice to look at. She kept track of everything. *Everything important.* Dad was the organized one, kept the day-to-day moving. Mom never got us anywhere on time, and dinner was always incredible and overengineered and way later than anyone would have preferred, but it's like she couldn't help herself from doing one extra thing, just to make it perfect. We never asked for it, but she lived for that stuff."

I smile and look up at Ian, but his eyes are distant again, his jaw tight.

"The first time she got sick, it was a total upheaval. Grant was four, and between him and her doctor appointments, I had to do a lot on my own. And I was *such* a dick about it."

He pulls off his hat, raking his fingers through his hair. His stress behavior. I wonder if he knows he does it. "When she relapsed, she and Dad didn't tell us until it was clear that she wouldn't make it." He tugs the cap back on.

"Did it progress quickly? Not that you got to know."

"It was fast. She chose not to do chemo. It wouldn't have given her much more time, and I get why she didn't want to spend what little she had left feeling like shit. Not that it kept me from being mad at her for not fighting," he grumbles. "I was hurt that she didn't tell us. Grant and I, we had no idea how bad it was. He was still just a kid. But I…" Another micro-wince, and this time, I can't help it. I place a hand on his, where it rests on the table.

He rubs his thumb along my pinky, absently. "I know she didn't want me to lose any time worrying about something I couldn't control, but if I'd known, I would have made it a priority to get more time with her. She shouldn't have taken that choice from me, I guess." His shoulders rise and fall as he shakes his head. "I don't know."

I nod. Her reason for keeping her sickness quiet resonates with me, but I can see Ian's side of it, the unkindness of her deny-ing him and Grant the chance to come to terms with it. They would have felt helpless in the face of it—anyone would—but they deserved to know.

My conscience clears its throat. This is an opening. An opportunity to tell him about my un-diagnosis, my eye, my fear. But that would mean hijacking this moment about his grief and his mom, and I'm not going to do that.

"She'd go overboard at Christmas," he says, and a smile tugs at his lips, sunshine peeking out behind the lingering sorrow. "We weren't even religious. But she loved dressing everything up. I bet you do, too. If you do Christmas?" he adds, hurriedly. Worry puckers his brow, and I nod, smiling as relief replaces the wrinkles.

"Yes and yes." I squeeze his hand before taking mine back. "Simple, but all-out. Garlands, white lights—"

"A tree?"

"I've never had a tree. But I buy an ornament everywhere I visit. My first tree will be very well-traveled."

"Mom did that, too. Bought ornaments on trips. Not the 'simple' though. Multicolored lights, no theme. Dad called it 'Christmas chaos.'" He's beaming now. "She passed before the blow-up yard decor got popular. She'd have *loved* those."

I redirect my attention to the photo again. But he's watching me, I can feel it. I don't dare look back at him. I *hate* those things.

He leans into me, and I elect to focus on the pleasant heat of him against my shoulder and not the burning dislike I have for the inflatable abominations. "I bet you can't *stand* them."

"They are not to my taste."

"Nah." He's smiling now, so big, I can make it out from the corner of my eye. "You *hate* them, I know it—"

"They're such a cop-out! Taking up as much space as possible and zero effort. They're never the right scale," I rail. "Like Macy's parade rejects. When they're on, the fans are loud and annoying, and when they're off, you have ugly heaps of nylon scattered around your yard. No one even tries to make them look cohesive, they're just dumb and inelegant, and yes, I hate them!"

He stares at me, then nods. After a moment, he heaves a sigh. "I can't believe you hate my dead mom's favorite Christmas decorations."

Panic detonates in my chest. "You said she passed before—"

"My dead mom's *hypothetically* favorite Christmas decorations." He can barely shape the words, he's trying so hard not to laugh.

The anxiety leaves me in a rush. "You *turd*. That was so dark!" I laugh, and he surrenders to his laughter, letting out a deep rumble that warms my insides. "That was fucked-up!"

He shrugs.

"Wow," I marvel. "I didn't know you had it in you to go there."

He chuckles, his gaze returning to the photo. He's looking at it differently now, no trace of the earlier sadness in his eyes.

"You should frame it," I say. "Hang it up somewhere."

He nods, placing the picture back on the table, but his eyes linger on the photo. He's still smiling, and there's something soft in his expression that I don't think I've ever seen before. It makes him look about as young as he was on that beach.

He taps the stack of clippings I wanted him to look over. "If you keep these out, I'll look through them this afternoon so y'all can get going on whatever it is you're planning with them." He fans them out, smiling to himself. "I haven't thought about this stuff in forever."

"I'd guess so, Captain Cock Sock," I say. "Those about gave me a heart attack."

He laughs, and while I know it's at my expense, I can't help grinning back.

Ian's still smiling at me, somewhere between amusement and something warmer that has me wanting to reach out and take his hand again, when his phone buzzes with an alert. He blinks, checking his watch. "Shoot, I have a personal training client in five. You good back here?" he asks, and I nod.

"There's one more bin to go through," I say. "Anything I should be warned about?"

"Nothing you can't handle." He heads for the door, but turns around before walking through. "Thank you, Ellie. For listening."

My breath catches a little. "Happy to. Thank you for telling me about her."

He nods, shooting me an almost-smile, then leaves.

The last bin is sadly void of anything resembling a cock sock. Just trophies, but there are a few medals that will look good on the wall, as well as a Best of Austin award for Best Group Classes, dated last year, still in a bubble-wrapped mailer. It's cute, with a hand giving a thumbs-up beside Firehouse's name. It's absolutely going up, too.

I tuck the mailer under my arm and pick up the shot of the family of four and the smiling woman in the center. Had she known then that the cancer was back? Had she suspected it? And when had she decided not to tell her boys?

My conscience gives me another nudge. I push back. This isn't the same. The worst-case scenario for me isn't death, but a life that doesn't look much like living. And why would I burden more people with that than necessary?

Ian's mom spared them for as long as she could. I still see Ian's side of it, the unfairness, but he'd said it himself: What could he have done?

I consider the dimensions of the picture. Probably a four by six. A standard print size. Easy to frame. I slide it into the mailer, easing it over the slick surface of the plaque, so it doesn't get bent.

Not for the pro shop. This will be just for him.

23

"KNOCK, KNOCK," HEATHER SAYS, stepping into the house early Saturday evening.

"Careful," I warn her, and she freezes with both feet on the doormat. "The floors are slick. We got the ratio wrong on the wood cleaner, and it's like an ice rink in here. Go barefoot if you want to remain upright."

"Or just embrace it!" Mark calls from the hallway. Heather and I turn toward his voice, and a moment later, he glides down the hallway on his belly, penguin-style.

"Nice distance," I say. He stands up, keeping a hand on the wall for balance.

"The guys gave me a push. This is actually a really good time," he says. "Human curling." He turns and shuffles back up the hallway on socked feet.

"And you're encouraging this?" Heather asks.

"The guys have already exceeded their entertainment budget for the month and were desperate for things to do. Outside of their multiple video game systems, the finest television and sound system setup this side of an actual theater—"

"You have the TV tonight!" Grant reminds me from the depths of the hallway.

"Only from eight to ten," I holler back. "Y'all have the entire internet at your disposal."

"We're bored of the internet!" Diego counters.

Heather laughs. "I'm not sure if that's great for society or terrible," she says, and toes off her sneakers. She eyes the shiny hardwood, then braves a step off the mat. Immediately, she drops into a crouch to keep her balance. "Good God, what did you use? Motor oil?"

"Might as well have. The floors look great, though."

"Until they're covered in my blood. Yeesh." Still crouching, she shuffles toward the couch and grabs hold of the arm, using it to tow herself to safety. She takes a seat, craning her neck toward the hallway as she settles. "How long have they been doing this?"

"About twenty minutes. It was Mark's idea. I attribute it to his improv background. Big 'yes, and' energy."

As we watch, fingers curl around the wall at the mouth of the hallway. A moment later, Diego slingshots himself into the living room, slowing to a stop before the couch. He flops onto his back. "I'm bored again. What else can we do?"

"For free," I remind him.

"Fine. What else can we do *for free*?" he asks. The other guys pad into the living room, Grant employing a skating motion to glide to the couch.

"Might I propose…" Mark plants both feet on the wall at the

mouth of the hallway, then launches himself into the living room, maintaining a casual side-lying posture as he eases to a stop. "Silence and Sabotage."

I catch Heather's eye, and she shakes her head. He's in auteur mode.

"It's a variation on tag. The person who is It is blindfolded. And everyone else is confined to a certain area, say"—he gestures around himself—"the living room. Whoever's It has to feel around for the others, who have to remain silent or otherwise keep who's It from figuring out where they are. Players may sabotage others by making noise, but do so at their own peril; create enough noise to draw the attention of It, and you may be found instead."

"Did you come up with this?" Heather asks.

"Absolutely not. I saw it on Instagram. But I did come up with the name."

"Just now?" I ask.

"*Just* now."

"Very cool," Diego marvels. "*Silence and Sabotage* is a great name."

"Thank you. In the version I saw, the evading party was confined to a couch, and the blindfolded person had a squirt gun, and while I suspect that Ellie would murder me if I proposed that—"

"You would be correct," I chime.

"—I think that having everyone trying not to bite it on the floor will be challenging enough." He looks around at each of us. "Y'all in?"

All eyes turn to me.

Regular Life Me rails against the idiocy of the proposed activity. My mind floods with visions of busted chins, cracked teeth, blood on the couch. But I also haven't joined the guys in any non-gym nonsense so far. This is what these six months are supposed to be about.

I press up from my spot on the couch. "I'll get some socks."

Silence and Sabotage is more fun than it has any right to be.

We're all treating it with the same deathly seriousness that Mark had when introducing the game. Heather is ruthless, sliding up beside other participants and making a noise, only to skate away while whoever's It closes in. She got me caught that way, which is why I'm standing with Alistair's backup—as opposed to *primary?*—sleep mask on, listening for a player to give away their location.

Someone in the room clears their throat nominally, the wet rumble coming from my left. I'm edging that way when I pick up on something else: footsteps on the porch. Heavy. Distinctive. I lean in the direction of the sound. "Is Ian here?"

Across the room, Diego mutters, "She knows his feet?"

A double knock sounds at the door, and then I hear it open. "Hey. You guys ready to go eat?" He pauses. "What is this?"

I wheel toward him, tugging off the eye mask. He's on the doormat, in faded jeans and a baseball tee with navy sleeves. I don't dare look at Heather; we've long championed the baseball tee as superior to all other male casual wear. It strikes the perfect balance of universally flattering crewneck and forearm-baring sleeves that demand some degree of musculature to fill out. Why all the love for the Henley, which, frankly, sits awkwardly on the neck and shoulders of all but a select few male forms, when the baseball tee is already doing the Lord's work?

Instead, I glare at each of my roommates, who studiously avoid my gaze. "Did you recruit him to take you out?"

Grant's focus is somewhere near his toes. "Maybe."

"I—" Ian begins, and starts to take a step forward, off the doormat. The entire room cries "No!" before his foot makes contact with the floor. He hops backward.

"We got a little overzealous cleaning the floor," I explain. "We're making the most of it."

"Ah! I was told that you'd come up with a way to keep them entertained for free." He eyes me. "And that you were being a fanatic about their entertainment budget."

"They're supposed to be learning how to manage their funds," I say, cutting my eyes at the guys again. "But it seems they've only learned to be sneakier when turning to you." I sigh. "And I'm afraid you're going to have to join in, now that you've been duped into undoing all my work toward molding these ding-dongs into financially responsible young men."

"I wasn't duped," he counters, face almost convincingly stern. "I was being a good brother."

"Pushover."

"Tyrant."

"Are we going to get back to the game, or do we have to wait for the sexual tension to diffuse, first?" Heather calls.

I elect not to dignify that with a response and ask Ian, who has somehow maintained a straight face through all of this, "You in?"

"Do I get to wear the eye mask?"

"No!" Diego calls. "I'm tired of hiding. I want to be It."

"Hey, Ian!" Heather shoots me a wicked wink. "Nice shirt."

My knee pops.

The unmistakable sound is like a gunshot in the silent room. Diego's head whips around like a predator catching a scent on the wind, and he grins. "Ellie!"

Shit.

He stalks toward me, posture hunched. Each step is taken in exaggerated slow motion, with Diego losing his footing every few inches and scrambling to recover. It's like watching a moose cross a frozen pond. I hold back a laugh. Across from me, Heather is convulsing with the effort not to let hers out, a hand over her mouth, eyes watering.

But he's getting closer. And I can't trust my creaky joints to risk moving again. The most I can do is lean back a tiny bit—

I'm so focused on Diego's progress that I almost miss Heather waving her arms. I meet her insistent glare, and she points behind me, mouthing, *Ian!*

I frown in confusion, and she makes a tugging gesture with both of her hands, grabbing at waist level, then driving her simulated grip into her hips—

Is that a *hump*? Involving *Ian*? Madam, this is no time to mime my secret thoughts!

I'm still frowning at her gesticulations when Diego takes two large steps forward, recapturing my attention. But then, warm hands close on my hips. Big hands. *Ian's* hands. I stare down at the fingers pressing into my hipbones. My immediate thought is *Eh?*, followed by an equally inarticulate *Is* this *a hump?* But then I begin easing backward.

A glance over my shoulder gives me a view of Ian, bent over fully at the waist, making use of his impressive torso and arm length to close the distance between our spots. He's achieved traction by going barefoot, the crafty guy, and as he pulls, I scoot ever nearer to him, my socks sliding soundlessly over the glossy wood.

I face forward, Diego has advanced. He's stalking straight for me, while Heather and Alistair—the traitors!—have scooched out of his way, leaving the path clear.

Ian adjusts his grip, fingers digging into my sides, and heaves me back. I careen into his chest, molding my back into his body while Diego gropes in the spot where I'd been not two seconds before. I shrink further into Ian, his arms banding across my chest and waist. He starts edging backward with me in tow, the motion rocking me side to side with each shuffle of his retreat. I am, essentially, being rubbed against the entire front of his person. I do not mind.

Diego pauses, doing birdlike head tilts, but for the moment, I'm out of his range. I tell myself it's out of relief that I let the back of my head rest again Ian's chest. But when I connect with that impressive swell of muscle, I am fused to the spot. I'm like a cat caught in a sunbeam, totally immobilized. God, he's warm.

Diego reaches out suddenly, swinging his hand so close, I feel the air it moves past the tip of my nose. Ian had been approaching a wall when I looked back at him, so there's only so much farther we can maneuver to get out of reach. I have no choice: It's going to have to be sabotage.

But with what? I have nothing on hand; my leggings don't even have pockets. But Ian—he might have something! I scour my brain, keeping tabs on Diego's proximity as I think. Car keys? Phone? Ah! His wallet!

I raise a hand, my index finger lifted in the universal—right?—symbol of *aha!* to let him know I've had an idea. It earns me a squeeze—which hijacks my brain for only a moment—and I change the position of my upraised hand, making a plucking motion before lifting my other hand, my two palms face-up, like a billfold. In a last-ditch attempt at clarity, I fan my left hand over my right palm to mime "making it rain dollar money."

He gets it, I think. He gives me a thumbs-up using the hand across my chest, so now, I need to make my way toward his wallet...but which pocket is it in?

While I feel that it reflects well on me as a modern woman of good taste who does not objectify her boss that the man's posterior isn't etched firmly enough into my memory that I can recall on which side he keeps his wallet, right now, it is an inconvenience. I tap on his right leg, getting no response, then his left. This gets me another thumbs-up, and I reach behind him. For the sake of propriety, I make as little contact as I can, walking my fingers down to his waistline. But I do not miss the way his grip stiffens as I edge toward my target. When I get to the pocket, I pause, waiting for any final objection. Another encouraging squeeze from Ian. In I go.

I try to maintain my minimal-contact spider fingers, but the fit over his well-formed posterior is too tight. So it's an open palm slide over firm, high glute for me. Ian shudders, the left side of his body contracting against me, and I have to remind myself to breathe. But then the very ends of my nails graze over something in his pocket. I go deeper and curl my claws, the tips digging into the leather of his wallet just enough for grip, and I lift up.

It's awkward going when I have to transition the wallet from my fingers to my palm, demanding a wriggling motion that results in some unavoidable prodding of Ian's butt cheek, but then the wallet is securely in hand. I free it from the pocket, the air of the room noticeably cooler outside the tush-warmed denim, and bring it in front of me. There's a sliver of candy wrapper stuck to it, the cellophane from one of the cinnamon things he's always sucking on.

I scan the room, trying to determine the most effective spot to toss my plunder, when I notice that everyone not blindfolded is openly gawking at me. Their eyes dart from me to the wallet, then past me, presumably, to Ian, and I realize that as far as they're concerned, I molested the poor man, then pickpocketed him.

Heather even mouths, *What the hell?*, which is fair.

I raise the wallet, then make a tossing motion to demonstrate my intention, pointing at Diego with my empty hand for good measure.

The critical reception softens to understanding. But Grant's head is still cocked.

"You're gonna *throw* that at Diego?" he asks. *Aloud.*

"Grant!" Diego spins on his heels, and, in a moment of unexpected agility, leaps at Grant. Or would, if he had any traction. His legs fly out from beneath him, and for a heartbeat, the man is suspended in the air, arms outstretched, Superman-style, before he drops. *Hard.*

This would have been bad enough for Diego, but Mark had

been edging behind him the moment the latter fellow spun around, and he ends up taking the bulk of Diego's not insignificant mass. Mark lets out a squawk upon impact, as Diego grunts, guessing "Ellie's man friend?" from his living landing pad.

The tension leaves the room in a whoosh of faintly hysterical collective laughter.

Ian collapses over me in relief. "When I guessed what you were going for, I didn't expect it to be so...thorough." It's murmured directly into the side of my neck, his lips shaping each word into the tender skin. For half a second, my laughter becomes a breathy, almost moan. *Jesus.* My entire body is tingling.

"I'm so sorry!" I say, and he straightens, loosening his grip enough that I can turn to face him while still in the circle of his arms. "I tried not to make more contact than necessary."

"You're good." He shakes his head. "But I think I lost consciousness the moment you cupped my ass."

"You what?" I ask. He's still holding me; my hands, one still brandishing his wallet, are high on his chest; and if not for the difference in our heights, we would be crotch-to-crotch. As it is, we're currently crotch-to-belly.

"Ellie! You were going to throw something at me?" Diego asks. And while I'd still like clarification on Ian's brief loss of consciousness, I face my downed roommate. Ian, ever the gentleman, keeps his arms around me.

Diego lies on his stomach. He's shoved the blindfold onto his forehead, and the band has bunched his hair into a bobbing black dome that gets a giggle out of me as he peers up, wide eyes fixed on the wallet in my hand as though it were a mace.

"I wasn't going to throw it *at* you," I clarify. "I was going to throw it somewhere to *redirect* you. You were coming straight at me. I had to do something."

"Ah." Mollified, he turns and smiles at Mark, still partly under him, giving him a friendly pat on the knee. "Sorry for squishing you. Thank you for breaking my fall."

We decide to end the game after Diego's moment of flight, determining that it was as close to disaster as we were willing to get. And in the spirit of avoiding potential disaster, I give Ian my leave to take the destitute trio out. Ten minutes later, I'm still dazed. There was just so much of him all up against so much of me. The press of his hands. The feeling of his butt beneath my fingers…

"Hey, horndog!" Heather snaps her fingers to get my attention. I come to to find her and Mark watching me, trying not to laugh.

Heather rolls her eyes, "We going to watch a movie, or should we spend the evening recapping whatever was going on with you and Beefcake Mountain?"

"My vote's for Beefcake Mountain," Mark chimes.

"You're going to be thinking about it, anyway."

"Probably." I sigh. "That was so much contact! Hands on parts—"

"*So* many parts," Mark agrees. "And when he wrapped his arms around you?" He fans himself. "Ellie, he got this look in his eye that was, like, I don't know what! It was some *me Tarzan, you Jane* propriety. *Big* protective instinct. So hot."

"*So* hot," Heather echoes.

"And your face said that you were into it," he says. "So why in the hell haven't you shimmied up that tall tree of a man?"

"Is it because he's your boss?" Heather asks, skeptically.

I wave that off. "The gym is a paycheck gig. I have zero concern for an imbalance of power. It's just..."

I frown. If my attraction to Ian were just physical, a fling with him would be perfectly in line with my six-month scheme. But I'm well beyond the physical with him. "He doesn't feel like 'break' material."

"Huh," says Mark. He shares a look with Heather, and I very much wish I'd chosen to turn on a movie earlier.

"Does he *have* to be break material?" Heather asks too carefully. "I know you've only known him a few weeks, but if you're into him, and he's into you, and he's the kind of guy who would parade shirtless to intimidate your ex—"

"You make it sound like he was peeing in a circle around me."

"Except that he wasn't!" Mark interjects. "You told us he did it because he recognized that someone who treated you poorly was the kind of trash who would be intimidated by shirtless parading, and that speaks volumes."

"He isn't Cole," Heather says. Her voice is hard and direct. "He's not the kind to bail."

"I know," I say. But that's the problem.

My mind goes to the family photo, framed and wrapped and at the bottom of my gym bag waiting for me to get up the nerve to give it to Ian. I keep thinking about his mom and what she didn't want for him. I know that it wasn't fair of her, but she didn't want to burden him with something he couldn't control. I don't want that for him, either. And if there's a chance that what's developing between us is more than physical for him, too, then telling him about my un-diagnosis will do exactly that.

That goes for everyone else I've invited into my "break" life. It's not just that I don't want them to see me as broken. I hate keeping this from them, but I'd hate it more if it weighed on them. If I could go back and spare Heather and Mark and my parents, I would. It's hell knowing that the people I care about are worrying about me.

For anything with Ian to play out in real life, I'd have to let him in on this. It would weigh on him the same, impotent way. I refuse to do that.

Mark grins, wicked enough to pull me from my turbulent thoughts. "Twenty bucks says you don't make it a week before you break."

"Prepare to pony up, friend," I say, and reach for the remote. "I am a pillar of restraint."

24

I AM A WEAK, weak woman.

I haven't *broken*, thank you, but halfway through my work-week there are cracks in my resolve.

I can recall every time he's touched me since Saturday. Monday, when his fingers brushed mine when he handed me a cup of coffee, and when his knee bumped me beneath the table when we sat down for lunch, we just…stayed put. Neither of us commented or made any effort to move, and we maintained the contact for the duration of the meal. I swear, I could feel the pressure of his knee against my thigh for hours after.

Tuesday almost broke me. He had me model an assisted lat stretch, where I hung on to the rig while he pushed me from behind. His hands pressed below my shoulder blades, sending me up and out, releasing tension across my chest and shoulders while inspiring a whole other kind of pressure below my waistline. When I dropped from the bar, my legs about gave out.

There's been no touching today, but I'm facing another challenge. He's programmed deadlifting. A brutish, grunt-heavy lift no one, not even Alistair, can perform without some degree of unflattering facial contortions. I'd hoped that Ian would do me the courtesy of providing a hint of grotesque when he lifted during the nine forty-five class, but nope. Just steel-eyed determination as he ground through a set of five at 80 percent of his own max, in lieu of the day's prescribed PR attempt, punctuated with guttural cries that had my toes curling.

Now, as I watch his deadlift demonstration in my own class, the relatively light weight he's using means there's no opportunity for weird faces, and his no-nonsense breakdown of the movement has inflamed my competence hard-on. Then, there's what the mechanics of the deadlift require of him physically. Tiny shifts, muscles rising and falling with each adjustment to his form. His shirt is so fitted that when he braces, I can see the muscle high on the outside of his ribs ripple like a cluster of pebbles.

He insists—literally—that we observe the engagement of his glutes as he initiates the lift. He stands, bar in hand, and those glutes I've been instructed to watch grab at the seam bisecting the seat of his shorts, closing around the line to create a perfect outline of the individual cheeks. My brain volunteers a little Cookie Monster *om-nom-nom!* at the sight. Because not only am I a nauseatingly horny wretch, but I have the humor of a six-year-old.

"Any questions?" he asks. Or repeats? Who knows; I'm thinking about some *om-nom-nom* of my own and how gladly I'd take a bite of that firm tush. Just a playful nibble! Maybe give it a little smack...

"Hayes! You gonna load up that bar?"

"On it!" I call back, coming to and realizing that I am the only attendee not retrieving plates. I scurry off for some fifteens. The warm-up rounds are easy enough, and I do the prescribed larger number of lifts with lower weights before cutting back on my reps as the load creeps up.

Ian catches me midlift and tells me, "Chin down. Not too much, just enough to have your neck in a neutral spine alignment."

I make the adjustment and am rewarded with a warm finger at the base of my skull, tracing down my spine to the collar of my tank top.

"That's what you want," he continues, like he hasn't just created a channel of heat that's set fire to my entire central nervous system. "A long, straight line."

I nod, a quick jerk of my chin, and rise, my posterior chain grabbing for the back of my own shorts. I reverse the bar path and reset, lifting again, and wondering, without looking or interrupting my set, if Ian is in a spot to appreciate the active engagement of *my* backside.

"Nicely done," he says, and moves on to Russ in the row ahead of me.

I unclip the collar on each side of the bar, sliding on another five-pound plate to each end. I'm not even doing math anymore. I know I'm close to the record I established when I started, but Grant assured me earlier that with the work I've been putting in, I'll blow past that today.

The next lift is a breeze. I switch out the five-pound plates for tens, and lift on autopilot as my mind continues down a very different track.

What if I'm reading all of this wrong? My stomach flops, and I lower the bar to the floor with a scowl. What if he isn't interested beyond casual, consensual, workplace flirtation, and I'm the horned-up weirdo who is imagining Cookie Monster *om-nom-noms* on this poor man's backside?

OH GOD, HE'S BACK!

I'm squatting beside my bar, sliding on another ten pounds, as he pauses to look over the plates I've loaded. Instead of tabulating the weight myself, I watch him do the math. His brows rise, and he presses his lower lip out approvingly. "Is this close to your last PR?"

No idea. I'm just doing my best not to let my attention drift to his crotch, which is currently at my eye level. "Yup!"

He smiles. "Still feeling strong?"

"Yup!"

"Great! I'll let you get back to it."

I stand and return to the bar. Focus, Ellie. No thoughts of nibbles or crotches or—holy hell, how is my blood still on fire from his finger? That was, like, what? Ten minutes ago? How long have I been lifting?

I grip the bar, ring and pinky fingers firmly on the rough section for grip, and rise.

The right side of my body flashes with heat. My head spins.

No!

The bar falls from my hands, the plates hitting the floor with a thud loud enough to hear over the bass throbbing from the speakers.

I gasp.

My vision has gone spotty, and the ground is uneven, rolling beneath me like a goddamn funhouse. I can't trust myself to stay standing.

I drop to a crouch and grab my bar for balance. Dr. Hartman's list of possible symptoms rifles through my mind. My eye, tingling in my limbs…sudden dizziness.

Panic rises in my chest, so fast and sudden, it closes up my throat. This is it. It has to be. This is the second nerve attack.

A whimper crawls up my still tight throat, and I force it down. I have to get out of here. The hysteria is bubbling beneath the surface, and I'm not about to fall apart in front of everyone in the class. Especially not—

Ian's head swivels in my direction.

I turn away. I keep hold of my bar, hoping it looks like I'm trying to keep it from rolling toward Russ, who's grunting through his own lift, but out of the corner of my eye, I see Ian heading toward me. He's not making a scene, but if he gets to me in this state, *I* sure as shit will. I have to get off the floor.

I rise unsteadily and keep my head down as I beeline for the supply room. I left it unlocked when I started the laundry, and it's a safer call than waiting it out in the locker room, which will be full of members when class wraps up. I step in, close the door, and lean against it, not bothering to turn on the light.

The right side of my face still tingles, like I've put some weird chemical peel on it, and my heart rate is sky high. But I don't cry. Which surprises me. I'd have figured that when this caught up with me, I'd finally have that emotional collapse I fought against the last few weeks.

Instead, my body shakes, rocking with full-body convulsions I make no effort to combat. I try to make a list, but the only thing I come up with is to call my neurologist. Every other to-do spins out from there.

In the gym, more weights hit the floor as athletes reach their limits. Someone rings the PR bell. Had I PR'd? Does it matter?

A broken sob pulls free from my throat. *It isn't fair!* I've only just found this new, powerful thing my body is capable of. I hadn't known I had it in me, and there's so much more I want to do. It's taking me four pulls to get to the top of the rope; I want to be able to do it in three.

My eyes sting, but still, no tears. I just shake.

So much for *while I can.*

25

I'M SITTING ON THE FLOOR, my back against the door, when there's a knock. "Ellie?"

It's Ian.

The dizziness has subsided, and the shaking has reduced to the occasional shudder, but it still takes enormous effort to force out a faux-casual "Oh, hey."

"What happened?" he asks though the door.

I sigh. I have no idea what I'm going to say to him, but what else is new? I get to my feet, taking some comfort in the fact that the movement is only accompanied by run-of-the-mill head rush, and pull open the door. I have to step back to keep from bumping straight into Ian. His gray eyes stare down at me intently, a concerned tug between his brows. I have to take another step back. It's overwhelming, being looked at like that.

I shake my head, still muddled by his expression. "I'm fine."

"*Fine* doesn't send someone to the storage room near tears," he says, voice hard.

I scowl. "You're inconveniently perceptive at times, did you know that?"

"Being able to accurately read someone's body language is a critical part of coaching."

That is a very Ian answer. A very *competent* Ian answer. So, while I'm still wading through my lingering panic, I can't ignore that I'm feeling a *touch* more appreciation for his knowledgeability than is appropriate, given the scenario. But it carries me above the fear, so I lean into my competence boner like a kickstand.

Which is a *really* gross visual.

I grit my teeth. I could fess up. *Should* fess up. Tell him about my eye and the possible MS and what this episode probably means for me, but I'm not ready to let go of the version of me I get to be here. I don't think I'll ever be. But I don't want to lie, either, so I go with the simplest version of the truth. "I got dizzy."

"Dizzy," he says, flatly.

"I thought I was going to black out. I haven't experienced anything like that before, and I didn't want to keel over in front of everyone, so I bailed. It scared me," I say, garnishing with specificity.

Ian nods slowly, seeming to take this in. "That was a high weight for you, right? You were close to hitting your PR?"

"Yeah." I shrug; might as well be truthful where I can. "Or maybe I'd already hit it? I wasn't paying attention to how much was on there."

"First, *never* do that. You *have* to stay aware of how much is on the bar every lift, or you're gonna get hurt. As for the dizziness…" He sighs, like my faux pas with the weight has made me unworthy of whatever he plans to say. "It's not uncommon. Especially when you've only been lifting for a short while."

"What?" I gawk at him, my fear suspended by a thread. "The dizziness? That *happens*?"

"If you don't breathe properly before attempting a lift like that, it can."

I continue to stare at him, unwilling to give in to the temptation of relief.

"The dizziness you described was probably because you didn't prep for your lift the right way. You gotta—" He pauses, sucks in an exaggerated breath, and braces, contracting his abdominals enough that he curls forward slightly. So, *so* much shifting among the muscles. "When you initiate a lift that heavy, you have to set yourself up. Which I did make a point of saying when I modeled it."

I frown, thinking back; nope. Nothing but *on-nom-nom*s. "I guess you did?" The larger meaning behind what he's telling me sinks in, and my fear is replaced by a flicker of hope. "So, you think that was it? Just my breathing?"

"As an actual expert, that is my expert opinion." He tips his head toward the gym. "Let's find out."

I frown. "What—now?"

"Your bar is still out there. C'mon." He reaches out a hand, the pink calluses stark against the lines of chalk still dusting his palm.

I stare at his offered hand. I'm afraid of trying and having the dizziness overtake me again. Of having it happen in front of Ian, when I can't deny the severity of the situation, and inevitably break down and tell him what's actually going on.

But…what if it *doesn't* happen?

"Humor me," he says.

I roll my eyes, but the out is a kindness. I take his hand, letting him pull me into the hallway, and he surprises me by releasing my hand to place his on my shoulder as we walk to the gym floor.

My bar sits alone in the corner of the room, near the plyo boxes. Everyone else has cleared out. I wonder if he shooed away any stragglers for my benefit.

"You switched the plates," I say, registering that the nubbly rubber plates with the weight in pounds have been replaced with the smooth kilogram plates I only ever see the more hardcore athletes use. I don't even know how many kilos are on the bar, not that I'd able to convert it anyway. It's what, 2.3 pounds to a kilo? Or…something?

"I don't want you thinking about the weight right now. It'll get you too in your head." He brushes his thumb over my shoulder, which does more to wave away my thoughts about metric conversions than logic ever could.

"You said I'm supposed to stay aware of the weight at all times."

"Unless *I've* set up the bar. Obviously."

"*Obviously*," I snark, but my heart's not in it. His hand's still on me.

"Just follow the motions."

I hesitate, and Ian gives my shoulder a squeeze. "I'll talk you through it. We've got this." He slides his hand to the center of my back, encouraging me toward the bar, and I step forward. "Get in close, bar over your shoelaces," he says, using the same instruction as he had in class, and I follow along. "Bend your knees, butt back like you're trying to find a chair. Good—down more," he amends, and I adjust. "Look about eighteen inches ahead of your toes. Now, brace, but only lift enough to take the slack out of the bar. You'll hear it."

I do, and the barbell clings against the metal ring at the center of each weight plate.

"Nice. Relax," he says, and I stand. "Shake it out a little." When I don't move, he eyes me. "Shake it out," he repeats, with the lilting reprimand of someone telling a dog to "drop it."

I screw up my face and shimmy, letting my arms flop.

"*Brat*. Back to the bar."

Smirking, I resume my earlier stance, feet shoulder-distance apart, and peer over to make sure the bows of my shoelaces aren't visible. "All right, I'm good."

"Now, really brace. Engage your lats. There should be more tension here." He places a hand at my side, just below the band of my sports bra. I tense at the contact. "Good." He removes his hand from me, then there's a touch on my spine. "Try to pinch my finger with your shoulder blades," he directs. I pull my shoulders back as far as I can, and I feel them graze his finger before he withdraws it.

"Now roll them down—imagine you're tucking your shoulder blades into your pockets."

"Weird," I say, just to feel like I've contributed, but I make the adjustment, feeling more muscles engage.

"Breathe"—I do—"brace"—I do—"take out the slack"—that, too—"and *go*!"

I feel every muscle engage, pressing the ground away as much as lifting myself to stand. I'm at the top of the lift before I even realize it.

"Good. Bring the bar back to the floor."

I reverse the steps, and the plates hit the floor with a dull thud.

"Let's add weight." He nods to the ten-pound plates on the floor by my bar.

"That's a twenty pound jump on top of whatever you already had on there," I point out.

"You've got it."

"If I fall over, it's your fault."

"Hayes, I can bench two of you. If you fall over, I can deal. Put. Them. *On.*"

Every word is a command. And damn it all, I want to do it. Whether to please him or in spite of him, or, perhaps, in response to the jolt my libido had given at his direct tone, but he's thrown down the gauntlet, dammit; I'm going to pick it up.

Also…he can bench two of me? Can we test that?

Once the bar is loaded, Ian nods, then clears his throat. "Approach. Brace. Slack. Lift."

I follow the steps one by one. It's tougher going this time—I'm feeling every one of those additional twenty pounds—but then, I'm at the top of the lift.

"Bring it back down," he says, with all the enthusiasm of someone reading off stereo instructions.

The weights clatter to the floor.

"Dizzy?" Ian asks, voice quiet.

It takes me a moment to make sense of the question. Then— "No?"

"You just PR'd by thirty pounds, Ellie."

I gasp. "It was that heavy?"

"You probably could have done more, based on your form—"

"I didn't get dizzy! I'm fine." Relief ricochets around my torso, bouncing off the walls of my rib cage. "You were right!" I jump at him for a hug, and he catches me easily. He holds me as I crush my arms around him, my anxiety and terror fleeing my system, replaced by giddy relief. He squeezes me to his chest, pressing a shuddering breath out of me. "Oh, my God. I'm okay."

"You're okay."

I nod into his shoulder. Tears sting my eyes. I hadn't realized how scared I was until I didn't have to be anymore. I sigh. I'm okay.

"I'm okay," I repeat aloud. The words replay in my mind on a loop. *I'm okay, I'm okay, I'm okay!*

"And you PR'd," he adds, like it's anywhere in my awareness.

I barely have the breath to let out my laugh. "You tricked me with the metric system."

"And it worked. Do—" He clears his throat. "Do you need a second?"

I nod again.

"Should I leave you alone?" His hold on me loosens almost imperceptibly, and I tighten my grip on him on instinct.

I shake my head side to side, still pressed to his chest. "Stay? Please."

"Okay."

No hesitation. He's here. Staying.

He cares.

"Thank you," I say.

His head lowers to rest against mine. "Happy to." His cinnamon-spice breath brushes the side of my neck like his lips did on Saturday night, the movement sparking across my skin.

Once again, I rack my brain for any details about the night we met. I hate that my recall is so hazy. The first new lips and hands I'd experienced in years, and so much of it has been lost in a Dionysian fog. I'm sure my own performance is best left buried, but to know what his hands are capable of in that context would be something.

His head drops to my bare shoulder, and his next exhalation rustles the fine hair on the back of my neck, setting off a new wave of tingles. I arch against him in response, the movement involuntary, but undeniable. His hold on me tightens.

Desire lashes through me. This feels inevitable.

"Should I let go?" he asks.

I shake my head again.

"Ellie." His voice is thick. "I think I should let go."

"I'm feeling greedy."

His laugh is a breath. There's something empowering about that, reducing a man of his size to a breathy half laugh. "Me, too."

Any relief I'd feel at the confirmation that we're on the same page is overwhelmed by the new peak in arousal it gives me. We're in sync there, too; pressed this close, I am keenly aware of a distinct hardness against my abdomen. Holy. *Hell.*

I consider pressing my hip against that hard heat. It would not be fair of me. Nor would it be professional. But we've agreed that we're being greedy, and I'm off the clock…

I commit to the hip press. The responding throb at the point of contact is immediate.

"Ellie," he rasps. My name is a plea.

I angle my head to look up at him, keeping my cheek firmly against his chest. His heartbeat thunders in my ear. Even at this awkward, low angle, the want in his gray eyes is clear.

His lips had been so soft that night. That I do remember. And I'd told him as much, tracing the fullness of his lower lip with the nail of my index finger before his mouth claimed mine. I hadn't even had time to move my hand out of the way, the pressure of our lips briefly trapping my finger between them.

"Tell me to stop," he pleads, but he's rocked against my hip. Whether he's conscious of the movement or not, the heat of him hardly makes his request compelling.

"You first," I say, watching his lips. I untangle an arm from my hold around him, sliding my hand up his chest, his neck, tracing his jawline. I let the nail of my index finger glance off the cleft of his chin, then press against the fullness of his lower lip. "I want to remember this time."

And just like that night in the bathroom, I barely have time to move my finger out of the way before his lips crush to mine.

I have zero control over myself. It's like the contact has invoked the muscle memory of that weeks-ago drunken scramble. I'm all impulse and need as I cling to his shoulders, hauling myself against him just as fiercely as he holds me, bracing a forearm between my shoulders and his other hand around my waist as we kiss.

I hike up a leg to finally realize my vision of climbing Mount Ian, and he is right there with me, shifting his hold to my rear and supporting my weight so things like "standing" and "maintaining my balance" won't interfere with my ascent. He's walking, wearing me, until I'm backed onto a hard surface—the plyo boxes? Don't know, don't care, because what it means is that his hands are free to roam, and so are mine.

I draw on his upper lip. He lets out a low sound, and the hand at my back goes to grip my shoulder, then moves to cradle my neck, his thumb kneading my jawline. I shiver, digging my fingers into the muscles of his shoulders.

Ian breaks our kiss, nudging my head back to kiss my throat as

I gasp for air. His lips trek to the low neckline of my shirt, setting fire to the skin as his hands work under my tank, fingers siding beneath the back of my bra band. He grips my shoulder blades before easing to my rib cage, holding me in place as he kisses his way to the center of my chest. I gasp.

And keep gasping.

The breath stretches on, and to my horror, my mouth opens wider. I turn my head away as I receive the largest, most inopportune yawn ever to be drawn into my body.

"No!" I cry, barely able to form the word around my still over-wide mouth. I hurry to cover it with a hand, but Ian's leaned back, still holding my sides as he laughs. My eyes water. "I'm sorry! I'm just not breathing enough? Or, I dunno. That freak-out kind of took it out of me."

"It's fine, Hayes," he says, and gives me another quick peck that I lean into to turn into more. The tip of his tongue teases the corners of my mouth, and I pull him close, hands under his shirt, relishing the heat of his skin against my palms—

My jaw tightens in warning of another yawn.

I try to stifle it, but Ian laughs against me. He breaks the kiss to nuzzle against my still-quaking jaw. "It's okay. I think your body is trying to tell you something."

"My body is telling me many things that are more interesting than yawning," I grumble, still fighting to keep the yawn contained. It happens anyway. Ian chuckles against me, the puffs of his exhalations grazing the sensitive skin along my throat.

He brings his hands from under my clothing, resuming his hold at my waist. He presses a kiss to my neck, then meets my eyes. "I think it's time for a nap."

26

I'M FAIRLY CERTAIN I'M HAVING an out-of-body experience, because a moment later, I'm in the stairwell to Ian's apartment. He opens the door ahead of me and steps back to let me pass.

I stay where I am, seized by the sudden awareness that this is
actually happening. "Are you sure? Aren't you afraid I'll try to
alphabetize your books?" I waggle my fingers at him with car-
toonish menace. "Rearrange your closet by color?"

"With those nails, that's actually kind of threatening." He tips
his head, encouraging me forward. "Generous of you to assume I
have books, though."

I laugh but stay put.

Ian must realize that I'm incapacitated, because he smiles,
coming down a few steps on the stairs. He stands two below me,
so that I'm slightly above him. "You okay?"

"I have...concerns."

He leans against the railing. "Let's hear 'em."

"I'm afraid that if I go in there and it's anything like the

Dawghouse was when I moved it, it will totally smother the crush I have on you."

His face lights up so completely at this, I can't be embarrassed at the overshare. "You have a crush on me?"

"*Obviously.* And whatever. You're crushing on me, too."

"True." He leans closer, his face distractingly close. "Full disclosure? There's a drawer open in my dresser," he stage-whispers. "I was just trying to figure out how to get in there and close it without you noticing. But I *did* make the bed—"

"That's my other concern! If you're secretly a pillar of organization, I don't know that I'll be able to stop from throwing myself onto this meticulously made bed of yours in surrender." I press out my lower lip, beseeching. "I'm only human."

"Hmm." The thoughtful sounds rumbles the space between us. He studies my lips, then seems to remember that we've broken the seal on kissing, because he smiles, half shy, half wicked, and plants one on me.

His lips a fraction of an inch from mine, he says, "Tell you what." Another brush of lips. "We're going to go inside."

"Mm-hmm," I say, eyes closed.

He kisses the corner of my mouth. "You're going to look around, take it in." His lips trail along my jaw, and I fumble for the railing with one hand, fingernails digging into the wood as I shiver. "Probably judge me for my books."

"Nonfiction?" I say, breathless.

"With the exception of Tolkien?" He nuzzles the hollow of my throat. "Almost exclusively."

My hands make their way to his chest, sliding to his shoulders.

"Shame." I flutter my eyelids open to find him smiling up at me. "At least you're pretty."

He laughs. "And then we're going to nap."

I knead the muscle of his shoulders, grounding myself in the heat of him. "You really think we'll get in a bed and *nap*?"

"*On* the bed. I'm not making it a second time today. And you were the one yawning in my face earlier," he reminds me. "We'll nap, and then, if we have the time, since we've been standing here forever, we will explore one another's bodies until I have to go down and coach."

Holy shit, that was decisive. So much so that it completely derails my anxiety. I nod.

"Excellent. Now, ladies first."

I turn and ascend the last few steps, Ian behind me. Inside, I find a bright studio apartment. *Very* bright; the windows and skylights let in so much sunshine that he doesn't even have to turn on a light as we move through the room that I am already committing to memory. To the left of the door, there's an L-shaped kitchenette with a farmhouse-style sink—unexpected—and a metal prep table. The fridge is a smaller version of the one downstairs, with a sliding door, like in a convenience store. The whole thing is just discordant enough to work.

I point at the fridge, which has a different energy drink logo emblazoned across the top than the lobby's. "Were you two-timing a sponsor?"

"They tried to get me, but this one tastes like someone ground a multivitamin into a La Croix. I couldn't have my name associated with something I couldn't bring myself to consume."

Hot. "You kept the fridge?"

"They never asked for it back."

"How do you do that?" I ask. "On the one hand, you kind of scammed your way to a free fridge, but on the other, you did so with a balance of personal integrity and dumb ol' practicality. That's hot, Ian. Like everything you do." I sigh. "It's so annoying."

His laugh is a surprised bark. I turn away, under the guise of studying the room. Unfiltered honesty is really working for me. Speak first, worry later. How Dawghouse!

I continue my inventory. Vaulted ceiling, exposed beams, so, *so* many places to hang plants. A bookshelf with a surprising number of good-sized hardcovers, though I force myself not to scan the titles. Past the kitchen is a living space with a tan leather couch and a flat-screen TV, as well as a coffee table. I wonder if the furniture had been purchased before or after his time with the guys.

I take in the bedroom area, dominated by a king-sized bed replete with a bed frame. The top drawer of his dresser is open, like he said, but otherwise, the space is neat as a pin.

He stands at the foot of the bed, arms crossed over his chest, "So?"

I mimic his stance. "So, what?"

He reaches for me, pulling me against him, and I wrap my arms around his neck. "Are you crawling out of your skin?"

"Are you going to show me the bathroom?"

"Absolutely not."

"Then—and be honest—do you keep your toothbrush in the shower?"

He half smiles. "It's *efficient*."

I cringe, fighting a shudder that's only partially for show. Ian laughs.

"It's on the *soap dish*," he continues, running his hands up and down my sides. "The toothpaste, too."

I shake my head, but it's at myself, not him. A shower toothbrush has never been a deal-breaker, but seeing one puts me on guard. At least it always has before. But not now.

Ian wiggles his brows, delighting in my torment.

This man.

I sigh. "You *really* want to nap?"

In answer, he grins, and tumbles back onto the bed, bringing me down with him.

I guess so.

I wake up swaddled in Man Mountain. He is a living weighted blanket, his heavy arm over me, forearm wedged between my boobs, his hand tucked beneath my cheek. I make an exploratory attempt to roll away, and his hold tightens, the flex of his arm securing me to him again. He grunts and nuzzles into my neck.

It's decided. I'll stay here forever.

As my body settles into its new residence, my mind reels with the impossibility of my morning. The dizzy spell. Ian's one-on-one lifting lesson. Our literal one-on-one. The fact that at this exact moment, I am on his bed, draped in his exceptional form, which was, not long ago, expressing base intentions toward my very receptive self.

He shifts, and the hand at my cheek drifts down my sternum, halting when he gets to my left breast. I stop breathing. Another grunt. This one...*curious.* A gentle squeeze, and my body reacts, arching against hand and hips encouragingly. His hips press against me in response, and there's no missing the rigid heat making contact with my rear. Oh, *my*.

Behind me, Ian's breathing maintains the steady rhythm of sleep. His hand continues to knead, and heat gathers low in my belly. His thumb brushes my nipple, and the intimate contact has me gasping. Good *Lord* I'm starved for this. Semiconscious groping through a sports bra and tank has me writhing like a cat in heat.

A mechanical vibration picks up on the bed, and I freeze. Ian's arm shifts below the pillow we share, and I watch him thumb the screen of his phone to silence the alarm. He lets out a snuffling sound, resuming his massage of my breast—

His hand stops mid-squeeze.

I laugh. "How's that boob treating you?"

"Oh, my God," he breathes. He releases my breast slowly, giving it an apologetic double pat. "I'm so sorry."

"You sure?" I shift my backside against the absolutely raging erection nestled against me. "This doesn't feel like *sorry*."

He groans, backing off just enough to separate from my tush. "It was a really good nap!"

"You don't say?" I roll over to face him. His expression is appropriately abashed, chin tucked and eyes wide. But he's trying not to smile.

"It's a really good boob, too," he says, losing his fight and grinning. "Since you asked."

"Thank you. We were enjoying your attention."

For a few heartbeats, we stay on our sides, watching one another. I wonder how much time we have before he has to coach. But I can't seem to look away from him long enough to check my watch.

Deciding that the activities of the past however long it has been means we're open to casual intimate contact, I press a hand to his chest. He holds it against him, taking in a long breath and exhaling slowly, eyes still locked on mine. His heartbeat is steady, but each throb punches against my palm.

My voice is thick as I say, "Hi, there."

"Hi. You sleep like the dead."

"Anything worth doing is worth doing right."

His brow arches, and his hand releases mine, closing over my hip, his thumb pressing meaningfully. I arch into the contact. "Is that so?"

"It's kind of my thing."

"Ah. Good point," he says, and tugs me closer. I drape a leg over his side, and he grabs onto it, hand smoothing up the length of my thigh to the leg of my shorts.

A faint twinge of anxiety goes off in my chest. As much as I'd like to linger in this lazy, sexy limbo, I'm too much Regular Life Ellie to tolerate its ambiguity. "What are we doing?"

He laughs. "Hayes, I swear, if you're trying to label this out of some kind of need for control—"

"I need parameters! I'm not in a good decision-making period." I squeeze my leg over his hip in emphasis, but it undermines my point; hugging onto him in any capacity feels like a really good call.

The hand on my thigh maneuvers to my rear. I was right. Excellent choice on my part.

"How 'bout we talk changes to our workplace dynamic?" I offer. "Or at least some discussion of discretion? Because I'm pretty sure that the flaunting of a physical relationship in the business place counts as harassment."

"You plan to flaunt this?" He sounds surprised.

"I'd be happy to, but I'm pretty set on a 'no grab-ass in the gym' rule. But there might be some slipups on my part," I admit, and tighten my hold over his hip.

"I didn't think you'd dispense with the physical stuff so freely."

"You—" I smile. "You thought about what I'd be like in this scenario?"

"*Here*, sure." His smile is wry. "But never *napping*."

"Ah! So you thought I'd dispense with sex freely enough, but not snuggling?"

"I don't think there's a safe way for me to answer that question."

I laugh. "At least there is no power dynamic to worry about. You are *technically* my boss, but I can't say that I consider you an authority figure."

"Ouch."

"You're still an authority on many things, which is very sexy," I assure him. Using the leg I have hooked over his hip, I lever myself onto his waist, nudging him to his back. He grips the backs of my thighs.

He cups my butt. "How does the 'no grab-ass' policy apply to surfaces around the facility?"

I open my mouth, a comment about workplace safety and cleanliness standards at the ready, and he silences me with a finger to my parted lips.

"Before you get in some smartass line, it's not just that. I want—"

I widen my mouth just enough to get hold of the tip of his index finger with my teeth, then close my lips around it. His eyes are huge as I suck on it, three languid draws, and a solitary press of my teeth before releasing his finger. It hovers in the space between us, and I press a quick peck to it in fond farewell.

He's staring at his finger as though he's never seen it before.

Then he grabs me.

In a flash, I'm on my back, pressed into the mattress, fully caged by his body. The sudden increased vulnerability sends alarm streaking through me, but it's expended just as quickly. This is *Ian*, the man who cried at *Inside Out*.

I grab on to his shoulders, savoring the feel of the sheer bulk of muscle beneath my palms. "Don't you have to work soon?"

His nod is distant as his heated gaze roams my face. The weight of him feels so good. I am again aware of a very specific warmth pressing against my thigh, and I'm reminded of how quickly the good feeling can turn into pain. My whole body fights a shudder.

"You okay?" he asks.

I grip his shoulders, again, hoping to ground myself. *Unfiltered honesty.* Or…some degree of honesty. "I should warn you about sex. With me," I blurt. "It can hurt. *Me.*"

His brows draw down.

"I have endometriosis. And sex can be painful." I laugh at the oversimplification. "*Existing* can be painful."

"What does that mean?" His voice is heavy with concern, and my anxiety flares; that could be for me or for his own gratification. But he lowers himself to lie beside me again, gently pressing a hand to the side of my face. He brushes his thumb over my cheekbone.

"Do you know what the condition is?"

"Not really."

"It's when the tissue that normally lines the uterus develops outside of the uterus. It can be on ovaries, fallopian tubes, intestines…" I grimace. "This isn't ideal pillow talk."

Another brush of his thumb. "This is about your body. And I

have both professional and *un*professional interest in your body's well-being," he says, which is disarmingly flattering.

"Each cycle, the tissue builds up and breaks down like it would if it were in my uterus—"

"Menstruation," he says, matter-of-factly.

"Yes. But when the extra tissue does it, there's bleeding inside of my pelvis. And that results in inflammation, swelling, and scarring of the normal tissue."

The tug of worry between Ian's eyebrows is as deep as I've ever seen it.

"The pain is only ever *bad* bad around ovulation. Day-to-day, it's kind of a dull ache? And I'm used to that—

"You're *used to it?*" He cringes. "Jesus. Are you in pain all the time?"

I shake my head. "I get a pain-free window of seven to ten days, from when my period stops until I ovulate." This does nothing to relax his face. "Other times, it's an uncomfortable pressure or a twinge of *blinding* pain. But when I have sex, depending on where I am in my cycle, or how shitty my body wants to be that day, or—" I sigh. "The whim of whatever fertility goddess I angered in a past life…"

Ian almost smiles at this, but the worry still mars his forehead.

"It can hurt. A lot." Unexpected emotion makes the words come out thick.

Ian smooths his hand over my cheek. "I'm sorry. That you experience any of this." His eyes widen. "Oh, shit. Are you in pain right now? Just, in general? Cycle-wise?"

"It's a dull ache kind of day. But…" I wince, dreading what I'm going to have admit. "Based on my calendar and some uncomfortable flares, it's pretty likely I'll be down for the count soon. I'm sorr—"

"Don't you finish that," he warns. "That is not something you apologize for."

It absolutely is something I apologize for, but I nod. "I only ask that you not treat me any differently, now that you know. That's been the pattern of things for me since I started experiencing symptoms," I say, skirting the rejection that's also part of that pattern, as well as the crippling panic spiral that can hijack intimate encounters; that's just a me problem. "It's been a nice change, not having people asking after me, wanting me to take it easy—"

"Oh, no. I'm not going to lay off you at all. Your snatches are still terrible."

I smile. "They are!"

"Okay. So…just tell me how you're feeling," he says with finality.

I let out a laugh. What a Dawghouse answer. Like it could *ever* be that easy. But for the sake of optimism, I nod.

"For now…" His hand trails up my thigh, over my ass to grab my waist, pulling me closer. "We have seven minutes. How would you—"

"I want you to take your shirt off, and then I want to put my hands all over your bare chest. Please. And feel, um—" I gesture toward his sides. "Whatever the muscles are high on the outsides of your ribs? Please," I repeat, and silently pray that this burst of unfiltered honesty wasn't a total mood-killer, because that was belligerent.

He kisses me hard. "Hayes," he says against my lips, and I wonder if I can change my answer or at least amend it to include more of this, because this is bliss. "It would be my pleasure."

27

I LOOK AT MY REFLECTION, the light catching gold thread in my navy bra and panties. In the light of the otherwise oppressive bulbs of my bathroom vanity, the set is as substantive as a heavy mist. *Exactly* what I was going for.

As if in response, my abdomen cramps brutally.

I sigh. I hate being right.

The pain flares started in earnest a few hours after Thursday's interlude with Ian, at an intensity that suggested they were making up for the relatively gentle cycle I experienced last month. I didn't even end up working out yesterday, though now I wonder if I should have given it a shot. I rallied for today's endurance class, and the external, objectively optional discomfort of the workout was at least a distraction from the pain that I had zero influence over, so…silver lining?

I uncap the ibuprofen on the edge of the sink, dry-swallowing two of the pills, then bend over to drink straight from the tap. Straightening, I give myself a few moments to admire the new lingerie. The package had been waiting on the doorstep when I got home from Firehouse. I figured I could at least find out if it looks good before putting it away until it can be of use.

I turn to the side and smirk. It does look *good*. And it sure as hell is going to be put to good use.

Eventually.

Outside of a few stolen moments between classes, Ian and I haven't had much time to enjoy one another. Seth, the evening coach, called out sick Thursday afternoon, leaving Ian to cover the p.m. classes, and a personal training client rescheduled his session to coincide with what should have been yesterday's nap time. Between our respective shifts at the gym and last-minute, time-sensitive responsibilities—a client in Tempe, Arizona, had to fill in for a summer school session and suddenly needed revised rubrics before the weekend—evenings haven't worked out. And while we are independent adults with our own personal living quarters, I haven't mustered the courage to propose a sleepover. Because I am a coward.

And now that the cramps have started—

Pain grips my abdomen, barbed wire snagging on something deep in my pelvis, and my grip on the sink goes white knuckle. I count my breaths, the searing pain lasting one…two…three cycles, fading to a dull ache by the fourth breath. When I catch my reflection this time, the sudden beading of sweat out-glistens the sparkly bra.

One more jagged inhale, and the ache is more manageable but still not something I can ignore. I wipe at the sweat on my brow, tears of frustration and pain welling in my eyes. It isn't fair! I have someone I actually want to be physical with, even if I'm secretly terrified of the prospect. And dammit, my boobs look great in this bra!

It's with a chest full of self-pity that I wail, "What a fucking waste!"

"Ellie?" Ian's voice is sharp, and the floor vibrates with rapid footsteps.

Shit! I turn and scramble for my robe on the back of the door. Before I can grab it, the half-open door swings open. I jump back, barely avoiding getting hit.

Ian halts in the doorway. "Oh, sorry! Are you okay? The door was open, and I heard…" His eyebrows go high as he realizes what I'm—or am *not*—wearing. "This a bad time?"

I shake my head, going for casual, but disappointment weighs on my chest. This is about to get really awkward. "No! I'm okay. Sorry. I was going to get my robe."

"Why would you be sorry?" he asks, taking a slow perusal of my scantily clad form. A libidinous smile pulls at the corners of his mouth, and I'm keenly aware of the negligible opacity of my bra and panties. The heat in his expression is a lure and a warning, my responding desire forcing me still, wanting him to look, while the prey animal in me freezes at the threat of danger. Not of *him*, not rationally, but of what so often accompanies a scenario like this. Pain. Rejection—

"You look amazing," he says, his voice thick.

I smile at the compliment. But reality brings me back to earth quickly. "I'm…" My brain provides the euphemism Cole used to use. "Out of commission."

Ian frowns, and I imagine he's parsing through my phrasing. After a second, his eyes go wide, and his gaze drops to my abdomen. Instead of changing the subject or, Cole's go-to, leaving the room entirely, he steps into the bathroom with me, closing the distance between us. My protest builds in my throat, but before I can voice it, he makes a sympathetic sound, placing one of his broad hands below my belly button. My relief is immediate; the man is a human heating pad.

"I'm sorry." He kisses my forehead. "You need anything?"

The consideration is a balm. No hesitation, no discomfort, just sweetness. "No. But thank you. I can…" I point toward the door and my robe, fumbling for words again. "I can cover up."

He frowns, pulling his hand away. "Why? Oh! Are you cold?"

Cold? In June? In *Texas?* But I take a cursory look down my front and have to concede; physical evidence would suggest a chill.

I bite the bullet. "Cole would get frustrated when I'd have a flare-up. When he'd see me like this, but we couldn't have sex."

Ian scowls. "What, like an animal?"

"I—" I never thought about it that way. "I guess?"

Disgust mars his handsome features. "Ellie, that's fucked-up. You look incredible, but it's not like I can't just appreciate the view." His expression lightens. "As long as you don't mind me appreciating it. You look…different."

"Different?"

"Some of it is what you're in. No tape this time, more…*you*. But your body's changed in the past few weeks."

He watches me for a second, chewing in his lower lip in thought. "Here, face that way." He points to the mirror over the sink. When I continue to stare at him in confusion, he leans closer, crowding me, and growls, "I've picked up that you're into the authoritative thing, but don't make me tell you twice."

My heart leaps at the sudden shift to Commanding Ian tone, and I suck in an involuntary breath of surprise.

He kisses my temple. "Seriously. Please don't make me tell you again," he says, his voice normal. "Because I can't think of a follow-up."

I bite back a smile and nod, moving toward the sink. Behind me, Ian closes and then locks the bathroom door. The sound of the bolt driving home makes me flinch, but I force my features to relax as he makes his way back to me. His arms wrap around my torso, and I back-burner my panic as the expanse of him scorches into me.

"As I was saying, there's more definition now. I have no memory of your serratus anterior"—he traces a finger along the muscle visible below my bra band, toward my ribs—"on the night we met. Though that might have been covered by the tape."

I shiver at the contact, swallowing hard as his hand makes a languid pass down my side. A low sound escapes me, and he does it again, eliciting the same response.

"There wasn't as much definition in your tone then, but your back..." He places his hands flat against my shoulder blades. "Your teres minor"—his thumbs run over a muscle high on my back—"and teres major—" He shifts to trace above the band of my bra, almost under my arms, the touch sparking across my skin. "Those were memorable.

"Your lats," he continues, sliding down from my bra to the waistband of my panties, "weren't as pronounced then." His hands move lower and freely massage my backside. "And your gluteus maximus," he says, dreamily. "I think it's higher now."

"I'll trust you on that." I'm starting to feel lightheaded. "It was a particular favorite of yours that night."

Ian nods, but the movement transitions to a shake. "Not just that night." He gives my ass a double-handed squeeze, then releases me to take hold of my hips, closing the space between us. The length of his erection presses against the channel of my spine.

Despite the confidence reinforced by every interaction I've had with this man, a swell of fear rises in my chest. Stress about *his* desire, *his* needs, my guilt, my pain—

"Ellie." Ian's direct tone has me meeting his eyes in the mirror. "I'd like to try something, if you're okay with it."

I nod, but he doesn't look convinced.

Worry tugs at his brows. "You can always tell me to stop. No..." He halts, changing the angle of his body. The hard heat of him leaves my back, taking with it the bulk of my anticipatory stress. "No pressure."

At his words, the tension gripping my chest releases, like a weight vest falling away. I take in a long breath, like I would for pain abatement, and stare at him.

"Is that what you needed?" he asks softly.

I nod. I didn't know that; how did *he*?

"Ah! I get it." He smiles, like he's proud of himself for solving a riddle. It's so disarming, I smile back.

"As you were?" I encourage and shimmy my shoulders.

His responding grin is feral. "With pleasure." Still maintaining his distance below the belt, he grips my shoulders and pulls me firmly against his chest. "You have more definition here, too, in your deltoids," he continues, and outlines the band of muscle from the back of my upper arms to where they arc toward each bicep. "And there's no missing these Twinkies." Before I can ask what he's talking about, he kisses the muscle between my neck and shoulder, which has grown more pronounced in the past weeks; bra straps have been killer. "You have the most beautiful trapezius," he mutters against my neck.

I giggle, but when he nibbles at the same spot, the sound turns into a whimper. His eyes are intent on my reflection as his hands trace down my sides, resting above my hips.

"Your waist—"

"I don't have a waist," I insist. "I'm built like a thumb."

"No, there's definite tapering between here"—he shifts his hands down to my hips, palms cupping my outer thighs—"and here." He reverses the route, palms moving slowly, emphasizing the slight—but not nonexistent—cinch at my waist.

He catches my eye, and I see a dark glint in his as he continues his upward traverse, his fingertips making a whisper of contact as they breach the center of my bra, barely grazing the inside of my breasts. "Your pectorals have filled out."

"Have they?" I reach around his neck, offering full access, while also emphasizing the swell of flesh over my bra cups. Thrust like this, the bra is practically transparent, my hard nipples obvious through the material.

Ian's approving growl rumbles against my back. He keeps the actual contact limited to the muscle high on my sternum, but the heat of his palms radiates against my breasts with cruel intensity. "I filed down my calluses earlier," he says, and plucks at the cup on the right side. My nipple is so tight, even this slight movement of the delicate fabric over the skin has me arching toward his palm, desperate for contact. "I won't rough up the fabric."

I'm about to ask him to clarify, but then his hands blessedly, mercifully, close on my breasts, and he begins to knead. I can't say anything. My head falls against his chest, and he nuzzles into my neck. We're both watching the movement of his hands.

He releases my left breast to trail his hand down my torso. "External obliques," he notes, mouth against my neck. His hand passes over the slight indentation of muscle in my abdomen. "Rectus abdominus," and lower, just above the waistline of my panties, "Tendinus inscriptions."

Instead of breaching the southern border, his hand trails toward my hip. I watch with hooded eyes as his index finger follows the slight channel that cuts in at an angle above my hip flexor. "The inguinal ligament. Very defined on you. Makes me want to follow them down." He watches the progress of his fingers for a few breaths, tracing down the length of the ligament, then up again, over and over.

He meets my gaze, a question in his eyes.

"Please," I say, breathless.

A growl of assent, and he eases past my waistband. He pulses his fingers against me, pressing and releasing as he makes his way down my pubic mound to cup my sex, his usually warm fingers cool against the relative heat of my opening. He smooths over the slick folds. "Do you think I can finish you like this?" he asks, tugging on my earlobe with his teeth.

Before I can respond, his fingers part me, sliding up to massage my clitoris. My legs threaten to give out.

He abandons my breast, reaching up for my right hand, still clinging to the back of his neck. He breaks my hold, lowering my arm, then tugs my bra strap roughly from my shoulder. My breast is bared, and then his hand is back over it again, massaging my nipple in the same rhythm as the fingers deftly maneuvering around my clit.

"Watch what I'm doing to you, Ellie." He licks up the side of my neck, kissing my jaw. "I won't need to put even a finger inside of you."

My insides clench, the ache inside of me demanding to be filled.

He chuckles. "I felt that. They want something to hold on to."

"*They?*" I pant, the delicious tension in my belly winding tight. "You know the names of so many muscles, but not the ones in the vagina." I catch his eye in the mirror and do my best to scowl. "What an oversight."

He increases his pace. My legs are shaking. His tongue is hot and insistent at my ear, and as I waver on the edge, his wrist presses low on my abdomen—"Bulbospongiosus."

I shatter with a cry wrenched from some primal part of me. I dig my nails into the back of his neck, my other hand gripping his backside, pressing his erection into my lower back as my body pulses its pleasure in spite of not having that thickness where it should be. Somewhere in the haze, I hear Ian emit a grunting roar, stifling the sound against my shoulder. He doesn't relent for a second, his hands continuing their wizardry for the duration of my climax. It's bliss and agony and endless.

When I'm finally spent, I release Ian to grip the edge of the sink. He's removed his hand from my panties, but he holds me firmly by the waist, curled over me, the hand that had been at my breast now crossed over my chest.

"Fuck, that was amazing to see," he breathes, and nips gently at my neck.

I'm blinking back tears. I gawk at our hunched reflections as he moves his lips over my shoulder, his head side to side, pausing intermittently to place a kiss. I'm still panting.

He meets my eyes and smiles.

I'm speechless. Mostly. "Bulbo…*what?*"

He barks out a laugh. "Bulbospongiosus. That's the muscle. One of them, anyway. Men have it, too, in a different configuration. In us, it controls erections." His eyes still on mine, he asks, with less bravado, "None of that hurt?"

"*No,*" I say. "No. Jesus, Ian. You sent me to another *plane.*" He grins. I love it so much, I keep talking. "I think I can taste colors."

That gets a deep, full-bodied laugh from him. "I hope that's good?"

"Would you like to find out?" I shift my hips meaningfully, though there's less resistance from him against my back than there was a moment ago. "I'd like to return the favor."

"You already did."

"What?"

His cheeks go pink. "Feeling you and watching you was hot as *fuck.* And I don't know if you noticed, but there was some writhing from you near the end." He gives me a full-body squeeze. "I popped off like I was fifteen." He shakes his head at himself, then looks to me, panic in his eyes. "Oh, shit. Sorry if that's gross."

"Eh. It's kind of flattering." I laugh, and he buries his red face into my shoulder with a groan.

I turn around and face him, resting my hands on his chest. His eyes drift over me. The cup of my bra has partly lifted back over my breast, but the strap is still off my shoulder. Watching him, I push the other strap down. I reach behind my back, unfasten the hook and eye, then drop my arms, letting the gauzy garment fall to the floor.

Returning to Ian, I take hold of the hem of his shirt. He catches on quickly, tugging off the tee in that uniquely male way, hauling the back up and over his head. The shirt joins my bra on the floor, and his arms wrap around me automatically.

I'm exquisitely aware of my body's reaction to being skin-to-skin with him, the lingering sensitivity of my orgasm in every pleasure receptor, and the general, full-body comfort I feel with him. When I hug him back, he lets out a quiet sigh. My heart squeezes. I could stay like this forever.

It's that last thought that has me letting go. Because this isn't going to be forever. It's only a reprieve. I have a handful of months of this. Hell, if I have another nerve attack before November, I might not even have that time. I'll be learning to cope, and there is zero chance I'll be tainting this dream with that nightmare.

"What's up?" Ian asks, bringing me back from my unwelcome thoughts.

All we have is now. Better not waste it.

I move his hands to hook his thumbs into my waistband. "Help a gal out?" I ask and kiss his chest. "We need to shower."

28

WE LOUNGE IN BED, clean and sated and languid with pleasure. I'm reclining against the headboard in my robe, and shorts-clad Ian, who, evidently, has zero qualms with raiding his brother's clean laundry, lies on his back between my legs in a pair of basketball shorts. His head's against my lower abdomen, the weight and heat of him combatting my pain.

I rake my nails through his hair, and he shivers, squirming against me pleasantly.

He squeezes my calves. "You've completely changed my opinion of those claws of yours," he says. "I had no idea they could be so *fun*."

I harumph, stilling my hand. "Decorative doesn't exclude functionality." He chuckles at this, and I feel the vibration of it against my inner thighs. Delightful.

He reaches back for my hand, moving it over his scalp. I smile and resume scratching.

We sit in silence for a few moments, me, enjoying the feel of his thick hair between my fingers, and him interrupting the quiet with the occasional grunt of pleasure. It's so...*calm*. I'm still aware of the unpleasantness in my abdomen, but I'm not as anxious about the days ahead as I had been. There's a story structure activity I still need to find resources for, and the gym's newsletter could use a final going-over before I send it off...and tell Ian that Firehouse now has a newsletter. I also need to confirm a time to do a run-through with Diego on his next livestream for Built Box. He floated a gimmick to them based on an idea from Mark, which could get...*improv-y*.

But I don't feel the need to get to work on any of these. I am at peace. Content. Lazy, even, beyond the sedative influence of post-release bliss. I feel physically lighter, the stunning slab of man currently employing me as a chaise notwithstanding. I have been *relieved*.

A swell of gratitude rises in my chest. I lean over to kiss Ian on the forehead. "Thank you."

"You're welcome." He beams up at me. "Are you thanking me for anything specific?"

I'm not sure where to begin, but I settle on "Earlier."

He waggles his brows. "For introducing you to the taste of colors?"

I laugh, lying back. "Well, that, sure." He rolls over, still cradled between my legs, and rests his chin on my stomach. "But for backing off when you did. I couldn't even identify that I needed it. And I don't know that I'd have asked you to ease off if I had." I frown. "So dumb. You're *you*; it's not like you'd get shitty once I told you I wasn't up for sex."

"I'm glad you know that," he says, his eyes firmly on mine. "I don't want you to feel like you can't tell me stuff like that. Or... anything," he adds.

A guilty pang goes off in my chest, so sharp and thorny that I'm tempted to lay it all out for him: my eye, the MS, the creeping dread that keeps me up nights after a day I haven't run myself ragged. The hopelessness I feel knowing that this life I've found is temporary...

"Ellie?" he asks.

I shake my head. *Coward.* "Cramp."

He makes a sympathetic noise and sits up, repositioning himself so he's draped over my left thigh, propped on his elbow. He reaches into my robe and rubs his free hand over my belly. It does soothe the cramping, but my guilt skyrockets.

"Having a hard time asking for something," he says. "I get that. I can't ask for help *ever.*"

I smirk. "You don't say."

His small smile is self-deprecating. "I'm just sorry you don't feel comfortable asking for what you need."

"It's not you—"

"I know. You..." He frowns. "You mentioned that Cole was weird about that."

"Yeah. I got into the habit of..." I grit my teeth. *Shit.* Every formulation of what I'm about to say sounds so demeaning. But it's what I have. "I'd try to work around it, initiate sex, even when I didn't want to. To, I dunno, have sex credit banked for when he'd want it while I was having a flare-up and would turn him down? I know it's stupid—"

"What's stupid is that he'd try to fuck you while you were in pain."

I blink. There's a dark edge to his words that I've never heard from him before. It isn't scary, just surprising. And for me.

"It's pretty deep-seated," I explain. "The endometriosis symptoms started in college. Just painful stretches around my period. I'd refuse sex with any guy I was dating. It became a deal-breaker pretty quickly. But with Cole, I thought I had someone who would stick around anyway."

A bittersweet nostalgia sweeps over me. "He was really supportive early on. It was like we were trying to crack the case together. He'd come with me to doctors' appointments, helped me research. But naming what was happening to me didn't do anything to fix it. The pain was still there. Treatment options are limited, and they only do so much, anyway. There's still unpredictable, sudden pain regardless of where I am in my cycle, just *blinding*."

Ian lets out a sympathetic sound, his hand still smoothing over me.

"So much of my relief was having something specific to point to; any symptom mitigation was gravy. For Cole..." I shrug. "Nothing changed as far as what we could do, physically. But it did take away something that we had in common. After so long, it was like the mystery of it was all we had. Once that was resolved, we didn't have anything to align against. And we started to drift. Those cracks I mentioned."

"Which I was a dick about," he says, plainly.

"It was a dick move," I agree. "There's more to the condition than just pain. The scar tissue, especially in cases as severe as mine, can make getting pregnant difficult. Or impossible. There are surgeries to, ah, clear the path, but it's not likely that anything would happen without major intervention. *So*," I manage, and force a smile. "That was in the background, too. Just one more thing I couldn't provide."

"You don't know—"

"I'm not willing to hope," I say, with enough iron that Ian stiffens. Seconds pass, the silence getting heavier, and my heart rate climbs. I feel a spiral coming on, like the panic in the bathroom, that I've fucked things up by being difficult, by asserting, and—

Ian squeezes my hip. "Okay. So." He gifts me a half smile. "You were drifting?"

I nod, grateful for the out. "I felt guilty because he'd already stuck by me through so much, and that was around the time that I decided to leave teaching and pursue my own business. I had a lot of guilt about that, too, having to take so much time to build up my backlist of lesson plans and try to get the word out. That's when I *really* started compensating. I did everything around the apartment. Prioritized his interests, his plans and activities."

Despite the bummer of the recall, I can't help laughing. "That's my villain origin story! I'd already been type A, but trying to prove to my boyfriend that I was worth keeping around turned me into a controlling nightmare."

Ian scowls, his hand going still. "Ellie, you're hardly a nightmare."

"Ah! I've fooled you," I say, laughing again, but it had been nice to hear.

"You're inflexible when it comes to the *Ellie Knows Best* angle," he says, hand beneath the robe shifting to hold on to my hip. "But it's only annoying because you're right so often."

"My cross to bear," I say.

Ian smiles, but it doesn't reach his eyes. "Did he ever ask? If you were okay?"

"What? Like, with sex or with anything?"

He frowns. "Sex, but, *shit*, I'd hope anyone's partner would ask how their day was."

"He would. But even that wore us down. At a certain point, 'How are you?' became indistinguishable from 'Can I fuck you?' Which was exhausting. For both of us, I'm sure."

I worry my bottom lip. "So I'd initiate. Even when…" I grit my teeth, bracing for the admission. "Even when there was a degree of pain. More than a degree. And he could assume I was okay because why would I have gotten the ball rolling if I wasn't?"

Ian's eyes are dark. "He still should have asked."

I shrug. "And I should have been honest. By the end, I suspected he knew and was waiting for me to say something. Calling my bluff."

Which only made me hate him. And myself.

I run my nails up and down the length of Ian's forearm, zigzagging a trail in the dark hair. "It ruptured something. I couldn't trust him. And I'd given him reason not to trust me."

I frown, realizing the truth in what I've said. I'd never considered the damage that had done to my relationship with Cole, certainly not my role in it. But the same way that relationships don't just happen to people, their endings don't, either. Both take effort. Or neglect.

"Is all this why you said you were sad? In the bathroom, that first night," he clarifies. "You said you were a lot of things, but mostly—"

"Sad. And scared." Another pang of guilt skitters across my conscience ahead of the half-truth I know I'm going to share, but it's already more than I've ever admitted to before. I can almost convince myself it's enough.

"I'd done everything I thought that I could do to make up for what I couldn't provide, and it wasn't enough. Not even for someone who, as my friends loved to assure me, had long since stopped deserving the effort. It wasn't *super* encouraging as far as future success."

Ian rumbles thoughtfully, an almost-smile teasing the corner of his mouth. "How did you know what he wanted? Did you ever ask?"

"I don't ask," I say, wryly, painfully aware of the irony. "I know best, remember? If I had to ask, then I wouldn't know everything. Can't have that."

"Hmm. No, you're right." The corner of his mouth quirks again. *"You,"* he says, pointedly, "can't have that."

I grimace. "Damn. Maybe I haven't fooled you after all," I say, and he chuckles. "I think I'm making strides, accepting a certain degree of fallibility," I continue, feigning pique. Kind of. "You were right that I needed to actually find out what the guys wanted, instead of imposing my standards, even if my standards are impeccable. So thank you for that."

"You're welcome. Since you're being so gracious, I'll admit that you've gotten me to accept help—"

"More than what I've offered, personally?"

"I'm in talks. So thank *you* for *that*," he says, and smiles. Withdrawing his hand from beneath my robe, he eases himself up my torso until we're face-to-face, one leg between mine.

I run my hand over his shoulder, following the shape of the resting muscle so obvious under his warm skin. "So, may I *ask*, is there anything I can *help you* with right now?"

"Honestly, I'm content. I have been since we got out of the

shower. Which is strange for me. There's always something I'm stressing over."

"Right? Me too! No intrusive thoughts—" Mostly.

"Well, that's great news." His eyes roam my face for a few heartbeats before meeting my eyes again. His brows twitch down for a second, and his voice is more serious than I expect when he asks, "Do you think you can do something for me?"

"Sure?" I ask, curious.

He draws his lower lip in between his teeth and I have the very real urge to lean in and do the same. "I'm not going to lie. The idea of sex with you is *amazing*," he says, and my body responds with a combination of delight and anxiety that would probably knock me over if I weren't already lying down. "But I want you to let me know when is good for you. For my part"—he clears his throat, chin raised slightly as he continues—"I do have experience being *careful* with partners." I arch a brow, and he shrugs. His expression is equal parts abashed and shameless as he says, "I'm not a small man, Hayes."

While our shower earlier had been more than perfunctory, there is something endearing about him feeling compelled to make clear what that cock sock had more than promised. "Your dad have a conversation with you about that, too?"

"I will neither confirm nor deny any such thing," he says, and I laugh. He grins. "For now, we can figure things out. I think we've proven that—"

I run my finger over his chin, tracing the rise and fall in the deep cleft. "Are you saying that you're content to shoot off in your shorts?"

"So, not *that* part, but I have faith in us to come up with alternatives. But I don't want you to have those same worries. Not with us."

I still my finger. *Us.*

"And I know that I'm going to ask how you are, because I'd like to know how you are. In general. That matters to me."

"Okay." My throat closes in around the word.

"I'm going to leave it to you. I trust you," he says, driving another bolt of guilt through my heart, "to tell me when you're good to go. *Really* good to go."

I nod, trying to acknowledge my guilt as the totally justified discomfort it is, but also feeling my attention drift to the erection pulsing against my thigh.

I give in to the pull of the latter. "At the moment, you feel *particularly* good to go. And I'd like to do something about that. So I'm going to *ask* if you'd like some *help.*"

The man's pupils dilate like I've given them a command. But he sounds convincingly cool when he says, "You're really asking?"

I slide my hand down the ridges and planes of his torso, lingering as I try to recall the vocabulary he used in the bathroom. "Pectorals," I muse, raking my nails over his chest, then light my fingertips along his side. His body tenses. "External obliques."

Lower still, I trace the channel above his hip bone. "What was this one?"

It takes him a moment to reply. "Inguinal ligament," he pants.

"Ah!" Continuing downward, I hold my palm to his lower abdomen, edging below the waistband of the borrowed shorts, my fingers spread in a *V* to either side of the base of his penis. I press firmly, and the thickness of him pulses against my wrist. "Bulbospongiosus, was it?"

His "mm-hmm" is strained.

I grip his shaft and smile; not a small man *at all*. "Anything in particular you'd like?"

"You know best," he says, sucking the words in between gritted teeth.

"You may be right about that." I use my free hand to nudge him onto his back. Keeping him firmly in hand, I straddle his legs, leaning in to kiss him fiercely. I nip at his lower lip. "Let's find out together."

29

"HELLO, MY STRONG FRIENDS!" Diego announces, smile broad and brilliant as he addresses the camera mounted above the screen Grant set up for us. "Tonight, we have an additional challenge! You remember Ellie, who has been such a help on these livestreams. This time, we'll be working without her input. At least, not her words, because she can't speak!"

I wave, smiling behind the piece of gaffer's tape over my mouth. It seemed better than the bandanna Ian offered, which was a little too close to gag territory for comfort.

Mark's idea of "see no evil, hear no evil, speak no evil" is as rooted in improv as I'd feared. Three of us will be working without one of our senses, as Diego takes on the role of host and commentator. I'm the designated "speak no," with Alistair, in a pair of noise-canceling headphones, as the activity's "hear no."

I peer around Alistair to check on Ian, who's donned a sleep mask to round out our hamstrung trio as "see no." Tonight's recipe called for an air fryer, one of the few kitchen devices I have yet to procure, but, as Diego pointed out during planning, one Ian *does* have. A few texts later, not only had Ian offered to let us use said air fryer, but had said that we were welcome to stream from his kitchen, and would it be okay with Diego if he participated? I could swoon.

Diego frowns at the screen, lips moving slightly as he reads a comment. "No, Suica99, I don't equate this with the silencing of a strong female. And"—he squints to read on—"I don't think she feels this way? Ellie!" He wheels toward me, the portrait of worry. "You aren't suppressing your voice or compromising yourself in concession to the patriarchy, are you?"

I roll my eyes. *No.*

"Well, that's good. I would never want Ellie to do that. No one should, with any woman in their life! Next, we have Alistair, who a lot of you remember because you're saying that you're sad that he is wearing pants. Sometimes, people need pants."

I nudge Alistair, who frowns at me before realizing he's been introduced. "Oh, hey, hi, Diego fans!" he shouts.

In his own headphones at the command center he's erected in Ian's living room, Grant flinches. In another installment of *Ellie's Massive Oversights,* I learned today that he's pretty damn tech-savvy, having shot, edited, and produced Diego's more involved posts. He scans the area around him, grabbing a lump of grip chalk from the coffee table, and chucks it at Alistair.

Alistair bats it out of the air in time to avoid getting beaned. "Dude!"

Grant points to the earpieces of his headphones, then makes a thumbs-down gesture. *Quiet down, you asshole,* he mouths.

Alistair wrinkles his nose. "Dick," he grumbles, but it's at a normal volume. He elbows me. "I've got an audiobook on. Have you tried them? They *rule.*"

Naturally, I'm dying to know more, but Diego gets back in front of the camera. "You might be wondering about the last member of our party. It's the great Ian Hammond! Ian, please introduce yourself."

Ian raises the mask to his forehead, giving the camera a wave with his free hand. "Hi, everyone. As Diego said, I'm Ian Hammond. If you've been lifting for a while and follow the sport, you might remember me from—really?" He interrupts himself as my favorite photo, *The Roar*, takes over half the screen. Grant brays a laugh from his corner. The chat erupts in fire emojis.

Diego winks at the camera. "I guess sometimes people *don't* need pants."

Ian shakes his head. The image disappears. "Now, I own and operate Firehouse Fitness in Austin, where I have the privilege of working with Diego. He's an excellent coach and a talented presenter, as you know, and if you don't mind my saying so here, Diego, I'm really proud of you."

My heart squeezes. I look at Diego on the screen, and he's trying to hold back a smile, fully retreating into humility mode.

"You've come a long way from the college freshman who just wanted to improve his bench press." Ian points to the camera, then gestures to the Built Box spread in front of us. "You've earned this. I hope you know that."

Diego opens his mouth to reply, then closes it. He clears his throat, and after a few seconds, nods, standing straight, his chin high. "Thank you, Ian. That's good to hear."

Ian nods, and my heart soars as I watch Diego take another couple of breaths to collect himself. I smile behind my tape. And to think that this moment of unfiltered masculine affection is being shared with an audience of dudebros.

Alistair pokes my arm. "Are we starting?"

Diego laughs, giving himself a little shake, and Ian pulls the blindfold back over his eyes. "Friends, that was really cool for me. Okay! Onward with our cooking!"

He explains the session's questionable approach to executing buffalo ranch chicken chalupas. "Will they be successful?" he asks his audience. "Will there be danger? We don't know! But we'll find out together!"

He remains smiling in the corner of the frame as the three of us...wait.

I really should have vetted this idea.

"Is anything happening?" Ian asks.

"What?" Alistair asks, semi-shouting again. Another piece of chalk flies toward us, and he dodges it. "Dude, if his *back* is to me, I can't read his lips. Are we *starting*?"

I tap the recipe card. I can't convey "aloud" with my eyes, so I make a thrusting gesture with my left hand, projecting it away from my face. He frowns. I point past him to Ian, then cover my eyes with one hand to indicate his handicap, and tug on an ear with the other.

"Oh!" Alistair points to his headphones. "It's *The Death of Ivan Illych*. Do you know it?"

I'm going to lose my mind.

Diego shakes his head, addressing the camera. "Friends, we may be in for some trouble."

For the next few minutes, I'm inclined to agree, but once

Alistair catches on, things start to progress. He takes on sauce duty, mixing and intermittently grumbling something about a "bourgeois Russian cog"—Mr. Illych, I presume. I intercede when necessary, mostly acting as eyes for to Ian, who is tasked with patting the chicken dry, and guide his hand to make sure the ranch seasoning he sprinkles over the chicken gets distributed evenly. We risk letting him try chopping some breast meat after its initial round in the air fryer, but after I make one too many high-pitched warning sounds, he suggests that Alistair take over.

"How's this look?" Ian asks, indicating the chalupa he's assembled. It's a little messy, but most of the filling has made it into the Built Box proprietary blend grain-free tortilla.

I pat his arm approvingly, and while I'm in the neighborhood, discreetly press my knee against his below the prep table. We haven't talked about how public we're going to be about this, and while I suspect that the guys would just roll with it, certain gym members are already more invested in the prospect of us getting cozy than is healthy. I'd rather not have to deal with their expectations while I'm still trying to understand my own.

Ian makes a low rumbling sound—oh, my *favorite*—and I—

Alistair is watching us. So is Diego. A cursory peek into the living room reveals Grant peering around his laptop screen. All three wear matching looks of confusion.

Until Alistair doesn't. "Oh, no shit!" he bursts, and Grant shoves his headphones off with both hands with a "Goddammit, dude!"

Using the business end of his knife, Alistair points back and forth between Ian and me. "You two are *doing it!*"

I freeze, Ian going still against me.

"We are not…doing it." Ian says, with an angle of uncertainty that makes the technically accurate denial more scandalous than the accusation.

Alistair laughs. "Whatever. You're definitely doing something."

"What are you— Oh!" Diego interrupts his question to read off the screen. "It's from BarbaraSells4U. I bet that's Babs! The coffee group was going to do a watch party at Tom's."

What!? I scramble forward to read the screen. Alistair's theory has inspired a number of strangers to comment, but I focus on specific names.

BarbaraSells4U: I KNEW IT!

HelenNOTofTroy: When did this happen?

BarbaraSells4U: YOU WERE SO OBVIOUS SATURDAY! HOW DID I NOT PIECE IT TOGETHER?

TOMMYnumber$: I knew

HelenNOTofTroy: Why are you typing? We're in the same room.

TOMMYnumber$: HAHAHAHAA

HelenNOTofTroy: Why am I still typing?

TOMMYnumber$: Ellie's going to have to be more discreet when she slips out the back stairs at Firehouse.

The back— My shoulders drop. Thursday, after nap time. Ian had walked me out via the back door, so we wouldn't be seen by anyone coming in for the one thirty class. We'd lingered in the doorway for a minute…or more. I just needed another feel of his pecs.

I shuffle back to my spot beside Alistair, and Diego places a hand on my shoulder. "Ellie, if you need privacy, let me know. I can wear my headphones. For *volume*. If that's something…" His cheeks flare scarlet. "That you do?"

I fold my arms on the table and bury my face in them. *Christ.*

"Could we please change the subject?" Grant asks. "You're making this *weird*."

"This is getting a lot of engagement," Diego observes. "Ellie, do you think that this is useful to Built Box?"

I let out a muffled scream.

"But you like her?" I hear Alistair ask, overloud.

"I like Ellie a lot, yes," Ian says, a self-conscious laugh in his voice.

My heart skips. I turn my head in his direction, peeking over my arms. That half smile of his hooks the corner of his mouth, and I prop my chin in my hands, wildly curious about what's inspired it.

Alistair's uncovered one of his ears. "Rad. Who made the first move?"

I bury my head again.

"Ellie!" Diego calls. "The comment section thinks that was very incriminating."

I growl. The comment section can eat me.

"It was fairly synchronous," Ian says. "But I had it bad for her early on."

Oh? I risk another peek. He's still smiling, but it's different. Sweeter. Soft.

"Like, when she came to Firehouse the first time?" Diego asks.

"More like...twelve hours before that? I went into the bathroom at your place, and there was the 'whole-ass woman' Alistair had told me was looking to move in. All he said was that she liked cheese, so I wasn't sure what to expect."

"She was..." He's smiling. Smiling so much, in fact, that the mask bunches over the rise in his cheeks. It's only when I feel the tape tugging against my face that I realize that I'm smiling, too.

"Regal," he concludes.

"*Regal* is a good word for Ellie," says Diego. "Ah! And Babs says that *smitten* is a good word for both of you! Oh, that's so sweet! This is getting so many hearts!"

"And these are gonna be sick!" Alistair cheers, pointing at the arrangement of fully assembled chalupas on the plate in front of him. He finished the entire batch. Sneaky. "Let's air fry these up!"

We relieve ourselves of our self-imposed handicaps to eat, and after we've expressed an appropriate amount of enthusiasm for the chalupas, which are, as per Alistair's prediction, indeed sick, Diego signs off. While I did avoid the comment section for the remainder of the stream, I appreciate that there is nothing further from my roommates on the subject of whatever it is Ian and I are "doing." Classic Dawghouse.

At least, not until after we've cleaned up and the guys start to head out. Diego smiles at me, then peeks down the stairwell, which Ian and Grant headed down to load up the equipment Grant brought over. "Ellie, if Built Box thinks more of you and Ian would be good for numbers, would you be up for it? Viewers were *really* responsive."

"Take your leftovers," I say, pointedly shoving a to-go container into his chest. "I'll see you in the morning."

"Oh!" A hint of his fuck-with-you face slips in. "A *sleepover*?"

"Goodnight," I say, and he descends, grinning.

Alistair steps up, his eyes on the floor, then he tugs his headphones around his neck. "Uh, sorry if I blew it for you guys."

I wave off the apology. "It was going to come out eventually. I'm more interested in *Ivan Illych*. Why?"

"It's recommended reading for med students. Like, to help see patients as actual people? I dunno. Have you read it?" I nod, and he tosses up his hands. "Do we ever find out what's killing this guy? It's driving me *nuts!*"

"It's been a while, but..." I think back. "What if it's less about what's killing him, and more about how he's being treated, and how he comes to terms with his impending death?"

"Huh." He frowns thoughtfully, which is a new look for him. His eyes widen. "Oh! Shit, I'll have to start this all over again." He sighs, tugging the headphones back over his ears. "Hey!" he shouts, and jogs down the stairs. "I'm gonna walk home! For more book time!"

I leave the door open in anticipation of Ian's return, then move farther into the apartment. I eye the window beside Ian's bookshelf, which overlooks Tom's porch next door. I edge closer, peering into the dark. I haven't dared look at my phone. Heather and Mark will have left who knows how many texts decrying my betrayal—and reminding me that I owe Mark twenty bucks—and I'm sure Helen and Babs have more thoughts than they shared in the chat.

Ian's steps sound on the stairs, and he comes back in, a wry smile on his face. "They ambushed me," he says, joining me at the window. "They're very protective of you. Diego demanded to know what my *intentions* are."

"If you said *pure*, I'm going to be very disappointed," I say, papering over the opportunity for that conversation.

His responding rumble is enough to distract me from my guilt. "How's your mouth after taking off that tape?"

I angle my head up, and he runs his thumb over my lower lip. I close my eyes. *Divine.* "Fine. I put ChapStick on first, so the tape wouldn't stick as much."

"Good thinking."

I smile as his thumb continues to stroke my lip, and curiosity gets the best of me. "Why'd you do this tonight?" I open my eyes. "I thought you didn't want to reward Built Box with your presence."

"There's a chance that even a has-been like myself can have some industry pull. Might as well lend it. And after you asked me about not wanting to be involved, I realized that I hadn't explained my reasons to Diego. Now he knows. Besides, I wanted to be around you."

He makes the admission so freely that my jaw drops, but I turn it into a grin. "Is it because I'm so *regal*?"

He hooks a finger into the waistband of my shorts, and I let him tug me closer, reaching up to twine my arms around his neck. "You're the one who declared herself *queen*." He bends down, and I angle my head up for a kiss.

He stops just shy of my lips. "But I like *smitten* even better."

I close the space between us.

I like smitten, too.

Too much.

30

"WHAT'S THE ONE ABOUT the lady who slept with the corpse of her fiancé?" Ian asks.

Smiling, I turn in my desk chair to face him. He's sitting in my throne, where he's been thumbing through a collection of short stories while I finish an email. "'A Rose for Emily.' Faulkner."

He nods, eyes distant. "We read it in class junior year, and you could track how quickly everyone finished by when they reacted to the ending. One of the cheerleaders audibly gagged." He laughs, returning to the book. "That single iron-colored hair will haunt me for *life*."

"It's a classic for a reason," I say, lingering to indulge in the sight of him. He's dressed almost exactly as he was the night we met, but in a darker sweater, and the T-shirt below doesn't appear to be cutting off circulation. I ended up in the same halter dress, mostly to see if "break" me is bold enough to forgo boob tape. Turns out, I am!

Tonight is supposed to be our first *date* date, which is hard to believe, given that we haven't spent a night apart since Diego's livestream last week. We usually end up here. He comes over for dinner, we help clean up and, after, hang out with the guys for a bit, streaming something on the TV or reading or working on assignments or projects. Last night, I finally showed them *The Proposal*. I was right: They loved it.

It's sweet and homey, and if I trade bubbly ladies for beefcakes, surprisingly close to what I'd been hoping for the day I spotted that glittery pink sign.

When we bid goodnight to my roommates, it rouses some cheeky commentary. Grant makes a retching noise, and Diego inevitably drops his line about wearing headphones. And while Ian and I do enjoy plenty of activities that would make his brother retch to consider, between the discomfort leading up to my period and the unkindness of menstruation itself, we haven't gotten to do anything at the Dawghouse requiring soundproofing.

That's where the privacy of Ian's apartment comes in. Like yesterday, when I installed the suction-cup toothbrush caddy I'd bought him. I attached the caddy to the wall of his shower, highlighting the clever design—It holds the toothpaste, too! No more soap dish!—and he thanked me by stripping off my clothes and bringing me to glorious, nonpenetrative climax right there next to it. The caddy didn't budge, not even when I grabbed on to it in the throes of orgasm. I may have to mention that when I post a product review; Ian did the same thing when I pounced on him, and frankly, that's incredible performance for one little suction cup.

The subject of an actual date came up not long after. I left it all up to Ian, though I did put in a request for somewhere with burrata. And while I'm excited for whatever he has in store, a rain check may be in order. My period tapered off this morning, and

I'm as pain-free as I get. Now, seeing him in my space, lounging with a book, I'm officially at my limit. I need this man inside of my body.

I am out of my mind with want for him. He turns a page, and I am riveted by the movement of his fingers, the care he takes with the worn paper. I glare at the whorish book, cradled in his capable hands, open and exposed to peruse at his leisure. I want to be in his hands! I want to be exposed! Peruse *me*!

He looks up, catching me creeping on him as I mentally slut-shame a Norton Anthology. "You ready to go?"

I start to nod, then shake my head.

His brows twitch down. "What's up?"

"Did you make a reservation?"

"Ah—" His look turns wary. "No. It's Sunday, so I figured we'd be okay..."

I take in a long breath. No reservation. He made no reservation, and this has done nothing to curb my appetite for him. Incredible.

"So, no time constraints?" I confirm.

"No?"

I stand and slowly start toward him. I can't make it to dinner. I can barely make it across the room. This is happening *now*.

He stays seated, his eye line forced upward as I approach. It's not an angle I've had much experience with, but I like it. The look in his eyes tells me he does, too.

I stop just shy of him. "Dinner is going to have to wait."

The book hits the floor with a hollow thump.

Watching him, I reach under my left arm for the tiny hook and eye at the top of my dress, unfastening it with my thumb and forefinger before taking hold of the zipper. I ease it down, feeling the teeth separate as the form-fitting garment loses tension, Ian following the descent of the pull with unblinking focus. He tracks my hand just as intently as I reach up and back for one of the trailing ends of the bow securing the halter, not moving as I coil the ribbon around my finger and pull.

The bow comes apart, but the tension I have on the ribbon keeps the dress from falling off me. I watch Ian's chest rise and fall with a long, controlled breath. And then another. I hear the pop of a knuckle, and glance at his hands, fingers white-knuckling the armrests of the chair.

I let the ribbon unfurl. The dress falls to the floor.

Ian stops breathing mid-inhale.

Points for boldness, Break Me.

Clad only in a lacy black thong, I step out of the circle of my dress, resisting the impulse to drape it over the back of my desk chair, my eyes fixed on my quarry. Still no sign that he's breathing, but the throb of his heartbeat is visible against his light sweater.

Speaking of…"I need to touch you." I nod to indicate the layer. "Take it off."

The unfinished breath rasps into him, and he's all action, sweater and shirt coming off in a blur, joining my dress on the floor. Bare-chested and panting, he leans back in the chair, awaiting further instruction.

Bending forward, I gently press his legs together. His eyes are impossibly large as I rest a knee to one side of him, then angle my opposite leg over him to straddle his lap, resting my rear on his thighs. I take his hands, the fingers still tense, and press them to my bare sides. He's stopped breathing again.

I run my palms over the expanse of his chest, raking my nails through the hair, kneading the slope of his trapezius, then cradling his face in my hands. Leaning in, I draw on his lower lip, nibbling it gently, and his hands relax as he kisses me back. After another moment of coaxing, his hands slide down to my waist and back up to my rib cage, thumbs gliding over the tender skin below my breasts.

I break the kiss, lifting my face from him just enough to ask, "How are you?"

He chokes a laugh. "How am I?" His right hand meanders along my side, coasting down my hip crease toward my center. His fingers smooth over the edge of my thong, and I whimper. But he doesn't go any farther. He just teases along the border of flesh and fabric. "I thought you didn't like that question."

"I don't like it being asked of *me*. But I couldn't come up with a euphemism for letting you know I'm"—a finger bypasses the elastic—"ready." He traces the edge of my opening, and I drop my forehead to his shoulder. "*So* ready," I moan.

"Are you?" His finger continues to skirt the heat of me as I pant, unable to speak as he traces up, circling my clitoris, then easing back down. "I think you could use some more time."

Incredulous, I roll my head to the side to glare at him. He laughs.

"Not *much* more," he assures me. "Not unless"—he runs a finger down my seam, parting me—"you want it?"

"*Please.*" The single, desperate word rips out of me, and gray eyes flash as one of his fingers enters me. I grab his shoulders, nails digging in. He eases in and out, gently, his focus on my face, and I can barely keep my eyes from rolling back.

"You're sure?" he says thickly. "You're not in any pain?"

"None."

"Then I think I should tell you about the stimmy."

The— I gawk at him, my face still half buried in his shoulder. He is manipulating me like a finger puppet, and the dumbest series of syllables has just fallen out of his mouth. *"What?"*

"It's a byproduct of your body's stress response. From lifting heavy. Like the back squats you did this morning."

"Why?" I shake my head, bewildered and probably oxygen deprived. "Why are you doing this *now*?"

"Because you're willing to skip a burrata for the chance to fuck me," he says, decisively. "The least I can do is make sure you're set up to get the most out of it."

I…can't argue with that? "Okay?" I concede, and force myself upright, gripping the back of his neck for support. "Then do some boob stuff, too."

His free hand cups my right breast, and I moan. "You're incredible, you know that?"

"Stress response?" I remind him.

He takes in a long breath, then continues, his finger stroking inside me, thumb caressing my erect nipple. "When you're going heavy, do you ever feel like you're being hijacked? You know that you're only squatting, but your body is screaming *battle!* and wants you to throw a car at an advancing army?"

Christ, this is strange, but I've legitimately wondered about this. "Yes!"

He lets out a thoughtful rumble, leaning in to kiss my neck. "That's the stress response." He presses the words into the column of my throat. "You're putting a significant amount of stress on your body, which your lizard brain interprets as a threat. So your brain, specifically, the hypothalamus, activates the fight-or-flight response."

"And my body prepares to fight."

"Just fight?" he asks, lips teasing below my ear.

"Are you calling me a coward?" I demand, impressed at myself for feigning indignation when my blood has abandoned my brain. "Are you"—I gasp as he pinches my nipple—"suggesting that I am predisposed toward flight? Because there's a car out there with your name on it."

He chuckles into the side of my neck. "Motivational behaviors drive the activity in the hypothalamus. The four Fs. Fight, flight, feeding, and—" He fully cups my sex. *"Fucking."*

I moan but try to turn it into something thoughtful sounding even as I grind helplessly against his hand. "I knew that once, I think. Biology was so long ago."

Ian kisses down my chest. "We call it the stimmy. It comes after lifting heavy, the post-battle, fuck-like-Vikings-while-the-boat-is-on-fire sex. And when you come..." He eases his finger from me, his hand leaving my panties, moving to my waist, holding me in place. "It's like a goddamn freight train." He draws my nipple into his mouth.

I arch involuntarily, my body demanding I hand myself over to the teeth and tongue at work against me. I have the sudden presence of mind that I, too, have clever parts and snake my hand down his body, pressing the flat of my hand against his length. His next breath sucks in between his teeth with a hiss that sends sparks across my sensitive nipple.

He lifts his head from me. "Bed," he says, not asking, and holds me to his chest. Standing, wearing me once again, he walks the few feet to the bed, kissing me as he lays me onto the comforter. He takes my hands, and my nails press into the back of his knuckles as he sweeps my hands over my head, claiming my mouth in a deep kiss. I'm vaguely aware when he releases one hand, only to recapture it in the other, clasping my hands together against the mattress. He breaks the kiss.

"*Stay,*" he repeats, with a playful edge of reprimand, but it zings through me like physical contact; I do so enjoy Commanding Ian. He takes his time backing off the bed, his hands trailing down my arms, over my breasts and sides, then pausing at the lace trim at the top of my thong. His eyes meet mine in question, and at my nod, his fingers hook into the barely-there waistband, dragging the last shred of clothing from my body as he stands.

I let my knee fall to the side, eliciting a groan from him. I giggle because, delirious, horny wretch that I am, it occurs to me that I have opened myself up like a slutty little book and have defeated that shameless anthology abandoned on the floor.

Ian undoes his belt, making short work of his fly, and then his pants are down, the length of him straining against the confines of his navy boxer briefs. A moment later, he's naked as well, and I am breathless.

His gray eyes roam over me, and I could feel self-conscious, but I can't spare a thought for what he's seeing because there is just *so much* of him to take in. His massive chest heaves with exertion, his eyes stormy with lust. Observing him from below, exposed, a tendril of fear laces my desire. Not a fear *of* him, not acknowledging an active threat, but an awareness of the power and scope confronting me. He is *so* much. And I want all of him. I *get* to have all of him.

For now.

I have to brace against the shudder that rips through me at the thought. More than "now" feels too much like hope. And if the worst does happen, I'm not going to be another woman he has to watch fade. Now is what I have. Now has to be enough.

Ian's brow wrinkles, concern shading the lust in his eyes. "You okay?"

I breathe in deeply, not minding when his eyes fall to my chest, briefly absorbed in the rise of my breasts. Desire burns through the remnants of his concern, turning my unwanted thoughts to ash.

"I am now. And I'm about to be a lot better."

"Condom?" he rasps.

I tip my head toward my bedside table, and he reaches for it. I let my eyes drift to the ceiling as I listen to the telltale sound of a package being torn open, and then he's above me again.

His fingers trail down the left side of my body, sending shock-waves over every inch of my skin. When he gets to the inguinal ligament, he uses the slight channel to guide him to the apex of my thighs. I whimper at the contact, his knuckles stroking my sex until I'm grinding against him, and he leans over to kiss me. His fingers leave me, a new heat taking their place as he positions himself at my entrance.

"*Slow,*" I gasp, acknowledging the other catalyst for my earlier thrill of fear: the possibility of pain. The specter of experience looms over us, threatening to smother my desire. Just because my body is ready doesn't mean it won't betray me.

Ian's eyes soften, still dark, but comprehending. He caresses my cheek, separating from me below. "We can stop. This doesn't have to happen now—"

The reassurance extinguishes my fear. "Don't you fucking *dare*. I need this. I need you."

He blinks, half smirking in surprise, but he still sounds guarded when he asks, "You'll tell me what you're feeling?"

"Yes." The single word is desperate. I arch my hips, and then he's against me again, his expression cautious, jaw slackening just slightly as he begins to ease in.

I gasp, squeezing his forearms at the sensation of his entry. Holy hell…

"Ellie?"

"Good!" I assure him. "So, so good. Oh, Ian," I pant. He's still watching me, waiting for my go-ahead. "Yes. More." I hook my heel behind his rear for emphasis, urging him farther in. *"More."*

He continues with torturous slowness, rocking slightly, in and out, as my body molds to accommodate him. I roll my hips in time with his, and the muscles of my sex clench and release, pulling him in deeper, my body betraying my impatience. But he takes his time. He moves with the thoughtful confidence of a man who knows he needs to maneuver carefully. And while my brain does produce the inconvenient realization that his is the kind of skill that requires practice to hone, I find that I have nothing but gratitude for every experience he's had that has led him to this particular performance.

I leverage my hips to meet each thrust, and we fall into a rhythm, my pleasure heightening, the pressure building, climbing—

Pain, sharp and piercing, erupts behind my navel. I flinch, my nails digging into the back of his neck. Ian stills.

"Ellie?" He begins to withdraw.

I shake my head, forcing my fingers to relax as the pain subsides. "Stay! Just..." It takes a moment to get my brain back to word making. "It's passing. It's—" I breathe in slowly, allowing my lungs to fill, bearing down internally to maximize the pressure. No pain. "It's over." I tell him. "Maybe...let me on top—"

I haven't fully articulated the request before he's shifted to accommodate it, holding me with one hand and rolling to his back without extracting himself. I gasp, gripping his sides with my knees, then relax, allowing the full length of him into me. We let out a sigh simultaneously, and I lean over to press my chest to his, needing a moment to adapt to being in a reality where I have access to an experience like this.

He runs his hands over my shoulders. "You're okay?"

"Perfect," I say, and then we're moving again.

Within seconds, I've resumed my position at my peak, so, so close to losing myself.

"What do you need?" he insists.

"Press—" He knows exactly what I'm asking, pressing the flat of his palm into the space between my pubic bone and my belly button.

Everything around me stops. There's only this moment as pleasure claims me, holding me in its grip as my climax washes over me. It's as endless as the other times we've brought me here, but complete in a way I hadn't known. Forget tasting colors. I'm manipulating time.

Somewhere in the void, I hear myself call his name, losing myself in the delight of it on my tongue.

Ian goes tense below me, and I fight to maintain my pace as a new crest appears on the horizon. "Ellie—" he rasps, gripping my hips.

I press a hand to the side of his face. "I want to hear you."

He roars. It's the sound I've been fantasizing about for more than a month, and I'm undone. I follow him into a second orgasm, and I'm giggling through it, because my God, this is nothing if not Vikings-fucking-while-the-ship-is-on-fire sex.

I collapse onto him, his arms tight around me, my face pressed into his damp chest. We lay there panting, for several seconds. Or minutes? What is time?

I smile. My right eye is fogged up.

"Holy shit," I croak, and kiss Ian's chest. "The stimmy rules."

"Yeah, it does." He gives me a squeeze, then laughs. "I hope Diego was wearing his headphones."

31

THE DOUBLE DOORS OPEN, the sound of the crowd assembling outside flooding the lobby before the doors clatter shut again, returning the din to a dull murmur.

"Ellie?" Ian's voice cuts through the darkened space, his form limned by the green glow of the exit light above the doors. The sight is cinematic, but distinctly genre, like things are about to get either very *spooky* or very *sexy*.

Or very judgy.

"Are you ready?" I ask. I sit on the couch dividing the shop from the communal lounge, and when I stand, it activates the motion-sensing lights, illuminating the pro shop behind me. The effect is really dramatic; I recorded my practice run to be sure.

Ian's attention is fixed behind me, his eyes tracking from left to right. "Wow," he says, his tone gratingly neutral as he starts toward the pro shop. I move to meet him, stopping to accept the kiss he plants on my temple, and one of his hands finds its way to my side as we move closer to admire the changes.

Even though I worked on the makeover all day, I'm still taken with how well our vision has translated into reality. It was truly a group effort, with every insurgent in the Coffee Coup staying after the Saturday endurance class to help, but they insisted that I present the final reveal on my own on the grounds that they wanted to help prepare for tonight's event. Plus, as per Babs, "Ian might want to *thank* you." Her suggestive tone inspired a round of faux-scandalized *oohs*. They really do need to find a better way to fill their time.

"Those are the rigs from storage," he says, starting in the left corner of the shop. We paired them with some banged-up barbells he'd retired, repurposing them into racks to hang T-shirts and tank tops. "Good call."

"We swiped two pairs of j-hooks." I point to where they hold the bars "So if we're ever short on the floor, we'll have to find another way to hang those."

He nods, moving to the cubbies, inspecting the shelves.

"Everything is arranged by size and color, biggest on the bottom, working up to extra smalls." I gesture to the rightmost column of shelves. "This design is the one we have the most of. Since you didn't nix the suggestion to comp shirts to new members and visitors, I figured we'd use these. It's a good strategy," I say, hoping to reinforce the idea, in case he had simply overlooked the note. "People love free stuff."

"Sure," he says, attention traveling along the shelves of newly organized protein powders and supplements to the right-hand wall of the shop. I try to read his body language, but this vantage point gives me nothing but his splendid rear view. He pauses in front of the wall, now adorned with rows of glittering medals and trophies: Ian Hammond's timeline of glory. "So this is where those photos and articles ended up."

"Jacob's a photographer," I say. "He mounts and frames his own work, and he took on all the magazine and newspaper articles the ladies and I culled through."

He moves to the corner, where the timeline kicks off with a plaque with a yellow duck mounted to it. "The Rubber Ducky Award from high school was worthy of inclusion?"

"It speaks to your lifelong commitment to fitness." I point to the group photo above the plaque, where a teenaged Ian stands a full head above the others on his track team.

"That's when I started lifting," he says. "Coach Smitty taught shop, knew *nothing* about track; had gotten stuck with it for some reason, probably budget cuts. But he committed. When he decided to incorporate a weight training element my junior year, I threw myself into it." He lets out a dry laugh. "Anything to keep myself out of the house. Sick mom, pain-in-the-ass little brother…"

Panic grips my stomach, but he smiles, and the tension releases. "By the next fall, I was so big, the football coach tried to recruit me. I stuck with track and helped the underclassmen in the weight room." He taps the bill of the duck. "At the end-of-season banquet, I received this as a thank-you."

We continue to move to the right, tracking his college years and professional career, including a discreet five-by-seven of *The Roar*. He arches a brow, pausing in front of the infamous shot.

"You didn't veto it," I remind him. "That was major! An international publication."

He chuckles, sliding his hand from my waist to give my tush a squeeze. "I like that you like it."

About two-thirds down, it switches from his time as an athlete to his coaching, though we elected not to mention the accident or the other gym. Instead, it starts with an article in a community paper about our grand opening. It's an entertaining read, half informative, half grumbling about the continued "erosion" of the neighborhood's historic properties, penned by Firehouse's favorite espresso-pulling diabetic. Tom had been mortified, which only made Babs more insistent that it went up.

I tap a pair of laminated plaques. "Your Best of Austin awards."

"When did the second one come in?"

"Last week. Surprise! I hid it."

"Of course you did," he says, but there's a smile in it. He nods to the empty wall space a few feet shy of where the shop transitions into the lounge. "Blank?"

"Intentionally. The Coup has *thoughts*. We could do a member of the month, write a special workout for them and a little Q&A to post here, or put up a calendar with member birthdays, mark any future community events you might plan…"

"You mean, events *you* might plan?"

"Events I'm already planning." I sidestep to the last portion of the makeover. "And here are the testimonials."

This is the project I left in the care of Babs and Helen. As I explain to Ian, I sent an email to members, asking if they were up for a survey, then passed their info along to the ladies, who handled the interviews and compiled the responses. I only intervened to forbid any glitter and to shoot down Babs's original plan, which was to arrange them on hot-pink poster board. She probably buys it in bulk.

"This is a *lot*," he says.

I nod. The project received almost 100 percent member participation, and their responses were above and beyond what I'd anticipated. As hard as it had been to hand the project over, I'm glad I did; I had to stop reading after about five of them. It was too much. Too open, too vulnerable, too…compelling. In the eyes of this community, Ian is everything from drill sergeant to life coach to personal savior.

My heart twists. Someone who deserves more than what life with me could mean.

I tap the profile photo beside Helen's submission. "That one almost made me cry."

"She had a lot of shit to work through when she first came in. And would be the first to admit that she still does." He steps closer to read. His brows twitch in surprise. "Wow."

His eyes shift to a neighboring submission, moving side to side as he reads. He reads another. And another. I watch as the surprise shifts to wonder, then something more. Realization.

He blinks rapidly, taking a step back, as though suddenly appreciating the scope of what's in front of him. "It's funny," he says, voice distant. "In this job, success is obvious. Clients set goals; you work together to plan a path to achieve them. In time, they're faster, stronger, leaner." His eyes are still on the display as he says, "But you don't know what it means to them."

I slide my hand up his back to his shoulder, resting my head against his arm. "People value what happens here. What *you* do here."

His arm comes around me, and I turn toward him. When I look into his face, I have to grip him more tightly. He's never been able to conceal anything, not with those exceptional eyes. And right now, the emotion shining through them is unwinding that twist in my heart, imploring me to give in to the greedy impulse to keep him, no matter what it might cost him.

"Thank you for caring," he says. "Caring enough to do all of this."

My throat goes tight. "Thank you for giving me somewhere to care about."

"And for caring about the guys. And…" He swallows hard, Adam's apple bobbing. *"Me."*

There's a question in the last word, and if I had an ounce of self-preservation, I'd simply say something reassuring and leave it at that. But because I don't, or don't want to, I pull him down to me. I kiss his Adam's apple first, because I don't know that I've done that before, and the way it moved just now was enchanting, and then his neck, and below his ear.

I nibble his ear lobe, giving it a gentle tug. "You make it easy."

He holds me so tightly, I can barely breathe. I hug him back just as hard, my eyes welling. Reading those testimonials was like being served with the world's most compelling character witness statements, but instead of seeking clemency, they were selling me on the reasons why I should bind myself to this man and never return to my real life. God, I want to.

Now isn't enough. It was never going to be. I'm too greedy for him. It started the second his eyes softened at my sadness that first night, and it's only gotten worse. I'm greedy for his skin, his incredible eyes, the way he makes me feel, and the rumbling laugh I can get out of him. I'm greedy for the casual moments, when he conks out on the couch here in the lobby, his head in my lap while I read, or at the Dawghouse, quoting along with Betty White's warning not to let the puppy out because the eagles will snatch him. I'm greedy for interactions that have nothing to do with me: helping Penny release a cricket; listening to Tom break down his most recent update to the billing system; handing Babs her preferred lacrosse ball at the end of class.

This man isn't break material.

And he doesn't have to be.

The thought teases through me, shifting and expanding until it threatens to become the one thing I've refused to let myself consider: hope. Hope that I'll be okay, that the next few months will pass without incident and the specter of my fear will go with them. There's still the five-year window, but after the six months, the possibility of MS drops significantly. It is possible. I can remain this version of myself, keep this life and the strange, wonderful community that's made me one of their own.

Keep him. Stay *us*.

I gasp at that. Ian meets my eyes, his look tinged with worry, then relaxing as I smile at him, stunned. I can hope.

"I have something for you," I say, and step back, however reluctantly, so he has to let me go. I scramble for my gym bag, left on the couch, and rummage through it until my hand closes on the slim package I've left languishing for too long.

I return to Ian and hand it off. "For upstairs. For you."

He looks from the gift to me, and back again. He slides a finger under one edge of the paper, prying it loose from the tape, and pulls the wrap away from what's inside. The light overhead glints off *The Hammonds Do Hawaii*, now behind glass.

Ian stills. "You framed it."

"Is that okay?"

He nods. "That was weeks ago. When—"

"I picked up the frame that day. I've been wanting to give it to you, but I needed time. To let myself..." I shake my head, almost afraid to say it aloud, like I might scare it away. *"Hope."*

"Hope?"

"For this? For you. That I could…" I don't have the words. "Keep you."

Ian's arms come around me, the frame still in one hand, and I grab on to him again. "Hayes. *Ellie*," he says, emotion cradling both of my names. "I—"

The double doors swing open. We pivot to face them, still clinging to one another.

Grant staggers into the semidarkness, vectoring toward us. "I'm so sorry! But we gotta do the unveiling now, or they're going to riot."

Ian releases one arm from me to give his brother a gesture that seems to convey "Fine," "Are you kidding?", and a possible threat of bodily harm, but Grant only seems to register the first one, responding with a double thumbs-up before darting out the still-open doors.

"It's your fault," I tell Ian, who turns to eye me. I smile. "It's this damn community you've put together. They're committed." He laughs but cuts a glare toward the doors again. Grant returns, hitting the lights, and members begin filing in.

"Duty calls," he says, and releases me, fingers slowly trailing down my arm.

I grab his free hand. "Will you be my partner tonight? For whatever this stealth thing Diego and Mark have put together is?" I was going to pair up with Heather, but she can deal. Right now, I can't be anywhere but with him.

He links his fingers with mine, squeezing gently. There's a tempest in his eyes when he says, "Hayes, I couldn't spend a second away from you tonight if I tried."

32

"I KNOW I GAVE YOU a hard time about the first community event being on a night I was working," says Maggie, her attention on Diego, who's sprawled on the hospital bed, an ice pack conforming to his forehead. "But you didn't have to bring the party to me."

Diego groans, and Maggie shakes her head, turning to Ian and me. "What were you even doing out there?"

The nurse at reception had asked something similar when our disheveled trio stepped up. I couldn't blame her. Diego's nose had bled all over my shirt, while Ian was sans shirt entirely, having sacrificed his tee to contain the nosebleed. Maggie found him a blue scrub shirt to wear while we waited. It does not fit him. At *all*.

Ian's eyes flit to mine, and I fight a smile, color rushing to my cheeks. There are several ways to answer her question. We'd started out playing the evening's activity, which, as per Mark's breakdown, was essentially hide-and-go-seek in the dark with the addition of the "seekers" being in cars. As one of the hiding pairs, Ian and I were trying to get from the gym to a park about a mile up the road without being spotted and collected by those seeking.

Easy enough. But because there was no telling which cars held seekers and which were simply passers-by, we scrambled for a hiding spot every time we encountered headlights. We dodged countless cars and spent several minutes squatting behind a dumpster to hide from what ended up being a food delivery guy crawling up the street trying to read house numbers.

I give Maggie the basics and shrug. "At that point, Ian's knee started to bug him, so we decided to wait it out behind a hedge in someone's yard."

Ian bumps my shoulder with his. I flush again. Not someone's yard, exactly. The house had a for-sale sign and a lock box on the front door. And when we realized we hadn't tripped a motion sensor light, we figured there were more…*satisfying* ways to enjoy our time in the dark.

I twine my fingers with his. I don't know what's come over me. It's one thing to striptease in the privacy of my own room, but seizing the cover of night as an opportunity to solicit my boyfriend with a "How are you?" and promptly going topless was entirely out of left field.

But—I squeeze his hand, and he squeezes back—I guess that's who I am now.

"Sure." Maggie's tone is knowing. "And Diego appeared…"

"From above," Ian offers. I nod. A vibration had picked up in the darkness, accompanied by the bright beat Diego uses for every alert, incoming calls, timers, alarms; the sound has started to haunt my dreams. It was enough to rouse me from, well… my arousal, and that was when I spotted a light outlining a shape among the lower branches of the tree above us.

"He dropped his phone. It barely missed us," Ian adds. He'd

looked up, too, and as the phone came hurtling our way, he threw his arm over me. A second later, we were rolling, stopping only when we hit the hedge.

"I tried to catch it," Diego wails. "I'm so sorry! Ellie, I wasn't watching, I promise. I didn't see your—"

"Did he even try to break his fall?" I ask over whatever it is Diego is about to assure me he hadn't seen. Because it was my boobs. And everyone in this room knows it.

"It doesn't look it," Maggie says. I don't know how she's kept a straight face through all of this. "Probably for the best. The skull is designed to take a certain amount of impact. If he'd put up his hands, he probably would have broken his wrists."

She nods at her patient. "I'm discharging him. There's no indication he's suffered a concussion, but just in case, wake him up every now and then to check for symptoms. Confusion, memory loss, emotional swings. Presuming that's distinguishable from his normal behavior."

"Any more paperwork on our end?" Ian asks, approaching the bed.

"Nope," she says. "Ellie's got it. You're good to go."

Ian looks at me in silent lack of disbelief, and I shrug. "I have photos of all their IDs, insurance cards, and emergency contact information on my phone. It seemed prudent."

His smile holds that same something I glimpsed back at Firehouse, before Grant interrupted. Something to hang a hope on. He nods at our charge. "Shall we?"

The moment we maneuver him into the hallway, Diego announces in Spanish that he has to go to the bathroom. Ian follows. "I'll go with him. Make sure he doesn't drown in a urinal."

"I'll meet you out front," I say, and point to the double doors below the exit sign. Ian nods, giving me the same look, and I remember what he said as everyone had filed into the gym. "So much for not spending a second apart tonight, huh?"

"I'll make it up to you," he says, and his eyes go dark. "That's a *promise*."

I'm feeling more than a little lightheaded when Maggie intercepts me at the nurse's station. "Ellie?"

"Hmm?"

She gestures me closer. I lean in, and she whispers, *"Your shirt's on inside out."*

I look down at my front, the rise of the tank's seams obvious in the harsh light from overhead. "So it is!" I chirp.

"There were some muddy handprints on Ian's chest, too. Just a heads-up for later." She winks. "Enjoy the rest of your evening."

"Will do!" I say and continue down the hall and out the doors.

Recognition sends a chill over my shoulders, sapping me of the giddy lightness so completely that I stagger to a stop. It's not the entrance we'd used earlier, but the main lobby, which separates the emergency room from the rest of the medical facility.

I know it well; countless trips up the leftmost hallway for my gynecologist, then, more recently, traveling down the right for the neurologist. I got to visit a whole separate wing for my MRI, where I pulled up an image of a coyote-proof dog harness for the receptionist; her back patio bordered a nature preserve, and she was concerned about leaving her Pomeranian outside. I wonder if she bought one.

It feels like a lifetime ago, or like someone else's life. But now that I'm here, it's all too real. This is no place for hope.

"Ellie?" asks a familiar voice. It's Dr. Selah.

I scan to spot the gynecologist a few paces away, emerging from the left corridor. "Hi, Doctor!" I send her a genuine smile, happy to see her at her full height and not seated between my legs.

"I haven't seen you in some time," she says, her eyes moving over me as she approaches. "Are you well?"

I frown, not meaning to, and quickly school my face into something less expressive of *seriously?*

But her eyes go soft. "I should know better than to ask that in this building." She looks at me more closely, and I clock the moment the blood on my shirt registers. "Oh, Ellie, are you—"

"It's not mine!" I assure her. "One of my roommates fell out of a tree."

Her forehead creases, and I suppress another frown. My living situation has changed *significantly* since the last time we saw one another.

"Cole and I broke up. It wasn't…" I don't know how to finish that sentence. Or why I'd started it in the first place. Was I about to claim that the reasons why I was going to her *hadn't* contributed to the demise of our relationship? "It's been an interesting few months."

"In any case, you look well." She studies me. "If you don't mind my saying so, you look"—she makes the double-fisted gesture generally used to convey muscularity—"fit."

"Yeah! I'm working reception at a gym. Membership is a perk. It's been nice experiencing *elective* discomfort." At her wary expression, I explain, "Being sore from back squats is preferable to extreme pain because my body has decided that my uterine lining should be on a kidney this month."

Her responding laugh seems involuntary. "You've always had a colorful perspective."

"It's either that or scream."

"Good point." She smiles. "It's nice to see that you've found a way to make peace with your body."

I tip my head, pretending to consider. "More like a temporary suspension of hostilities."

"I'm glad. Especially given those exchanges I had with Dr. Hartman's office. I'm so sorry," she says, placing a hand on my arm. "I meant to follow up with you—"

"It's fine...*now*," I say, and Dr. Selah's hand returns to her side. "Another item on the list of maladies."

"Oh, Ellie!" Diego's voice calls from behind me, and I turn to watch him half jog toward me, one hand still clutching the ice pack to his face. "Ellie, I didn't know where you'd gone!"

Ian rolls his eyes as he saunters after him. "He was *very* concerned."

"Ian, this is Dr. Selah," I say, taking note of the tastefully appreciative glance the doctor sends Ian. That scrub shirt is fighting for its life. "And Diego—"

"Ellie is my roommate," Diego explains. "There are three of us! And she's been teaching us how to cook and be adults. I can make an omelet!"

To her credit, Dr. Selah just keeps smiling. She has a wonderful smile; she hasn't had much use for it during my visits. "A good omelet is one of life's pleasures. Pleased to meet you both. Ellie, always a delight." She cocks her head thoughtfully. "You really do look well."

"Thank you," I say. "I feel...great."

"I'm glad to hear it. And hoping that I *don't* hear from Dr. Hartman's office again."

I raise a hand, crossing my fingers. "Ditto," I say in parting.

Diego waves at her broadly, and she waves back with a laugh, then heads for the exit. I watch the double doors part as she approaches, then shut behind her.

I turn to find Ian studying me, a question in his look. "She's who diagnosed my endometriosis," I explain.

He nods, brow still pleated. "Sure. Let's go."

33

"WELL, I JUST FISHED GRASS out of my bra," I say, stepping out of my bathroom. "That was a first." I look at Ian, perched on the corner of my desk. He's frowning at his phone.

Unease creeps over me. He'd been quiet on the drive. I wanted to believe it was how he was coping with Diego's running monologue, but there was a tension to his silence. It was still thick while we got Diego situated in his room, and I hoped it would run its course while I took my time cleaning up. But he turns his frown on me. My stomach drops.

"Why was your doctor talking about a neurologist?" His voice is too calm.

My stomach bypasses the basement and plummets to the subcellar. "How—"

"I looked up the hospital's directory. Only one Hartman." He holds up his phone. On the screen is a photo of the good doctor, as well as information about his hours and the number for his office. He has a five-star rating from patients. Good for him.

I cross my arms and lean against the doorframe of the bathroom. "A little *invasive*, don't you think?"

"Forgive me for having some sensitivity around the woman in my life receiving specialized medical care." It comes out of him sharp, but then he sighs and closes his eyes for a beat. When his gray gaze returns to me, it's softened. "I'm sorry," he says gently.

My heart joins my stomach somewhere subterranean. The hope that had felt so promising back at Firehouse seems like such a fragile thing. That whole scenario it generated was hung on never having to tell him at all; I don't know that it can support the truth.

I start small. "When we met, I couldn't see out of my right eye. Optic neuritis. Inflammation on the optic nerve keeping what my eye was seeing from getting to my brain."

"That's...that's why you'd cock your head."

"You noticed that?"

He frowns. "It's you, Ellie. Your body. Of course I noticed." Before I can unpack that, he continues. "You haven't done that for a while...the vision came back?" He sounds hopeful.

I grab on to the hope and white-knuckle it. "Yeah! It still gets foggy when I overheat. That puts pressure on the nerve. So, a good workout, or particularly athletic sex. We've left me half blind more than once," I say, relieved to be able to contribute some levity. It rouses a smirk from him, but the upturn vanishes a beat later.

I rest my head against the doorframe. "Other than that, I don't see color as brightly on that side now. And I get a phantom flash in the corner of my vision when I look really far to the right. Which is weird. That's the only area I could see during the nerve attack."

"Nerve attack?"

"That's what it was. It took three doctors to get the diagnosis, but Dr. Hartman"—I nod to the phone still in his hand—"he figured it out."

He nods, and I hope against hope that this will be the end of the subject. My eye was weird, now it's not; end of story. But when he meets my eyes again, he wears an expression of such obvious hurt, it's like I've kicked him.

"Why didn't you tell me?" His voice is quiet. "I asked you, when we talked about your goals at the gym, I asked you *directly* if you had any medical conditions. You said no."

"You asked me if I had any injuries or anything that would restrict my movement."

"You were *blind* in one eye, Ellie."

"I knew how to accommodate it."

"But I didn't! The guys and the others working out around you didn't! Any one of us could have been in your blind spot and interfered with a movement, and you or someone else could have been hurt."

"But that never happened," I insist.

"It could have been a liability for the gym. Had you considered that? If something had happened, it could have been on the facility. It would have been on *me*."

The oversight dulls some of my defensiveness, and I sag a little, the ridge in the doorframe digging into my shoulder. "You're right. I'm sorry about that." I really am. And I also really want to defuse this situation. "I was already the newbie, coming in, knowing nothing. My fucked-up insides have made me the damaged one for years. I didn't want to be that here, too. And it's fine now—"

"What if your eye goes out again? Could that happen with this nerve thing? Would you tell me?"

I scoff. "If it happens again, I'll have different priorities, I assure you."

I should not have said that.

"What does that mean?" Ian's question comes out flat. I don't answer. "If it happens again, will it...will it be permanent? Ellie, oh shit." He's at my side before I can react, hands rising to cup my cheeks as he looks down at me. It's more than worry on his face. "Oh Jesus, babe, I'm so sorry." He pulls me into a hug. "I hadn't thought about that."

"It's okay," I say. Tears have sprung to my eyes. Joy and panic war in my chest. He cares. So much. *Too* much. And I want it too much.

He holds me more tightly, and I realize that I'm shaking. One of his hands smooths over my back, and the rush and relief I get from it is cruel.

I've let this go on too long. I've forgotten who I really am, and what it is to be the real me, always on time but never a good time. I don't get to have this life. I don't get to have him. I don't get to hope.

I straighten enough that he has to loosen his hold. "The vision loss could be permanent. But symptoms could take any number of forms. In any case, a second flare-up would mean that I have multiple sclerosis."

Ian's arms stiffen. He steps away, his hands falling from me like I've shrugged out of a jacket. "What?"

"Half of the time, the eye thing is the first sign. The MRI I had two months ago showed no damage that would correspond with MS, which was great," I say, lightly, "and when the six months is up, I'll have a second MRI and they'll look again. But if I have another nerve attack in that window, I'm diagnosed. That's why I lost it the day I got dizzy. I—"

"You thought it was the second nerve attack," he finishes for me. His face is so hard. "And when I asked you *directly* then," he bites the words out, "you said that you were *scared.*"

"I *was,*" I say, defensively.

"But that wasn't all."

"What does it matter? It didn't end up being anything."

"It was a lie of omission."

Why is he being so hostile about this? And why am I arguing with him? "How, Ian? How would knowing this have been useful?"

"You've had this hanging over you this whole time, and you never said anything to me!"

That his instinct is to point out that this has been a burden I've been shouldering alone does not elude me. He was annoyed by the eye thing, but this is different. He's mad because I left him out of something massive in my life. Because I wouldn't let him help.

I get back on the defensive. "What could you have done?"

"Been aware! Known to look out for signs—"

"What signs, Ian?" I ask, weeks of sidelined fears creeping in, the past decade of crushed hopes overwhelming his credentials. I think I'm going to throw up. "I don't even know what signs to look for. I just get to obsess over every minor glitch in my already fucked-up body and hope it goes away. There was no reason to burden you with this, too."

He's shaking his head. "I've heard that line of logic before, Ellie. It was bullshit when my parents used it, and it's bullshit from you. When my mom relapsed, she and my dad decided that Grant and I didn't need to know the severity of it. So when she went from 'a little sick' to terminal, it was a pretty huge shock."

"This isn't like that. This isn't a terminal diagnosis. There isn't even *a* diagnosis! It's just a maybe. It's a maybe for the next few months, less of a maybe for the next five years—"

"Five *years*?" He stares at me. "How long does it take to get a fucking diagnosis?"

"If something doesn't happen in the next few months, there's still a 20 percent chance of it developing in the next five years."

His eyes bug. "And you're just going to live with that?"

"I don't see any alternative."

He runs his fingers through his hair, tugging it. "I can't believe this."

"This isn't even for you to take on, Ian. All this was only temporary, anyway. This whole thing, renting the room here, working at the gym." I point back and forth between us. "Whatever this is—"

"Us."

"Everything! All of this was a break from my life while I waited out the window. It's a fantasy. It's not who I am. I make to-do lists and go to bed by ten. I don't skate on the living room floor and have a fling with my hunky boss!"

But...I do. Or, at least, I do now.

The color drains from his face, his expression going slack. I don't think he could look more stunned if I'd slapped him.

His eyelids flutter, and his head shakes slightly, eyes going hard. "So you've just been passing the time, then? All of this. Like you said. Everything. Us. None of it has mattered."

I know that this is my chance to nip this in the bud. I can just agree and it will cut him so deeply, he'll be severed from me completely. But some sentimental, stupid part of me says, "I didn't say it doesn't matter."

"But it's not real. Not for you."

The *you* is an accusation. And a contrast. It's not real for me, but it's real for him.

But we can't be real because the *me* in it doesn't exist. With him, I'm Break Ellie. Not Real Life Ellie. So it doesn't taste like a lie when I say, "No. Not for me."

His face is bloodless. I feel the color drain from myself as well, but I call on the scaffolding I've spent the past decade-plus erecting. I hadn't known it, but it had all gone up for this. Because no matter how many times I try to tell myself differently, he *is* the one who will stay. It won't matter how hard things could get, how far I might deteriorate, what shell he might be left caring for. He'd stay through it.

And I won't do that to him.

We stay in our stunned silence: Ian, white faced at my cruelty; me, erect in defiance of the seismic shift that's taken place inside of me. For so long, I've been afraid that I'd be alone. That my ruined insides or broken personality would keep getting me left behind. That was the pattern until now.

Now I have the man I know won't walk away. But I can't bear the thought of him staying. Not for what this could look like. I won't ask that of him. I want more for him.

"Then you're fired," he croaks. His voice is so broken, it takes me a second to process that he's even used words.

I blink. "Excuse me?"

"We're done," he says, his voice tight, but his own again. "Completely. If none of this has any significance to you, then I don't want you on the team."

"The *team*? That's your concern? That I'm going to be a drag on morale? Fuck that. You can't fire me! I quit."

"Fine!"

"Leave!"

"I am!" He sputters, and starts for the door to the side yard, me on his heels. He turns so suddenly, I almost run into him. And it's a mercy I don't, because if we'd collided, I'd be collapsing into him and I don't think I'd be getting up again.

He points at me, his face fierce. "And don't even *think* about coming back to the gym."

"I'll just work out here, then!"

"Fine!" He flings open the door and storms out. I stare into the darkness, listening to his angry footsteps on the gravel path.

I want him to come back. I want to go after him. But I told him to go.

And now he's gone. Because that's what happens.

I end up collapsing anyway.

34

THE DAYS THAT FOLLOW are agony.

Not just emotionally. My body has completely rebelled, attacking me with the full force of barbed wire across the kidneys that makes getting out of bed an eye-watering ordeal. I spend Sunday and Monday holed up, mainlining ultra-strength Tylenol and cursing my maker. And crying.

And screening calls. My absence from the gym does not go unnoticed, and on Tuesday, I admit to Babs and Helen via text that I'm basically bedridden with pain. Within the hour, I've received a care package containing three pints of ice cream from Jeni's and a selection of Haribo chewy candies, which tells me that Heather and or Mark had been asked about my preferences. Accustomed to my inoperative periods, they send me messages of sympathy and offers of Taco Bell, but I demur. They know too much, and one look at me will tell them exactly what's going on. I reply with appreciative gifs and promises to keep them updated. I am an asshole.

When I do emerge from my miserable isolation that evening, the guys tiptoe around me. I worry what I might be modeling as far as expectations regarding the menstrual cycle. Diego roasts a chicken for dinner. Alistair watches me like he might one of those extreme driving videos out of Russia, with a combination of anticipatory anxiety and morbid curiosity. Grant avoids eye contact. Ian is not mentioned.

I'm at the Ping-Pong table for a change of scenery Wednesday evening, testing out all 240 of my felt-tip markers to see which are out of ink and how long I can commit myself to the task before lobotomizing myself with one. Habit has me glancing at my phone every few minutes, but I turned it off when a new group chat populated. Babs, Helen, Heather, and Mark. Helen asked Ian how I was doing. He didn't know. She would like to know why not. Theories abound.

Grant joins me at the table. He sits, picks up one of the scraps of cardstock I'm using to test my pens, and turns it over between his fingers. "I talked to Ian."

It takes me three tries to recap my cyan. I want to ask, "About me? Has he asked about me? How is he? Forlorn? Pining? Indignant?" but manage a cool "Yeah?" instead.

"About what I want to do. Education, and all of that."

I put down the pen, giving Grant my full attention. "How did it go?"

"He was surprised. Worried that it would be a lot of responsibility for me. But he...got it?" His brow puckers, as though he still hasn't worked out how this conclusion came to be. "He understood that, like, helping to establish that foundation of fitness is part of why I want to do it. Because it is!" He leans in, face alight. "Ian helped me figure out how to express that. I want to introduce kids to how awesome it is to move their body on purpose."

"To move their body *with intention*?" I ask, unable to help myself.

Grant snaps his fingers, pointing at me. "Yes! Oh, that is a great way of putting it. Yeah! *How awesome it is to move their body with intention*," he echoes.

I doodle the phrasing for him on another scrap of cardstock, angling the pen for a flourish. I push it to him over the table, and he picks it up, still beaming.

"Rad."

"So he really wasn't…" My first thought is *butthurt*, but I go with "Put out?"

"Nah. I mean, it's not *that* different, you know? And he understands my motivation. He relates to that. He's just thinking ahead, to me, dealing with parents and school districts and even getting a job in the first place. But he said I'd be good at it." He sits taller. "He's stoked on the kids' classes for the gym, too. He's going to look over my notes and stuff, but he thought it was a great idea. He said he was proud of me for figuring all this out, and my commitment to it. That was cool."

"I'm glad."

He turns the little card over. "It's so crazy that I stressed about telling him for so long."

I shake my head. "He's your big brother. You look up to him, and don't want to disappoint him. And there was a chance that not following in his footsteps would come across as rejection, and no one wants to be responsible for that kind of hurt."

I'd know.

"Um…" He worries his bottom lip, and I concede to the obvious follow-up. "I haven't asked Ian, but what happened with you two?"

"We…didn't work."

Grant sits back in his chair, brow furrowed again. "He's been in a real dick mood since you stopped coming in," he adds. "That's part of why I talked to him. Figured, he was already grumpy, might as well just get it over with."

"Bold strategy."

He nods, the motion more a reflex than sign of agreement. "It's just a bummer. I hoped that being with him would mean you'd stick around longer."

This tugs at my heartstrings. "Oh, you guys are fine. You hardly need me."

"We don't need you for stuff," he counters. It stings, literally stings, like an actual punch to my chest, and it's a struggle to keep my face placid. "Not that it isn't awesome. Your eggs are still better than Diego's. But we like having you around, just, like, *being* you. It's cool, coming home and knowing you're here, seeing your stuff around. It's cozy." He grins. "*You're* cozy."

The word wraps around my aching heart. "I like *cozy*. Thank you."

Grant's smile broadens, then wavers. "I liked that for Ian, too. And *you*. This one time—" he falters. "This is gonna sound like some real creeper shit, but I swear, I just happened to look at you two. You were on the couch in the lobby, and he was out, like old man–style, head back, mouth open—" He drops his head back, mouth agape, to demonstrate, and I laugh. I have absolutely caught Ian in that position.

Grant lifts his head and catches my smile. "Anyway, the way you looked at him…You smiled all soft, like it was the best thing ever to be on some shitty pleather couch with my brother. And you cuddled into him, and I think you fell asleep, too. And you were smiling. *Cozy*," he emphasizes. "Like, how having you here makes the house cozy, but for you, being with Ian made you *feel* cozy. And the same for him."

Anything I might say in response is lodged among the tangle of emotions in my throat. Cozy is right. Cozy is what I felt, among so many other things.

Grant excuses himself to go shower, and I nod, keeping my eyes on the table as he stands, hoping that he doesn't see the tears in my eyes.

A sharp *yip!* echoes in the hall. "Jesus, Alistair! You scared the shit outta me!" I look up to spot roommate number two entering the room from the hallway. Grant's voice grows faint with distance as he grumbles, "Lurking in the dark like a fucking weirdo."

I cock my head as Alistair takes Grant's seat. *"Alistair,"* I chide. "Were you lurking in the dark like a fucking weirdo?"

Alistair doesn't say anything, but he's angled himself slightly toward the hall. A door closes, and the bathroom fan switches on. He lifts his chin at me. "Is it MS? The diagnosis you're waiting out," he clarifies, like he hadn't slapped me with the initial question.

Ice prickles over my shoulders. My silence probably answers for me, but I nod. How the hell does he know?

"Fuck." The expletive draws out as Alistair falls back into the chair. He crosses his arms over his chest. "I've been noodling on it since I overheard you talking to Mark and Heather when you moved in. It wasn't until the eye thing that it clicked for me. But you never brought it up, and I figured that meant you didn't want to talk about it. I don't blame you. That *sucks.*"

"Thank you," I say, not quite grasping how we're having this exchange; I was still settling into *cozy.*

"What do you know about the condition?"

"Generalities. Loss of mobility and feeling. Exhaustion. I—" I suck in a breath. I feel winded every time I try to approach this. "I've avoided researching because I know that once I go down that rabbit hole, I'll never come out again."

"Yeah, that sounds like you." He drums his fingers against the table, pausing the rhythm to point at me. "Have you ever had mono? Like, when you were younger."

I nod, remembering the article my mom sent. I still haven't read it. "Seventh grade."

"Did your neurologist ask you that?"

"No. Why?" I ask, wariness creeping in on my confusion.

"Huh. 'Cause a few years back a study linked Epstein-Barr to MS. It was a *huge* study. They worked from something like ten million blood samples, and found that individuals who were *not* infected with Epstein-Barr virus virtually never get MS. It's only *after* Epstein-Barr virus infection that the risk of MS jumps something like twenty-five-, thirty-fold? Of all infections, it has the clearest connection."

I shake my head, not following, and not sure I want to. "So, is Epstein-Barr mono?"

"It's usually what *causes* mono. But other viruses can cause it, too," he adds, hastily. "And it's not like everyone who's had Epstein-Barr gets MS. It's just…"

"Everyone who has MS has had Epstein-Barr," I finish for him.

"Pretty much."

I do not care for this new information. And it looks like Alistair regrets having brought it up; his handsome features pucker like he's bitten into something from Built Box before Diego's doctored it.

"Your eye was what had you getting checked out?" he asks,

voice tentative. It's the least confident I've ever heard him. I nod, and he grimaces.

"It's cleared up since. Now I get to experience the joy of waking up every morning, afraid to open my eyes in case my vision's gone again, instead."

"Ugh. Fuck that." He frowns. "When was that... It's a nerve attack, right?"

"Yeah. It was the week I moved in with you guys."

"Was it why your boyfriend broke up with you?"

The allusion still stings. "It was the straw that broke that particular camel's back."

He nods, eyes going bright, like I've done more than answer a question; I've confirmed a suspicion.

"You been noodling on that, too?" I ask, dryly.

He makes a dismissive sound. "Not that it caused *that* breakup."

"What do you mean?" I immediately regret asking.

Alistair leans back in his chair, resting it on its back legs. I arch a brow. He knows I hate that. Which is why he's doing it; his responding smirk is all challenge.

"Does Ian know about the MS stuff, or did you nip that particular camel in the bud?"

"You're mixing metaphors."

His front chair legs land hard against the floor. "Doesn't matter. In any case, you've made the decision for him." At my sustained scowl, he elaborates. "You either dumped him out of the blue before he found out, or he found out, and you *freaked* and left him before he had the chance to do what your shitty ex-boyfriend did. It's a fucked-up move either way."

"And there's no third scenario?" I counter, though I'm rattled. "Just me, being a cowardly asshole."

"You and I both know that Ian wouldn't leave you over this. You *know* him. You know his past, which, come *on*. That only makes this worse." Some of the hostility leaves his expression. "If this was just about you being scared, that would be one thing. But Ian's *in* it. That dude cares about you. And you are throwing that away because you're being a little bitch."

"Excuse you? Just because you've turned your brain back on, you think you get to dole out insight? You don't know. You don't know what I've already had to deal with, what this fucked-up body has already cost me—"

"Oh, what? A dickhead boyfriend? Some loss!"

Tears spring to my eyes. "Ian's already had to accommodate enough." The words barely make it through my clenched teeth. "I'm not asking for more."

For the first time in this exchange, or ever in the time I've known him, Alistair seems surprised. His eyes widen, going distant, his mouth shaping something my comment has evidently made irrelevant, because he doesn't voice it. He just stares at me, and I stare back, conceding to the tears already on my cheeks. I don't know when they fell.

Alistair blinks, lips pressing into a line. After another beat of my wretched silence, he stands. He shakes his head, disappointment clear in each side-to-side movement. "Then I guess you never really knew him. Because if you did, you'd never believe that you'd ever have to ask."

35

"ABSOLUTELY NOT," I SAY, retreating to the back door. "Nope. No thank you."

"Ellie Hayes, don't you *dare*," Babs calls after me.

I turn back around. The entire Coffee Coup has assembled in the backyard. They're dressed to work out, which was what I was hoping to do after Diego knocked on my door, inviting me to try a kettlebell set Grant wanted to test. It had been a ruse.

I level a glare at my roommates. Grant and Diego look appropriately abashed, though Alistair raises his head, defiant. *Traitors*. But while my roommates are at least impressionable enough to consider forgiving, Heather and Mark, who are also here, should really know better.

Heather raises a shoulder. "You're not the only one who can activate a phone tree."

Fine. I focus all my ire on Mark; he always breaks first, anyway.

"We haven't shared any business that isn't ours to share. But…" His shrug conveys some degree of remorse at least. "Come on, Ellie. We're worried about you."

"I don't know what you're talking about," Babs scoffs, hands on her hips. "We're here for some evening kettlebells. So, I propose that we start moving these weights, and if Ellie decides to explain why she thinks she can simply vanish into the ether at the same time that Ian transforms into a complete ogre? Well! We'll just turn down the music to listen."

Helen frowns at her. "An ogre? Really?"

"He's been grumpy," offers Russ. "Mostly, he looks miserable. Lots of moping."

I am dying to know more. But I'm not giving in to their manipulation so easily. I turn to Grant. "We warming up or what?"

"He misses you," Helen whispers. I check my watch; she made it a whole four minutes.

I pivot my curtsy lunges to the opposite direction. It puts me face-to-bug-eyed-face with Bleu Cheese the Frenchie, who Jacob is using as a weight.

I scratch the dog's chin and smile at his owner. "Thanks again for taking care of matting and mounting all those clippings," I say, to get ahead of anything he might have on deck for me. "They look amazing. Are you sure the petty cash covered it?"

"I was happy to do it," he blurts. "Firehouse means so much to me, and I think you did such a beautiful job. What you've done for the gym, and how Ian—"

I pivot again. This time I'm facing Maggie. She raises her brows.

Nope.

I'm about to circle back to my starting point when Grant calls time. The Coffee Coup spreads out, choosing from the kettlebells we have on hand and deciding who's going to share which weights.

"I'm looking forward to these endorphins," I tell Diego, because he's the only person in the vicinity not actively watching me for some sort of performance.

"That's good! Because…endorphins make you happy! And I like for you to be happy." His eyes are wide and imploring. "And…for Ian to be happy?"

"Oh, Diego, I—"

The music cuts off suddenly.

Babs stands beside Grant. She's taken his phone, her finger on the green Pause button dominating the screen. "Oh, I'm sorry. Ellie, dear, were you about to say something?"

Anger lashes through me. This is stupid. I don't owe anyone anything. I am well within my rights to go back to my room and ignore the meddlesome horde gathered in my backyard. But at the same time…they're my meddlesome horde. They're here because they care. And I care about them. And now I've hurt someone we all care about.

"It's my fault," I say. "Ian being in ogre mode. Well, not my fault. His behavior is his own," I amend, making eye contact with each of my roommates in turn because this is an important distinction to make. "But I wasn't honest with Ian about some things that I'm going through. And when he found out, I downplayed our relationship." I sigh. "When we started seeing one another, I was treating it like a fling—"

"Ooh!" Diego crows. "Just being *sexy*."

"Yes. But…" I throw up my hands. "It's *him*. I don't think there's a way to keep things *just* sexy with him."

Grant scowls, I assume, at the mention of the word *sexy* in conjunction with his brother. But then—"You love him!" He is belligerent with delight, his smile massive. "You *love* Ian!"

The backyard is a chorus of approving *aww*s.

I sigh, the sound starting somewhere near my toes. I'm not admitting that to them. Not first, anyway. That's for him. "I've really screwed up."

Diego nods, sagely. "You told him about just being sexy. And that hurt him."

"That's—" I look to Alistair, who shrugs. "Yeah. More or less."

"Less," Alistair grumbles.

I glance at Heather and Mark, who smile encouragingly. It's mine to share. And even if it's been pulled from me semi-unwillingly by a crew of well-meaning busybodies, I think I want them to know. Because they're my people now, too. Not just Break Me, but...me.

"This is going to take time to explain. Should we—" I indicate the porch, where we might all take a seat, but Diego and Grant plop down on the ground, sitting crisscross applesauce, and look up at me as if ready for story time. After a moment, the others follow suit, arranging themselves around the yard.

"Should we still keep working out?" Diego asks. "While you tell us this?"

"Crunches!" says Grant. "Ellie, you continue, we'll do crunches. Everyone, ready? Go!"

I crunch, too. "When I met y'all, I could only see out of one eye," I begin, and lay out the saga of my un-diagnosis, from that first cycloptic morning to the day it cleared up. "I'm fine for now," I conclude. "But it's a waiting game."

"That's why you wanted the lease to be six months," Diego surmises. "Next exercise?"

"Air squats?" offers Jacob.

I look around as everyone stands up, though I avoid catching Maggie's eye; if there's any opinion I don't want, it's that of a medical professional. There are frowns, some confusion. Babs and Helen watch me with the same sad wariness I got from folks when I'd first share about my eye and what it could mean. I see it for the care it is, but part of me hates it, too. Back to being broken.

It's quiet as we begin our squats, the only sounds the errant pop of ankles and knees as we lower ourselves to parallel and stand back up again.

"Ian got upset because of Mom," Grant says. "He's talked about that. How unfair it felt, not knowing how sick she was."

A fresh wave of guilt washes over me. "I get that. And I get where she was coming from, too. There'd already been such a disruption to your lives the first time she'd been ill, I can see how she wouldn't want to subject y'all to that a second time. Especially when there wasn't anything you could do about it." I grimace. "But it was also an unkindness. It was unfair. And while my situation isn't the same—"

Alistair clears his throat.

"—it treads on some of the same sensitivities. And not disclosing about my eye was also something that could have been bad for the gym. I hadn't considered that, but mostly..." I shake my head at myself. It had been really dumb of me not to think of that, but my vision wasn't the real issue. It never was. "I was afraid to tell him."

It is a mercy that no one asks me why.

"Would…" Grant's voice is tentative. "Would you like some cheese?"

I laugh. "No, but thank you."

"Do you want to cook him something?" Diego asks. "I read that the best way to a man's heart is through his stomach. It was in the margin of a cookbook."

"Good call," I say. "But I think that a simple apology might do the trick."

Diego stands, shaking out his legs. "I don't know. If his blood sugar is low, he might not be receptive. That wasn't in a cookbook. That's just true with him."

A number of others mutter in agreement. I smile.

"So…" Helen sits back on her heels. "Are you going to go over there?"

My smile twists into a grimace, but I nod. I'm the one who hadn't been honest. I'm the one who'd known better. I'd admitted as much to Ian the afternoon he introduced me to the taste of colors. That however flawed my relationship with Cole had been, my not being honest with him about my pain had damaged what we had.

I'd given Cole reason not to trust me. And now I've done the same to Ian. If I go to him now, he'll have every right to turn me away. But I have to try. Because I love him.

"Good." She lifts her chin, like she's shooing me off. "Go."

"What, now?" I shake my head. "What about my endorphins?"

"You can run!" Grant suggests.

"We can all go!" says Babs.

"But...just on the run," Diego adds. "You need to do the talking on your own. And the *sexy*."

I look around the yard. A sea of beaming faces—plus Alistair, who just looks smug—shines on me, awaiting my verdict.

I hold up my palms in defeat. "Let's go."

36

I LOOK UP THE LENGTH of rope to where it's anchored directly above the window outside Ian's apartment.

This is about to get very, very stupid.

"You've got this, Ellie!" Diego cheers, his tone hushed.

"Sure," I say. "It's only *twice* the height of the rope *in*side, but why worry about that?"

"Nah." Alistair nods at the rope. "It's poetic. One of the first things he showed you was how to climb a rope. This is some full-circle shit."

"Can you not use this?" Mark points to the keypad between the bay doors. "Or knock?"

I shake my head. After being-fired-slash-quitting, I don't feel entitled to using the code for downstairs, and I can't bring myself to knock on the outside door to the stairwell. Ian might not even want to see me; I'm actually pretty confident about that, which is why I forbade anyone to warn him that I was on my way.

But he forgot to take down the rope, and seeing it feels like the universe has issued me a challenge. A feat of strength to prove I'm worthy of the gentleman in the tower…or…something. I'm sure there's a literary reference I could use.

"Alistair's right," I say. "Some full-circle shit."

"Plus, it's gonna look rad," he adds. I nod. The rad factor is also a mark in its favor.

"Thank you, all of you, for the moral support," I say, and look over the group. "I could say something about how desperately y'all need to learn to mind your own goddamn business, but—" I return to the rope. "I have a gesture to make."

The assembly responds with almost silent cheers, and I initiate my climb. I lift, lean, crimp, and stand my way up the line, the movements smooth, even if the rope isn't. But the whispered support keeps me moving, and I'm at the window in no time. I peer in.

Ian stands in his kitchen, drinking a Topo Chico. A quiet night in. Hope he wasn't too attached to the idea.

"Is he there?" Diego asks, and I look down—big mistake—to see him cupping his hands over his mouth to amplify his whisper.

"He's there," comes a new voice, and the group swivels en masse to spot Tom on his porch next door. He nods at me. "He moved past that window on my side just a minute ago. Looks miserable, too, by the way," he adds.

"Thank you, Tom," Babs says. "He stayed behind to be lookout in case you ended up making your way over here."

I free a hand to give a thumbs-up, and take in one last steadying breath before I knock a rapid shave-and-a-haircut against the glass.

Ian's head pivots toward the door, where knocking would make sense, but when I rap a second time, he looks to the window. I wave. His responding *"Jesus!"* is very loud.

Ian jogs to the window. He fumbles with the latches that unlock the pane, and then he's lifting it up, leaning out and reaching a hand toward me. "What the hell are you doing?"

My stomach lurches, but I force a smile. "Hi! I need to talk to you."

"I—" He looks down. I follow his line of sight to my supporters. *"What?"*

"Dude!" Grant hollers. "You left the rope out! You'd have totally chewed us out for that."

Ian ignores this, attention returning to me. "I have a door. You have the key code."

"You fired me! I didn't want to overstep. But I am questioning my approach." I take his still-extended hand to tow myself toward the window ledge. I let go to brace myself when my rear settles onto the alcove but maintain a death grip on the rope with my other hand and feet.

"Get in here." He grabs me around the waist, and I release the rope to wrap my hands around his shoulders as he hauls me through the window. I'm still holding on to him as I find my footing inside.

Arms around me, he leans his head out the window. "You are a terrible influence!"

"Whatever, man," Alistair fires back. "You know that was *sick.*"

"You good, Ellie?" Heather asks. There's an edge of concern to her voice.

"A few rope splinters, but I'm cool," I assure her, even though that wasn't what she'd been asking. "Thank you for everything, folks. You're dismissed."

Diego claps his hands, commandeering the attention of the group. "Okay, friends! Let's make the most of this and get in another mile! Tom, are you joining—" A door slams. "Okay! No Tom! Everybody else, say good luck to Ellie!"

"Good luck, Ellie!" they call, and I'm reminded of my first haggard morning at Firehouse. We've come so far from the army of the dead.

Heather, Mark, Helen, and Babs linger, and I bid them farewell, promising to call. Mark and Heather send their love, Helen blows me a kiss, and Babs—

"Ian Hammond, you get your mopey head out of your ass and listen to that girl. And Ellie?" A hot-pink talon pierces the night. "You better grovel *good*."

"You mean *well*!" I holler back, and then they're off, too.

Locked in our awkward semi-embrace, Ian and I watch the figures vanish into the darkness. His attention is still out the window when I look up at him. Now that the grand gesture portion of the evening has concluded, it's on to the soul-baring, emotionally vulnerable main event. The prospect should be terrifying—it *is* terrifying—but I'm more than willing to take the risk.

Ian meets my eyes, and in the moment before his expression shutters, he's all softness and hurt and so painfully *him*, my chest aches. His hands leave my sides slowly, and I interpret it as reluctance. "You could have called," he says.

I don't know if he's referring to tonight or the past three days, but in either case, my answer is the same. "I didn't want to." His mouth presses into a flat line, and I lift my chin. "I needed to get yelled at by Alistair, apparently." I keep my eyes on his when I say, "I'm sorry."

Ian doesn't move, nor does he appear moved. "Sorry for what?"

The dull tone cuts a bit, but fair's fair. "A lot." I take in a long breath. "I was unkind to you, and that wasn't okay. I said terrible things, *untrue* things, out of fear and…I don't know. Old habits? And I hate that I did that. It hurt you. *I* hurt you, and that is unacceptable to me."

His face is still stony as he gives me a tight nod. "Thank—"

"And I'm sorry that I didn't tell you about my eye." I say it quickly, the words tripping over one another. "You're right, it could have been a liability, and it was inconsiderate of me not to acknowledge that. But I don't know that I need to apologize about keeping the MS stuff to myself. At least, not initially. But when we started seeing one another…maybe I should have told you? I don't think it was fair of me."

Ian's eyes soften, and a cruel ember of hope flickers to life where my heart should be. "I don't know that I get to be upset that you didn't," he says. The hope burns brighter. "If it is just a possibility. But Ellie, I don't want to be left in the dark about something that serious. Not if we're going to be…" His face closes off again, but the *together* resonates in the silence as clearly as if he'd said it aloud, right beside the days-old echo of my insistence that we were not.

"Is that all?" His voice is as stony as his expression.

I shake my head. "What I said about who I am, or who I *think* I am; that wasn't fair, either. Who I am with the guys and at the gym and with you, it's who I *want* to be. For so long, I've seen myself in a specific way. I've defined myself by certain traits, but I think it was more how those traits had always been received, or the shitty reasons they developed. And I don't think it's a good metric.

"And you, Ian. Jesus." I huff out a laugh, but I barely have the breath for it. "When we caved, I told myself it wasn't serious. That it couldn't be. You're not real—"

He leans back at this, bringing a hand to his chest like he's testing for tangibility.

"You're too good to be true," I clarify, before the man tumbles down an existential spiral. "You are a monument to physical perfection. You're kind and thoughtful and *so* good at your job. Do you know how hot that is? You are both master of your body and how to achieve that mastery! And you use it to enhance the lives of others! And you care about everyone who comes in. Sure, it's your business, but there's something altruistic about it that's arousing to me.

"I want you so much. The way I feel with you? I've never felt more whole. Or seen. Or cared for or challenged. And I don't want to lose that."

I grip the back of my neck with both hands and tug. "I'm not doing this right. It's just...*you*. Not that you're 'just' anything. You're everything wonderful I didn't know could be in one person. And I love you."

Ian just stares at me.

I stare back. I said that out loud. I was saving my *I love you* for him, but I hadn't expected it to come out like that, at the end of a belligerent rant.

Seconds pass. And we're still just...staring at one another. Staring at one another in an increasingly uncomfortable silence.

My pulse thunders in my ears. I may pass out. I just told him that I love him. And he's given me zero reaction. Maybe he's keeping it in? Like how I'm containing the screaming in my head right now because I've ripped open my rib cage to bare my heart to this man and he's standing here as though I've said nothing.

Self-preservation finally kicks in, the dizzying medley of emotions lighting up my stress response, and I pick flight.

"So." I force out a little laugh that teeters precariously close to hysterical. "That's what I needed to put out there. An apology, an *un*-apology, some soul-baring, and a declaration of my love. For you." I hold up a finger for each item, like I'd been tallying them. "I'll go?" I point toward the door. "I'll take the stairs this time, if that's cool."

Ian nods. The movement of his head is the only motion, otherwise the man appears to have turned to stone.

"Great!" I chirp. My chest aches in time with my heartbeat. "Good talk."

I slink toward the door, blinking back tears. I don't know what I thought all that would amount to. I know what I'd *hoped* for, but since when was hope something I could cling to?

The blood whooshes in my skull so loudly that it's by the shuddering floorboards alone that I register Ian's heavy, hurried footsteps toward me. I turn, and the movement propels me into his chest.

"Hayes." His voice is so quiet. "I'm still hurt," he says, and I nod, my eyes averted from his. He holds high on my left bicep and brushes his thumb over the path where the muscle of my shoulder carves into my upper arm. "And I don't know how long it will take to get over that." His hand slides to my shoulder, the backs of his fingers stroking the side of my neck, then lighting under my chin. He gives the gentlest nudge, tipping my chin upward, and I finally meet his eyes.

He runs his thumb across my lower lip. "But I love you, too."

"Oh!" I don't know what I was going to say, and it doesn't matter anyway because his lips are against mine.

I roll over and raise the corner of the frame from where we placed it face-down on the nightstand. Four sun-pink faces smile back at me before I lay it down again. As touched as I'd been that Ian had held on to my gift in spite of my abhorrent behavior, having his family watch me make it up to him was a bridge too far.

Over in the kitchenette, the lid of the trash can snaps shut, and Ian strolls back to the bed, still naked and sweaty and glorious. I lift the throw I'd snuggled under for him to slide in beside me, and smile as his brow quirks in appreciation of my own bareness before he joins me. The man was literally inside me not two minutes ago, but he still takes pleasure in a peek.

He props himself up on his elbow, cool fingers tracing below my right eye. "How are you?"

"Are you asking if we fogged me up? Because that's an affirmative." I close my left eye, and my vision goes hazy. "Go team *us*."

He laughs, but it fades quickly. "I meant how you're feeling about the MS possibility. I might have spent the past few days sulking, but it did occur to me that this is probably really fucking scary for you, and that I was being an asshole not acknowledging that."

I open my good eye. His concern is as naked as we are. "I am scared. *When* I let myself think about it. Mostly, I hate not knowing. And then knowing that even if I get through the next few months, there will still be that slim chance MS may develop looming over me for years. But it's something I have to live with. Honestly, since moving in with the guys, I've gone days at a time without thinking about it."

"If it happens, it's going to be hard," he continues. "I've read up since the other night. I didn't know that there were different kinds. Some folks have flare-ups, where they're just symptomatic for a few days or weeks, then totally fine for months. Others are more frequent. Others—" His lips press to a pained line.

"Deteriorate," I finish for him.

The worried tug pulls at the center of his brows. "I know that it could get bad. But I'm not going anywhere."

My eyes well. He didn't need to say it. But I definitely needed to hear it.

He strokes the side of my face. His voice is soft when he says, "I don't want to see you uncomfortable."

A peal of panic rings through me, his words too close to echoing Cole's bullshit: "I don't think I'm strong enough for this, too." But this is Ian, not Cole. And if there's one word to describe Ian, it's *strong*.

I blink back the tears. "For now...just don't tell me to hold back at the gym."

"You're planning to come back to the gym I banished you from when I fired you?" His lips quirk in a half smile.

I plant a kiss where his smile has hooked itself, darting out my tongue to brush the spot. "You can't fire me; I quit," I say, echoing my childish retort from the other night.

"Then we appear to be at an impasse."

I chew on my lower lip in feigned thought, not missing when his eyes track the movement. I nudge his shoulder, and he rolls onto his back. I ease onto his torso, straddling his waist, and edge myself toward his groin. "I have a feeling I'll be working my way back into your good graces."

I make contact with the head of his penis, which is unsurprisingly, conveniently, erect. It twitches so violently, it bumps me in the butt. "Is that a yes, or are the two of you going to have to chat about it first?" I rock my hips back again, inspiring the same response. This time, I even hear the gentle pat of dick-to-tush, and suppress a giggle.

"Yes, Hayes," he groans, and I sway my hips side to side. "You can come back."

"That's more like it," I say, and kiss him again. I do us the courtesy of reaching into the nightstand for a fresh condom and make quick work of unwrapping it.

Tossing the foil aside—but tracking where it lands—I pinch the tip, holding it up in offering. "May I?" I ask. In response, he lets out a groan that I find most flattering.

I roll it down his impressive length, frowning a little at the tingling in my hands—that rope outside sucks—but when the curled edge comes into contact with the base of his penis, I'm all smiles.

I straddle him again, and ease backward toward my target.

"I love you," I say, because it's true and because I can. And it doesn't matter that I'm still scared. The hope I have now is stronger than that fear. I may even be okay in the long run.

And if I'm not?

Ian holds a hand to the side of my face. I press against it, enjoying the scrape of the calluses just below his fingers. "I love you, too," he says.

I have that. And it's strong, too.

37

I CURL UP BEHIND IAN, pulling myself to his back with a grip around his waist. His laugh rumbles against me, and I smile, my cheeks pressing against the sleep mask. Between the skylights and the proximity of the city's northernmost moon tower, eye coverings are a must the nights I sleep over. Which, in the month since my dramatic ascent to his window, is most nights.

"It's good effort," he says, "but I don't think that 'big spoon' is in the cards for you."

"How about a jet pack?" I ask, and his laughter jostles me again. I kiss his shoulder. "What time is it?"

"Four fifteen. I'm going to have to coach soon."

"Boo, that." I snuggle closer.

"I'll get coffee going?"

I huff into his shoulder. "Less boo. But not a lot less."

"Glad to see I rate above caffeine."

"Only you."

He squeezes the arm I've draped over him, and I squeeze him back before releasing him to his noble task. I hear the lamp on the bedside table click on and lift the left side of the mask to peep at him. He pulls on a pair of shorts, cutting off my view of his impeccable backside. I whine my disappointment.

"Creeper."

"Oh, are you shy now?" I laugh, pushing the sleep mask up and off my head, and rub my eyes. "You were flaunting it around here pretty casually last night, Mr. Let's Try the Counter."

He chuckles, and I hear him pad to the kitchen. "I think we can agree, that worked out pretty well."

Grinning, I open my eyes—

My entire body flashes cold. *No.*

Wrong.

My vision is wrong.

I jerk upright, eyes wheeling around the room, desperate for something to explain the vacant sensation on my right side. I close my eyes, bringing my free hand up to cover my left. I recognize it as muscle memory; the first thing I did every morning during my bout with optic neuritis. I'm shaking so badly, my hand rustles against my lashes.

The coffee grinder starts. Ian says something, but I can't make it out over the grinding and the blood in my ears and the screaming in my skull. Every muscle tenses. My hand starts to get clammy.

The grinder stops. A small, desperate sound escapes me, but I open my right eye.

The room is replaced by a shadowy haze.

The world falls out from beneath me.

But this time I'm caught.

"What can you do now?" Ian asks.

"What?" We're on the bed, my legs across his lap, Ian holding me to his chest. I don't know how long we've been like this, but when I sit up, my ear has left a pink imprint high on his left pectoral.

"You plan." He says it plainly, but his voice is strained. There's tension in his face, too, pain in his eyes. He's fighting to keep it together for me. His chest rises in a long breath, but it takes him a moment to continue speaking. "So, what's the first thing you're going to do?"

"I'm…" My mind churns. Canes. Fatigue. Memory loss. Urge incontinence. Paralysis—

"What can you do, Ellie?"

I shake my head, trying to disrupt the spiraling symptoms. None of that is up to me. What can I control? What can I do? "I have Dr. Hartman's cell phone number. It's on his card. I have that in my wallet. He told me to call him if"—I suck in a sob, and Ian's hold tightens—"this happened."

"I'll get your wallet. Then what?"

"I don't know. A lot will depend on when I get in with him, and then what he says—" My throat closes around the rest. But there is no rest. That was it. One thing. I could only come up with one fucking thing. There's nothing else I can do.

My breathing starts to pick up, my body going tense—

"Okay." Ian runs his hands over my back, and something crinkles against me before he releases it to the bed beside us. It's the coffee filter. He came to me so quickly, he hadn't even put the damn thing down.

He cares. It's a given. Not presumed, or taken for granted, but as much of who he is as his strength and his eyes and his capable hands. He cares so much, about so many people and things. It's what he does. It's what made me fall in love with him.

But it's too much. I don't want this for him.

"What else can I do?" he asks. "What do you need from me?"

Not "Now what?," but "What can I do? What do you need?"

The questions break me and mend me in the same breath. I need him here, but I don't want this. Not for him. I don't have a choice, but he does.

I stare into his face, his exceptional eyes watching me, forehead marred with worry. My head shakes. Or my whole body does. The thoughts start to spiral again. I shouldn't have gone to him that night. It was selfish and shortsighted, and I knew better than to hope. It isn't fair. It—

One of his hands goes to my cheek, but I keep shaking. I can't get it out. I can't let him go, but I can't let him stay. Not for this.

"Speak to me, Hayes."

"I don't want this for you!" I force it out on a sob. Tears fall down my face, heavy and hot. "I don't want you to have to do this. This is why I told you to go. Because I knew you would never leave over this. But I—" I squeeze his hand, and I know I know I know I should let go, but I can't. I'm too greedy for him. "This is too much. I don't want you to have to take this on."

He cradles my face in both hands now, thumbing away the tears. "It's part of you," he says, his voice unsteady but firm. "If it's part of you, I'm taking it on."

"I'm going to need you too much."

"There's no such thing."

I grab his other wrist but still can't make myself move either of his hands away. "You don't know that! We don't know what this means! We don't know what it's going to end up looking like. I already—" I halt, hating the question I haven't even braved asking yet. "What about kids, Ian?"

He blinks. "What?"

"Have you even thought about what being with me will be like long-term? What it could really mean. What I already probably can't do. And now this—"

"We'll figure it out," he rasps, brushing away more of my tears.

"You're already doing too much! You're supposed to be coaching!" I remind him. "But you're here instead. Because of *me*."

"Because I'm not going anywhere. I told you that." His hands leave my face, but I don't let go. "The class will be fine. Tom and Babs know the door code. You wrote the workout on the board before we came upstairs last night. I'll call one of the guys and they'll be here before five a.m.'s even finished the warm-up."

The fear has its claws firmly in me, but damn it all, that was a competent response. I want to climb into his skin.

A gentle hope softens his eyes. "Did that kind of work for you?"

I nod, weakly, a sense of defeat mingling with the terror. I release my grip on his wrists, and he slides his arms around me. He starts to pull me closer, but I resist, the final, unspoken fears holding me back from surrender.

"What if it's bad?" I whisper. "Really bad?"

"You're thinking about the worst—"

"Because that's what I always get."

"And you always find a way. You had a bad time teaching, but now, you have your own business doing what you loved most about that experience. You moved into the Dawghouse and turned it into a functional household. You found a disgusting bathroom and got me."

I choke out a laugh.

He half smiles. "You saw value in what I do, and got me to see it, too."

"I told you." I can feel the praise softening me. "You make it easy."

He runs his hands up and down my arms. "Your body has betrayed you before, but you adapted. And you're going to do that here. I hate that you're going to have to do it. But if there's anyone who can, it's you."

"But what if I'm not me anymore?" The question is wrenched from me in pieces, bringing with it the last, ruinous truth. "Ian, I could lose *everything* that makes me who I am. And I'm only just figuring it out. There's still so much that I don't know if I can do! I want to climb ropes and carry stupid, heavy shit and have stimmy sex with you after and be useful to the people I care about in ways I haven't even come up with yet. A few months ago, I didn't even know any of it was possible. It's new and incredible and empowering and I love it, and I might lose *all* of it."

"Not all of it," he says. "And not me."

I push back one last time. "I don't want this for you."

His eyes are intent on mine, gentle, but utterly resolute. "You don't get to make this choice for me, love."

I close my eyes, letting the brutal, exquisite truth of that wash over me. One more thing I have zero control over. Surrender has never been such a relief.

My body goes slack, and Ian pulls me against him. I cling to him, shuddering against his chest. And I cry. Again, I lose track of time. He holds me and I cry and shake until I think I'll break myself apart, but his grip is so solid, and I hold him so tightly, that I stay in one piece.

EPILOGUE

December

"WE HAVE TO STOP MEETING like this."

I grin, and turn—and keep turning, since he's on my right—to find Ian filling our bathroom doorway. I recap my eyeliner with a *click* that echoes in the tiled space and toss it into my makeup bag. "I don't know. Bathrooms seem to work for us."

"Especially when you're on the counter," he says, and I shift, letting my feet dangle off the side of the surface as he steps between my knees. I hook my finger into his belt loops, pulling him closer. He grins. "Should I shut the door?"

"I was hoping you were coming in to free me from my banishment," I say. "I'm losing my mind in here."

"It'll be another few minutes. Everything looks great," he assures me. "I took care of the locker rooms, Heather and Mark are en route with the last of the small plates Diego had back at the Dawghouse. Barbara—"

We both flinch as the sharp shriek of feedback comes in from the open window in the bedroom.

"—is about to get fired from playing deejay. And Grant and Tom have the kids working on your surprise in the lobby."

"I still can't believe that Tom filled that position," I say. Tom's not only come to the rescue on the accounting front, but is providing all childcare coverage now that Grant's courseload has doubled, courtesy of his education classes. He's taken to it like a particularly curmudgeonly duck to water, and the kids adore him—especially Penny, which Grant is more than a little testy about.

"It boggles the mind. Speaking of, Alistair is dressed like an elf? Or, what he's calling an elf, which does include a little hat, but is otherwise limited to shorts and suspenders."

"No shirt?"

He scoffs. "*Never.* He's not really contributing, but there a good chance he's putting Helen at risk of preeclampsia. That poor woman swoons every time he walks by."

"I hope she's seated."

"As a matter of fact, she may not be able to get out of the armchair. Her words. I think this last trimester is going to be rough."

I stick out my lower lip in sympathy. The pregnancy had been a happy surprise, but Helen found out a few days after we'd spent a lunch detailing our respective medical histories. She had been so delicate in telling me that she was expecting, it was practically an apology. I appreciated her sensitivity, but at this point, whether my body is up to the task of reproducing is the last thing on my mind.

"So, rest easy about the success of the first annual Firehouse Fitness holiday party, and tell me." He half smiles. "What *are* you doing up here?"

"My eyeliner. I have to angle the cabinet mirrors to see my right side, and it takes forever to get the wings symmetrical." I frown. "I hate having to relearn it every relapse. You'd think I'd have the muscle memory by now."

I grimace the moment the complaint is out of my mouth. Ian gives me a reassuring squeeze, but I sigh. "I'm an asshole."

"You're not an asshole."

"I'm griping about *eyeliner*. There are people with this who can't walk or see or live independently, and I'm bitching about nailing a cat eye."

"Your MS is *your* MS. It isn't a competition."

He's right, but I sigh again, anyway.

Dr. Hartman had gotten me in first thing that nightmare morning, and an MRI and spinal tap confirmed my condition. Relapsing-remitting multiple sclerosis. I experience flare-ups, during which my immune system attacks the myelin protecting my nerve cells, as well as the nerve fibers within. This interrupts signals from getting to the parts of my body where they need to go, my optic nerve evidently being the go-to, though new symptoms may pop up. This can last days or weeks, which has been my experience so far, or longer, and then I go into remission, where, again, so far, the symptoms go away. As with all things MS, this is simply a matter of luck; I could be symptomatic even outside of an attack. I just get to wait and see.

Ian takes my hands, squeezing them and running his thumbs from my knuckles to my wrists. "Are your hands behaving?"

I shrug. My eye might be my body's preferred victim, but this relapse, a tingling has picked up in my hands. It's maddening, pins and needles dancing along my fingers and palms. I end up wiggling my fingers or curling and relaxing them to relieve the sensation. Five days into this flare-up, and I don't even notice I'm doing it. But Ian does.

"It's fine," I say. "I just didn't do enough with them today."

As ever, movement is my savior. Beyond the relief I get from simply keeping my hands active, the tingles are hard to focus on when I'm cursing workouts like Barbara, which, as per its namesake, really does suck. For now, I'm going as hard as I reasonably can for as long as I reasonably can. The only change is that the guys spot me during overhead movements, especially with this flare-up's twitchy fingers, and I'm expressly forbidden from rope climbs without Ian and the crash pads below me, which, c'mon—don't threaten *me* with a good time.

I curl my fingers around his. Unfiltered honesty has gotten a lot easier now that I have nothing to hide, but admitting weakness still grates my pride. "I don't like that there's a new symptom. It feels too soon for something new. And I feel guilty because…I should be so lucky that it's just something really, really, annoying and not debilitating. And I'm scared. Because the next symptom might be."

Ian opens his mouth, doubtless to say something reassuring, but I shake my head.

"I know that it isn't likely. Not now. But even with my medication, it is the eventuality." The vast majority of RRMS patients transition to a progressive form of the condition, where the relapses stop being relapses and become their life, the symptoms permanent. In most cases, that takes time, ten to twenty-five years, and that's not nothing. One can fit a lot of living into that, and I'm going to.

"But whether it's a decade before that happens, or two, *or,*" I emphasize, leaning on the still-tender hope I've been nurturing, "MS is miraculously cured in the meantime, now is all I can depend on anyway." I smirk. "I could get hit by a truck tomorrow, regardless of my MS progression."

"Let's not do that though, okay? This is Texas. There are a lot of trucks."

"Good point." I slip my hands around his sides, squeezing his waist with my legs. "It's a crappy part of my life, but still only part of it. It's not all that I am. I can still apply eyeliner. And walk. And run. And climb a rope. And move stupid heavy shit and have stimmy sex with you after—" I shrug, smiling as his hands slide up my back. "For now, that's pretty damn good."

"I agree," he says, and leans down, brushing his lips to mine.

I nip at his lower lip. "And I can be helpful, too, if those brats will let me."

"This is *for* you," he reminds me.

I let out a huff, and Ian laughs, jostling me at every point of contact. The feeling revives Break Me, which was really just *me*, anyway, and I squeeze him between my thighs with a little more intention.

"We still have a few minutes?" I ask, and he nods, his smile growing lascivious. "Excellent." I tiptoe my fingers down to his rear. "Let's put these fingers to use."

"Okay!" Diego's excited voice comes from my left, accompanied by the faint tinkle of jingle bells. I bite in my smile, imagining him in the little Santa hat he was wearing for the Built Box holiday video we recorded this morning. It was the first kit he'd designed, courtesy of the nutrition training he's taken on, and one of many kits and features of his extended contract with Built Box. "We'll count down, and then you can look! Guys, start from *three!*"

On his cue, a masculine chorus chants, "Three, two, one!"

I open my eyes and gasp, immediately blinking back tears. Erected in the lobby between one of the boxy armchairs and the couch is a monstrous fir tree. I'd smelled it the moment Ian guided me out of the stairwell, my eyes closed, as per request, but in no way was I prepared for the sight of it, even at 50 percent functionality.

It is, without a doubt, the most poorly decorated tree ever to have been adorned. It is a crime; it could be used to support an argument against ever cutting down a tree for Christmas consumption.

And I love it.

Before I can fully process the cacophony of contrasting elements the poor tree has been subjected to, Grant steps forward. He gestures to the cluster of balls and paper chains that have been more or less thrown at the lower limbs. "I let the kiddos do this part," he says. "They've been making ornaments during the childcare hours the past couple of weeks. The chains, too," he adds, begrudgingly. "It was *Tom's* idea."

I nod in a way that I hope is sympathetic.

"Anything that looked fragile was kept out of their reach," Alistair adds. He is, indeed, wearing next to nothing, and I wonder how the med school panel he interviewed with the other day would react to him in his tiny elf hat and short shorts.

He points to the top half of the tree. "Check it out."

I do, coming to stand beside Grant, letting my eye fall over the ornaments higher up. I gasp again. The Gorgon's head from Bath, the miniature Rose Window from my trip to Notre Dame, and the delicate palm tree that had miraculously made it back from the Keys without losing a glass frond. They and all my other ornaments have been rescued from the underbed bin and finally put on display.

My first tree.

But not just mine. The childproofed section is full of unfamiliar ornaments from places I've never been but have seen in Hammond family photos. It's their mom's collection. My heart swells. I look at Ian, and I'm grateful for my deep aversion to the multicolored lights illuminating the tree, otherwise I'd be a mess. It's *our* first tree.

"Christmas chaos." He says the words with a sigh aching with memories. His arm comes around my waist, and I find myself softening to the profusion of color, if only to bask in the joy it brings him.

His joy, however, transitions to something closer to his fuck-with-you face. "Hey, Grant?" he asks. "Would you mind hitting the button on the cord? It's close to the plug."

Grant peers at the floor, nudging something below the tree with his foot. A moment later, the lights are a tasteful soft white.

"Oh, thank God," I sigh, sagging in relief.

Ian laughs. "I thought you'd feel that way. This seems like a good compromise, yeah?"

"I love you," I say, firmly. "This was very clever, and I love you for it. Do know that I love you anyway, and I love you for this."

"I love you, too," he says, and leans in, kissing my temple. While he's close, he adds, quietly, "And we'll take no offense to you moving around ornaments if you need to."

"Thank you." I kiss the corner of his mouth. "The ball distribution is *killing* me." I look back at the tree. "But it's kind of great as-is?" Facing the guys, I say, "Thank you, truly. It's perfect. It feels—"

"Cozy?" Grant offers.

Fresh tears spring to my eyes, and I nod. "Yeah. *Cozy* is perfect."

"We don't want to keep you from the party for too long," he says. "We just wanted to be sure you got to see it first. It's our thank-you. To you. For…a lot."

I wave this off, painfully aware of the ongoing threat of tears. "You guys were keeping the toilets pristine even before I moved out."

"Not that! Well, not *just* that," Diego says. I'd been right about the hat.

"You inspired us," says Grant, and he smiles, holding a hand aloft. "To be *more*."

"You believed that we could be," Alistair adds, then shrugs. "I mean, I knew I'd get around to med school *eventually*, but, I dunno. You were that extra push—shit, you're crying."

"Mm-hmm," I wipe under my eyes.

Alistair shakes his head. "You always do this now. You used to be so hard!"

"Not *hard*! More like…*insulated*." I say, and sniffle. I don't have to be anymore.

I smile. "I'm so proud of you, what you're learning and doing, and it is humbling and really gratifying to have contributed to that in any way. I love you to pieces." I take in a long, shaky breath, and laugh. "And none of you can hug me right now because I'll fall apart and also, Alistair, honey, is that the shimmer again?"

"It's *festive.*"

"Fair. Just…keep it off Mushu? It can't be good for his leaves." I look at each of them in turn. "Thank you for letting me into the Dawghouse. And into Firehouse, and into your lives."

My roommates smile back, and my whole body hums with gratitude for them. Alistair, dazzling as always, literally so with his bronze shimmer; Diego, soft-faced and sweet, his cheeks encroaching on his eyes; and Grant, who opened the door between me and this weird, wonderful, empowering environment, his smile so much like his brother's, and all the more endearing for the ways it's his own.

His eyes widen, and his smile spreads to uniquely Grant proportions. "We should shotgun a beer! For old times' sake!"

All eyes land on me, the onetime resident killjoy, who maybe never was all that bad. "Well," I say. "Only if there's cheese, too."

Diego throws his arms up in victory. "I made miniature caprese! On toothpicks!"

The collegiate cave-pups whoop and jingle their way to the double doors. As they file out, the sound of the gathering outside floats in, conversations between some of my favorite people, my community, my support, overlapping with "Rocking Around the Christmas Tree" and a shriek from who I suspect is one of the other childcare kiddos fleeing from Penny, who has upgraded from capturing bugs to handling them. It's chaotic. And a little invasive at times. But just like the truly bonkers tree beside me, I wouldn't have it any other way.

There's room to be scared, but surrounded by all of this, I can't find it. I'm not sad, either, and as the door closes on the din outside, I'm definitely not alone. I look at Ian, who watches me with a mix of curiosity and adoration, and when I wiggle my brows, I find that I am coy. His eyes smolder back, and it turns out, I'm also a little sexy.

"Thank you," I say, and turn to face him fully, wrapping my arms around his neck. "For being strong enough for all of me."

"Ellie Hayes," he says, and kisses me. "You make it easy."

ACKNOWLEDGMENTS

Thank you to my longtime readers, who were with me from beginning to end. To Beth, who will be the only one coming to this book to be surprised by the reveal that Ian is Man Mountain. I'm so glad that you got to have that experience, and so, so glad that you messaged me immediately from your hair appointment to relay your shock and delight. And to Tricia, aka @readingrowans, whose Instagram handle I include here because she really should get all the ARCs and beta reader offers because she knows everything Romance. The next patio will be better, I promise. And Tracy @readingwithtracy, thank you for the encouragement with my early chapters. It's come a long way!

Thank you, Mumsie. Always.

To my Austin readers. Angela, thank you for running the Austin Romance Writers group. From chatty meetings to prolonged writing sessions, field trips, and unrelenting children's musical acts, it has been such a treat to have this group. Thank you, Nealy, for your thorough notes and constructive feedback, and for strong-arming the Jane Austen Society into reading my debut.

Thank you, Madeleine, editor extraordinaire and recognizer of *Legally Blonde* quotes. You cracked the code with me; all you have to do is tell me I'm funny and I'll make any changes you want. And Grace and Caroline and Dana and everyone at the Forever team, thank you for taking the time to hang out with me when I came to visit. Here's to functional trash and the hope that Patti LuPone wouldn't actively dislike us if we ever had the honor to be in her presence.

To my agent, Tara, who managed not to lose her mind during the nine-month period I reworked the first three chapters of this thing. Thank you for believing in this project long after it was reasonable to do so.

To Margo, who picked up *A Certain Appeal*, and so kindly gave notes on early chapters around the time I was both lost in the forest and blind to the trees around me. That was so, so generous of you.

To the coaches! First, the good folks at Sanitas, onto whom I imprinted like a gosling reared by a particularly convincing puppet. Antonio, Butts, Courtney, Dwight, Elissa, Faisal, and Laura, I can't thank you enough for turning me into the brawny broad I was always meant to be. None of you are Ian. Don't make it weird. However, I cannot rule out that some himbo behavior was informed by things overheard and observed while in your company. I leave it to y'all to determine which of you told me that my snatches were "slow as shit." I regret to inform you that they still are. And while you, Tom, aren't why there's a book Tom, True's love-on for you as childcare provider is the basis of the Grant/Penny dynamic.

And to the crew at Dane's: Ashley, Beth, Blair, Chad, Dane, Keith, Lauren, Mark, Monica, and Stormie. Thank you for everything you do for our fitness community. I promise, I have told no one where the key is. None of you are Ian, either. Sela, I borrowed your name. Hope you don't mind!

To my fellow 5 a.m.ers. Call it a shared need for endorphins early in order to be nice, call it a trauma bond. In either case, it is an honor and a joy to sweat beside you. Thanks for humoring me when I insist you take off your running shoes to lift and for indulging my whims, like "How about we start a gourmet group and I'll be the dictator?" Friday coffee feeds my soul.

And Diego, thank you for the loan of your name. I also gave my Diego your hair. Speaking of, you should really consider a scrunchie or two; I think the look would work for you.

To Sarah MacLean, who does not know me. But when I was ready to give up on this project, I started listening to the Hell's Belles series, and I was so enthralled and inspired that I had to get back to writing. I have a thank-you gift. It is *Moonstruck* themed. I promise, I'm not weird.

To the podcasts that keep me sane when I'm not writing. The gals at *Heaving Bosoms*, whose regular use of "competence boner" made me comfortable applying it here. Shout out to the boys at *Overdue*, whose decade-plus of weekly episodes means I always have something to listen to. My daughter and I still growl, "Grubs!" and your coverage of *The Death of Ivan Ilych* is why Alistair is reading it here. And to the ladies at *Worst Bestsellers*, whose read of Pamela Anderson's memoir had me screenshotting the captions to record, "Love is the quality of attention we pay to things." I wrote entire chapters around that, including the elevator scene, for which I am particularly grateful.

To my daughter, True, who will be taller than me by the time this is published. I hope you don't mind that I've fictionalized your insect fascination. I love you, Goof. Keep track of your rib cage.

To my husband, Derek. Thank you for the time and space to make writing possible. Thank you for asking, "Writing go well today?" when I'm in a particularly good mood. You were right when you told me I'd love CrossFit. It took me three years, but I'm so glad I caved. And thank you for holding me when I was too scared to ask for it. Without you, there is no Ian. Without you, I wouldn't even know where to start. I love you, Boo.

ABOUT THE AUTHOR

Vanessa King is the author of *A Certain Appeal*, a *Pride and Prejudice*–goes–burlesque novel based on her experiences as a stage kitten at NYC's famed Duane Park. She's since traded pasties and pumps for power lifting and cross-trainers but maintains that red nails go just as well with a chrome barbell as they do fishnets. *Ellie Hayes and the Himbos* is set in her new hometown of Austin, Texas, where she lives with her husband, daughter, and two objectively terrible cats that she can't help but love anyway. When not writing, she enjoys reading, convincing anyone within earshot to listen to her favorite podcasts, admission-free hours at Barton Springs, and pre-dawn workouts with her five a.m. crew.